PERFECTLY TWISTED

KRISTINE MASON

ISBN: 0-9906543-6-2
ISBN: 978-0-9906543-6-0

For Liz…

I'll never forget the day I met you. I actually felt kind of bad. You were shy and, well, my family doesn't know the meaning of the word. The thing I remember the most about that day was liking you instantly, and discovering a new friend. Here we are, eight years later. You're now Grandma Liz. The special things you do for me, my kids, and especially my dad, mean the world to me. If I could be as creative as you, I'd make the most fabulous hat for you. A big one that made a statement. One that would let people know how much you are loved and appreciated. You're a good person, and a good friend. I'm honored to know you. Plus, if it wasn't for you, I would only own one purse. XO

ACKNOWLEDGEMENTS

Thank you Crystal Jardine, of Jardine Funeral Home and Cleveland Cremation, for giving me a tour of the funeral home and crematory. I respect what you do, and appreciate the insight. Special thanks to my cousin, Philip James, for helping me enlist my hero in the U.S. Army. Your recruiting knowledge truly helped mold my hero, and I hope that I honored the men and women who serve our country. I respect you, Phil. Thanks for your years of service. I'd also like to thank Donna Stevens for naming Above the Law's headquarters. It's a perfect name for this ragtag group. Thank you Tessa Shapcott for your editing skills. Elle Rossi, from EJR Digital Art—lady, you know how to design a fabulous cover! Tessa had summed up the cover perfectly: "He's a very handsome snake, but menacing all the same." I want to give a shout out to Sherry for proofing Perfectly Twisted. Thanks for catching those little things my tired mind had missed. Special thanks to Jamie Denton. I know I drove you nuts with this book. Thanks for sticking with me on this one, and for all of your help. I don't know what I'd do without you. As always, I want to thank my husband and kids for cooperating with me as I wrote this book. I know I can get a little crazy when my deadline is looming. I'm so happy you guys still love me—crazy and all. Lastly, I'd like to thank my readers. I write because I love creating stories, but it wouldn't be fun without you!

KRISTINE MASON

THE YOUNG REVEREND

Every great story seems to begin with a snake.

—Nicolas Cage

Easterville, Tennessee
Thursday, 5:24 p.m. Eastern Daylight Time

"I HATE YOUR mama."

The young boy wiped the tears from his face and stared at his daddy. "I do, too," he whispered. Worried his mama would hear him, he looked around the room. She was just down the hall in her bedroom folding laundry. As it was, if she knew he was sitting, rather than kneeling on the cornmeal she'd sprinkled on the hardwood floor, she'd whoop his butt.

"How long did she make you kneel this time?" Daddy asked, and rubbed the boy's red knees.

He shrugged. "Since after school. I'm still supposed to be kneeling." He started to rise and move back into position, but his tired legs gave and he plopped back onto his rear. "I don't want to get in trouble," he said, fresh tears burning his tired eyes. "Help me, Daddy, before Mama sees me sittin'."

"Don't you worry about your mama. I'll take care of her for us." Daddy wrapped an arm around his shoulder. "Would you like that?"

"What do you mean by takin' care of her?" he asked. Even at eight, he understood what his daddy was suggesting, but wanted to be sure before he answered. He'd witnessed his daddy in action, and knew his temper well. Daddy had never raised a hand to him or even to Mama, but just last week he'd pistol-whipped the pastor of The Church of Jesus Christ. Daddy had never liked Reverend Clarence Bramson. He hadn't, either. The man was a little too friendly with Mama. Plus, Daddy was a pastor at the Church of the Living God. Since Mama no longer believed in Daddy's teachings, she'd started going to Pastor Bramson's church. Daddy hadn't liked that. Not one bit. What would Daddy's congregation say about his wife spending her Sundays at a different church? That'd be as bad as cheating on Daddy. But it no longer mattered. That pastor wouldn't be preaching anymore. He also wouldn't be tattling on Daddy, not when the sheriff was a member of Daddy's congregation, and a firm believer in Daddy's teachings.

Daddy smiled. "Boy, you ain't dumb. Why, you're the smartest kid I ever done seen. I think you know. But I'll tell you anyway, 'cause if I'm gonna do it, I want you to be there with me." Daddy hugged him close. "Me and you. That's all we need. Your mama? The only good thing that woman has ever done was give me you."

He looked up at his daddy, and swallowed hard. "You want to…kill her?"

His daddy's eyes shined with laughter. "Our Lord says killin' is a sin. But God does forgive His children, don't He?"

He leaned forward and looked toward the hallway to make sure Mama wasn't listening around the corner. Sure they were alone, he rested his back against Daddy's arm. "I thought you don't believe in God," he whispered.

"I don't. Do you?"

"Mama does. She says the only way to salvation is through Jesus. That's why I should read the Bible every day, and when I'm bad…" He glanced to his red knees. "I should pray."

"You were kneeling for over two hours. How much prayin' did you do?"

"None."

"Then what was you thinkin' about?"

He twined his fingers together and twisted them, just like his belly was doing now. Twisting up, like one of Daddy's snakes might do before they struck. "I don't wanna tell you."

"I'm your daddy, you can tell me anything. You don't judge me, and I'll never judge you. Hear me?"

He nodded. "I was thinkin' what it'd feel like to hurt Mama."

"How'd you want to hurt her?"

He shrugged and looked to their brand new Curtis Mathes TV console. No kid in Easterville had a TV like theirs. Daddy had even bought them a Beta VCR so they could tape stuff.

Daddy let out a quiet laugh. "Boy, I hear the gears grindin' in that head of yours. Come on now and tell me."

He looked to his twined hands. "I was wonderin' what might happen if I pushed the TV onto Mama when she was dustin' it." He looked at his daddy. "I wouldn't do that. I know how much you like your TV, and I wanna be able to watch *The Real Ghostbusters*."

"I know you do, son." His daddy patted his shoulder and laughed again. "Yeah, it'd be a shame to ruin our TV, and I'll be honest, I've thought of a few ways to hurt your mama, too. You know she was gonna leave my church, right?"

He nodded. "That ain't right. You're a better preacher than Pastor Bramson."

Daddy narrowed his eyes. "How do you know?"

"'Cause Mama made me go to one of his Wednesday evenin' sermons."

"When?"

"The time you was gettin' the rattlers from Mr. Jimmy."

That night had been a bad one. He'd been forced to listen to Pastor Bramson's boring teachings, then pray for an hour while Mama met with the preacher. Once they were home, and Mama saw that Daddy had brought more snakes into the house, she'd screamed and yelled at Daddy. He'd thought for sure Daddy would hit her. Daddy hadn't. But *he* had wanted to. He'd wanted to take one of Mama's cast iron frying pans and shut her up—for good. She'd made him betray his Daddy by going to another church, and he wasn't stupid. He knew how babies were made, and he'd bet his baseball collection that Mama hadn't spent an hour praying with Pastor Bramson that night.

"Hmm. Well, that's mighty interestin' news. I guess it's a good thing Bramson won't be preaching no more, huh?"

"I think so."

"But what do you think about gettin' rid of Mama. I know you're young, but you're old for your age. Smart, too. You also gotta know she don't approve of my snake handling ways."

"She says you blasphamitize the Lord's teachings with them snakes."

Daddy chuckled. "I think you mean, blaspheme. But that's okay. It's a big word, with big meaning. I'll let you in on a little secret. I don't *blasphamitize* anything. I use the Bible to get what I want." Daddy looked to their new Curtis Mathes. "Like our TV. How do you think I paid for that? Well, I'll tell you how— my congregation. Your mama is a pious, self-righteous bitch. She'll sit and read the Bible, pray to her god, then turn around and beat the shit out of you. How is that Christian-like?"

"It ain't."

"Nope, not at all. See, I might take money for preaching bullshit I don't believe in, but in the end, my congregation leaves my church satisfied. I give them a show." He raised his hands to the ceiling. "I hold my snakes up high and show them that with God on our side, even the venomous serpent can't hurt us." Daddy wrapped his hand around his shoulder again. "Mama knew what I was when she married me, but she got religion in her head and hasn't been right since."

"What do you mean? What were you when you two got married?"

"A con-artist. Know what that is?"

He shook his head.

"I take people's money, and I want to keep takin' my congregation's money. I want my church and what I preach to expand across Appalachia. And I want my boy by my side while I do it. Hell, I'll ordain you and you could become the youngest reverend in history."

The youngest reverend in history? He pictured himself holding one of Daddy's snakes and preaching right alongside him. The congregation would fall to their knees and pray before them and maybe give them enough money so he could have a TV in his room. "Will you teach me how to pretend to speak in tongues?" Since he could remember, he'd watched his daddy talk gibberish in front of the mirror. Daddy had once told him it was a crowd pleaser, and that was all he'd needed to know. But now he wanted to know all of Daddy's secrets. He wanted Mama gone from their lives so they could preach together and make lots of money.

"In time, boy. But first we need to decide what to do about Mama. She won't like me ordaining you. I'm worried what she'll do to you when I ain't at the house."

More kneeling. More praying and reading the Bible. More whoopings. "We don't want to ruin our new TV."

"No, we don't."

"And I don't want you gettin' caught for doing something bad to her." He turned to his daddy. "What do *you* want to do to her?"

Daddy had one of those faraway stares he'd seen his grammy do when she would go inside her old head. "I think you're too young to know."

"No, I ain't. Tell me, Daddy. I won't tell no one." He used his finger to cross his heart. "I promise."

Daddy looked at him and smiled. "I know you won't, and you're right. If you're going to join me on my mission, you're old enough to know." Daddy leaned close to his ear. "I want to gut your mama and watch her bleed."

A shiver ran through him. He'd pictured hurting Mama, but *never* like that. "You'd get in trouble for sure."

"I know I would, so I ain't doin' it. Nothing wrong with dreaming, though."

"What if a snake bit her? That'd kill her for sure, wouldn't it?"

Daddy sighed. "Boy, I knew I could count on you. Why, Mr. Jimmy even found a rattler when he was huntin' yesterday. It'll do the trick." Daddy stood, then helped him to his feet. When his knees buckled, Daddy picked him up in his strong arms and sat him on the couch. "No time like the present."

Goose bumps coated his skin and his stomach twisted up again. "You're gonna do it now?"

"I don't have to, but why wait? Do you want to spend tomorrow on your knees again?"

"No, sir."

"What'd you do to deserve it anyway?"

His cheeks grew warm and he looked to his red knees. "Mama caught me lookin' at the bra and panties section of her JC Penney catalogue."

Daddy grinned. "That's my boy. Ain't nothing wrong with appreciatin' a woman's body. So how 'bout it? You want me to take care of Mama?"

He considered his mother and pictured her face. She wasn't pretty like the women in the catalogue and had these deep parenthesis around her mouth that made her look ugly. He also couldn't remember the last time she'd smiled at him, or hugged and kissed him like his friends' moms would do. All she did was yell and quote stuff from the Bible, and put down Daddy. He hated her. Hated the way she treated him and Daddy. Hated the whoopings.

"Yes," he said.

Daddy rested a hand on his shoulder. "You're a good boy. We're gonna do great things together." He stepped away, then turned on the TV. "I won't be long," Daddy said, then walked down the hall.

Alf played on the TV. The show was kind of dumb, but his legs ached too much to stand up and change the channel. As he watched the show, his stomach settled and the knots disappeared. Daddy was going to make everything all right. He'd take care of Mama and make it so she couldn't hurt him again.

His mama screamed. He shot upright and tensed. Waited. Should he go see what happened? Or should he wait for Daddy? Daddy said he'd take care of Mama, and Daddy always made good on his promises.

By the time Daddy came down the hallway *Alf* was ending. He stared at Daddy, unsure of what to say or ask.

"She ain't dead. Yet," Daddy said, and plopped next to him on the couch. "Let's watch a little TV before bed."

"Okay, Daddy."

Together they sat on the couch. As *Alf* ended and *The Hogan Family* began, Mama cried and pounded on the door. Scared she'd live and hurt him, worried his Daddy would go to jail, he moved close to Daddy.

Daddy wrapped an arm around him. "Don't worry, son. By morning, she'll be gone."

Church of the Living God, Easterville, Tennessee
Saturday, 10:47 a.m. Eastern Daylight Time

Daddy had been right. With a little help, Mama had died sometime during the night. All her pounding and crying had driven him and Daddy nuts, so Daddy had given her a bonk on the head to keep her quiet. By three in the morning, she'd gone to her god in the sky. Today, she'd go into the ground.

"That was an excellent sermon, Reverend." Lyle Gessup, one of Daddy's hunting buddies, as well as a member of his congregation, shook Daddy's hand. "I'm sorry for your loss."

"Thank you kindly, Lyle," Daddy said, then frowned. "It's a shame my wife didn't believe enough. Had she put her faith in

God, the venom of the snake wouldn't have harmed her."

"Amen." Lyle nodded. "Are you worried about her salvation?"

"I admit I have my fears. If the Holy Spirit runs strong through your body, there ain't nothing to fear. God will protect you and deliver you from all that is evil."

"Amen," Lyle repeated, and shifted his gaze to the wooden casket displayed on the small altar. "Your wife was a devout woman. Her death makes me wonder if I have enough of the Holy Spirit in me. It also makes me wonder what'll happen to me when I die." Lyle shook his head. "My apologies, Reverend. This ain't no time for this kinda talk."

"That's okay, Lyle. I think we all wonder what will happen to our souls upon death. If we're free of sin, though, there ain't no need to wonder," Daddy said with a reassuring smile.

"But your wife, what with as devout as she was, she still couldn't handle the venom." Lyle let out a breath that was laced with whiskey. "I think I need to go pray for her."

"You do that," Daddy said, and gave Lyle a pat on the shoulder.

After the man walked away, the boy looked to the altar, stared at his dead mama, and thought about what Daddy had said to Lyle. "What does happen to us when we die?" he asked.

Daddy led him to the casket. The rest of the congregation, made up of thirty-five or so, hung back, praying or talking among themselves. "What are you askin' me, boy?"

"If we don't believe in God, what'll happen to our souls?"

"Don't know. Could be as soon as we die we're reborn as someone else." He smiled. "Maybe even an ant or bird. Or, it could be we just die, which is why we should make the most out of livin'."

"What about going to Hell?"

"Well, if there ain't no such thing as God, how can there be a Hell?"

"I guess you're right, but are you worried about what Mr. Lyle said?"

"What's that?"

"He thinks Mama was a better Christian than him."

"We know that ain't true."

"Yeah, but aren't you worried the congregation will start wondering about what'll happen to them if they ain't got enough Holy Spirit in them when they die?"

Daddy hugged him to his side. "Boy, you sure are a smart one. I could use your mama's early demise to give my congregation hope that there's salvation even if we die with sin stainin' our soul. I'll have to think how to do that."

"What about the snakes? You could put one in her casket before she gets buried."

Daddy grinned. "I could put one in her belly."

He touched his stomach. "How would you do that?"

"I did say I wanted to gut your mama. I could open her up and put the rattler inside." He snapped his fingers. "And let the beast swallow her sins and cleanse her soul."

Daddy was the best preacher ever, even if he didn't believe a word of what he preached. "Will you get in trouble?"

"Don't you worry, son. I'll talk to the sheriff. In the meantime, I want to do something special." He turned toward his congregation. "Before I take my beloved wife home and bury her in the family plot, there's something I need you all to do for me."

Daddy stood behind him. "Since my wife loved Jesus so much, I know she'd would want me to do this now. I need y'all to gather around. My son is just as Christianly as his mama. I want him to work by my side and learn my ways so he can carry on this church when I'm old and gray. I want his mission to start now. Today, my boy will become a reverend."

As the congregation approved and applauded, the boy's small chest filled with pride. He had a mission, and he'd work side-by-side with his daddy. After Daddy had finished the ceremony, which the young Reverend was sure had been made up on the spot, he pulled aside the sheriff. He couldn't hear what Daddy said to the man, but when the sheriff nodded, and shook Daddy's hand, the boy had a feeling the sheriff approved of their idea.

"We're all set," Daddy said to him. "We're gonna take your mama's body home and perform the ritual there. The sheriff is letting some of the members know what we're doing, so we'll have several handpicked, honorary and trustworthy witnesses."

The young Reverend still worried. "What if people talk and word gets around town?"

"Hell, boy, the Catholics have their exorcism, now we got ourselves our own ritual. Don't you worry about people talkin'. I'll be sure to let our members know that I'll unleash the wrath of God upon them if they spread rumors."

No. Daddy would pistol-whip or take a bat to one of their heads. He'd do the same if Daddy asked him to. He and Daddy might not believe in God or what Daddy preached, but the Church of the Living God belonged to them. Its members worshiped Daddy and his teachings, and maybe one day, if he worked hard, they would worship him, too.

"So what are you gonna call the ritual?" the young Reverend asked.

Daddy tilted his head as if he were thinking. Then he patted his shoulder. "Got it. We're gonna call it the Ritual of the Serpents." His eyes glittered with laughter. "What do you think about that, boy?"

He loved it, and to think his Daddy would include him. "I think Mama would hate it," he said with a smile.

"Which is why it's so perfect. Come on, son. Let's head home and gut the bitch."

THE RITUAL OF THE SERPENTS

Twenty-six years later...

Ochopee, Florida
Saturday, 8:07 p.m. Eastern Standard Time

"SHE'S DAMNED TO Hell."

The Reverend stared at the old fool in front of him. Back in Easterville, Tennessee, Harlan Reed had been a devout follower of his father's church. About fifteen years ago, the widower had remarried a woman half his age and, a few years later, had moved to Ochopee, Florida, with his bride and her six-year-old daughter from a previous marriage. The only reason he'd bothered to see ol' Harlan was because the man, thanks to winning an asbestos lawsuit against a previous employer, had money. Lots of money.

"You mentioned during our phone conversation that your stepdaughter has been gettin' into trouble." The Reverend rested a hand on Harlan's shoulder. "But only God can decide whether she belongs with the damned."

"Amen." Harlan nodded. "You're right. I ain't got no place to decide. But you, as your father's son, do. How is your daddy?"

Old. Dying. The Reverend sighed. He didn't know what he'd do once Daddy was gone. It'd been just the two of them for nearly three decades, and he sure did love the man. Daddy was almost bedridden now, but when he'd told his daddy about Harlan's call, the old man's eyes had brightened. He, too, knew Harlan was worth a pretty penny. "Thank the good Lord he celebrated his eightieth birthday last month. As you know, he's retired." He tapped on his chest. "The spirit is there, but the physical strength ain't what it used to be." He grinned. "Hell, my daddy jokes that he can't even lift a baby garter snake, let alone an adult rattler."

Harlan nodded. "He's a good man. I remember how he ordained you at your mama's funeral, then when he made it official a few years later. *You're* a good man. Thanks to you, he don't need to do any heavy lifting no more. Not when he has you to carry out his calling."

His calling.

His daddy's *calling* was for the ignorant and the fanatical. Who in their right mind would ever think that God wanted His followers to use the serpent that He had cast as the lowliest of creatures to do work is His name? Fools. He knew it, his daddy knew it, and together they exploited the stupid and righteous.

"Which is why I traveled here to see you, Harlan. You've been good to my daddy's church, even after the police shut it down years ago. Without supporters like you, he wouldn't have a roof over his head."

"I'd give your daddy my house if he needed it." Harlan closed his eyes. "When you were just a youngin', maybe ten or twelve, I witnessed the way God worked through your daddy." When Harlan opened his eyes, they glistened with that familiar awestruck, distant stare that he'd seen more times than he could count. "I watched him preach, heard him speaking in the tongues of God's angels, and when he raised that rattler and it bit him?" Harlan shook his head. "Your daddy didn't flinch. And he survived that bite. God Almighty. He *survived.*"

His daddy survived because the snake was too sickly to release enough, if any, venom to kill him. His daddy's trick?

Keep the snakes malnourished and it made them, along with their venom, weak. As for speaking in tongues? His daddy had taught him how to speak gibberish, but he'd never been as good at as his father. If the man wasn't as ugly as the backside of a monkey's ass, his daddy would've made a fine actor. "I was actually fifteen when that happened and I remember it well. If I recall, you were dealing with your wife's cancer."

"I was," Harlan said, his tone melancholy. "She was a good woman, just like my Sally."

Harlan's second wife, Sally, had died eight years after they'd moved to Ochopee, leaving him to raise her daughter, Katie, who he'd adopted when they had married. "You've suffered plenty, Harlan. And now you're suffering because of your daughter."

"No child of God should ever act so...foul."

"Define foul for me."

"Sex, drugs, alcohol."

While the Reverend had no interest in drugs, he was rather fond of sex and alcohol. "What a shame she's strayed so far from God's path."

"You got that right. Katie just turned twenty-one. I kicked her out when she hit eighteen, but the girl keeps comin' back. She can't hold a job. She's stolen money from me, along with her mama's jewelry. That girl would do anything to get her hands on them drugs she worships."

"Such a shame." The Reverend shook his head. "Where is she now?"

"Sleeping off whatever she was drinkin' or smokin' last night. She's down the hall in her old bedroom."

The Reverend rose from the dining room table, then peered around the corner of the modest ranch-style home. "Do you think she'll talk to me?"

"She has no choice. I warned her last night when she stumbled in from only God knows where, that you were coming. I told her she needed to heed your advice and accept the Lord Jesus, or I was going to change the locks and call the sheriff if she ever came 'round here again."

"Then I best go and speak with her. I'd hate to see you having to involve the law."

Harlan also stood. "She's in the last room at the end of the hall." He looked to the ventilated plastic container on the tiled floor. "You takin' your snakes?"

"Not just yet. We'll talk first," the Reverend said, then started down the hallway. When he realized Harlan was following him, he turned to the man. "Alone."

Harlan stopped and nodded. "Understood."

The Reverend continued on, and when he reached the closed door, he knocked.

"Go away," a woman shouted.

He opened the door and quickly found the light switch. "Mornin', Katie," he said, and smiled when the girl pulled the pale pink and green comforter over her head. The Reverend glanced around. With pink paint on the walls and a dollhouse bookshelf in the corner, the room looked as if it were for a ten-year-old girl. The only evidence a slutty young woman lived here was the spiky set of heels and a little black leather skirt on the floor, and the pack of cigarettes on the nightstand. "I hear you've been gettin' into some trouble."

Katie didn't respond. She kept the comforter over her head and rolled on her side.

He sat on the edge of the bed. "I know Harlan told you about me. I suggest you sit up and listen to what I have to say."

When the woman remained silent, he grabbed a fistful of the comforter and tore it off her. "Get out," she yelled, and quickly scrambled to her knees. "I don't care who you are or why Harlan wants you here."

She wore nothing but a skimpy tank top and panties, revealing plenty of bared flesh. Her skin was so pale he had no problem finding the track marks along her arms and legs. Her makeup was slightly smeared, making the dark circles under her eyes more prominent. The girl was skinnier than he liked, but even in her disheveled state, her dirty hair sticking up at multiple angles, there was something attractive about her. He glanced to her pert breasts. Yes, very attractive. "Harlan's worried about you," he said, meeting her gaze.

She snorted. "Yeah, right."

"He also claims that you're abusing drugs, and that your abuse has gotten so out of hand, you're stealin' from him."

"He's full of shit."

"You didn't take money or your mama's jewelry?"

"I did, but my mama gave me her jewelry before she died. Kinda hard to steal something that belongs to you."

"What about the money you stole from Harlan?"

"He's got enough to go around."

Yes, he did. By the time he left today, he'd have a nice portion of that money. "Katie, what you're doing to your body is unhealthy. God—"

"Fuck that. I don't want to hear any preaching. Now get the hell out of my room."

He grabbed her by her shoulders and gave her a shake. "This ain't your room or your house. Everything you see around you belongs to Harlan. *You* belong to him."

She struggled to free herself. "I don't belong to nobody."

He released her. "I'm guessin' the money and jewelry you stole are long gone. So, who gives you the junk you put in your veins? How do you afford it if you don't have a job?"

Katie glanced away. "None of your business."

"I'm making it my business. Are you selling yourself?"

"Get out," she said, keeping her gaze averted and crossing her arms over her small breasts.

Holy hell. Harlan's little girl had grown up to be a whore. Who would've thought? "When Harlan finds out you're prostituting yourself for drugs, I can't see him allowing you to ever enter his home again," he said, rising from the bed.

She gripped his arm. "I'm not a prostitute."

"And I'm not stupid. How do you afford the drugs?"

Her chin trembled. "You don't understand. I've gone to him for help, but he just turns a blind eye. Please, he doesn't need to know. I…I can stop."

"The drugs or whoring?"

"Both. Don't tell him. This is the only place I've got. It's the one place I feel safe," she said, her glassy eyes imploring. "I know I've done a lot of bad things, but I can change."

Well, shit. With the way Harlan had spoken on the phone, he hadn't expected the girl to confess so damned quickly. If he was going to earn the five grand Harlan had promised, he'd have to stretch out this coming-to-Jesus moment a little longer. "You'd be willin' to enter a rehab program?" he asked.

She looked away again. "I'll try it out."

"Not good enough." He shook her off him and stood. "I'm going to recommend tough love. I think Harlan should force you on the streets until you crawl back to him begging for help."

Katie hurried off the bed and stopped him at the door. "Please. I'm begging you. Don't tell him. He knows I'm not a virgin, but if he knew the truth, it'd kill him."

He smiled. "You almost sound like you care."

Her eyes filled with tears. "Because I do. I've wronged him. I know it. I know it every time I shoot up or spread my legs for a fix." Tears trickled down her pale cheeks, causing her mascara to run. She ran her hands along his chest. "Please. Talk him into giving me a second chance." She shifted her hands to his crotch.

He grabbed her wrists and stopped her before she could stroke him through his pants. Although he could use a quick lay, even he had standards. He'd rather be bitten by one of the rattlers he'd brought with him than catch a disease from a drug-abusing whore. "I need to reflect and pray. I suggest you do the same."

She dropped to her knees, and reached for his belt and pants. "I'll pray," she said.

He pushed her away. "Katie, if you want me to talk to Harlan, then you better straighten up and quick. Trying to seduce one of God's disciples ain't gonna help you none. Understand?"

Tears streamed down her cheeks, along with more mascara. She nodded and stood. "I'm sorry. I just thought—"

"You thought wrong. Now get some pants on and wait for

me. I'm going to talk to Harlan, then I'll be back in a few minutes," he said, and left the room.

"Well?" Harlan asked when the Reverend reached the dining room.

There were two ways he could play this—be a good preacher and help Harlan and Katie, or go for the money. Since he loved money…"She's worse than you thought."

The old man's eyes widened. "How bad?"

"She's whoring herself for drugs." The Reverend rested his hand on Harlan's shoulder. "She even offered herself to me if I could keep you from kickin' her out of your home."

"Dear Lord."

"We need to pray for guidance, Harlan. And you need to decide what you want to do with her."

"If people find out…" Harlan shook his head. "I can't be connected to a whore. The drugs were one thing. But whorin'?" He let out a sigh and looked down the hall to the closed bedroom door. "Can you do what we discussed when I called you? You know, help me out like your daddy helped Lyle Gessup's wife, like he helped your mama?"

Lyle Gessup was as bat-shit-crazy as the rest of his father's congregation. He'd also witnessed what he and Daddy had done to Mama before they'd buried her in the family plot. When Lyle had discovered his wife had been cheating on him, and that the child she'd recently birthed wasn't his, he'd asked Daddy to perform the Ritual of the Serpents.

Now, Daddy had only done the ritual once, and that had been on Mama. But the members of the congregation who'd been selected to watch the ritual hadn't a clue. That day, while Daddy had cut into Mama's belly, making up the ritual as he'd performed it, the members of their church had stared at him with awe and fear—no one wanted to be a sinner. "Be pure of heart and soul, lest God releases his serpents to swallow the evil within you," his daddy had told the congregation. Then, after he'd finished working on Mama, he'd gone on to cite a few times when such a ritual had been carried out. Every story had been utter bullshit. Even so, the congregation had believed

Daddy. Especially Lyle. Apparently Harlan had, too.

"I can perform the ritual, Harlan, but these are different times and we ain't in Appalachia no more. What you're asking me to do could have the law after us. Non-believers just don't understand our ways."

"I'll pay you double."

Double? For what he was risking he'd need more money. "Make it fifteen thousand and I'll take care of Katie. She'll be pure of heart and soul within no time."

When Harlan agreed without flinching, the Reverend wished he'd set his price higher. That was okay. They might no longer have a bricks-and-mortar church, but thanks to his daddy's legacy, they still had believers in over a half dozen states they could fleece. There'd be plenty of money coming in over the years, plus, once Daddy passed on, he'd have total control over his father's half-million dollar bank account instead of the modest monthly allowance he currently received.

"Her soul will be clean?" Harlan asked.

"As a newborn baby's."

Nodding, Harlan wiped a hand over the bald spot in the middle of his head. "This life ain't no good for her. She needs to be with her mama."

While he didn't agree, he wouldn't back out now. He could use the fifteen grand. Half to pay off his gambling debt, the other half to treat himself to a nice vacation. Maybe he'd take a cruise or go to one of those all-inclusive resorts.

"I think you're making the right decision," the Reverend said. "If you're ready, I'll need a few things for the ritual." After he instructed Harlan to cover the dining room table with plastic garbage bags and to bring him the sharpest knife he owned, the Reverend placed the duffle bag he'd brought with him onto the dining room chair. He set a needle, threaded with fishing line, on the table, along with several pairs of latex gloves. When he was finished, he looked to Harlan. "You're sure about this? Once the ritual begins, I can't take it back."

"I've been praying on this for a long time, Reverend. I know in my heart it's the right thing to do."

The Reverend glanced down the hall. "I promise this won't take long."

He walked toward Katie's door, then entered her room. Now wearing a pair of low-riding jeans, she stood by the opened bedroom window smoking a cigarette. After he shut the door, she turned. "How'd it go?" she asked, then dropped the cigarette butt into a can of Mountain Dew. "Does he want to see me?"

"He does."

"Did you tell him I offered myself to you?"

"No. I told him you're a lost soul who needs mending. Harlan's willing to give you a second chance." He held out his hand. "Come here, Katie." When she reached him, he smiled. "The first step to getting better is for you to open the door and face your demons."

She drew in a deep breath. "Thank you. I meant what I said. Harlan…Dad has been good to me. I don't want to be forced to live on the streets." She gave him a shy smile. "I'm sorry I offered to…you know…" she finished with a shrug.

He didn't believe one word. Not one. He knew people hooked on drugs. She was lying to him, and would lie to Harlan in order to keep from being booted from the house. Did she deserve what was coming because she was a lying, whoring drug addict? Nope. But he couldn't pass up fifteen grand.

The Reverend placed both hands on her shoulders. "You're welcome." He slid his hands up her neck. "You'll soon see, when you leave this life behind, you'll be in a better place," he said, then kneed her in the stomach.

She grunted and doubled over. Keeping his hands around her neck, he threw her to the floor, then climbed on top of her. As he held her down and choked her, she swung at his face, then tried to grip his hands. Worried she'd mark him or that his skin might end up embedded in her fingernails, he slammed her head against the tile floor until she went still.

He bent his head to her mouth. Still breathing. Now that she was unconscious he could kill her without injury to

21

himself. After a few more minutes of squeezing, he checked her breathing and her pulse.

Finally dead. He'd killed four people. The two men he'd killed with his bare hands hadn't taken as long as Katie to die. Who would've thought this little slip of a girl who'd treated her body like shit had that much fight in her?

He climbed off Katie, then opened the bedroom door. After he lifted her lifeless body in his arms, he carried her down the hall and into the dining room.

Harlan stared at Katie. "Is she…?"

"Yes," he said, and laid her on top of the bags.

"Did she suffer?"

"No. From here on out, there will be no suffering." He rested his hand on Harlan's shoulder. "Especially for you."

The Reverend picked up one of the pairs of latex gloves he'd left on the table, then handed the other to Harlan. "Put these on. I might need your help. Be prepared. What I'm about to do isn't for the faint of heart," he said, snapping on the gloves. "But I promise I'll be quick."

Before he'd come to Ochopee, Florida, his father had explained how to execute the ritual. Although the Reverend had been by his daddy's side the three times they'd done the ceremony, he'd never done it himself. According to Daddy, how quick the process would go depended on whether he had the balls to cut the woman. Considering he'd had no problem choking the life out of her, he doubted he'd have a problem slicing her body.

Out of respect for Harlan, he shoved the girl's tank top up, keeping her breasts covered. He picked up the knife, stabbed Katie in the stomach, then sliced her abdomen horizontally. When he moved the skin apart, making a larger, deeper cavity for him to use, Harlan gasped and turned away. "Almost finished, Harlan. Hang in there."

Satisfied with what he'd done to Katie, he stepped away from her body and nodded to the container holding the snakes. After he instructed Harlan to open it, he bent, grabbed the largest, sickliest rattler by the head and yanked it from its temporary home without fear. "This is the most important part of the ritual," he said. "Close the lid and come pray with me."

Harlan did as he'd been instructed, then raised his hands in the air.

The Reverend held the malnourished rattlesnake over his head. "*Behold, I give unto you power to tread on serpents and scorpions,*" he began, quoting Luke and forcing his voice to shake as if the power of God ran through him, "*and over all the power of the enemy: and nothing shall by any means hurt you.*"

"Amen," Harlan murmured.

Since he couldn't remember what other bullshit prayers his daddy had used, he made up his own. His prayers assured Katie's spirit would be free of the demons that had possessed her in this life, and reassured Harlan that God would forever look over him. When he finished, he told Harlan to open the container again. He set the rattler back inside, then quickly grabbed one of the baby rattlers his daddy had recommended he bring. Considering the snake he'd used for his prayer was about four feet long, there was no way in hell it'd fit in Katie's belly.

After Harlan closed the lid again, locking the snakes inside, he stared at the skinny, one-foot rattlesnake he held. The young ones could release venom, and since this one was still healthy, it could cause him serious damage, should little bastard bite him. But at least it would fit.

The Reverend used his free hand to widen the slice along Katie's belly, then shoved the snake's head, along with the rest of its body, inside.

Keeping one hand over Katie's stomach, which shifted slightly as the snake moved, he ordered Harlan to hand him the threaded needle. He pulled Katie's skin together and began stitching. Her blood made the needle slippery, so he took his time in order to make sure he didn't prick himself and leave any of his DNA behind.

When he finished, he released a deep sigh and looked to Harlan who had grown ashen. "You good?" he asked.

Harlan wiped a hand down his face. "Yeah, I'm good. I was

just remembering what a sweet girl Katie used to be before the devil infested her soul."

"She wasn't that girl no more." The Reverend took off his gloves. He placed them in one of the plastic freezer bags he'd brought with him, along with the needle, thread and knife. "The baby rattler in her belly represents the Devil. It'll feed on the evil rotting Katie's soul. Once the serpent is full, it'll die and free Katie, sending her straight into God's arms." Hot damn, he was so good at this he almost believed his own bullshit. "Remember the good times and be thankful that she won't suffer no more. Understand?"

Harlan met his gaze. "I do. So now what?"

Give me my money so I can get the hell out of here. My congregation is waiting for me.

He picked up a clean pair of gloves. "Now we get rid of her."

PART I

Marriage is like putting your hand into a bag of snakes in the hope of pulling out an eel.

—Leonardo da Vinci

KRISTINE MASON

CHAPTER 1

Two years later…

Cap'n Ryan's Airboat Tours, Everglades City, Florida
Wednesday, 2:42 p.m. Eastern Standard Time

SHANE MONAHAN COUNTED his steps as he walked toward the porch of Cap'n Ryan's Airboat Tours. When he noticed the kids standing around Vlad Aristov, the Russian stray his brother Ryan had hired, he counted how many there were, then quickly combined the amount of kids with the number of steps it had taken him to walk from his truck to the porch.

Eighteen.

"Stop," Vlad shouted, making the two smaller children jump. "Polina no toy." The Russian stroked the small alligator he held as if it were a furry cat rather than a reptile. "Vlad will let children with small hands hold Polina."

When the four kids reached the gator, Vlad raised Polina away from them. "Once a time or Vlad take Polina away."

A girl, with bright red hair and enough freckles to keep Shane counting for hours, tugged at the large Russian's shirt.

27

"Who's Vlad?"

The Russian frowned. "Vlad is Vlad."

The girl looked to the redheaded boy—likely her brother—next to her, who shrugged. "What's a Vlad?"

"Vlad *is* a Vlad," the Russian said, and pointed to the pocket of his uniform shirt where his name had been stitched. "Maybe small child should not play hooker and go back to school to learn to read."

Hooker? Shane wiped a hand down his face. His brother should *not* let Vlad around the public.

"I know how to read," the redheaded boy said with offense, then scrunched his forehead and turned to the girl. "What's a hooker?"

"I don't know," the girl said. "I'll go ask Mommy."

Oh, sweet Jesus. "Hold up there, kiddo." Shane rushed over and set a hand on the girl's shoulder. "Lemme clear a few things up for you. This big guy here," he began, giving the Russian a light smack on the back, "is Vlad. Polina is his two-year-old gator. So he's a little protective of her. I'm sure he'll let each one of you have a turn at holding Polina. Right, Vlad?"

The Russian nodded his blond head. "Да."

"English for the kiddos."

Vlad rolled his eyes and sighed. "Yes. Vlad let child hold Polina."

After Vlad handed the gator over to the redheaded boy, the kid turned toward the two adults near the pier. "Look at me, Dad," he called to the man taking a picture of the airboat docked in the canal.

As the father swiveled and took a couple of shots, the redheaded girl asked, "So what's a hooker?"

"I know." Another boy, who in no way resembled the two redheads, stepped forward. "It's—"

"Not what you think," Shane said. "Vlad's not from around here and his English isn't the best. He was referring to playing hooky."

"That's not what he said," the kid insisted. "He was talking about hook—"

"Hey, guys," Harrison Fairclough, his brother's other new stray, rushed down the porch steps. "Cap'n Ryan's treasure chest is open for his maties. Ask your parents if it's okay to go into the ice cream shop and pick a small souvenir."

As the other kids rushed off to pick out free junk, the redheaded boy handed Polina over to Vlad. "I think your alligator is cool."

Vlad nodded and held the gator to his chest. After the boy ran off to join the others, he sighed. "Small children," he began, "are pain in Vlad ass."

"*You're* a pain in my ass," Harrison said, keeping his voice low. "I heard the hooker thing from inside the souvenir shop. Hell, even the customers inside heard you. You've gotta get over this obsession with Polina, otherwise Ryan's not going to let you do this anymore."

The Russian kissed the alligator's head. "Vlad no care."

"Lola will," Harrison countered, and shoved his light brown hair off his forehead. "Don't screw things up for us over a frickin' gator."

Harrison shook his head and looked to Shane. "You've got two tours on your schedule, then we're calling it a day. The first one is in about twenty minutes. Barney wasn't sure if you'd make it back on time, and readied your boat for you."

Shane nodded, then glanced to Vlad after Harrison walked back into the souvenir shop, which was also where customers signed up for their airboat tours. "If you don't like kids, why are you doing this?"

"Vlad like kid. Vlad no like when kid touch Polina," the Russian said, and placed the gator in its cage.

Shane stared at the man's massive back and shoulders. According to Ryan, Vlad was a former heavyweight boxer and a friend of Ryan's fiancée, Lola. Based on the man's size, he hadn't doubted his brother. How Lola had managed to talk Ryan into letting the Russian work for the airboat tour company, showing off his alligator, he still didn't know. Same went for Harrison. Neither man had a set job, but at least Harrison helped in the shop and scheduling tours. Still. Mel or

Barney could handle that end of the business, just like they had before he'd gone away.

"Then maybe you shouldn't bring Polina here," he said.

Vlad finished locking the cage, then stood and faced him. "Then what Vlad do all day?" he asked, frowning.

Shane shrugged. "Don't know. What'd you do before you worked for my brother?"

"Vlad live in Orlando by your Mickey Mouse Land."

"Right. You told me that before. But what did you *do* in Orlando?"

The Russian winked. "Misty."

"Misty?"

"Да, Misty. Blonde with big titties and bad attitude. Misty smash Vlad phone and took baseball bat to Vlad car." He sighed. "Then Misty broke Vlad heart."

"I'm not asking about the woman you were doing when you were living in Orlando, I'm asking you how you made money. You know, what kind of job did you have?" When it came to Vlad and Harrison's background, he could never get a straight answer from either man. Even his brother had been tightlipped about them, only mentioning Vlad's boxing gig, and that Harrison was great with computers.

Vlad placed a hand on Shane's shoulder and looked out into the parking lot. "Vlad love Kiss."

Shane tensed and knocked off his hand. "Sorry, buddy. I don't swing that way."

Vlad laughed. "Vlad say he like big titties, not penis."

"No, you said you love to kiss."

"No. Vlad say he love Kiss. Picture Vlad with makeup," the Russian said, then stuck out his tongue.

"I'm going to throw up on you if you do that again."

Vlad turned him toward the parking lot, just as the woman Shane had been fantasizing about for the past eight days stepped out of her small SUV. She rested her knee on the driver's seat, then leaned back into the vehicle to reach for something on the passenger side, giving him an excellent view of her rear. He instantly pictured her with her shorts around her ankles, his hands on her hips and his dick buried—

"Is not the woman stalking Shane name Beth, like Kiss song?"

"Yeah," he said, Vlad's actions and words clicking into place. "So you don't want to kiss me and the tongue thing was your attempt to mimic Gene Simmons from the *band* Kiss."

"Да." Vlad nodded his blond head. "*Beth* Vlad favorite Kiss song."

"Thank God we got that cleared up." Shane took a step off the porch, then stopped when he remembered what else Vlad had said. "And she isn't stalking me."

Vlad crossed his arms over his massive chest. "Shane work for Captain Ryan eight day, no?"

"Yeah, so?"

"How many time Kiss Beth do boat tour?"

"She's not stalking me," he repeated. "Ryan and Barney both get repeat business and tourists requesting them as their captain all the time."

"Vlad think Shane in the Nile. Time to awake and smell what in coffee mug." He leaned forward and sniffed. "Vlad think Shane should make use of shower or baby wipe. Shane smell like engine."

Considering he'd spent the majority of the morning and early afternoon working on his Cessna Skyhawk, he probably did smell greasy. And since this was the third time he would be taking Beth on an airboat tour, Vlad could be right. The woman might be interested in him.

Who the hell was he kidding? He'd seen the way Beth had checked him out and had loved every second of it. He hadn't been with a woman in seven years and he wanted this one. Not just because he wanted to tangle his hands in her long, wavy brown hair as he buried himself deep inside her sexy body. While he wouldn't deny his physical attraction to her, or the way his stomach tightened when he pictured her, she was more than a pretty package. He was turned on by her confidence, curiosity, killer smile and genuine laugh. Plain and simple, Beth was fun. After seven years of being locked in a prison cell, he needed fun in his life.

"I'll be right back," he said, and headed into the souvenir shop. Ignoring the customers checking out t-shirts and trinkets, he moved into his brother's office, then began searching the closet for something to make him smell better.

"What are you looking for?" Harrison asked.

"Do you know if Ryan keeps cologne in here?"

"No, but Lola has some hand lotion that smells nice."

"I don't want to smell like a woman." Shane closed the closet door and stared at Harrison. "Why didn't you tell me Beth was my first tour?"

"Beth? Your stalker? Sorry, man. I didn't book her tour. Barney hasn't left. Do you want me to see if he'll take her out?"

"No. And she's *not* stalking me."

Shane made his way out of the office and toward the exit. When he reached the porch, Beth was bent down next to Vlad, checking out Polina. Her tank top gave him a nice view of her ample cleavage. He glanced away from her breasts and quickly slipped on the sunglasses he'd hooked to the pocket of his uniform shirt.

"Afternoon," he greeted her.

She looked up and smiled. He drifted his gaze to her mouth. He'd love to know if her lips were as soft as they looked. He'd love to see her breathless, her lips parted as he learned every inch of her body with his hands and mouth.

"Hey there," she said, and stood. "Since it's just me again, are any other tourists joining us?"

During Shane's first day back to work, he'd taken Beth and her friend on a boat tour. She hadn't requested him as captain. Instead the tour schedule had worked in his favor. That day, he'd been lucky enough to spend an hour listening and watching Beth and her friend laugh and have a great time as he veered them through the Glades. Three days later, Beth had come back for another tour. She'd been alone and had requested him as her boat captain.

Harrison had planned to add a family of four to Beth's

tour, but the family had declined, saying they would prefer to wait until they had the boat to themselves. When he'd found out about Beth's request, he'd told himself not to read too much into it. Maybe she liked the adrenaline rush that sometimes came when he took the boat to full speed. Or maybe she just liked being in the Everglades. He wanted to think she was interested in him. But after years of being labeled a piece of shit, his confidence wasn't all there. When her tour had ended, he'd been tempted to ask Beth for her number, but hadn't had the balls. If he'd read her wrong and she became offended, making a pass at a paying customer would look bad for his brother's business, not to mention a blow to his already deflated ego. Besides, what woman would want to go out with an ex-con?

"No other tourists today," Shane said. "I'm afraid you're stuck with me."

Beth grinned. "I asked for you, so I think it's the other way around."

The Russian stood. "Vlad know Shane like Kiss Beth on boat."

Beth's sunglasses hid her eyes, but her creased forehead spoke volumes. "I'm sorry, what did you just say?"

Before Vlad dug himself into a deep hole, Shane touched Beth's arm and motioned toward the wooden ramp leading to the dock. "Don't mind Vlad," he said, once they'd distanced themselves from the Russian.

"It's kind of hard not to when the man said that you'd like to kiss me on the boat."

"That's not what he said."

She stopped when they reached the dock. "That's what I heard."

Damn it. He was going to have to have a serious conversation with his brother about Vlad. "I apologize if Vlad made you uncomfortable. I never told him I wanted to kiss you. Vlad has a thing for the Kiss song *Beth*. He also does this weird thing with peoples' names. He calls my brother Captain Ryan, and my future sister-in-law Asian Lola."

"Why does he call her that?"

"Because she's Asian."

Beth laughed. "Isn't Vlad the master of the obvious? I love it. Okay, so Vlad nicknamed me Kiss Beth and you don't want to kiss me. Gotcha."

"I didn't say that." *Smooth, Monahan.* Fuck it. He wanted to see her away from the boat shop, take her out to dinner, find out more about her and, yes, kiss her.

When her lips tilted in a sexy smile, he relaxed. She turned and climbed onto the airboat, then settled on the cushioned bench seat. "For the record, I wouldn't turn down a kiss from you," she said, and reached for the headphones used to block the loud sound of the airboat.

Maybe not right now, but once Beth found out about his past, she would probably run in the other direction. What woman would want to kiss a convicted murderer?

I can't believe I just told Shane I wanted him to kiss me.

Bethany Price held the headphones tight in her hand, as Shane veered the boat into the no-wake zone. Never in her life had she been so forward with a man. Sure, she went after what she wanted. And, yes, this was the second time she'd requested that Shane captain the boat for her tour, so he had to know she was interested in him.

If he didn't, he sure does now.

Oh, well. She couldn't take the words back, and honestly didn't want to. It had been a long time since she'd dated. Between work and school there hadn't been much time for a social life. Plus, when most guys had found out what she did for a living, they ran in the other direction. Not many men were interested in dating a cop.

"Since this is your third time out," Shane began, "how about we go a different route and see some new sites."

"Sounds good to me," she replied, glad he'd finally said something to break the block of ice she'd put between them.

"Does this mean you're not going to tell me about the infamous albino alligator or the elusive coonther?" During her first two tours, Shane had told her tall tales about the made-up gator and deadly hybrid raccoon-panther creature that lurked in the darkest recesses of the Everglades.

With a chuckle, he shook his head. "Those are the best stories I've got. Actually, I stole them from my brother, and Barney, the other boat captain. He has a couple about alien experiments and the zombie apocalypse he likes to tell. If you're interested, I can spice up the ride with tales of zombies rising from the sawgrass and attacking campers."

She raised a hand. "I'm good. I don't do zombies."

"Aliens?"

She grinned. "Instead of making up stories, why don't you tell me yours?"

"Mine?" he asked, waving at a passing boat. "Not much to tell."

"How long have you been driving an airboat?"

"I learned how when I was a kid. My dad had one, and was good buddies with Barney, the other captain I was telling you about. They both taught me and Ryan everything we know about boating and the Glades."

"So, Cap'n Ryan is your brother?"

"Yeah, younger by about ten months. Since this is the busy season, I've been taking shifts to help out." He picked up his headphones. "We're almost out of the no-wake zone. I feel kinda funny sitting up here by myself. Why don't you sit in the chair next to mine. If you want, I'll let you steer."

"Really?" Not waiting for an answer, Beth stood, then moved around the two sets of bench seats. Shane helped her onto the higher platform. His hand was big and rough. Before she pictured him running his hands along her bare skin, she quickly sat, her arm brushing against his.

"Ready?" he asked, and put on his headphones.

After she did the same, she nodded, then quickly gripped the armrest when Shane shifted the stick between them forward. As they sped through the narrow canal, the mangrove trees lining the shore created a cool tunnel effect. When he increased the speed and took the boat over drifting logs, water sprayed her face and tiny droplets clung to her sunglasses. Considering the temperature hovered in the high eighties, she welcomed the cool water and warm breeze. What she loved the most was sitting next to Shane.

She'd first gone to Cap'n Ryan's Airboat Tours with her friend, Erin. Actually, she'd dragged Erin with her. As an Ohio transplant, Beth had wanted to know everything she could about Florida. In the five years she'd been here, she had hit every beach within a three-hour radius. Once she'd switched from being a paramedic to a deputy for the Collier County Sheriff's Office and some of her cases had taken her into the Everglades, she had decided to explore the area.

There were dozens of airboat tour companies along Florida's southwest coast. During the past year, she'd been on tours with at least half of them. After the first tour, she'd been hooked. She loved how the airboat moved, but mostly she loved the eerie beauty of the Everglades. While each boat tour had been different and a total blast, the ride Shane had given her and Erin had stuck with her the most. Okay, Shane had stuck with her.

Although she was normally attracted to men with short, dark hair, Shane had become the exception. When she'd first spotted him by the dock, desire had immediately curled through her belly. Like today, he'd worn his shoulder length, dark-blond hair slicked back away from his face. His dark-blue, short-sleeved uniform shirt had hugged his biceps and chest in a way that had her fantasizing about what he'd look like shirtless. Hair or no hair on his chest? She could care less. She wanted to stare at his naked chest as she lay beneath him. Then there was the short beard. From the moment she saw it, her fingers had itched to touch his face. Was his beard soft? How would it feel brushing against her inner thighs?

She glanced away from his strong profile, and back to the water. She wanted to be bad with this man. Growing up the youngest of five, and the only girl in the bunch, she'd never had the opportunity to be bad and take a walk on the wild side. Despite his cool, quiet exterior, she suspected Shane had a wild side to him and she wanted him to unleash it on her.

She wasn't looking for love or a major relationship, but wouldn't pass either up if the right man came along. For the past five years, her sole focus had been on work and night school, leaving her little time to date or find the right guy for her. Since she was graduating in the spring, and her course schedule this semester was light, she was ready to have some fun and start dating again. But would Shane be interested? He didn't deny that he'd like to kiss her, yet he hadn't exactly confirmed it. During their last boat tour, he had stopped the boat in a marsh so she could check out the alligators and other animals in the area. They'd remained there for a while talking about nothing and everything. Later, when the tour had ended, she'd thought he might ask her out, but had been wrong and she'd left Cap'n Ryan's disappointed.

Erin claimed third time's the charm, and that men could be clueless. Her friend also suggested that Shane might have wanted Beth to do the asking. After all, the tour company could have a policy against employees dating customers, which Beth could understand. The last thing Shane's brother would need is a sexual harassment suit against his business.

Because she'd sensed a connection between them, and she'd sworn Shane had checked her out, she'd taken Erin's advice and had decided to come for one more boat tour. Once they were back at the dock, she'd ask Shane if he'd like to see her again. If he declined, that'd be a damned shame.

He slowed the airboat when they reached an open stretch of water surrounded by more mangroves and tall grasses. "Ready to drive?"

She looked at the two sticks between them. "Will you get into any trouble?"

"Maybe if you crash and sink us," he said with a smile.

"Not funny. I'm being serious."

"You'll be fine. Here," he said, taking her hand and wrapping it around the right stick. "This is the throttle. The other one steers the boat. If you push the throttle forward, we go. If you pull it back, we slow down." Keeping his warm palm over the back of her hand, he pressed forward, which caused the boat to move, then he eased back, slowing them. "See. Nice and easy. Now on to the steering. Forward is right, back is left. Keep it in a neutral position and we'll go straight. Got it?"

Forward right, back left. Forward fast, back slow…

"Yeah, I think I've got it."

"Then go for it."

She moved the throttle, not much, and took them at a mild pace. Then she practiced her steering. After a few minutes, and confident she wouldn't crash them into the mangroves, she increased the power and speed. Her heart rate kicked up a few notches and she couldn't stop smiling as she took the boat across the water. Knowing the airboat could turn on a dime, she decided to mimic Shane's skills. Pushing the left stick forward, she whipped them to the right, causing water to splash into the boat. Shane let her loop around the marsh several times before he gave her a nudge with his shoulder and placed his hand over hers, easing the throttle back until the boat slowed.

"You did good. Told you it was easy." He kept one hand over hers and used the other to take off his headphones. "If you like planes, maybe I'll take you up in mine and let you give that a spin, too."

Did he just ask her on a date? Maybe wasn't concrete enough for her. "I didn't realize you were a pilot."

"Yeah, I own a Cessna Skyhawk. It's a single engine and seats four. I give aerial tours over the Everglades, or fly folks to the Keys or Miami. I fly out of Everglades Airpark."

"That's really cool. How long have you been flying?"

Keeping his hand over hers, he took them away from the marsh and into one of the many canals that made up the Everglades. "Since I was seventeen." He looked to their joined hands. "Ready to make this thing cook?"

When she nodded, he eased the throttle back, then,

unfortunately let go of her hand and picked up his headphones. She did the same, which meant no more hand-holding. That was okay. Once they both had on their ear protection, Shane took them for a fantastic ride. Twenty minutes later, he eased the throttle back, slowing the boat as they approached the no-wake zone. While Beth slipped off the headphones, nervousness settled in the pit of her stomach. She'd already requested Shane as her tour guide twice. Since she didn't want him or the people he worked with to think she was a stalker, there wouldn't be a third time. Now that the ride was over, she wasn't sure she had the nerve to ask him out. She could handle rejection, but damn it, she liked Shane and wanted to see him again.

"Did you have a good time?" he asked, as he steered the boat toward the dock.

"Absolutely. Thanks for letting me drive. I'm sure it gets boring for you, but I loved it."

"Not at all. I get a kick out of watching the tourists having fun." He slowed in front of the dock. "Especially the kids."

With his rough, rugged exterior, she hadn't pictured Shane as the type of guy who liked children. Then again, what did she really know about him? He drove a boat and flew a plane, which gave her the impression that he liked adventure. But what else did he like? Her?

"Sorry you didn't see any gators." He hopped off the boat and quickly secured it to the dock. "The last two times I took you out, we got lucky."

She drew in a deep breath and decided to shove her nerves aside and go for it. "I didn't come out for the gators," she said. "If I want to see one, I can hang with Vlad and Polina."

He took her hand and helped her off the boat. "So why'd you come for another tour?" he asked, still touching her.

Her stomach flipped. With her free hand, she dug into the front pocket of her shorts for the tip she had ready for him. Although he'd refused her money the last time, she didn't want to assume he would again. She held up the fifteen dollars. "This is for you," she replied, suddenly too chicken to admit the truth. She might be blunt and usually had no problem going after what she wanted, but if Shane had no interest in her outside of boating and *maybe* flying, she'd rather not make a complete fool of herself.

He plucked the money from her hand, then reached between their bodies and stuffed the fifteen dollars back into her pocket. "I don't want your money." He settled his hand on her hip. "I want your number."

Oh. My. God. Her heart tripped. "Don't feel obligated because I've been here twice to see you."

When Shane took off his sunglasses, her breath caught. The hunger in his gray-blue eyes had her licking her lips and aching to kiss him. "The first time I saw you, I went to bed that night with you on my mind. After the second time, I couldn't sleep because I was too busy kicking my butt over not asking you out for coffee or dinner." He inched his hand up to her waist. "Now that you know where I stand, I'm going to ask you again, why'd you come for another tour?"

"Because the first time I saw you, I went to bed that night with you on my mind," she said, repeating his words and telling him the absolute truth.

Despite the bright sun, his eyes darkened with unmistakable desire. "I wonder if we were both thinking the same thing?"

She grinned. "Maybe we should compare our thoughts over dinner?"

As he leaned forward, she inhaled. Damn, he smelled good. Like grease, saltwater and pure hardworking male. "Tonight?" he asked, pulling her a fraction closer.

Wow, the man moves fast. "That works for me."

The laughter of kids floated from the parking lot to the dock. "Sounds like my next tour is here. Can I get you an ice cream or something to drink?" he asked.

"Thanks, but I'll pass. I have a few things to do before we go out. Where and when do you want to meet? I live in Marco Island. How about you?"

"I'm here in Everglades City. What'd you say I head your way? Is The Fish House still around? That should be close to where you live."

A five-minute drive. "Pretty close," she said, instead. Between being a paramedic and a cop, she'd seen enough to know never to trust strangers. No matter how attractive they were. "What time is good for you?"

"Does seven work?" he asked, letting go of her hand.

"Perfect," she said with a smile, then turned when one of the tour company's employees, Harry, according to Vlad, led a group of five toward the dock. "I'll let you get to work. See you later."

"Looking forward to it," he said, his eyes holding promise. Then he slipped on his sunglasses and greeted the tourists.

As she headed for her RAV-4, she saw Vlad standing at the side of the building smoking. He quickly put the cigarette behind his back, and waved. "Bye-bye, Kiss Beth," he called.

She smiled and waved back. Once she was inside her car and had the AC cranked, she pulled her cell phone off the car charger, then called Erin.

"Well, how'd it go?" Erin asked, as Beth drove out of the parking lot, then onto County Road 29.

Beth couldn't stop grinning. "We have a date tonight."

"See, I told you third time's the charm."

"Technically, this was my second time to see him. The first time I didn't know he existed."

"Doesn't matter. Give me the details."

She turned north onto U.S. Route 41 and filled Erin in on what had happened during the boat ride. When she finished relaying what had gone on once she and Shane were on the dock, Erin let out a dreamy sigh.

"Wow," her friend said. "That's hot. Are you going to bring him home tonight?"

"God, no. I might've already had sex with him in my head, but I'm not a slut."

Erin laughed. "Considering you haven't had sex outside your head in what? A year? I'd definitely say slut is the last word I'd use to describe you."

"What about desperate?" Beth asked. "Let's face it. I didn't exactly play hard to get."

"No, you did what you do when you want something."

"Yeah, but we're not talking about a job or a condo. This could be a pity date. He might not even show tonight."

"Would you stop?" Erin sighed again, this one bordering on frustrated. "C'mon, Beth, why are you second-guessing this? He's all you've been talking about for the past week."

"I'm not second-guessing myself."

"Then what's the problem?"

"I like him and he doesn't know I'm a cop."

Erin chuckled. "Look, I know you've had bad luck with men. The guys who took off the moment they found out what you do for a living were dickheads."

"Shane could be a jerk, too," she countered.

"If he is, move on. If he's not, then maybe he could end up being someone to have fun with in between work and school."

Or maybe not. Shane wasn't just a carefree boat captain, but a pilot and business owner. She loved a man who had drive and wasn't afraid of hard work. Fun could turn into something more serious, which might not be such a good thing. Once she graduated from law school in May, she would have to study for the Bar exam and search for a job as a law clerk, leaving her little time to focus on a relationship.

"And," Erin began, "if you're worried Shane's going to walk when he finds out you're a cop, then don't tell him."

"I'm not going to lie."

"I didn't say you should. I'm saying keep him distracted and off the topic of what you do for a living. Keep in mind," Erin continued in a taunting tone, "you haven't had sex in a year."

"It's been longer than that," Beth admitted.

"What? I thought you and Paul—"

"Didn't happen." Two years into her job as a deputy, Paul had been the first guy who hadn't acted as if her profession bothered him. For a few months, she'd actually thought they might have a good thing going, until a routine traffic stop. She and her partner, Ricky, had pulled over a car speeding through an intersection. To her surprise, Paul had been in the car with his wife and kids. "Remember, he was the cheater?"

"Oh, that's right. You were seeing him when I was about to give birth to Jackson. Sorry, impending motherhood had me a little self-absorbed back then."

"You were not." She loved Erin. When she'd first become a paramedic, Erin had been a dispatcher for the Collier County Sheriff's Office. Her husband, Trey, was a fireman. When they'd met at a mutual friend's house for a barbeque four years ago, they'd hit it off and had been best friends ever since. Calling Erin—who would do just about anything for her or anyone else—self-absorbed was like calling Beth a slut. Neither description fit.

"So how long has it been?" Erin asked.

"For what?"

"Sex."

Too long. "I'm just about home. I'll call you tomorrow and let you know how tonight went."

"Bethany Ann, you better tell me."

"Or what?"

"Damn it. I don't know. I can't think straight. Payton's teething and Jackson's acting like frickin' Pig Pen. My house is a mess and, since I quit nursing, my hormones have been going ape shit." She paused. "It's not a good combo, so you should probably tell me the truth."

"Three years."

"Three years," Erin repeated. "That's ridiculous. The only people who go that long are priests, nuns and prisoners. Even some prisoners get conjugal visits."

Beth laughed as she turned down the street leading to her townhome. "Although this conversation has been riveting, I'm almost home and need to do a few things before my date."

"You know, Shane might be different," Erin said. "He seemed like a cool guy. Maybe he won't care that you're a cop."

Beth pulled into the driveway she shared with her neighbor and hit the garage door remote. "True. But with my luck, he'll want me to bring out the hand cuffs and play dirty cop."

Erin chuckled. "That wouldn't be too weird." Payton wailed in the background. "Sounds like naptime is over," she said. "Before I go, what are you going to wear?"

"I haven't gotten that far."

"Speaking of far…how far are you going to let things go tonight?"

Beth climbed out of the car. "Go take care of your daughter, and I'll call you tomorrow."

"You're no fun. Send me a text when you get home. I want to make sure you're okay."

"Yes, Mother," she said, then after saying good-bye, she ended the call and headed into her townhome. She was met with utter silence and suddenly envied Erin's loud, chaotic house.

She'd grown up in a large family where everyone vied to be heard and missed the noise.

Maybe she should adopt a cat. While she considered herself a dog person, a cat would be easier to take care of with her schedule. But did she really want a pet to ease the loneliness? Not really. She just wanted someone to hang out with once in a while.

She glanced at the clock and decided to take a quick shower, then give the homework assignment due tomorrow another read. As she stood under the warm shower spray, she couldn't stop thinking about Shane, their date, or how he'd react to her job. By the time she was seated at her kitchen table, books open, laptop in front of her, she decided the hell with it.

She looked from her lanai toward the setting sun. If Shane was intimidated by her being a Collier County deputy and blew her off, that'd be his loss.

She let out a sigh. And a damned shame.

****

Naples, Florida
Wednesday, 4:32 p.m. Eastern Standard Time

His dead lover called to him. He stood naked in front of the bedroom mirror, staring at her lifeless body in the reflection. The soft glow of the candles on his nightstands gave her pale skin the illusion of warmth. But he knew her body was cold to the touch. Blood no longer flowed through her veins and had been replaced with formaldehyde.

He looked away from his lover and glanced down at his erect penis. His hand shook as he stroked himself.

"This is so wrong," he whispered, and closed his eyes.

She'll feel so right.

Morally, ethically what he was about to do defied everything he'd been taught. He'd been raised to respect the dead. He'd been educated to help the living. Doctors hadn't been able to save his lover. Some might say a higher power had taken her. While he believed in a higher power, clinically, ventricular fibrillation had caused her death.

He opened his eyes and glanced at the young mother of two. Such a shame. She'd had so much to live for.

She deserves to rest in peace.

With disgust, he released his erection and looked to the boxers he'd left on the hardwood floor. He should dress, take the woman, along with the other two bodies resting in the fifteen cubic foot freezer in his garage, and remove them from his house.

What man became sexually stimulated by the dead?

A sick one. A vile, morally debased creature infected by lust, by disgusting desires.

But was he truly a bad person? Was it his fault his body couldn't react normally in the company of a beautiful, *living* woman?

Besides, he wasn't doing this for himself. He was taking a lover for Gabriela. The image of his longtime girlfriend filled his mind. Her long black hair, olive skin, dark-brown eyes and gorgeous smile. He loved her body. Only he couldn't *love* her body in the way she desired. Impotence wasn't the problem. He pressed down on his erection. Clearly he had no issues with erectile dysfunction. Yet he still couldn't make love to Gabriela.

He had performance anxiety. Plain and simple. He wanted to marry Gabriela and have children with her. What woman would want to be married to a man who couldn't give them children without artificial insemination? What woman would stay with him if he couldn't give her pleasure? Toys and oral sex had helped sustain their relationship, but Gabriela was a young, passionate woman. If he didn't give her what her body desired, would she eventually find a man who could?

White-hot jealousy had him gripping his erection. He'd seen the way the men at the country club had ogled Gabriela's curvy body and full breasts while she'd sunned herself by the pool. There had been hunger in their eyes, and he'd imagined them undressing her, tearing off her bikini, groping her breasts and rear.

He let out a harsh breath. Right or wrong, to save his relationship with Gabriela he *had* to give this a try. He had to take his lover and prove that he could perform like a normal man. Viagra hadn't worked, neither had seeing a sex therapist. Would the lifeless body of an attractive woman stimulate him enough to finally reach an orgasm without the use of his hand?

Gabriela had never complained about their sex life—yet— but the women from his past had, which had only heightened his anxiety. The dead couldn't complain. They couldn't bitch about not having an orgasm, or pat him on the back and tell him that maybe next time the sex would be better.

Ignoring the boxers on the floor, he drew in a deep breath and walked to the bed where his lover lay on the center of the mattress surrounded by silky gray sheets. He'd painted the woman's finger and toenails the same shade of red Gabriela liked to wear, and had dressed her in the red bra and panties he had bought for Gabriela last week. The tags were still on the lingerie. Whether this experiment worked or not, he still planned to gift Gabriela the bra and panties, and pictured how incredibly sexy she'd look wearing them.

Keeping Gabriela in mind, he ran his hand along the calf of the woman, then spread her legs wider. When he looked up at her face, he realized this was all wrong. He quickly moved away from the bed, grabbed the brand and color of lipstick Gabriela preferred, along with a bottle of her favorite perfume. He returned to the bed, then climbed onto it and moved toward the woman, whose name—according to the paperwork he'd found with her body—was Darla. He moved her long hair, which draped along her shoulders and chest. He'd noticed the two small incisions above her clavicle bone on the left side of her body earlier when he'd dressed her in the lingerie. One incision had been made at her carotid artery to pump the formaldehyde into her veins. The other cut had been to her jugular vein, where her blood had been expelled from her body as the formaldehyde replaced it. He gave the area where the incisions were located a small spritz, then did the same on her right side. Once his lover's skin held the delicate scent of lilies, peonies and jasmine, he set the bottle of perfume aside, then pulled the cap from the lipstick.

The embalmer had done an excellent job of making the woman look pretty, even in death. He'd used the perfect sized eye caps to keep her eyes from sinking, and had sutured her mouth in a way that made her lips look pleasing. As he applied the lipstick, he realized the embalmer must have injected a compound into her mouth to help with the natural effect. Darla had pretty lips, and he momentarily pictured how they would have looked puckered as she'd prepared for a kiss.

Guilt crashed into him. How many times had this woman kissed her husband and two young children? Who was he to take those intimate moments away from her or her family?

Before he made a mess with the lipstick, he quickly capped it, and tossed it next to the perfume bottle. Despite the guilt, his penis had grown painfully hard. For the first time in his life, he could take his time and do as he pleased—without judgment from his lover.

When he'd stripped Darla of her funeral attire and had

dressed her in the bra and panties, he had done so with a clinical mindset. He hadn't lingered at her nipples or labia. Instead, he'd pretended she was a mannequin. As despicable as his plans were, he'd wanted to prove to himself he had some semblance of control, no matter how much he'd ached to touch and caress.

But now there was no need for control. He ran his hand along her breast. Excuses were no longer necessary. He'd made his decision. As wrong as it was, he would follow through with his experiment. His lover couldn't tell anyone. He certainly would never reveal his loathsome secrets, and the young man he'd stolen the bodies from couldn't identify him. Even if the man went to the police, the mask he'd worn when he'd confiscated his lovers was now in the murky swamps of the Everglades. The stolen car right next to it.

He moved the lacy bra aside and revealed a nipple. Yes. No one would know.

Or would they?

This is wrong. So wrong.

"So wrong," he murmured, and cupped the woman's breast anyway. Her skin was hard and tight, not as soft and warm as Gabriela's. He closed his eyes and replaced the dead woman's image with Gabriela's.

His breath came in ragged pants. How many times had he wanted to make love to Gabriela without worrying he couldn't perform? How many times had he touched her in this way, let her soft sighs and throaty moans wash over him? Only it hadn't been enough. Her sounds of pleasure had merely intensified the worry. Had she been faking? Had she really enjoyed his touch?

Darla wouldn't make a sound. She wouldn't complain. She would lie on his sheets and allow him to touch her in any way he desired.

Control. So much control.

He slid his hand down her torso, then paused when his palm met with the sutures at her navel. The stitches were a reminder that the embalmer had used a trocar on his lover.

He'd pierced her skin with the long, narrow, hollow instrument to aspirate the fluids from her organs, then had refilled them with a stronger concentration of formaldehyde.

The thought should disgust him. With his fingertips at the edge of the lacy panties and his penis harder than it had ever been in his life, it didn't. Careful to not tear the lingerie he would eventually give to Gabriela, he slid the panties from his lover, then he gently shoved the cups of the bra aside to reveal her breasts. Remembering the condom and lubrication he'd left on the dresser, he rushed from the bed to retrieve them. He quickly tore open the condom package, then sheathed his erection. After rubbing the gel along himself, he approached his lover. Imagined Gabriela spread out and waiting for him.

The mattress dipped as he placed his knees on the bed. He widened his lover's legs, then poised himself above her. Doubt crept in as he stared at her closed eyes, at her unmoving mouth...at her lifeless body.

Then he entered her.

CHAPTER 2

Shane's Rental House, Everglades City, Florida
Wednesday, 6:07 p.m. Eastern Standard Time

FRESHLY SHOWERED, SHANE stood naked in front of the bedroom closet. Before he'd been released from Haynesville Correctional Center ten days ago, Ryan and Lola had transferred his clothes from storage to the house he now rented from his brother. After he had been sentenced to five to seven years, his brother had taken care of selling his house, furniture and motorcycle. Shane had then had Ryan reinvest the money into the airboat business. Using Shane's part of the return on his investment, Ryan had taken care of paying for the hangar where Shane's Cessna, truck and boxes of clothes had been stored all these years. He'd also snake-sat Shane's ball python, which Lola had been eager to see leave the house she and Ryan shared.

Now he was starting over with a plane, truck, snake and a couple of grand. Things could be worse. He could still be in prison. But until he had his plane back in the air and new business coming in, what did he have to offer a woman? A whole lot of baggage.

He pulled a pair of jeans off the hanger, along with a white short-sleeved, button-down shirt that still had the tags on it. He'd bought the shirt a week or so before he'd gone to pick up Ryan from Norfolk, Virginia. At that time, Ryan had just resigned from the Navy SEALs. Instead of allowing his brother to take a bus or rent a car to make his way back to Everglades City, he'd driven to Norfolk to treat Ryan to a well-needed weekend of R & R that included too much alcohol, good food and women. They'd accomplished the booze and food, but hadn't made it to the women part of the weekend program. Being arrested for killing a man had put a dent in their plans.

It had put a huge dent in his life. He'd lost seven years, and had spent those years sitting in a prison cell contemplating what life would have been like if he hadn't swung at the man who'd coldcocked his brother, and then had gone after him.

He pulled a pair of underwear from the dresser drawer. Where would his business be today had he been around to enjoy it? Based on the money he'd been making before his arrest, the house he'd had Ryan sell could have been paid for by now. Maybe he'd even have a wife, and a kid or two.

"Anyone home?" Ryan called.

"Damn it." Shane put on the underwear, then shoved a leg into his jeans. "I'm in the bedroom. Be right out." He loved Ryan and appreciated all that he'd done for him, but walking in unannounced had to come to an end. After spending seven years in a fishbowl where anyone walking past his cell could see him doing his business, he needed privacy.

Grabbing the button-down shirt off the hanger, he plucked off the tags and left the bedroom. He entered the kitchen, just as Ryan popped the top off a beer bottle. "Holy shit, man," Ryan began, staring at Shane's chest, "I knew you bulked up over the years, but I didn't realize how much. Put your shirt on before you make me feel like a pussy."

Shane chuckled as he slid on the shirt, then bent down to give Ryan's dog, Sadie, a scratch behind the ear. "I don't know what you're talking about. You're bigger now than when you came home from Pakistan. Plus, with the way Lola's always touching you, I don't think you have anything to worry about."

Ryan grinned. "Yeah, Lola's awesome."

With his carefree lifestyle and issues with commitment, Shane had never thought his brother would fall so damned hard for a woman. He didn't begrudge Ryan and was nothing but happy for him. And maybe a little jealous. Lola was smart, pretty, had her shit together and made it obvious she was in love with Ryan, too. She'd also been nothing but cool to Shane. The first time he'd met her, she'd broken down in tears and had hugged him. She'd made sure the vacation rental—that he was now living in—had fresh sheets and towels, and she'd even stocked the fridge and pantry. Yeah, she was definitely alright.

"Where's your awesome fiancée?" Shane asked, and after giving Sadie a final pat on the head, finished buttoning his shirt.

"Working on her *jiu jitsu* at a gym she found in Naples. She won't be back for a couple hours, so I thought I'd drop by and have a few beers." He raised the bottle of Budweiser, toward his mouth. "But it looks like you have plans tonight," he said, taking a drink.

"I'm heading to Marco Island."

"Meeting up with your stalker?"

Shane looked to the ceiling. "She's not a stalker," he said, then went to the fridge for a bottle of water. "How do you even know about her?"

"I stopped by the shop to pick up today's cash and checks from the safe. Both Harrison and Vlad told me she came for another boat tour."

"Those two need to mind their own business." Shane twisted the cap off the water bottle. "I still don't get why they're working for you. Harrison seems to do all right, but Vlad? He told a kid he shouldn't play hooker, but go back to school to learn how to read."

Ryan coughed on his swallow of beer. "Shit."

"I don't know why you're keeping him around. In the week

I've been back, that guy's screwed up way too many times."

"Vlad and Harrison are Lola's friends. They're good guys and I'm helping them out until they find some other line of work."

"Tell them to get a job at McDonald's."

Ryan stood, then put the rest of the six pack he'd brought with him into the refrigerator. "In a few weeks you won't have to deal with them."

"I might want to deal with Harrison. He's maintaining your website, right?"

Ryan sat back down, and reached for his beer. "Yeah. He could also set up the same accounting program Lola's using to keep track of the business."

"Good to know. I'll talk to him about it when I see him tomorrow. The Cessna cleared inspection this morning. If everything goes okay, I could be up and running by the first week of March."

Although he'd been flying since he was seventeen, because he'd been grounded for seven years he had to tally up hours with an instructor. Since he was tight with the pilots at Everglades Airpark, he'd breezed through flight training. In between hours in the air and working for Ryan, he'd reapplied for all of his business licenses and permits needed for the Federal Office of Civil Aviation and the Federal Aviation Administration. Then there were the permits he needed from the state of Florida and setting up a bank account. Right now, the biggest problem he faced was spending what little money he had on restarting his business.

"Just in time for Spring Break," Ryan said. "If I remember, that was a busy time of year for you."

Shane shoved a hand through his hair and realized he needed to do something with it before he left to meet Beth. "Yeah, I'm hoping to get some charter flights to the Keys or Miami, but I'm really hoping to rebuild my tour business." That had been his moneymaker: a one-hour flight over the Glades, drop the passengers off, and take the next group in the air. At a couple hundred a flight, with four or five trips in a day, he'd be doing just fine. "The problem is, I'm short on cash. I applied for a bank loan and the dick denied me as soon as he found out I had a felony record. I got the 'you've committed a crime of moral depravity and henceforth will not receive a small business loan at anytime in the foreseeable future'."

Ryan frowned. "Why'd you go to the bank? You don't need to take out a loan."

"I'm not taking money from you. You're planning a wedding, have a couple of new employees and are renovating your house. Don't worry about me. I'll figure it out."

"No, what I meant is that you *have* money. You don't need a loan from me or anyone else."

Shane's chest tightened. "What the hell are you talking about?"

"Didn't you go through the envelope I gave you?"

"Sorry, man. I didn't feel like dwelling on the past seven years of my life," he said, picturing the thick, manila envelope sitting on his dresser untouched.

Ryan leaned forward and rested his elbows on the table. "You wouldn't have done those seven years if it wasn't for me."

Shane slammed the water bottle on the table. "Don't start with that shit again. You didn't take a swing at that guy, I did. Let it go."

"It's not that easy."

"It is that easy. Get over it. I spent too many years thinking about what I could've been doing. Now that I'm out, I don't want to think, I want to do. Got it?"

"Yeah, I got it. What you don't get, since you didn't bother going through the envelope, is that you have plenty of money."

"How much?"

"Little over thirty grand."

He quickly pulled out a chair and sat. "How the hell did that happen?"

Ryan grinned and shrugged. "The airboat business is doing well. Plus, I reinvested some of your money into my rental properties. Even after paying off the hangar, I was able to make sure you saw a return on your investment."

If he wasn't leaving for Marco Island in the next fifteen minutes, he'd have one of those beers Ryan had brought and celebrate. "No bullshit?"

"None. And, if you're interested, Lola wants to invest in the boat shop. She could buy you out and you'd have that money, too."

He picked up his water and drained half of it. Holy shit. Ryan was right. He no longer needed that dickhead banker. He had plenty of money to restart his business and possibly buy a house. The motorcycle would have to wait until he was bringing in some income, but that was okay. Right now, his problems were solved. Well, except for the woman he was meeting tonight. He'd let his hormones get the best of him when he'd told her he had wanted her number. He might have money, and he might have a legit business that would hopefully be back on track in a few months, but he was still a murderer.

"Done," Shane said. "If Lola wants in, I'm good with that."

"I figured as much. She also suggested we tie in our tours. You know, add an additional fee and your passengers could take one of our airboat tours at a discount, or vice versa."

"Down with that, too." He looked to the clock on the stove. "Can we run through the numbers tomorrow? I'm supposed to meet Beth at seven."

Ryan drained his beer, then stood. "You haven't been home long. Do you think it's a good idea to get involved with this woman?"

Hell, yeah. Beth was cute, sexy and funny. Hanging out with her would beat the shit out of sitting on his ass watching TV. "I'm going out for dinner, not putting a ring on her finger." When Ryan just stood there, his eyes downcast, he said, "Say what's on your mind."

"This woman—"

"Beth," he reminded him.

"Right. Sorry. Beth's a customer."

"Are you worried she'll leave a bad review if our date

sucks?"

"You're making me sound like an ass."

"Then don't act like one." Shane smiled to soften the blow, and stood. "I like her, and she likes me enough to go to dinner."

"Does she know?"

"No."

"Are you going to tell her?"

He picked up the water bottle and drained it. When he finished, he shook his head, and asked, "Why the hell would I say anything?"

"If you like her, you'll be honest."

Shane tossed the empty bottle in the trash. "So, should I tell her after I ask her what she'd like to drink, or after I ask her to pass the salt?"

"How about before you sleep with her?"

"Christ, I'm not going to have sex with her tonight."

"Maybe not tonight, but don't you think you owe it to her to be honest?"

What the hell had warped Ryan's brain? *Lola*. "Look, I think it's great you have Lola, but I don't need your fiancée in my head."

Ryan folded his arms across his chest. "Meaning?"

He grinned. "Simmer down, badass. No need to get defensive. But just because you've got it all going on right now, watch how you judge me."

"I'm not judging you."

"Sure sounds like it. Actually, I think you *are* worried Beth is going to have sex with me, find out I'm a convicted murderer, then get all pissy about it and leave a bad review for your company."

Ryan turned and opened the fridge. After he retrieved the beers he'd brought with him, he called Sadie to his side. "Buy your own fucking beer."

Shane blocked him. "Now that I know I have money, I'll buy a fucking keg."

"And the woman? If you're looking to get laid, Mel said

she'd take one for the team."

Shane almost threw up in his mouth. "Mel? Good God, I'll stick with my hand." Melanie Scarlet was like a cousin to him and Ryan. They might not be blood-related, but the thought of having sex with the woman gave him hives. Although gorgeous, she was crazy and vindictive. Years ago she'd used the pointy end of a nail file to slice a guy who'd tried to cheat during a poker game. Fortunately he'd been there to stop her from lopping off the guy's balls. To add to her crazy, when she wasn't serving ice cream at Ryan's boat shop, she was chopping cars and boats, and acting as if there wasn't anything illegal about it. "For the record, she already offered up her vagina to me."

Ryan burst into laughter. "Get out of here."

"I'm telling you the truth. It was the night I came home and she said it, just like that. 'Shane,'" he began, hitching his voice to mimic her sultry southern accent, "'if you need to make up for seven years of no sex, Mel's vagina is open for you.'"

When Ryan laughed harder, Sadie barked. After his brother had soothed the dog and wiped the tears from his eyes, he shook his head. "What's funny is she probably hasn't had sex for about as long as you."

Mel had always talked a good game, but wasn't as promiscuous as she acted. It probably didn't help that her dad was even crazier than her, and had a compound set up in the swamp geared for Armageddon. Rumor had it that her dad's swamp had also become the final resting place for anyone that messed with him or his daughter. "What happened to the repo guy?" Shane asked. "They were still together when I was locked up."

"Don't know. She took their breakup hard and holed up at her dad's for a couple of weeks. When she finally came back to the shop, she acted like nothing happened." Ryan pulled his keys from his pocket. "Sorry I called Beth a stalker and got into your business. Are we good?"

"We're good. I also get where you're coming from and don't want you worrying about Beth. I know nothing will come out of tonight."

"Then why're you going?"

"Beth's pretty and fun." He shrugged. "I like her and want to spend one evening pretending I'm a normal guy, not an ex-con."

Ryan squeezed his shoulder. "Who knows? Maybe she won't care that you have a record."

"We'll never know, because I don't plan on telling her. I just want one night, that's all."

"So one and done?" Ryan asked, and started for the door.

"That's the plan," he said, wishing it wasn't the case. Beth, her smile, her sexy curves…he wanted her. Based on how she'd pursued him, he suspected she wanted him, too. If she did, his gut told him nothing would happen between them once she found out about his past, and he wasn't that much of a bastard that he'd have sex with her or lead her on without telling her the truth.

"Well, I'll let you get to your date." Ryan opened the door, sending in a warm breeze. "When you have the chance, go through that envelope."

After he said good-bye to his brother, Shane headed into the bathroom to do something with his hair. When he saw his reflection, he stared at the mirror. On the outside, he'd changed. If he cut his hair and shaved his beard, he'd still look like he had before he'd been arrested, only harder. He had just turned twenty-nine when he'd been sentenced. Doing time had deepened the lines around his eyes and along his forehead. He looked away from the mirror and finished readying himself.

So he'd aged, so his life was fucked up. At least he had his plane, truck, a roof over his head and money in the bank. Since he couldn't turn back the clock, he needed to stay focused on moving forward and finding the normalcy that had been stripped from him the night he'd killed a man.

And his date with Beth was the first step in the right direction, even if it would likely be the last one he had with her.

The Fish House, Marco Island, Florida
Wednesday, 6:55 p.m. Eastern Standard Time

Shane entered the restaurant, then searched the small lobby and crowded bar for Beth. When he didn't see her, he gave the hostess his name and told her he'd made reservations, but that he wanted to wait for his date.

As more people arrived and filled the lobby, men and women bumped into him. He tried to ignore the way the walls began to close in on him by counting the number of old photographs hanging on the walls. It did him little good. His armpits grew sweaty, along with his forehead. When a couple walked from the bar into the foyer, staggering and laughing, and clearly drunk, he tried to step aside. The man swayed into him, and Shane instinctively raised his hands to shove him. Warm fingers grasped his forearm. He flinched before he connected with the man and looked down and to his right.

Beth grinned up at him. "Little crowded tonight."

He relaxed and smiled, relieved Beth was here and they could head to their table. "Just a little." He took her hand. "I made reservations. Come on, our table is ready." As they followed the hostess, he kept her hand in his. If he only had one evening with Beth, he wanted to take advantage of every skin-to-skin contact he could, even if it would only be hand-holding.

"I've noticed you've grown a couple of inches since this afternoon," he said, glancing at the heels on her sandals, then to her toned calves. She wore a denim skirt that came to her knees and a fitted, short-sleeved V-neck shirt that accentuated her breasts. Tonight was the first time he'd seen her with her hair down. He loved the way the thick long waves fell around her shoulders and could imagine pulling her hair back and kissing her neck.

She smiled at him. "And here I was thinking you'd shrunk."

He chuckled, and when they reached the table, he held the chair out for her, then took the seat opposite from her. "Is this okay?" he asked.

"Absolutely. This is a great table," she said, looking out toward the boat dock, which was lit up by rows of globe string lights. "From here, I bet the view of the sunset was awesome tonight."

"Can you see the sunset from where you live?"

"Right from my lanai. That is until the condo building behind mine hides it."

Their server stopped by and took their drink orders. Beth ordered an iced tea. As much as he'd like a beer or something stronger, he went with a Coke, even though he'd served his full prison term, and wasn't on probation. He could have a drink or walk into a bar. Hell, he could even be around weapons—he just couldn't buy one. But he had a thirty-minute drive home and refused to risk a DUI.

"Do you drink?" he asked, then quickly added, "Sorry, none of my business."

"It's okay. I do, but I have to be up early and I don't want to be fuzzy. You?"

"Same here."

"How was your last boat tour?"

He told her about the family he'd taken out on the boat, and how they'd seen a twelve-foot gator, along with a family of raccoons. From there, she began asking him more about growing up in the Everglades. "I love living there," he said. "There's no place on Earth like the Glades. But you have to show it respect. If you don't know what you're doing when you're hiking or boating there, you could wind up in serious trouble."

"I can see that just from the airboat tours I've been on. I couldn't imagine going in there without a guide." She stopped talking when their server returned with their drinks, then after they'd given her their orders, she said, "Everglades City is a small town. What'd you do for fun as a kid?"

"Boating, fishing, hunting. My brother and I used to capture snakes. I take it you don't like snakes," he said when she wrinkled her nose.

"I prefer a pet that I can snuggle with on the couch, not

one that is capable of wrapping itself around my neck and choking me while I'm watching a movie."

"Then I guess I better warn you that I have a snake." He grinned when her eyes widened. "Should I cancel our order?"

"That won't be necessary." She shook her head and smiled. "I suppose there are worse things than owning a snake."

Like murder?

"I'd like to think so," he said, reaching for his Coke. "If you're not into snakes, what kind of furry pet would you want snuggling on your lap?"

"Funny, I was just thinking about getting a cat today. I'd prefer a dog, but cats aren't as needy and are more self-sufficient."

"We had a couple of cats growing up. One disappeared—Ryan and I think a gator got her—the other two used to catch mice which we'd feed to the snakes we kept hidden from our mom."

"Your poor mother. Did your dad know?"

"Yeah, he bought us a terrarium for the snakes and kept it in the shed out back since our mom never went in there. He also gave us a book on snakes so we could learn which ones were venomous and know the ones to leave alone."

"Sounds like something my dad would've done for my brothers."

"Brothers? How many do you have?"

"Four, all older than me."

He leaned back in his chair. "Your house must have been crazy."

"Oh, it was loud and chaotic," she said, just as their food was delivered. When the server left the table, Beth picked up her fork and knife. "Then one by one, my brothers went off to college until it was only me, my folks and our dog."

"What's the age difference between you and your oldest brother?" Shane asked, and sliced his blackened stuffed grouper.

"Thirteen years. I was, as my mom likes to say, God's surprise package," she said, then cut into her swordfish steak.

After she took a bite, she hummed. The throaty sound had him staring at her lips and imagining them against his.

"Good?"

"Delicious."

Relieved, he began eating his own meal. "Are you from the area?" he asked, then took a sip of his Coke.

"Nope. I'm from Cleveland. My parents retired to Naples about five years ago. Since none of my brothers stayed in the Cleveland area, I decided to follow my mom and dad to Florida. The summers here are a little too hot and rainy for me, but I'll suffer through July and August to avoid snow and zero-degree temperatures." She picked up her glass of iced tea. "Plus, I couldn't imagine being so far away from my parents. They're in their early seventies, and I don't want to have to hop on a plane to see them. Bottom line, I don't want to have any regrets should something happen to one of them."

"I get it. We lost my dad ten years ago."

"I'm sorry to hear that," she said, sympathy in her eyes. "But your mom is still around?"

"Yeah, she has a boyfriend who keeps her company. She moved away from Everglades City a few years ago, and is living with him in Fort Lauderdale." He'd seen his mom right after he'd returned home. When he'd found out that she hadn't spoken to his brother in nearly seven years, blaming Ryan for Shane's incarceration, he'd been beyond pissed and had it out with her. Fortunately, she and Ryan had reconciled their differences, but Shane suspected his brother still held a deep amount of resentment toward their mom. He didn't blame him. What had happened that night hadn't been Ryan's fault, but his alone. Between what his brother had dealt with while he was still a SEAL, and the ridiculous guilt he carried over Shane's imprisonment, Ryan hadn't deserved their mother's crap.

As they continued with their meals, they did more of the getting-to-know-you small talk, which was fine with him. He hadn't been interested in carrying on a deep conversation, and had discovered Beth had a great sense of humor and not an arrogant bone in her pint-sized body.

She pushed her plate aside. "I haven't been here in a while. I'm surprised they have a band on a Wednesday night," she said, as the band began to play Van Morrison's *Brown Eyed Girl*.

He set his napkin on the table. "'Tis the season for tourists." He nodded toward the patio where tables had been moved to create a makeshift dance floor. "Do you dance?"

"Horribly." Beth glanced toward the dance floor, as a trio of giggling and well-inebriated women who Shane placed in their mid-fifties started to move to the music. "Of course, get a few drinks in me and then I've got it going on—at least in my mind," she said. "How about you?"

He shook his head. "I've been told I look like I'm having a seizure."

She laughed. "I'm sure you're not *that* bad."

"And I think you've got it going on, whether you can dance or not."

She gave him a shy smile and looked away. "Thanks."

He leaned forward. "What's that about?"

"I don't know what you mean," she said, meeting his gaze.

"Where's the confident woman who came to see me today?"

"She's still here, just not feeling as confident." She let out a breath. "Honestly, I feel a little foolish."

"Because?"

She fiddled with the small container of sugar packets, and he quickly counted five Sweet N' Lows and eight regular sugar packets. "I like you."

His stomach tightened with both anxiety and excitement. He liked her, too. But if she wanted to continue to see him, that meant he'd have to tell her the truth about his past. "I like you, too. So what's the problem?"

"The problem is that I don't want you to get the wrong idea about me." She pulled out a sugar packet—the pink one. "I'd say I made it clear I was interested in you outside of being my boat captain."

"If I recall, I made it clear I wanted to see you." He took

the sugar packet from her hand, then twined his fingers with hers. "I told you I've been going to bed with you on my mind."

"I believe I said the same thing." Her mouth tilted in a sexy smile. "Is this the point where we compare what we were thinking about?"

"We could, but I don't want you to slap my face."

Her throaty laughter made his balls tighten. "I have no idea what to say to that," she said, just as the cover band began to play Eric Clapton's *Wonderful Tonight*.

The women who'd been dancing hugged each other and began swaying together. A few other couples rose from their chairs and moved onto the dance floor. Still holding Beth's hand, he said, "Then dance with me."

"I told you—"

"Stop. Dance with me."

Her eyes lit with excitement and uncertainty as she stood and let him lead her onto the dance floor. He drew her into his arms, kept her hand in his and wrapped the other around her waist. When she stepped on his foot and apologized, he pulled her closer, pressing their bodies together. "Don't think about your feet, just move with me. Remember, I can't dance."

She relaxed in his arms and slowly moved to the music. He'd imagined plenty of things during his time in prison. This wasn't one of them. His finances, his business, flying, fishing and hanging with his brother had been on his mind. He'd never imagined he'd have a beautiful woman in his arms so soon after his release, and he wanted to hold onto this moment for as long as he could. Because once Beth found out everything about him, he'd be right where he was weeks ago.

Alone.

She sighed and wrapped an arm around his neck. When she moved her cheek from his and stared up at him, he fought for control. The desire in her eyes had him aroused to the point where he had to shift his hips away from hers. Beth. She was too damned good for him. Seven years ago, he wouldn't have thought that. Instead, he would have been expecting nothing but desire. He'd had it going on. Successful business, money in the bank, nice house and toys. He could have all that again, but the stigma of his felony would forever weigh him down, and any woman who chose to be with him.

He pushed those thoughts from his mind. He didn't want to think about tomorrow or next week, not with the way her breasts pressed against his chest, the way her body fit so perfectly to his. And that smile. He didn't have a poetic bone in his body, but wished he did so he could put to paper the beauty of her smile and how much it made his heart beat hard, his body ache from wanting her and his head cloud with indecision. Beth was a nice girl, a sweet person who deserved better than being in the arms of an ex-con.

As the song ended, he cupped her cheek. Before he told her what he was and she walked away, he needed to know if her skin was as soft as it looked. Her grin filled his palm and he couldn't help smiling, too. After the cover band segued from Eric Clapton to Three Dog Night's *Joy to the World*, and the three intoxicated women started dancing and singing along, he led Beth back to their table. When their server stopped by and they both declined coffee and dessert, he wished he had a reason to keep her in his company. He wished he had the nerve to be honest.

"Are you sure you don't want anything else?" he asked, as he paid their bill.

"I'm good. It's too bad we both have to be up early," she said, and stood. "I'd love to hang out with you some more."

"Where do you work?" he asked, realizing the topic had never come up during dinner.

Her eyes widened a fraction, before she looked away. "I…um—"

"Beth," a man called from two tables over.

Shane looked to the guy, pegged him to be somewhere in his mid-twenties, then glanced back to Beth to gage her reaction. If the guy was an ex who Beth wanted nothing to do with, he didn't want any issues. For whatever reason, a surge of protectiveness thrust forward, and he pictured the man, nose bleeding and flat on his ass.

Then she smiled and waved at the guy, who stood when a blonde, twenty-something woman approached and joined him at his table. Shane set the money for their dinner on the table. Man, he needed to keep himself in check. He wasn't on the inside anymore. Not everyone was a dick waiting to prey on the weak.

Beth walked toward the table where the couple sat. He followed behind, keeping his gaze on the man and woman when he really wanted it on Beth's ass. But then *he'd* look like an ass if the couple caught him staring.

"How are you?" Beth asked when she reached the table. "This is my friend, Shane. Shane, this is Austin and his girlfriend, Jazz."

"Great. Did you finish your paper?" Austin asked.

"It's done," Beth said, hooking the straps of her purse over her shoulder. "But when I get home tonight, I'm going to give it another read through. How about you?"

Austin grinned. "I wouldn't be out if I didn't."

"Is the paper for Schwartz's class?" Jazz asked.

When both Austin and Beth nodded, Jazz rolled her eyes. "I hated his Contracts course. I had Schwartz last semester. Totally boring."

"No kidding." Austin nodded. "His classes are about as fun as watching paint peel."

Beth chuckled. "He's not *that* bad."

"Says the star student already sporting an A."

"Whatever," Beth said, then hooked her arm through Shane's. "We're calling it a night. I'll see you in class."

Of course it made sense Beth was a student. That would explain why she had been able to come for airboat tours in the middle of the day when most people were working. They made their way through the bar area, which was now less crowded, since most people had moved to the outside patio where the band played.

"Where'd you park?" he asked, once they'd left the restaurant.

She pointed to the left, toward the tall lamppost lighting up the corner of the parking lot. Smart girl. He and Ryan used to ride Mel about parking lot safety, and had always told her to park by a light. While this was a nice area, even decent places had their criminals.

"So what are you getting your degree in?" he asked as they made their way to her car.

"Law."

Fucking awesome. Yeah, what attorney wouldn't want to date a felon? "Good for you," he said. "How much longer before you graduate?"

"This May." Keeping her arm hooked through his, she glanced up at him. "Did you go to college?"

"Nope, joined the Army right out of high school."

"Army?" She gave a chunk of his hair a playful tug. "Would've never guessed."

He tucked that same chunk behind his ear. "Yeah, it's probably about time for a haircut."

Shrugging, she said, "I like it, but you're the one who has to deal with it. There've been days when I'd love to cut my hair off and go with something short and easy. But I'm too chicken."

When they stopped at the backend of her SUV, he pushed a lock of her wavy hair off her shoulder. "That'd be a crime."

Her lips tilted into a small smile as she looked to the gravel. "So what did you do when you were in the Army?"

"Flew rescue and recon missions."

She met his gaze, the light from the lamppost darkened her hazel eyes. "I'm sure you have plenty of stories to tell."

If only she knew. He'd spent the majority of his twenties flying a Blackhawk behind enemy lines, then his thirties in prison. Yeah, he had plenty of stories. Too bad none of them were good. "We'll save that for another time." Unable to resist the softness of her skin, he touched her face again. "You have a paper to finish."

"Does this mean you'd like to see me again."

God, he wanted to. But he also didn't want to string her along. "Absolutely," he said, not wanting to hurt her feelings.

Damn it, he shouldn't have started this. He should've taken her tip after the boat ride, played dumb and acted as if he had no clue she was interested in him.

"I'm free Friday night, if you are," she said. "This time I'll come out your way."

"Friday works," he said, knowing he could've lied and told her he had other plans. From there he could have made up excuse after excuse as to why he wouldn't be able to meet her. Bottom line. He *wanted* to see her. He wanted to hear more about how she'd grown up in Ohio with a big family. What she'd been like as a kid. Why she'd decided to go to law school and her plans for the future. Tonight's date was an appetizer, a teaser, almost like a movie trailer. He'd learned just enough about her to make him want to know more.

"Same time?" she asked.

"Can you do earlier? Maybe we can watch the sun set." When he'd been in prison there hadn't been a chance in hell to watch the sun set. Since his release, he'd made an effort to catch the sunrise and sunset almost every day, and he'd love to have the opportunity to watch both with Beth. There was something special about the rising and setting sun. To him, it defined freedom.

"I'd love that," she said, then pulled her cell phone from her purse. "Why don't you give me your number and I'll send you a text so you have mine. Since we'll be in your area, you can pick the time and place."

After he rattled off his number, she slipped the phone back into her purse and hugged herself. "Thanks for dinner. I didn't expect you to pay."

"My pleasure. Thanks for going out with me," he replied, wondering if he'd totally lost his groove. After not dating for nearly a decade, he was at a loss for words and couldn't remember how to act at the end of a date.

"Okay, then," she said, then stuck her hand out in front of him.

He glanced from her eyes to her extended hand. Not once had he ever shaken a woman's hand at the end of a date.

Deciding to play it safe and by her rules, he took her hand in his. As if they'd just agreed on a contract negotiation, she gave him a quick, firm handshake.

"I'll text you later." She took a step backward, avoiding the bumper of her car. "Thanks again for tonight. I had fun."

He fisted his hand. Damn it. He didn't want a handshake. "Beth," he said, stopping her before she reached the driver's side door.

She hugged herself again and stared up at him. "Yeah?"

From his position, the lamppost was still bright enough to make out the disappointment in her eyes. God, he was an ass. He should walk away. Now. Because if they continued to see each other, he'd really disappoint her once she found out who she was dating.

"I don't want a handshake," he said anyway. He wasn't ready to walk away. Not yet.

The corner of her mouth tilted in a sexy smile. "What *do* you want?"

He took a step closer and sifted his fingers into her silky soft hair. "I want to kiss you."

She dropped her arms and settled a hand on his hip. "I want you to kiss me, too."

His stomach tightened with both desire and dread. In the past ten days, he'd had to relearn how to drive a car, an airboat and fly a plane. He'd had to adjust to using metal silverware, along with plates and cups that weren't plastic. He hadn't kissed a woman in over seven years and worried he'd forgotten how to do that, too.

He let go of her hair. With his heart kicking up in pace, he slowly leaned his head forward. The subtle scent of her perfume, a seductive blend of wildflowers with a hint of vanilla, teased his senses. He'd love to strip her naked, taste her, touch her, then walk away with her perfume still clinging to his skin.

He stared at her lips. Needing to know if they were as soft as her skin, anxious to rediscover the art of kissing, he inched his face closer. As her warm breath grazed his mouth, he brushed his lips against hers.

They were as soft as he'd imagined.

Aching for more, he tasted her. Taking his time, he learned the contours of her mouth with a deliberately slow, coaxing kiss. She matched his easy pace, but gave him the lead. Let him continue to make love to her mouth.

With only their lips touching, he didn't think he'd ever been more turned on his life. Her kiss held so many promises. Too damned tempted to shove her against the car and show her how much he wanted her, he pressed his hands on either side of her head along the driver's side window to keep himself in check and in control. When she parted her lips, he grazed his tongue along hers, and realized how much he'd missed the intimacy of a simple kiss.

But as their tongues and lips moved in an excruciatingly unhurried rhythm, the hunger inside him turned voracious. There wasn't anything simple about this kiss or the complexity of emotions filling his head with thoughts he had no business thinking. He was leading her on, which made him an ass. He should have stuck with the handshake and walked away. He should end the kiss now and do just that.

Damn, he didn't want to. Her soft sighs, her even softer lips, her intoxicating scent…

With reluctance, he gave her a final kiss, then rested his forehead against hers. "Sorry," he murmured. "That went on longer than I'd intended."

"Not long enough," she said, shoving her hands through his hair and pulling his head down. She parted her lips and kissed him with so much passion and urgency it took everything in him to not tear his hands away from the window and show her exactly what he'd been thinking about when he went to bed each night. Dick hard, heart rate high, he kissed her back. Tangled his tongue with hers until they were both breathless.

She gave him a couple of lingering kisses as she removed her hands from his hair, then she looked up at him. The uncertainty and desire in her eyes confused him. He took a step forward, finally allowing himself to be flush with her body. "What's on your mind?" he asked.

"I, ah, sorry," she said with a slight chuckle and shake of her head. "I might've been a little aggressive. I don't normally hang out in parking lots assaulting a man's mouth."

"You're great at it." His palms had grown slick from how hard he'd been pressing them against the window. He should step away and give her space. "Remember, I'm the one who couldn't be satisfied with a handshake."

"You're right. This is your fault." Her mouth slid into another sexy smile. "I *am* curious. Why'd you keep your hands against the car?"

He pushed off the SUV, then took a quick step back. "If I start touching you, I won't be able to stop." He brushed his knuckle along his lower lip, still moist from her kiss and took another backward step. "Looking forward to Friday night," he said, then turned and headed for his truck.

He might be an ass for wanting to keep his date with Beth, but he didn't care. He'd had a small taste of her tonight and needed more. He might also come to regret his decision, but he still didn't care. He needed Beth. He needed to erase the past seven years and rebuild his future.

Would Beth be in his future?

He climbed into his truck.

Damn. Not after she found out about his past.

CHAPTER 3

Naples, Florida
Wednesday, 9:56 p.m. Eastern Standard Time

"DINNER WAS DELICIOUS," Gabriela said, as they entered her townhouse. "And I love, love, love the shoes you bought for me." She set her package on the travertine-tiled floor, then yanked at his tie, drawing him down for a kiss. The scent of her, like lilies in full bloom, reminded him of his dead lover and the pleasure he'd taken from her this afternoon. He pressed a hand on the small of Gabriela's back, pulling her closer and deepening their kiss. When she groaned, the semi-erection he'd had since leaving his lover in his bed hardened further.

Breathless, she let out a throaty chuckle and ran her hand along his chest. "That was nice."

"I have something else for you. Why don't you make us a drink?" He gave her rear a gentle squeeze. "I need to run back to the car and get it."

"A present? What's the occasion?" she asked, leaning into him and running the tips of her fingers along his jaw.

"Can't I give you something just because?"

She grinned. "You won't hear me complain." After giving

his chest a light tap, she stepped away and started for the living room. "Hurry back."

He stared at her rear, loving the way her tight aqua blue dress hugged her curves. She had a fantastic ass. He knew it, and so did every man at the country club. He also knew several of those men were just waiting for the chance to pounce on her, should she ever leave him. Gabriela wouldn't go for them, though. She wasn't the type to play mistress to a married man, and he'd also noticed that she didn't care for men old enough to be her father.

He stepped outside, then walked toward his car. No, his concern was for the younger men who worked for the country club. Whether she was at the club's bar, restaurant or pool, the wait staff doted on her. Those men didn't bother him, either. Financially, they couldn't offer her what he could. But the two golf pros who catered to the members could. They had money—not as much as him—and were single and good looking. Yes, they could be a problem.

He opened the rear door of his Mercedes for the package he'd wrapped this afternoon. Anxiety and remorse twisted his stomach as he made his way back toward the townhouse. But he *had* to do this. He needed to prove to himself that defiling a corpse and going against everything in his moral code had been worth the effort, along with the risk. If he were caught, being able to sustain an erection would be the least of his concerns. He'd be ruined and go to prison.

He let himself in and headed for the kitchen. Gabriela had already poured herself a glass of wine and was currently filling a lowball tumbler with scotch. "Do you want more ice?" she asked, setting the bottle on the counter.

"No, that's perfect," he said, then handed her the package.

Her brown eyes sparkled as she stared at the gift. "I must've been a very good girl."

"I'm hoping later you'll be a very bad girl."

Smiling, she tilted her head. Her gaze drifted to his crotch. "I like that idea." She picked up her glass and rounded the L-shaped kitchen island. "Why wait until later?" she asked, running a hand along his chest.

"Because I want you to open your present first."

She moved her hand lower and rubbed his arousal. "Does my present have anything to do with being a bad girl?"

He sucked in a breath when she cupped him. "Open it and find out."

After taking a sip of her wine, she set the glass back on the counter in exchange for the package. While she tore the wrapping paper, he reached for the tumbler of scotch, then took a drink. His anxiety and remorse turned to excitement as she lifted the lid from the box and sifted her fingers through the tissue paper.

Gabriela gasped, then looked up at him. "Naughty," she said, setting the box on the high back chair in front of the kitchen island. She lifted the lacy red bra from the box, then the matching panties. "Very naughty."

"Do you like them?"

"They're beautiful and sexy, but they look so tiny. I hope they fit me," she said, checking the label. "Oh, my God, you bought me Fleur of England lingerie? Honey, this is too much money."

Enjoying the way Gabriela ran the tips of her fingers along the lace, he took another sip of his scotch and imagined her full breasts filling the cups of the bra. "Not for you," he said. While he thought spending over four hundred dollars on lingerie was ridiculous, Gabriela and her pleasure were worth every penny. "If you're worried about the size, why don't you try it on?"

Clutching the bra and panties to her chest, she rushed to him, then gave him a kiss. "Give me a few minutes before you come upstairs," she said, and, taking her wine with her, walked toward the steps leading to the master bedroom.

Once she disappeared, he drained his scotch. He was fucking sick. A sick, twisted, vile bastard. He loved Gabriela. And how did he show his love? By gifting her lingerie previously worn by a dead woman. He refilled his glass, then rubbed his crotch. He penis was already as hard as it had been this afternoon, but would it stay that way once he was naked and between Gabriela's long legs? God, he hoped so. They had a great relationship and he wanted to make her his wife. The only thing that had been stopping him from proposing was their sex life. She was a passionate woman and deserved a man who could keep her sexually satisfied.

"I'm ready," she called.

Anticipation spiraled through his stomach. After months of planning, the moment was now here. Glass in hand, he walked across the kitchen and toward the stairs. He was out of ideas. If this didn't work, other than disposing of the bodies in his house, he didn't know what he'd do next. Breaking up with Gabriela wasn't an option. The thought of leaving her, of some other man enjoying her body, made his chest ache.

When he reached the second floor, he paused outside Gabriela's bedroom. What if having sex with his dead lover ended up being the answer? What then? How could he continue along such a disgusting path without someone discovering his secrets?

"Aren't you coming inside?" Gabriela asked.

He took another sip of the scotch, then entered the room. She had closed the plantation shutters and lit several candles, which she'd placed on top of her dresser. The lamp on the nightstand bathed the room in a soft glow. When he looked toward the master bathroom, he nearly dropped the tumbler. Gabriela stood in the doorway. The light from the bathroom silhouetted her body. She stepped forward, and his gaze was drawn to her long legs and the black heels she wore.

"Well, what do you think?" she asked, sliding a hand along her breast, where her tanned flesh spilled from the lacy bra cup, then down her flat stomach. Her nails, the same shade of red as the lingerie and her lipstick, teased the waistband of the panties.

He set his glass on the dresser. "You look beautiful." He loosened, then pulled off his tie. "Turn around."

When she did, revealing the thong and how it rode between her cheeks, he approached her. "Absolutely perfect," he said, grazing his hand along her rear.

She tossed her long dark hair over her shoulder, then reached behind and stroked him through his pants. "Mmm. I can tell you approve."

"I more than approve." He kissed her bare shoulder. "Get on the bed and let me show you how much."

She turned in his arms instead and kissed him. While he loved kissing her, he wasn't in the mood for foreplay. He wanted to make sure his erection lasted long enough until they both came.

Still kissing her, he moved her backward toward the bed, then eased her onto the mattress. She laid back, her hair spreading across the cream-colored sheets. When he looked down at her, he was instantly reminded of how his dead lover had looked on his bed. Same bra and panties, similar hair and body. Only this body wasn't dead. Gabriela's skin was soft, tan and warm, not hard and cold. He slid his hand between the apex of her thighs. Warm and wet, he wouldn't need to lubricate her or himself like he'd had to do to his dead lover. But he *would* have to please her.

She groaned as he rubbed her sex. "Get undressed," she said, her tone husky.

He quickly shed his clothes, then slipped off her red panties. Normally he'd perform oral sex because he could never maintain an erection long enough to have sex. Hard and ready, today he'd skip going down on her. But as he climbed on the mattress, she pushed his head toward her out-stretched thighs.

Raising his upper body so his head was out of her reach, he looked down at her. "Later. I need to be inside you. Now."

She ran her manicured nails along his chest and met his gaze. "I understand," she said with pity on her eyes.

He didn't need her pity. He needed to fuck her and prove that he was man enough to keep up with her insatiable needs. Gripping his penis, he pressed it against her vagina. No longer as hard as he'd been seconds ago, he blew out a breath and stroked himself.

No, no, no!

Not now. Not yet. Stealing the dead women, having sex with one of them—it couldn't have been for nothing.

"Close your eyes," he said, an idea occurring to him. "Keep them closed and don't move." He reached for her breast, and as he'd done to his dead lover, he moved the bra aside to reveal a nipple. "Keep very still."

A smile curved her lips. "Is this a kinky Sleeping Beauty fantasy?"

No. A sick, kinky pretend you're dead so I can fuck you fantasy.

"Something like that," he murmured, and tweaked her nipple.

"I'm game," she said, and closed her eyes.

With her body completely still, he gazed down at her and pictured her dead. As he played with her nipples, then her sex, he imagined all the sexual and, yes, kinky things he could do to her body. He could violate her any way he wanted and she couldn't protest, making her the perfect lover.

His penis grew hard again. He spread her legs and poised himself at her entrance. "Remember what I said, don't move. Keep your eyes closed and don't make a sound."

"Whatever you need," she said, her voice breathless.

Confidence rushed through him as he stared at her closed eyes, at her unmoving mouth...at her body that appeared lifeless.

Then he entered her.

Everglades City, Florida
Wednesday, 10:27 p.m. Eastern Standard Time

Lola Tam tossed the paper plate into the trash can, then sidestepping the box of tiles that would eventually cover the kitchen floor, she walked toward the kitchen island where Ryan's empty beer bottle and paper plate sat. "You've been quiet since I came home. Anything wrong?" she asked, taking his plate and bottle.

"You haven't said much, either."

She tossed the bottle into the recycling container and the plate into the trash. "Not true. I told you how I hated the gym." The place hadn't been what she'd hoped for. She'd wanted to spar and sweat, and get her *jiu jitsu* on, only the place had been filled with novices, and the instructors had been more interested in trying to pick her up than sparring.

Ryan shook his head. "That's all you said. What else is on your mind? And please don't start with the kitchen renovation. I hate what a mess the house is, too."

She glanced to the partially finished backsplash Ryan had put up this evening while she was gone. "It's not the house. It's Ian." Her boss and future stepfather. "Now, 'fess up," Lola said. "What's on your mind?"

Ryan sighed and stood. "Shane."

Lola opened the fridge and reached for two bottles of beer. "What'd you say we compare our issues?"

"You go first," he said.

She entered the living room, which was filled with boxes of pots, pans, dishes and other kitchen items. This weekend Ryan and Shane were supposed to hang the new custom cabinets—if they came in—and then they could once again reclaim the living room. After handing Ryan a beer, she took a seat next to him on the couch. Their dog, Sadie, sat on the chair angled toward the TV, her head on the armrest, her loving eyes on them. Lola loved Ryan's dog and now thought of the Golden Retriever as her own. She patted her leg and made a kissing sound. Sadie jumped off the chair and in a few strides, was snuggled next to her and Ryan.

Lola took a sip of her beer, then set it on the coffee table. "I talked to Ian on my drive home."

"And?"

"And my mom is doing great. She's been approached to do another play." Back in the 80s, her mom, Camilla 'Cami' Carlyle, had made her fame in campy horror films. Several years ago, Cami had reinvented herself and had taken to the stage. Now the former scream queen was selling out shows and receiving rave reviews. Lola still couldn't believe that less than two months ago she and Ryan had been hunting a killer who'd tormented her mom and had later shot Ian. Other than a hairline scar on her mom's leg and arm, no one would know that the famous Cami Carlyle had been sliced up by a psychotic ex-con who'd had a vendetta against Ian.

"As for Ian," Lola continued, "he's feeling fine and business is good. He also mentioned that he and my mom think they might be close to setting a wedding date."

"That'd be nice. Once they have a date, we can pick ours."

"Barney's a licensed minister. I still think we should have him take one of the airboats out into the middle of the Glades and marry us there." Lola didn't want a big wedding like the one her mom and Ian planned to have. She wanted something simple and memorable, not all the expensive, stressful pomp and circumstance. She had an unpredictable business to run and didn't want it to interfere with her and Ryan's special day.

"Your mom would have a fit."

She sighed. "I know."

Ryan put an arm around her shoulder. "So if Cami and Ian are good, what is it? Are you feeling homesick?"

She kissed his cheek. "Since this is my home, not at all," she said, and rubbed Sadie's head. "Don't get me wrong, I miss seeing my mom's face, but we can Skype or FaceTime."

"And you can visit whenever you want."

"Right. Just not in the winter months. I'm good with never seeing snow again."

He chuckled, then took a drink from his beer. "I hear you on that." He gave her a squeeze. "So what's the issue?"

"I dunno...I'm supposed to be running a super-secret organization and we haven't had an assignment yet."

Eight months ago she'd been living in Chicago and had just joined CORE (Criminal Observance Resolution Evidence), Ian Scott's private investigative agency. At the end of her last CORE mission, which had brought her to Everglades City, where she'd thankfully met Ryan and had helped save her mom and Ian from a killer, Ian had asked if she wanted to lead a crew. Under her lead, Ryan, Harrison, Vlad, Mel and Ryan's longtime friend and confidant, Barney, were supposed to work cases that would not involve outside agencies like the police, the FBI, or even CORE. According to Ian, no one was supposed to know they existed. Harrison, a big Steven Segal fan, had called their group Above the Law or ATL, after one of the actor's movies. The rest of the group agreed to the title, and it had stuck.

"Our headquarters isn't complete," Ryan reminded her.

Ian had bought the rental house where he and her mom had been kidnapped from, then placed it in Lola's name. Since she and her team might be forced to bend the law to help solve whatever cases came their way, Ian hadn't wanted himself or CORE linked to her crew or the house. On paper, she was a landlord, renting to her tenants, Harrison and Vlad. In reality, the house was her team's headquarters.

"It's getting there," Lola said. "The team is ready, even if the house isn't. Plus, I think Vlad needs something to do other than show off Polina to tourists."

"Yeah, he's an issue. Shane told me today that he messed up playing hooky with hooker to a group of kids."

She laughed, causing Sadie to lift her head from Lola's lap. "No, he didn't."

"Apparently he did." He took another drink. "Shane's been asking questions about Vlad and Harrison, and brought them up again today."

"What'd you tell him?"

"That they're your friends and I'm just helping them out until they find something else."

"Did he buy it?"

Ryan set his beer on the table. "He suggested they get a job at McDonald's."

She laughed even harder. "Oh, my God. Could you imagine Vlad working the drive-thru window?"

Grinning, Ryan shook his head. "Right. Picture this…a mom, with a crap-ton of screaming kids in her minivan, pulls up to the drive-thru. What does Vlad say as he hands her the food?"

"Vlad hope Minivan Mom have nice day," she said, mimicking the Russian's accent.

Ryan chuckled. "Okay, now picture this same mom being told she has to pull off to the side and wait for her food, but she blows him hell and tells him she won't pull off and wait."

"I don't think I want to picture that. At all. Shane's been around Vlad long enough to know he—"

"Shouldn't be around the public," Ryan finished for her. "My exact point. We need to do something about Vlad."

"I know, but he really loves coming to the boat shop and showing off Polina. I tried having him work with Mel in the ice cream shop, but she threatened to dispose of his body in her daddy's swamp if he so much as stepped foot behind the counter." With a sigh, she rested her head on Ryan's shoulder and scratched Sadie behind the ear. "Hopefully we'll have something from Ian soon and we can put Vlad to use."

"You mean you, not we," he said, and kissed her head. "This is your baby."

While she might be in charge, she loved and trusted Ryan, and wanted his input where ATL was concerned. "Do you think Ian changed his mind?" she asked.

"About ATL?"

"And me running it. Maybe there won't be any assignments. Maybe this was his way to get me off his regular CORE team and—"

He touched her cheek and forced her to look at him. "You know how ridiculous you sound, right? You're a born leader. I know this, so does Ian. Stop doubting yourself and enjoy the calm before the storm. Months from now, you're going to be wishing we didn't have any assignments and we could lounge on the couch, sipping beers and just BS-ing."

God, she loved Ryan. He always knew the right things to say and at exactly the right time. She gave him a kiss. "Thank you. Now let's switch focus from me to you. What's going on with Shane?"

"I'd rather keep kissing you."

She smiled. "I'll let you, *after* you tell me about Shane. I might even let you do more than that."

"Then I guess I better make it quick," he said, giving her another kiss. "Okay, so I went to Shane's thinking we'd have a few beers while you were at the gym. But he was getting ready for a date."

"Really? That's great." Since her future brother-in-law's release, she'd seen him every day, except for today. She liked Shane. He was a good guy who'd been in the wrong place at the wrong time, which had cost him seven years. She could understand why Shane would be in the need for female companionship and was happy for him.

"It's not so great. I mean, it is, only the date is with a customer."

"Oh."

"Exactly." He let out a sigh and kissed her head again. "I want my brother happy, you know that."

"Of course," she said, curling into his chest.

"He's been through things I don't want to even imagine."

When he didn't say anything more, she raised her head and looked up at him. "What's the problem?"

"The problem is that he's still adjusting. I think it's too soon for him to be dating." He shook his head. "He's been so busy logging in flight hours, getting his business up and running, and doing whatever the hell else to get back to normal, that he didn't even go through the paperwork we'd left for him."

"You're kidding me."

"Nope. He had no idea how much money he'd earned while he was in prison."

"Did you mention my offer?" Lola had used the sale of her Chicago condo to help renovate her and Ryan's house in Everglades City, but she still had the sign-on bonus Ian had given her for taking on ATL. Since she helped with the accounting end of Ryan's airboat business, along with his remaining rental property, she knew investing with Ryan would be a solid plan and had wanted to buy out Shane's portion of the business.

"I did and he was all over it."

She shifted and met his gaze. "Are you sure you're good with me being an investor in your business."

He gave her another kiss, this one longer. "My business is your business."

"Vice versa," she said, snuggling even closer and running her hand along his chest.

"Good, because I want to tell Shane about ATL. I don't like keeping secrets from my brother, and I'm tired of avoiding the truth when it comes to Vlad and Harrison."

"Maybe we should ask him to join us." When he tensed, she raised her head and looked up at him. "How do you feel about that?"

"I don't want him going back to prison. Plus he can't carry a gun, so I'm not sure what he could do for ATL."

"He can fly a plane and offer his input when we're discussing cases. Since I doubt Ian's going to buy us our own private jet, there might be times when we'll need a lift, and I'd love it if Shane could pilot for us."

"That's not a bad idea. If he agrees to join us, I won't have to worry about keeping things from him."

She'd been wanting to bring up the subject of Shane being a part of ATL for the past few days, but had also wanted to wait. As Ryan had said, his brother was still adjusting to life outside of prison. But if Ryan was cool with including Shane, she was, too. She also didn't like keeping secrets from Shane. "I know this has been bothering you. If you want, we can tell him together. We can bring him to the rental house and have the rest of the crew there. This way he'll have a better understanding of what we're doing." At least on paper, since they hadn't had an assignment yet.

"Good idea. Tomorrow morning is bad, so why don't we have everyone meet Friday before the boat shop opens?"

"Perfect," she said, rested her head on his shoulder, and continued to rub his chest.

"As for Vlad…"

"Can we talk about him another time? Asian Lola want Captain Ryan," she said, once again mimicking Vlad.

Ryan hauled her onto his lap. "I like that plan."

Naples, Florida
Wednesday, 11:23 p.m. Eastern Standard Time

With a drink in one hand, bottle of Jack Daniels in the other, he staggered into his bedroom. Gabriela's perfume stuck to his skin, along with the cloying scent of her sex. He'd given her multiple orgasms before finding his own release. He should be relaxed, sated…happy. For the first time in more than a year, he'd been able to have normal sex with his girlfriend. Only what had excited him enough to sustain an erection hadn't been normal and he wasn't even close to being satisfied.

He wanted more. More Gabriela, more control.

Is this a kinky Sleeping Beauty fantasy?

As his gaze drifted back to the dead woman on his bed, Gabriela's teasing words taunted him while his actions haunted him. He took a drink straight from the bottle. Before college, he'd had no issues with sex. Then he'd met Cassidy, a pretty angelic blonde, who'd hailed from Rochester, New York. He'd fallen in lust with her and they'd eventually begun dating. When they'd finally had sex, it had been the best night of his life. Cassidy, as it had turned out, had been no angel. She'd been much more experienced than him, which hadn't bothered him in the least—he was getting laid and that had been all that had mattered. Until the night he'd overheard Cassidy making fun of him to one of her roommates.

Cassidy hadn't known that he'd been let into her apartment, and the girl who'd invited him inside had left in such a hurry, she'd never bothered to tell Cassidy he'd arrived. So he'd stood near Cassidy's closed bedroom door, listening as she made fun of him. She and her friend had giggled over his inexperience, at the way he had apparently grunted and groaned while on top of her, and the strange facial expressions he'd made during sex. Humiliated, he'd left Cassidy's, questioning whether what she'd said was true or not. Cassidy had been the third girl he'd been with, and he'd had no plans of calling the previous two to ask them if he sucked in bed.

He raised the bottle to his lips and took another swig. He'd never spoken to Cassidy after that, but what he'd overheard had stayed with him. Six months later, he'd met another girl he'd been attracted to, and after dating for a few weeks, he'd gone back to her apartment. So concerned how he'd perform, he hadn't been able to stay hard long enough to have sex. He'd pleased her in other ways, and had left her satisfied. But he hadn't been. He'd spent his teenage years—as most boys do—masturbating, except he wasn't a teenager by then, and had wanted the sexual fulfillment that came from having a lover.

He'd hated Cassidy for what she'd said about him, and hated himself even more for allowing her to fill his head with self-doubt. Still, he'd pushed forward. He'd kept dating, kept trying to have sex, only he couldn't. He could become aroused, but had always gone flaccid at that moment when it had mattered. Until the night he'd walked in on a room filled with five guys taking turns having sex with a drunken, unconscious Cassidy.

Stunned and horrified by the way the men were using her, he'd backed his way toward the door to contact the campus security. He'd wanted them to stop the abuse, but had also worried they'd beat the hell out of him if he'd tried. If that had happened, then there would have been no way for him to help Cassidy. But as he'd moved closer to the door, he hadn't been able to stop himself from taking a moment to watch.

He'd studied the other men, observed their faces and listened to their grunts, groans and heavy breathing. They hadn't looked or acted any different from the men he'd seen in porn films, and he couldn't see how his noises and facial expressions could've been any different from theirs. His confidence had grown, but when one of the guys had asked if he'd like a turn, he'd fled the room.

After he'd contacted the campus security, he had rushed to his apartment. Once inside, he'd stripped off his jeans and had masturbated. Rape was wrong, yet he hadn't been able to deny how Cassidy's unconscious body had turned him on. She hadn't been able to move or speak. If he'd had sex with her while she'd been passed out, she wouldn't have been able to make fun of his grunts or facial expressions. She wouldn't have had any control over him.

He glanced to his dead lover. *He* preferred the control.

As he recalled that night, he took another drink. The whiskey burned a path down his throat and into his stomach. He wiped the back of his hand along his mouth where some of the Jack Daniels dribbled from his numb lips, then went to the dresser. He swayed, rattling the contents on the top, and set down the bottle and glass. When he saw his reflection in the mirror, and that of his dead lover, acid rose in the back of his throat. For years, he'd used the memories of that night to help him have sex with conscious women, and would perform without issue. Eventually those memories had faded and had no longer worked. Maybe it was due to his age—he wasn't in his twenties any longer. Or maybe he'd needed *fresh* memories.

He might have issues, but he wasn't a rapist. According to the psychology books, he was a somnophiliac. Somnophilia, better known as Sleeping Beauty Syndrome, was a sexual fetish where someone unconscious sexually aroused a person.

Despite the queasiness in his stomach, as well as the self-loathing, he laughed. He'd graduated from somnophilia to necrophilia. He stripped off his shirt, popping a few buttons in the process, then reached for the bottle. His laughter died when he saw his reflection again. The problem was, sex with the dead woman had fixed his performance anxiety issues. He'd been able to give Gabriela what she'd need and wanted. He'd made love to her, fucked her, had given her orgasms. In the processes, he'd had an orgasm, too. Something that rarely happened unless he was alone.

"So now what?" he asked his image, his words slurring. He

had two other bodies in the freezer. One was a woman who had died at seventy-nine, the other was a woman who had died in a tragic car accident. Her face had ended up concave and she'd sustained burn marks over sixty percent of her body. While the phrase, *Beggars can't be choosers*, might apply to his predicament, he still wasn't sure if he could make the damaged woman appealing. Since her lips were missing, and her hands looked like skinny over-cooked chicken wings, even with a dark wig matching Gabriela's hair, no amount of lipstick or nail polish could make her pretty.

Maybe he didn't need these other women. His memories of Cassidy had sustained him for a while. His current dead lover could, too.

He looked at the woman on his bed. Although drunk, his penis hardened. He could do anything he wanted to her. Take her in every way imaginable and she couldn't complain.

He grabbed the bottle of Jack off the dresser and took another drink. Wiping his mouth again, he set the bottle down, then unbuckled his pants. Although his lover had been embalmed, and the AC had been running in his house throughout the day, he couldn't keep her much longer—maybe another four or five days—without having to put her back in the freezer. But he had the old woman and the car crash victim in there, the temperature hovering around forty degrees to keep them from becoming popsicles.

"No room at the inn," he said with a chuckle. He could remove the car crash victim and keep his current lover and the old lady on ice, but that wasn't an option. If he were to follow through with his plan, he needed to rid himself of all the bodies at the same time. The risk of planting one body, then later another was too great. When one left his house, they all would.

Too drunk to think about it, he shoved his pants down his hips, then kicked off his shoes. He used the dresser to keep himself steady, then, once naked, he turned around and stared at the woman on his bed. He reached again for the Jack, then thought better of it. He was already drunk and didn't want to waste his erection.

He grabbed a condom off the dresser, tore it open as he approached the bed, and tripped over his discarded clothes in the process. After he sheathed himself, he climbed on the mattress.

His lover looked like a mannequin, only she wasn't made of fiberglass or plastic. She was flesh, minus the blood. After having her once, he needed her again. Being with Gabriela had been beyond exquisite, but his girlfriend hadn't obeyed his rules. As he'd pleasured her, she'd eventually opened her eyes and had stared at him, yes, with passion, but it had screwed with his momentum.

Did she like what she saw? Was he making strange faces? Was he too noisy? Was she thinking about him or one of the golf pros?

As he'd tried desperately to dispel those thoughts and enjoy the moment, she'd started to direct him, saying, 'Just like that.' Or, 'Harder.' He'd never once considered himself a selfish lover, but tonight, he'd wanted to be. He had wanted her to lay still and keep quiet. He had wanted Gabriela to play opossum.

He ran a hand along the woman's calf, up her thigh, then grazed his fingers along her sex. He obviously didn't want Gabriela dead like this woman. He loved her so much, if something were ever to happen to her, it would break his heart. He positioned himself between the woman's out-stretched thighs and pressed his penis against her labia.

This is wrong.

His conscience broke through his drunken, lustful daze.

What if I get caught? What if Gabriela discovers what I've done? What if my dead lover isn't enough?

He'd been too careful. No one would know about his secrets, especially Gabriela. He'd planned out everything and even had the perfect fall guy.

And if he needed another dead lover, he'd find one.

Eventually, everyone died.

CHAPTER 4

Collier County Sheriff's Office, Naples, Florida
Thursday, 7:48 a.m. Eastern Standard Time

BETH SLID INTO the passenger side of the cruiser and placed her coffee mug in the center console cup holder. Her partner, Ricardo Cruz, had already turned the ignition and had the AC on high.

"Geez, Ricky. Are you having a hot flash?" she asked, redirecting the vents away from her. Later in the day, when the temperature was supposed to hit the upper eighties, she'd change them back. For now, she'd rather enjoy the cool morning air and keep the windows open.

"Our air conditioning unit broke down yesterday afternoon," Ricky said, pulling out of the parking lot. "My house is so damned hot, this morning I was sweating even after a cold shower." He adjusted the vents until the air moved the left sleeve of his dark-blue uniform. "Once I cool off I'll turn it down."

Ricky had a wife and two daughters, ages eight and six. "Is someone coming to fix the unit today? You guys can't be without AC. It's not good for the girls."

"Alice's cousin is going to take care of it this morning. It's an old unit, but I'm hoping he'll just need to add coolant. If we need a new one, I'm praying he'll give us a family discount. I don't want to have to pick up another side job."

She could only imagine the fit Ricky's wife, Alice, was having over the broken AC and the potential cost. The two of them couldn't catch a financial break. Last year had been rough on them. Their car had died in February. In May, their septic tank had backed up, costing thousands of dollars in damage to part of their house and yard. Then Alice's mom, who had been living with them since she'd moved to Naples from Puerto Rico six years ago, had passed away in July. Because Alice's mother had had no money and no life insurance, Ricky and Alice had to pay for the funeral. Between the six thousand dollar funeral, and the debt they'd accrued, Ricky had been forced to work extra side jobs. Alice worked, too, but even with both incomes they couldn't move ahead and had little time together.

"If you can't get it fixed today, you guys can stay at my house," Beth said, wanting to help them. She and Ricky had been partners for four years, and during that time they'd become good friends. She loved his wife and kids, and considered them extended family.

Ricky chuckled and shook his head. "Thanks, but I wouldn't do that to you. My girls would destroy your house."

"Honestly, it's no problem. My class was cancelled tonight, and my parents are out of town for the week. I can crash at their place."

"No class tonight? How'd that happen?"

She picked up her coffee mug. "My professor emailed this morning saying he had a family emergency." If only he'd sent out the email last night before her date with Shane, that way she could've suggested they meet tonight instead of Friday. After the way he'd kissed her, she didn't want to wait another day to see him again.

"What about the paper you've been working on?" Ricky asked, flipping on the right turn signal when he stopped at the intersection.

"I emailed it to my professor this morning."

As the light turned green, a female driver in a dark-blue Honda Odyssey traveling south blew through the intersection, thankfully before Ricky had made the turn. "You've got to be kidding me." Ricky switched on the lights and siren. "I was starting to finally cool off and now I've got to get out and battle the heat."

"It's seventy-two degrees," Beth reminded him, and used the mounted laptop computer to search the Odyssey's Florida plate. "If you're worried about melting, I can handle a speeding ticket."

"Nope, it's my turn," he said, veering off to the side of the road where the Odyssey had slowed to a stop.

She and Ricky had an agreement. Unless they suspected trouble, they took turns each time they had to pull over a vehicle for a traffic violation. Of course, he would end up first today. She preferred dealing with the female drivers than the males. Most men either tried to sweet talk her by complimenting her eyes or smile, or they tried to intimidate her. Neither worked. If anything, their actions made her want to find additional violations to tack onto their citation.

"Fine." Beth studied the computer screen. "The van's registered to Tracy Thomas." She glanced up and at the back of the van. "Oh, boy. Looks like she's got a bunch of kids with her."

He rolled down the window. "Yeah, I see them," he said, and opened the cruiser's door. "I hate it when there're kids in the car."

She did, too. She couldn't stand it when the little ones started crying because they thought their mommy or daddy was going to be hauled off to jail. What was even worse was when they actually *had* to arrest mommy or daddy.

Her cell phone chimed, indicating a text message. Keeping her gaze on her partner, she slipped her cell from the pocket on the door, then quickly read the message and smiled. Movement from the front of the cruiser caught her attention. She dropped the phone in her lap and looked up just as Ricky walked back toward where they were parked.

"Here." He handed her the woman's driver's license. "Mind running this through Dispatch?"

She reached for the radio handle. "No problem."

"I need three suckers from the glove box, too."

"I take it the kids are freaking out?"

He nodded. "Same with Mom. She's late for preschool."

After handing Ricky the suckers, she contacted Dispatch. While she waited for Dispatch to return, she also typed in the woman's information, this way she could see everything Dispatch would, except for local warrants.

Ricky leaned against the cruiser's door. "How's she look?"

She read the screen. "Hasn't had a ticket in seventeen years. I doubt Dispatch will come back with anything else." At that moment, Dispatch returned with the same information. "Are you going to let her off?" Beth asked.

"Yep."

"Softy," she teased, knowing she would've done the same. Unless they were total jerks or had multiple speeding tickets over a short period of time, she rarely handed out tickets.

While Ricky walked off to handle the driver, she picked up her cell phone from her lap and reread the text from Shane. Desire and anticipation curled through her stomach.

Had a great time with you. I know you have class tonight...wondered if we could meet for coffee after?

Last night's date had been too short, same for their kiss. A kiss that had been one of the hottest and sexiest she'd ever experienced. She'd loved the way he'd teased her by keeping the kiss chaste and controlled, even if she had wanted him to shove her against the car and possess her.

If I start touching you, I won't be able to stop.

When he'd told her that after she'd him asked why he hadn't touched her when they'd been kissing, her knees had grown weak. Once she was home, she hadn't been able to stop thinking about him, and not just the way he'd kissed her. Dinner had been relaxing and fun. She'd loved talking with him and how he'd made her laugh. She'd loved dancing with him and had wished the song had been longer. As if they'd known each other for years, being with Shane had been comfortable and she couldn't wait to see him again.

Hoping he'd like to meet her earlier, maybe for another dinner date, she replied back that she'd also had a great time and that her class had been cancelled. When Ricky climbed back into the car, she placed the phone into the door pocket.

"Playing Scrabble?" he asked.

"Wouldn't that be a wise way to use the county's tax dollars?"

"It beats what my old partner used to do," he said, pulling the car back onto the road.

"What was that?"

"He'd place bets with his bookie."

Beth shook her head. "Nice." Her phone chimed. Ricky looked at her and raised a brow. "You know I don't normally text when I'm on the clock," she said.

He grinned, then refocused on the road. "Airboat guy?"

Her cheeks grew warm. "I knew I shouldn't have told you about him."

"Probably not. So, is that who you were texting?"

Busted. "Yes. We went out last night, and he wants to know if he can see me again tonight."

Ricky adjusted the AC. "He's cool with you being a cop?"

She glanced toward the passenger window. "He doesn't know. At this point, he thinks I'm a law student."

"Which you are, except you also happen to wear a badge." Ricky took the ramp onto the freeway. "It's none of my business." He let out a sigh. "But I can't keep my mouth shut on this subject."

She looked at her partner. "Only this subject? Check yourself, Ricky. You've got an opinion for everything. Go ahead and say what's on your mind."

"Fine. I'm proud of being a cop. Maybe I get a little offended when you try to hide who you are because you think someone might not like you."

"I don't try to hide the fact I'm a cop."

"Then why doesn't the airboat guy know?"

Damn it. "I hate it when you're right and I'm sorry if I ever offended you. I love being a deputy and couldn't have asked for a better partner."

"Since I'm the only partner you've ever had, that doesn't say much," he said with a chuckle, then added, "Look, Beth, I'm not telling you what to do. But if this guy doesn't like you for you, then he's an asshole and you're better off moving on."

"I know." She really did. She was proud of what she'd accomplish. She had her bachelor's degree in criminal science, had been a paramedic before becoming a deputy, and was now only months away from graduating law school. In the nearly twelve years since graduating high school, she'd not only given herself a well-rounded education, but had had hands-on experience in both the medical and law enforcement fields.

Her phone chimed again, reminding her she still had an unread text message.

"Aren't you going to check that?" Ricky asked.

She grabbed the phone. As she read the new text from Shane, she couldn't stop smiling.

"Well?" Ricky asked.

"It looks like he's taking me flying."

"Flying? He's a pilot, too?"

"Yes, he has his own charter business." she said, and sent Shane a quick text.

"Impressive. So are you going to tell him?"

She placed the phone back into the door pocket and tried not to think about the way Shane had held her while they'd dance, or the way he'd kissed her. "Like you said, if he doesn't like me for me, then I'm better off moving on." She hoped that wouldn't be the case, because she liked Shane and could see herself spending a lot of her spare time with him.

Before she could dwell on her upcoming date, or how he might react to her being a cop, Dispatch notified them of a three-car accident. Beth switched on the cruiser's sirens and lights, then picked up the radio. Her love life would have to wait. She had a job to do. A job that might turn off Shane, but that'd be his problem, not hers.

Cap'n Ryan's Airboat Tours, Everglades City, Florida
Thursday, 8:17 a.m. Eastern Standard Time

Shane smiled as he read Beth's response.

"Why Shane all full of smile?" Vlad asked, as he stepped onto the airboat Shane had been cleaning. "Wait." The Russian raised a hand. "Let Vlad guess for answer. Is smile for Kiss Beth?"

Shane ignored Vlad and responded back to Beth, giving her the address for Everglades Airpark, and agreeing to meet her there around five. The timing would be perfect, since there was nothing more spectacular than watching the sun set from the air.

"Shane man of few word. Vlad understand."

"Vlad understands what?" Shane asked, and wiped the dew off the airboat's cushions. "Look, man. You seem like an okay guy—"

"Vlad not okay," the Russian said with a sigh.

Christ. His day was packed. As it was, he probably shouldn't have contacted Beth. But, damn if he didn't want to see her again. He couldn't get that kiss out of his mind and had gone to bed last night imagining what could have happened if they were at her place or his, and not in a parking lot. He'd also considered what a fool he was for pursuing her. She was in law school. Even if she accepted and disregarded his past, once she'd graduated and found a job, then what? Would the people she worked for give her a hard time for dating an ex-con? What if she had hopes of going into politics? Yeah, talk about skeletons in the closet. He could see the headlines: *Judicial Candidate Married to Murderer.* Not that he was thinking about marriage. At this point, he'd be good with just hanging out with her. And kissing. Lots of kissing. Touching would be nice. Maybe a little—

"Yes, Vlad has bad day."

Damn. The man couldn't take a hint. "Okay, why is Vlad having a bad day?"

"Harry."

Shane looked toward the souvenir shop where he'd seen Harrison earlier. "What's his problem?"

"Harry Vlad roommate. That the problem." The Russian glanced over his shoulder toward the shop, then leaned toward him. "Harry want Vlad to quit smoking."

"That's probably not a bad idea."

"Vlad agree. But, Harry no understand. It not easy for Vlad."

"How long have you been smoking?"

"Since Vlad fourteen."

"Jesus, man. That's long time. Listen to Harrison on this one."

Vlad raised the sleeve of his uniform shirt. Several circular patches coated his massive upper arm. "Harry bought Vlad nicotine bandage. It do not work."

"How long have you been wearing them?"

The Russian checked his watch. "One hour."

Shane shook his head and smiled. "Give it time. If that doesn't work, try the gum."

"Vlad," Harrison called from the window. "Can you come up here?"

The Russian rolled his eyes. "Of late, Harry is on Vlad nerve ending." He started toward the shop, then turned. "Vlad wish Shane luck with Kiss Beth."

Shane watched the man lumber along the pier. Maybe he shouldn't have been such a prick to the Russian. The guy was trying to make friendly small talk, but he'd learned in prison that friends were hard to come by. He'd made two during the entire seven years he'd been incarcerated. If it hadn't been for them, he might've gone crazy.

At least he wasn't counting as much. When he'd been in prison, he'd realized early on that he would need to keep his mind sharp. If he hadn't been reading, he'd been counting.

He'd taken to calculating his steps, counting the cinderblocks that made up his cell wall, the number of footsteps, coughs or sneezes he'd hear throughout the night. Now that he was out and his mind was preoccupied with trying to reopen his business, he didn't need to count every little thing that had crossed his path. Well, at least not as much.

What he hadn't counted on was finding a woman like Beth. Beautiful, sexy, smart and fun to be around. He didn't deserve to be in her company. Seven years ago? Maybe. Now?

He grabbed the towels and cleaning supplies from the boat and hopped onto the dock. He'd tell her about his past this evening after their flight. If she didn't want anything to do with him once she knew the truth, then that would be that.

As he made his way across the dock and toward the shop, he saw Barney sliding out of his old station wagon. Shane hadn't seen much of the man over the past few days, and he'd had to run several boat tours for him. Ryan had told him that Barney had been doing work on the rental property Lola owned, and where Vlad and Harrison currently resided.

"How ya' doin', boy?" Barney called, as he approached.

"Good. What are you doing here? I thought I was covering your shift this morning."

"Got that right." Barney nodded, and pulled off his baseball cap, which had a Vietnam veteran logo across the front. Barney adjusted the strap attached to the eye patch he'd been forced to wear since losing his eye in combat. "Came by to pick up Vlad. I need him to help me move something at Lola's house," he said, covering his thick, curly gray hair with the ball cap.

"Lola and Ryan's house, or Lola's rental property?" Shane asked.

"The rental property. Anyhow, where can I find—" Barney grinned and looked toward the porch that surrounded the ice cream and souvenir shop. "There's my man," Barney said to Vlad as the Russian approached, then he did a few boxing movements. "C'mon, Ivan, get in the wagon. I need those muscles of yours."

"Vlad have watch your Rocky Balboa movie and see this Ivan Drago. Vlad no find it funny."

"You ain't findin' anything funny since Harry forced you to quit smoking."

"Not true. Vlad find it very funny when Polina bite Harry toe this morning."

Shane laughed, along with Barney. "Is that why Harrison was hobbling around earlier?" Shane asked.

Vlad nodded. "Harry big baby. Polina not even crack skin."

"Well, you sure as hell crack me up," Barney said. "Now get in the wagon. We've got work to do."

"Exactly what are you working on?" Shane asked.

Barney and Vlad answered at the same time, only they each gave him a different one. Barney claimed the boat dock, Vlad, the kitchen. "Which is it?" Shane asked.

"Vlad mistake. Barney right. Boat dock," he said, then with a wave the Russian walked toward Barney's station wagon.

Shane shook his head. "What's going on, Barn? I keep feeling like everyone is hiding something from me."

"Nope. That's just you being paranoid. If I recall, you were just the same way when you came home after leaving the Night Stalkers."

"I suppose you're right," Shane said. "I'll catch up with you later."

As he and Barney went their separate ways, Shane considered what the man had said. Shane had been part of the U.S. Army's 160th Special Operations Aviation Regiment known as the Night Stalkers for a large portion of his Army career and had piloted MH-60M Black Hawks. They usually operated at night, using high speeds and low altitudes to avoid enemy radar, and their missions had ranged from attack, to assault, to recon. He'd dealt with his share of stress, fear and adrenaline during those years of service and he'd had a hard time adjusting to civilian life once he'd returned home to Everglades City. The only thing that had kept him grounded and the nightmares at bay had been his Cessna and getting his air charter business literally off the ground. Ryan would've, too, but he'd still been with the SEALs at the time.

Shane had been paranoid back then. Why, he'd never understood. During the seven years he'd been in prison, he had also dealt with stress, fear and adrenaline, only for different reasons. Still, he swore his brother and Lola, along with the rest of the crew who worked for Ryan, were doing something behind his back. Except that didn't make sense. Barney was a good ol' boy, who was handy with any tool, medical kit, weapon or steering wheel—no matter if the vehicle moved on water or land. Aside from constantly telling BS stories about things he claimed to know, there wasn't a thing about the man Shane didn't like. Hell, he even liked when the man fed him line after line of bullshit.

Then there were Lola's friends, Harrison and Vlad. He still hadn't figured out how the computer geek and the Russian knew Lola, or what type of jobs they were waiting to take. All he knew was that those two had a strange bromantic relationship and didn't belong here.

Lola was another issue. Ryan had given Shane a lame story about how he and Lola had met at a bar in Everglades City while she had been on a business trip. She claimed to be an accountant. He'd seen her practice her *jiu jitsu* in Ryan's backyard, so maybe she was more like a ninja accountant. He honestly didn't care what Lola's profession had been before she'd moved in with Ryan. She made his brother happy and that was good enough for him.

Still, something wasn't right.

As he made his way toward the boat shop, a minivan pulled into the parking lot. Since he was the only boat captain present, the van likely meant his first tour had arrived. He had five back-to-back tours, then he'd be free to leave. After that, he'd head home and shower, then drive to the airpark and prep his plane. He looked forward to taking Beth in the air. With the way she was nothing but smiles during the airboat rides, he imagined her reaction would be the same once he let her fly the Cessna.

His chest tightened with unease. He pulled a rubber band

from his pocket, pushed a hand through his hair and tied it back. Beth might enjoy the flight, but he doubted she'd be smiling once he told her the truth about his past. He didn't have to tell her anything, but damn it, he liked the woman. A lot. He didn't want to be that dick who strung her along for weeks, maybe months, then confessed that he was an ex-con. Even worse, a murderer. Like he'd decided earlier, he would make his confession and if she didn't want to see him again, then that was that.

Only *that* would be miserable. He'd had a taste of her lips. He'd checked out her curves and was dying to see her naked, have her beneath him. On top of him would suit him just fine, too. He didn't want to ruin his chance with her, yet he couldn't continue to see her while worrying one of his co-workers or the people around town might let it slip that he'd just spent the past seven years doing hard time. He might be a murderer, but his mom had raised him to treat women with honesty and respect. Then again, his mom *was* in Fort Lauderdale…

Naples, Florida
Thursday, 8:23 a.m. Eastern Standard Time

His head throbbed as if someone had used it for a game of soccer. The piercing to his temple was even worse. He rubbed his eyes, yawned and stretched, then jerked upright. He stared at the dead woman lying next to him. Memories of yesterday, of last night, collided together. He scrubbed a hand down his face, grazing the beard stubble with his palm. Looking down at his body, realizing that he was as naked as the dead woman, he quickly scooted off the mattress.

"What was I thinking?" he mumbled, and glanced at the Jack Daniels sitting on the dresser, barely a few swallows left in the bottle. He looked down at his flaccid penis, still sheathed in a condom—a broken condom—and gagged. He rushed to the master bathroom and reached the toilet just in time to vomit the booze and whatever had been left over from dinner with Gabriela.

Gabriela.

Bile burned his throat. He retched again and clung to the toilet bowl. He slid to the cool tile floor as guilt and remorse continued to agitate his stomach. What kind of man needed his woman to play dead and wear his dead lover's lingerie?

He wiped his mouth with the back of his hand. How could he have done that to her? How could he have given her a gift worn by a corpse? What he'd done last night hadn't been an act of love. He'd been selfish and cruel. Gabriela might not know this, but he did—the evidence of his depravity was still lying on his bed.

"She has to go." He winced. Talking made his headache worse. Using the counter to steady himself, he rose from the tile, then tossed the used condom into the toilet. Since Gabriela was spending the day with her two sisters and their kids, and he had nothing on his agenda until later this afternoon, he would have plenty of time to make the dead women go away. His plan might've worked, but he couldn't continue on with it.

Memories of taking the dead woman in a way that he would never, ever even suggest to Gabriela had his penis stirring. He closed his eyes and allowed those memories to run free. Yes, his plan had worked and, despite knowing sex with a corpse was wrong, given the chance he'd do it again.

He pulled his toothbrush and toothpaste from the vanity drawer, then proceeded to vigorously brush his teeth. What the hell was he even thinking? He couldn't do this again. He should have never stolen the bodies in the first place. The moment his ridiculous plan had entered his mind, he should have dismissed it. He'd tried. Desperately. But it was his desperation and curiosity that had led him to where he was at this moment. Sexually sated by a dead woman.

Fucking disgusting.

His lover and the other two bodies in his freezer had to go.

Screw his plan. He was better than this. How he performed sexually didn't define him as a man. He was wealthy, successful and a prominent member in the community.

He finished brushing, then headed into his bedroom. He wanted the dead women out of his house. Today, not a week from now as he'd originally planned. He needed to erase any trace of them, along with any reminders of how low he had sunk and how debased he'd allowed himself to become.

He grabbed the silky sheet lying haphazardly on the bed and tossed it over the woman's body, then searched his pants' pockets for his cell phone. When he found it, he dialed the pet store first, confirming that they were still interested in purchasing his snake terrarium, and making sure he could drop it off today. After he ended the call, he contacted the U-Haul dealer and rented a four-by-eight cargo trailer. From there, he called a local car rental company and asked if they could rent him an SUV with towing capacity and deliver it to his home. By the time he set his cell phone onto the dresser, he had in place all the necessary details in which he could rid himself of the bodies.

He considered the broken condom, then went back into the bathroom and turned on the faucet to the sunken garden tub. As the tub filled, he returned to the bedroom, tore the sheet away from the dead woman, then lifted her in his arms. The smell of semen and remnants of Gabriela's perfume had his queasy stomach cramping and his throat tightening with the urge to vomit again. After rushing into the bathroom, he gently set the body in the tub, then shut off the water. Using a washcloth and soap, he cleaned her, taking extra care when he reached her vagina and rectum. Hung over and disgusted by his actions, he shouldn't have found the act of bathing the dead woman sensual, yet he couldn't stop his body from reacting or for wanting her one more time.

He wouldn't use her again. He'd used her enough. Once her skin and cavities were cleaned, he washed and rinsed her hair, then pulled her from the tub and lay her on the clean towel he'd placed on the floor. As he dried her, he avoided her sex and temptation. When satisfied he'd washed away any evidence, he dropped the towel on her body. Remaining naked to avoid leaving behind DNA on his clothes, he went to the garage where he kept his freezer.

When he opened the lid, cool air and the foul odor of decay touched his face and nostrils. He stared down at the old woman who, like his dead lover, had been embalmed. She lay on her side in the fetal position, the car crash victim beneath her. Since the car crash woman's face had been so badly mutilated and the majority of her body had been burned, her family had requested that she be immediately cremated and the body not to be present for the memorial service. Which meant there was no reason to embalm the woman and that she was the source of the stench. Fortunately he'd had the sense to keep the car crash victim in the body bag provided by the coroner's accident investigation team. He'd still have to clean and air out the freezer, but the mess could've been worse.

An hour later, the three bodies—all of them cleaned and properly prepped—lay on the floor of his master bathroom. The bodies could eventually be discovered, he wasn't foolish enough to believe otherwise. If that ended up being the case, he'd needed to make sure they looked a certain way in order to pin the dead women onto his fall guy. He had also showered and dressed, and now he had to ready the snake terrarium before the rental company dropped off the SUV.

The doorbell rang. His stomach twisted in a knot.

They're early.

He checked his reflection in the bathroom mirror. Certain he didn't look as if he'd spent the past hour cleaning and abusing corpses, he left the bathroom, shutting the door behind him. When he reached the tiled foyer of his four thousand square foot house—a home too large for one person, but the size carried with it status—he opened the door. He glanced past the man wearing a golf shirt with the car rental company's logo embroidered on the left side of his chest to the SUV in his driveway. Once he'd signed the necessary paperwork, he went back into the house to gather his wallet.

After he'd made sure his house was locked, he took the rental to retrieve the trailer.

Another hour had passed by the time he returned home. He'd had a hell of a time backing the SUV with the attached trailer into his driveway. But he needed the trailer to be in the garage. If he were only transporting a terrarium, where the trailer was located wouldn't have made a difference. But since he had extra cargo—

"Morning," his next-door neighbor, Ned Baker, called as he pulled his golf cart from his garage. "Whatcha got going on over there?"

"Hi, Ned. When's tee time?"

"Twenty minutes. Mike had to cancel. We can use a fourth, if you're interested."

If he wasn't hung over and didn't have bodies to dispose of, he still wouldn't have taken Ned up on the offer. Considering it was just after eleven, by the time Ned and the rest of his group made it past the ninth hole, the temperature would likely reach eighty-eight degrees and he hated golfing in the scorching heat. "Thanks, but I need to return this trailer before I head into the office later. Keep me in mind for Sunday. I'm free then."

Ned drove his golf cart across the lawn, which pissed him off. Thanks to his neighbor, he'd already had his landscaper out twice this year to fix the damage the golf cart had caused, and it was only January. "So what's with the trailer?" Ned asked.

"I sold one of my snake terrariums."

Ned made a face, which caused his large nose to appear even larger. "I hope the snakes, too?"

"One of them." He hadn't sold the four-foot snake, but intended to set it free. He didn't need his snake's DNA leading back to him. "I promised Gabriela I'd get rid of the snakes. I'm attached to them, so I'm taking baby steps."

He'd had his California King snake for nearly eleven years. Due to her curious and gentle nature he'd always preferred the pretty, black and white female over the larger male he also owned. But months after she'd laid eggs last June, he'd noticed a lump developing near her head. He'd taken her to the vet and, after testing, had been told she had cancer. The surgery would be risky and her chances of surviving were low. Plus, he couldn't commit to caring for her after such a delicate surgery. Gabriela had thought him ridiculous for even considering spending over five hundred dollars to help his snake. He could afford it, yet hadn't wanted the snake to suffer. So instead of euthanizing her, he would now let her live the remainder of her life outside of captivity.

Ned shook his head. "Don't know how anyone could be attached to a snake, unless the snake's attached to your neck," he said with a chuckle.

"They're interesting creatures and don't require much maintenance," he responded. "I've had snakes since I was a kid. But if I'm ever going to get Gabriela to move in with me, they have to go." All of this was true. Gabriela hated the snakes and had told him they gave her nightmares. What he'd always found fascinating was the dichotomy of her reactions to them. They terrified her, yet when she had been in the room with them, she couldn't stop watching the snakes or commenting on how they moved. To him, the snakes represented various religions and cultures. More than that, he enjoyed the simplicity of the complex creature.

"If you're trying to get Gabriela to move in with you, does this mean you're finally thinking about popping the question?" Ned asked.

He'd been doing more than thinking, and had a three-carat diamond engagement ring stowed away in the hidden wall safe in his bedroom closet. "I'm not getting any younger," he said with a smile and edged toward the garage.

"You're just a baby," Ned said. "Hey, I've got a few minutes. Need help carrying the snake cage?"

Terrarium. "I could use a hand. I'd planned on taking it apart, but that'd be a pain in the ass."

Ned turned off the golf cart, then climbed out of it. "No problemo. Where we heading?"

"My office," he said, leading Ned into the garage and toward the door that would take them to the utility room.

"Nice freezer," Ned said. "What the hell do you need something this big for? Dead bodies?"

He chuckled and stopped at the freezer. "Not quite. I ordered it online, but didn't realize just how big it would be. Gabriela has a thing for lobster. I bought this to hold the order I'd placed from Maine."

When Ned opened the freezer, his heart rate increased and his stomach seized. Although tempted to slam it shut, he refrained. If he didn't act suspicious, no one would suspect.

"Hell, you could put a whole goddamned cow in this thing," Ned said, inspecting the freezer's interior. "It's not very cold though."

Playing dumb, he looked at the temperature settings on the inside wall of the freezer. "I guess I'm a bit of an idiot. I just plugged the thing in and didn't think about turning the temperature down." He made a quick adjustment to the dial. "I'm glad you said something. That would've been bad if I hadn't caught it before the lobsters arrived."

"I'm glad I can help. It's good to know you have this. We're planning a party next month, so keep the weekend of the twentieth open. If you don't mind, I might need to lease some freezer space for ice."

"You've got it," he said, leading Ned inside the house.

Within a few minutes, he and Ned were loading the terrarium—snake included—into the trailer. "Thanks, Ned. I really appreciate the help."

"Anytime." Ned climbed back into his golf cart. "If we're setting up tee times for Sunday, I'll give you a call."

He waved to Ned, then let out a deep breath.

Ned didn't smell a thing.

Regardless, he'd still clean the freezer. If he ended up at Ned's for a party, he had no intention of having a drink using the ice stored in a freezer that had once contained dead bodies.

He stood in the garage contemplating his next move. The moment he'd started prepping the bodies for disposal, he'd realized he'd been rash. Impulsively contacting the pet store, then renting the SUV and trailer had been a mistake. How the hell was he going to hide bodies in the middle of the day? He couldn't wait until tonight and couldn't leave the snake in the trailer all day, not with the temperatures reaching into the high eighties. Although reptiles thrived in the heat, they could also die if their environment became too hot. While he might be setting his California King free, he didn't want to see anything happen to her.

Which brought up the crux of his problem. He took a few steps toward the terrarium and watched his snake. Did he attempt to release the snake and dump the bodies during daylight hours, or wait until tonight? Come three o'clock, he would be busy until at least nine or ten. His neighbor knew his plans, and he'd already called the pet store to let them know he'd drop off the terrarium today, which meant he really had no choice but to take care of business now.

He glanced to his other neighbor's house. Ron and Liz were in the Keys for the weekend. Ned was golfing, and he knew Ned's wife played bocce ball with a group of women every Friday morning, then had lunch afterward. The land across the street hadn't been developed yet, so he didn't have to worry about anyone seeing into his garage. He ran a hand along the trailer, then gave it a tap.

Yes, his decision to take care of the bodies today had been hasty, but it had also been necessary. Besides, the place he'd chosen to release his snake and dump the dead women wasn't a high traffic area. Shell Island Road, a short twenty-two-minute drive from his house in Naples, cut through thousands of acres of undeveloped land and was used by some boaters and fishermen to access the free boat ramp located at the end of the road. He'd driven through the area on three different occasions and had never seen a car. Hopefully today would be no different.

After entering the house, he headed upstairs. Once he'd disposed of the bodies, he would need to put what he had done behind him and forget it had ever happened. Gabriela loved him for him. While he believed sex was an important part of a relationship, he also believed there was more to a marriage *than* sex. And he wanted to marry Gabriela. They'd been together for nearly two years. Not once had she ever complained when he couldn't perform. What he'd done to his dead lover, in a horrible act of desperation, wasn't worth facing felony charges, losing Gabriela or corrupting his morals any further.

When he reached the master bathroom, he glanced at the dead women on the floor. Looking at the naked bodies of the old woman and car crash victim made him sick to his stomach. The seventy-nine year old could be someone's mother and grandmother.

He quickly blocked the memory of what he'd done to the woman, along with the car crash victim, then turned away and covered his mouth. Bile climbed up the back of his throat as those memories surfaced anyway. He swallowed it down and dragged in a deep breath.

He had a limited amount of time to take care of business.

Now wasn't the time for emotion.

Now was the time to hide the bodies.

CHAPTER 5

Somewhere Over the Everglades, Florida
Thursday, 5:42 p.m., Eastern Standard Time

BETH'S CHEEKS HURT from smiling. She'd been on a plane many times in her life, but never one this small, and never behind the wheel. The cockpit, which wasn't the traditional type she'd glimpsed while boarding a commercial airliner, was tight. So tight the left side of her body was in constant contact with Shane's. She wasn't complaining. After the way he'd held her while they'd danced last night, she wanted him touching her, even if it was only due to their close quarters.

"What do you think?" Shane asked, his voice coming through the headset she wore.

"This. Is. Awesome."

When she'd first arrived, she'd been nervous. What did she really know about Shane? The man could kill her and dump her body over the Everglades. Instinct told her she could trust him. If he had his own charter business, he clearly had the appropriate licensing and knew how to fly. As for becoming a swamp murder victim, she needed to switch off cop-mode for a couple of hours and enjoy the ride. She'd wanted wild and fun, and Shane was delivering.

She glanced from the front window to the one on her right side. She'd experienced the Everglades from an airboat, but to see it from the air? From the numerous airboat tours she'd taken, and the reading she'd done on the area, she knew the Everglades encompassed a huge portion of southern Florida. Something like seven hundred square miles, if she recalled correctly. On a map, the Glades looked huge. From the air, it looked massive, beautiful and foreboding. Brackish rivers, canals and channels cut through the dense clusters of dark-green trees, giving the impression that a mammoth snake had once left its imprint on the wetlands.

As she stared down, she couldn't imagine hiking, camping or kayaking through the Glades. She knew people who had, but now realized they were nuts. She couldn't find one building or outpost, not one indication that humans had ever been in the area. Talk about a great place to dump a body.

Shane nudged her shoulder, stopping her from heading into cop-mode again. "We're flying over what's known as the Wilderness Waterway. Starting from Everglades City, people canoe or kayak the ninety-nine mile route all the way to Flamingo, at the tip of Florida."

"Ninety-nine miles? That's insane. How long does it take?"

"About a week, unless the weather's bad. There're campgrounds along the way, so it's not too bad."

She looked to his profile. "Have you canoed the waterway?"

"Ryan and I did it with kayaks the summer before I left for the Army. We had a great time, but I don't need to do that again. At eighteen, it was cool. At this point in my life, if I'm going to take a week of vacation, I'd rather go to a resort where there's a swim-up bar and the suites have room service."

She chuckled. "I'm not much of an adventurer. Like you, I'd take a resort over kayaking through this," she said, looking back to the landscape below them.

"I don't know. Being the youngest of five had to have been an adventure."

The quick memory of this past Christmas popped in her

head. Since her brothers all lived in different states and had families of their own, finding the time and location for all of them to reunite was difficult. They'd made it work in December. Christmas had ended up being crazy, loud and a reminder of how much she loved being part of a large family.

"It was," she said. "My brothers were over protective, yet teased me mercilessly. Especially my brother, Phil. He's the youngest of the boys and five years older than me. I used to follow him and his friends around, which my older bothers didn't like. Phil had no fear, neither did I."

"How many broken bones?"

"I only had one, my ankle. Phil had two, and I think between the other boys the total comes to seven. Don't even ask about stitches."

"Do your parents have any hair left?"

"Surprisingly enough, they do," she said, thinking about her mom and dad. She and her brothers had pooled their money together and had sent their parents on vacation for their forty-fifth wedding anniversary. She hoped they were having fun on their cruise to the Caribbean.

When Shane nudged her again, she looked at him. "Ready to take this for a spin?" he asked.

"Are you sure? This isn't like the airboat. At least if we crashed we were already on land, or at least near it."

"Yeah, I'm sure. You'll be fine. Just take the control column in front of you."

She placed both hands on the W-shaped wheel. "Okay, now what?"

"Now you're flying."

She glanced at him and realized he no longer held the wheel in front of him, then quickly looked ahead. "Please tell me I don't have to do anything with the pedals on the floor or the stick next to you."

"Nope," he said, and as she gripped the wheel tightly, he explained the primary flight controls. When he started talking about pitch and roll and yaw, then all the little devices on the control panel, she gently elbowed him. "Too much?"

"A little." Her palms had grown sweaty. "Maybe you should take the wheel."

"That's fine. There's something I want to show you." He moved the joystick next to him and gave the wheel a slight turn.

As the plane tilted and began to veer left, she wiped her palms on her shorts. "What should I be looking for?" she asked, her gaze on the wetlands below them.

"It's not down there, but up here."

When she looked up, her breath caught. She'd seen the beginning of plenty of sunsets, but never like this. In the distance, the orange sun hung heavy in the sky, its rays touching on the smattering of clouds and the dark-blue waters of Chokoloskee Bay, which ran along the west side of Everglades Airpark. "Absolutely beautiful," she finally said.

"That's why I wanted to take you up at this hour. There's no better place to watch the sun rise or set than from the air. Seeing the sunset from here, it's something special."

And he had wanted to share this with her. With his rough exterior, Shane didn't seem like the kind of guy who would stop and appreciate a sunset. There were more layers to him than she'd realized. She'd like to peel back those layers and discover more about him. During the time they'd spent together on the boat, having dinner last night, and now today, he'd talked, but he hadn't been *talkative*. Most men she'd dated were interested in telling her all about themselves, and hadn't known that it was okay to take a breath and ask her a few questions about her likes and dislikes, or where she came from, or where she wanted to go. Shane, on the other hand, was a quiet man, whose actions spoke volumes.

She really liked him. A lot.

For the next fifteen minutes, they flew in silence watching as the sun slowly dipped. When they neared Everglades Airpark's small landing strip, she couldn't help the disappointment. Being in the air with Shane would likely go down as one of those special moments in her life. He'd shown her a part of himself and had gifted her with Mother Nature's beauty.

As he descended the plane and the landing strip grew closer, she relaxed. Her earlier nervousness about flying in a plane with a stranger, along with thoughts of swamp murder, had been replaced with absolute trust. He'd promised her a great time, and he'd delivered. While she'd love to stay in the air with him, she now looked forward to the rest of their evening.

After the Cessna touched down and Shane slowed the plane, he circled the airport then parked in the grass. "Did you have fun?"

"Loved it," she said, unbuckling her seatbelt as he shut down the plane.

"What's better, the airboat or the Cessna?"

"Tough call." She rested her head against the leather seat, closed her eyes and brought to mind images from her last trip in the airboat. "What I love about being in the airboat is feeling that connection with nature, being able to pick up the different smells, and having the sun and wind against my face."

"And the Cessna?"

From the air she hadn't experienced that connection to nature. Instead, she'd felt wild and free, like a bird who'd just escaped the confines of its cage and could now spread its wings and soar. She rolled her head to the side and opened her eyes. Her cheeks grew warm when she realized he'd been watching her. "If I knew how to fly, I'd go everyday. Being in the air...there's something freeing about it."

His eyes held approval, along with something else she couldn't name. Keeping her gaze locked on his, she shifted and touched his jaw. His beard was soft and brought back memories of their kiss last night. "Thank you," she said. "I had a great time with you."

He leaned his head forward. "Sounds like you're ready to call it a night."

"Not at all."

"Good." He tucked her hair behind her ear, then caressed her cheek. "I thought maybe you were gearing up to give me a kiss good-bye."

She grinned. "Do all of our kisses have to be at the end of a date?"

"I don't think so. In my humble opinion, we should be kissing at the beginning, multiple times in the middle, and then, of course, at the end."

She leaned forward and kissed him. Not like she had last night, when she'd speared her hands through his hair and practically assaulted his mouth. Instead, she let her lips cling to his in a lingering, almost chaste kiss. "That was for the beginning," she said when she moved her mouth a fraction away from his.

He shifted his hand from her cheek and cupped the back of her head, locking her in place. "We're in the middle of our date now."

"Yes, we are," she murmured, and couldn't stop the smile tugging her lips. "If we should be kissing multiple times during the middle of our date, we should probably kiss again."

He drew her head closer and brushed his lips against hers. "Absolutely," he said, then he kissed her. Slowly. Sensually. As if he were trying to learn the contours of her mouth, or what she liked and didn't like. He'd kissed her this way last night. While she loved the way he was kissing her, she wanted hot and raw. Taking his lead, she caressed his jawline, then ran her hands through his hair and up his neck.

He kissed her harder, but kept his mouth closed. If only he knew how much he was driving her crazy. She needed more. She wanted to show him how much she wanted him touching and kissing her. If he was teasing her, playtime needed to come to an end, and soon. She liked Shane and had been fantasizing about more than kissing for a week.

Deciding *go bold or go home* would be this evening's motto, she gripped the front of his shirt. When her fist pressed against the hard slab of muscle along his chest, she couldn't pass up the chance to touch him. She released his shirt and ran her hand along his pecs.

Oh. My. God. His chest was bigger and more solid than

she'd imagined. If only they weren't in his plane and had layers of clothes separating them. She'd love to be naked and pressed up against his body.

Not ready for their middle of the date kiss to end, she slid her hand up his chest and twined her arms around his neck.

He fisted her hair in his hand and gently drew her back. She met his gaze. The hunger in his eyes in no way matched the way he'd been kissing her. Desire zipped straight to her sex, making her ache for him to touch her there and soothe the need rushing through her body.

"I'm trying to be good," he finally said.

"And I'm trying to be bad."

The corner of his mouth tilted in a sexy smile. "Now that I know that—" He crushed his mouth against hers. She opened her lips and welcomed him. Moaning her approval, she once again matched his pace. Tangled her tongue with his in one of the hottest open-mouthed kisses she'd ever experienced. Moments passed before he took the kiss right back where they'd started. Sweet, innocent and so damned sexy.

"I think we covered one of the middle kisses for now," he said, his voice husky.

She grinned and kissed the corner of his mouth. "For now."

Smiling, he leaned back. "Come on. I promised you dinner. If we're lucky, we'll catch the tail end of the sunset."

Twenty minutes later, after she'd followed Shane to Camellia Street Grill in Everglades City, they were seated on the back deck overlooking the water, sipping iced tea, picking at their appetizer of calamari and watching as the sun finally sank below the horizon.

"I'd love do this everyday," she said, and leaned back in her chair. "I wish I could retire now, instead of waiting until I'm in my seventies like my parents."

Shane reached for his glass. "Wouldn't that be the life?"

"Yeah, but you *do* get to enjoy this," she said, waving her hand toward the water. "And your Cessna. If I had a job like that, I wouldn't see any reason to retire. You could pick up and fly off to anywhere." Seriously. The man had it made. She wasn't knocking his profession and realized there were ups and downs when it came to running a business, but how could he have a bad day when he was either boating through the Glades or flying over it.

"I've thought about it."

"You mean flying off to wherever?"

He nodded, then leaned forward. "But I love it here. Ryan's just a few minutes away, same with the boat shop and airpark. I have this little slice of heaven, and if I want to head to a bigger city, it's just a drive or a short flight away."

"I get it. Honestly, I was okay staying in Cleveland. The winters were horrible, but I still have extended family in the area and there's that hometown familiarity. When I followed my parents down here, I truly understood the whole fish out of water expression. It took me weeks to learn my way around, months to find a townhouse that would be a good location for school and my job." She sighed. "It took even longer than that to make friends." She grinned as she remembered those first few months after the move to Florida. "My parents had been coming down here for a few years during the winter months, so they were established. I spent my weekends hanging out with people more than double my age. If you need to know where to hit the early bird specials in Naples, I'm your go-to girl."

Chuckling, he asked, "You go to law school and work? How do you manage that?"

She'd purposefully mentioned she had a job and he'd taken the bait. Now it was time to find out if her being a deputy mattered to him. "I go to night school. My first year down here, I went to law school fulltime and worked as a paramedic part-time, which was what I was doing when I was living in Cleveland. But I didn't like the stress that went along with being a paramedic." Her stomach knotted, but she ignored the nervousness wreaking havoc to her insides and pushed forward. "When I heard there was an opening for a deputy's position with the Collier County Sheriff's Office, I jumped at it. I figured, once I graduated, being a cop and understanding the system could eventually help with my law career."

"You said you graduate in May, right?" he asked, his expression never wavering.

"Yes. Normally night school would take five years. I'm doing it in four, since I did a year fulltime." She sat there for a moment, waiting for him to react like the men she'd dated in the past. Those guys would either grow distant until the date was over, or tell her being a deputy was too dangerous for a woman or, better yet, find a reason to end the date early.

"I'll be honest," he began, "I would've never pegged you for a cop. Now that I know you are one, I guess I better get rid of the marijuana plants I've been growing in the backyard."

She grinned and relaxed. She'd had herself so damned nervous over telling Shane about her job, and it had been an unhealthy waste of energy. From where she sat, he showed no indication that her job bothered him. Was it possible she'd finally met a guy open-minded enough to accept her career choices?

"Ah, now it's clicking in place. You grow the weed and ship it via the Cessna. I thought I smelled something funny on the plane."

"Busted," he said with a grin. "So tell me more about being a deputy. Do you have a partner?"

As Beth told him about her partner, Ricky, Shane leaned back into the chair and watched her. How could this beautiful, pint-sized woman, who had been the star attraction to his week long fantasies, be a cop?

A motherfucking cop.

Damn it. This sucked. Badly. He liked Beth, more than he'd expected to and now he'd have to end things between them. He could give a shit what she did for a living, and could care less that she was cop. Just because he was an ex-con didn't mean he had a beef with the law. Honestly, his issues were with attorneys. Especially the prosecutor who had gone to great lengths to make sure he'd served his full prison sentence, along with his clueless defense attorney who'd done dick to help him.

Prison guards were an issue, too. Not all of them had been pricks, but there had been a few who had taken pleasure in his misery.

No, he wouldn't stop dating Beth because she was a Collier County deputy, but because if the people she worked with discovered she was dating an ex-con, her career would be ruined. He could tell her about his past and let her decide if she wanted to continue to see him, but saw no point in doing that. Instead he'd pretend everything was fine, enjoy the rest of their date, then the next time they were supposed to see each other, he'd cancel. So it was the pussy's way out. He didn't care. He didn't want to hurt her. He might hurt her feelings anyway, but at least she could simply think of him as the dick who'd never returned her calls, rather than question whether she was a bad judge of character for hooking up with a murderer.

As the evening went on, he'd managed to pretend that everything was cool, even if his body was tense and he wanted to punch a hole in the fucking wall. He'd finally met a woman who he wanted to know past the first couple of dates. They'd connected, and he hated to sever that connection. He'd loved taking her in his plane, watching the perma-smile on her face as he'd flown her over the Glades and showed her the setting sun. He didn't even want to think about that kiss in the cockpit. He'd loved touching her, tasting her, and wanted more. More time. More Beth.

He might be a free man, but his felony record still held him prisoner to certain pleasures in life. Beth was now one of them.

They finished dinner. Since they both had to work in the morning, they'd decided to once again call it an early night. As he walked her to her car, she hooked her arm through his and leaned into him. "Thanks again for taking me in your plane and for dinner. I had a great time."

"Me, too," he said. When they reached her SUV, he glanced around the parking lot. Since the restaurant would be closing soon, the parking lot only was almost empty. He looked toward the sky. Unlike the parking lot they'd been in last night, this one wasn't as well lit, which allowed the stars to be seen more clearly. "It's a beautiful night."

"Noisy, too," she said. "Are those frogs I hear?"

"Frogs and insects." When he'd first returned home, he'd forgotten how loud they could be and had slept with the windows closed. But then the nightmares had started. Some from when he'd been with the Night Stalkers, others were bad memories from when he'd been incarcerated. Now the bugs and frogs helped him fall asleep. The white noise hadn't stopped the occasional nightmare, but concentrating on trying to pick up individual sounds, or counting the number of frog croaks, usually cleared his mind and made sleep come sooner. "You get used to it," he said.

"In my development I'll hear the occasional dog or cat. It's a nice area, but I wish I lived closer to the water." She slid her hand into his. "So…"

Right. So now what? She was a cop. He was a convicted murderer. Weren't they the perfect couple?

"What's your schedule like this weekend?" he asked, because that was the right thing to do.

"Tomorrow and Saturday I work until four. If you're free, maybe you'd like to come to my place and we could grill out."

Dinner at Beth's. Damn it. He could go. He could spend another evening with her and enjoy her company and her kisses, maybe even more. Doing that would make him an even bigger dick. He didn't want to lead her on or torture himself by spending time with a woman too good for him.

"Tomorrow works for me. What time?"

"Anytime after five."

"Let's make it six. Text me your address later and let me know what I can bring."

She wrapped her arms around his waist. "My treat. Just bring yourself."

Tell her the truth.

Indecision and guilt caused his head to ache. Knowing he wouldn't go to Beth's tomorrow evening had his chest tightening with anger and self-loathing. One bad decision had cost him seven years of his life. Now it would cost him the chance with a special woman.

He ran his hands along her arms, then settled them on her hips. She had curves in all the right places. Needing to take advantage of touching her this one last time, he pulled her closer. "I had fun with you today. More fun than I've had in a long time."

She moved her hands from his waist, then up his back. "We only had one middle kiss," she said, taking his memories back to the cockpit of the Cessna.

"Then maybe we should double up on our goodnight kiss to make up for the ones we missed in the middle," he suggested, and edged her back until she was against her car.

She pressed her breasts against his chest and hugged him closer. "That's an excellent idea," she said, and rising to her tiptoes, grazed her lips along his. "What are we waiting for?"

"Who's waiting," he said, then captured her lips, angled his head and deepened the kiss. When she parted her lips, he slid his tongue into her mouth. She quickly tangled her tongue with his and let out a throaty moan that had his balls tightening and his dick hard. Needing more contact, he moved his leg between her thighs and pulled her hips closer. He wanted her to know what she did to him. He wanted the heat of her sex warming his leg.

Still not enough.

He shoved one hand through her hair, used the other to grip her curvy ass. Unable to resist, he slipped his hand beneath the leg of her shorts and smoothed his palm over the back of her thigh until he reached her silky panties. Deciding he'd gone this far, and determined to take as much as he could from her, he slipped his fingers beneath her panties and gripped her bare ass.

She let out another moan, pushed her fingers through his hair, and ground her heat against his leg. She kissed him with the same passion and urgency that coursed through his mind and body.

Still not enough.

He moved his hand from her hair, dragged his mouth away

and kissed her face and neck. After he cupped her breast, he went back to her lips for another taste. She smelled so damned good and her body...her body was made for his. Her full breast fit perfectly in his hand. If he were a bigger bastard and they weren't standing in a parking lot, he'd love to shove up her shirt, move aside her bra and take her hard nipple into his mouth. Instead, he gently tugged at her nipple through her cotton shirt, making it harder, making her moan some more. Damn, the little sounds she made, the way she kissed him, rode his leg...she drove him crazy. He wanted to make her his in every sense. He wanted—

He sucked in a breath when she moved her hand between their bodies and cupped him. It had been so long since he'd been with a woman, he worried he'd come in his pants if she didn't stop. Instead of concentrating on the pleasure she gave him, he focused on her other breast, her rear and her mouth. He slid his hand beneath her shirt, along her ribcage until his fingers grazed the lace of her bra.

Voices floated from the restaurant's exit. Worried they'd be caught and Beth would be embarrassed, he kissed a path along her neck and removed his hand from under her shirt. "I should let go of your rear," he said against the crook of her neck.

She moved her hand from his crotch and hugged him. "Probably."

He rested his cheek against hers and grinned. "That's not a yes or no answer."

"You didn't exactly ask a question, and I happen to like where your hand is."

"Me, too," he said, but took his hand off her butt and out of her shorts anyway. He'd already tortured himself enough. As it was, he hated himself for kissing and touching her under the pretense that they would see each other again tomorrow. "Do you think that kiss made up for the ones we missed during the middle of our date?"

"I could kiss some more."

He chuckle and, bypassing her lips, kissed her forehead. "So could I. Problem is, if we start up again, I'm going to have a hard time stopping at just a kiss."

"Then it's a good thing you're coming to my place tomorrow. We won't have to worry about getting busted making out in a parking lot."

"A very good thing," he said, disgusted with himself for leading her on and lying. But better to end things with her now, than before either of them became too attached. The pisser? He could see himself attached to Beth. He could picture them dating, flying, boating and making love. He could imagine falling asleep to her soft curves and waking up to her pretty smile. For seven years, he did plenty of imagining and it infuriated him that he had a beautiful woman in his arms, a woman who clearly wanted him, and he was still stuck with only his imagination and out of reach fantasies.

He gave her one final kiss, hoping to sear the softness of her lips onto his brain so he'd at least have his memories to keep him going for a while. "Good night," he said, then hugged her. After he pulled away, she unlocked her car. He opened the door for her and once she was seated inside, he closed the door.

She turned the ignition and rolled down the window. "Good night. See you tomorrow," she said with a smile and a wave, then backed out of the parking spot.

As he watched her taillights disappear, regret amplified his anger and guilt. Hadn't he suffered enough? Hadn't he served his time?

He walked to his truck, then climbed inside. Wallowing in self-pity wasn't normally his thing, but tonight, with the company of a six-pack of beer, he'd go home and do plenty of wallowing. He might've only met Beth a week ago, but he wasn't ready to let her go.

Too bad he had no choice.

****

Naples, Florida
Thursday, 10:26 p.m., Eastern Standard Time

Breathing hard, he rolled off of Gabriela and stared at the moving ceiling fan. She curled her warm body against him, then rested her head on his shoulder. "That was wonderful," she said, and wrapped her leg over his. "Can you spend the night?"

Since he didn't have to work in the morning, and he no longer had to worry about the dead bodies in his house, he had no desire to be anywhere else but with her. "Nothing could drag me out of this bed and away from you," he said, and kissed the top of her head.

She ran her hand along his chest. The soft glow from the lamp on the nightstand reflected off the three-carat, emerald-cut platinum engagement ring she now wore.

"I love how the ring looks on you," he said, taking her hand and studying the way the ring sparkled.

She kissed his shoulder. "And I love you. But I still think this ring is too much. It had to cost a small fortune."

The twenty-five grand he'd spent on the ring hadn't mattered to him. Making Gabriela his wife and keeping her happy had been and would continue to be his only concern. "You're worth it."

She let out a small sigh. "Now for the fun stuff. How soon do you want to set the date?"

"I suppose it depends on when you want to get married. I vote no to the summer months. The weather is too unpredictable."

"Rain and heat are not a good combo. I'd love a fall wedding, but that puts us in the middle of hurricane season. What about next January?" she asked. "That would give us a year to plan the wedding."

"I think that's a perfect idea."

She shifted onto her elbow and faced him.

"What's wrong?" he asked, when he noticed the worry lines along her forehead.

"You've been so generous. I have money saved, but you know my parents won't be able to help with the wedding expenses."

Her parents had emigrated from Mexico about ten years before they'd welcomed Gabriela into the world. While they'd been in the U.S. for nearly forty years, her parents, Rosa and José Fuentes, had never had it easy when it came to jobs and finances. They were good, hard working people, whose religious convictions were as strong as their love for their four children.

He smoothed a lock of dark hair from her face. "You know I don't care about the money. I want you to make that clear to your mom and dad." He raised a finger. "Before you ask, I called your dad and asked him for permission to marry you."

She grinned. "Thank you. He's very traditional, which brings up another touchy subject."

"I know exactly where you're going, and I've already promised your dad we'd get married in a Catholic church and raise our kids Catholic, too." Although he wasn't Catholic and would have preferred to have a quiet wedding on the beach, he'd do his damnedest to make sure there wouldn't be any issues with her parents.

She leaned in and gave him a kiss. "Then I guess it's settled. We'll get married next January in a Catholic church."

"We'll also have to sell your townhouse so you can move in with me. Unless you want to keep it as a rental property."

"That might be a good idea," she said. "It could be an extra source of income, or I can put the money toward retirement." She gave his chest hair a gentle tug. "One big problem, though. I don't think I can live with your snake." When he looked down at his penis, she laughed. "You know exactly which one I'm talking about."

After an exaggerated sigh, he said, "I can't believe I'm going to part with my last snake. I must really love you."

"Yes, it's definitely true love when a woman comes between a man and his snake." She gave him another kiss, then started to rise. "I'm going to brush my teeth and wash my face."

"I'm going to grab a bottle of water. Need anything?" he asked, and climbed out of bed.

"Water would be great," she said, then disappeared into the master bathroom.

After he put on his boxers, he headed downstairs to the kitchen. Before grabbing them waters, he made sure the front door was locked, then checked the sliders leading to the lanai. Except for the light over the kitchen sink, the downstairs was dark and he was able to see out into the backyard. There had been a full moon three days ago. That had also been the night he'd stolen the bodies. Tonight, the moon was still big, and with the skies clear, the stars shone brightly. A perfect end to what had started out as an imperfect and stressful day.

He'd dumped the dead women without issue, had taken care of dropping off the terrarium to the pet shop, and had even managed to return the U-Haul trailer, along with the SUV he'd rented. Afterward, he'd gone into the office. At first he'd been paranoid, but had realized the ridiculousness of it. No one knew what he'd done. He had never considered himself cocky or arrogant, but he was confident. Even if the bodies were discovered, the police and anyone who knew him would never suspect him and would blame his fall guy.

Now he was lucky enough to be engaged to Gabriela, the beautiful and intelligent woman who he planned to love for the rest of his life. His dead lover's image suddenly surfaced, though fortunately the guilt didn't. He would forever be in debt to her and wished he could have given her a proper burial. Being with her had allowed him to break past the barriers of performance anxiety and to have the confidence to properly make love to his new fiancée.

Last night, he'd wanted Gabriela to play opossum in order to recapture the time he'd spent with his dead lover. Tonight, none of that—not even the memories of his dead lover—had been necessary. Like a normal man, with a normal sexual appetite, he'd made love to Gabriela with the lights on and had encouraged her to look at him, had asked her to tell him what she'd wanted in order to make sure he'd pleasured her as much as possible.

He quickly said a silent prayer, thanking whatever higher power watched over them for his dead lover. With her, sex was now possible.

"Did you get lost down there?" Gabriela called from upstairs.

He grinned and turned away from the glass doors. "I'm coming," he said, then chuckled at the double meaning. Thanks to his dead lover and his sexy fiancée, from now on, he'd definitely be coming.

CHAPTER 6

Shell Island Road, Naples, Florida
Friday, 8:46 a.m., Eastern Standard Time

BETH CLIMBED OUT of the police cruiser. As she closed the door, she scanned the area, then settled her gaze on the two men standing next to a silver late model Dodge Ram. With tanned, weathered faces and graying hair, she placed both men in their sixties. Since the Ram was towing a small fishing boat, it didn't take a genius to figure out why they were on Shell Island Road.

Last year, the county had paved the majority of the gravel road that cut through land belonging to Rookery Bay National Estuarine Research Center and Marco Island. At the end of the road was a free boat ramp. Since the road had been paved, more people had begun using it. With those people came trash, which conservationists had been complaining about for the past year. If the conservationists thought litter and barrels of refuse were something to complain about, she could only imagine how they—along with the rest of Collier County— would feel about three dead bodies.

Ricky met Beth at the tail end of the cruiser. "Let's hope these guys are wrong," he said, opening the sedan's trunk.

"Take these just in case." After he handed her latex gloves and foot protection, they made their way toward the men who had reported the bodies.

"Morning," Ricky greeted them. "Which one of you is Gil Daly?"

"I am," the skinnier of the two men said. "This is my buddy, Denny Hackett. Me and Denny fish here a couple times a week. We also like to take some time to check out the trash people dump."

"We reuse other people's trash, fix it up nice and sell it at flea markets," Denny explained. "You'd be surprised by the things we've found here or on curbs during trash day."

Ricky looked to her, his left brow rising slightly above his sunglasses. "So where were you garbage picking this morning?" he asked the men.

Denny pointed east. "About twenty yards from the side of the road, near the cluster of trees."

Another deputy cruiser pulled behind theirs. After Deputies Busch and Collins approached, Ricky told them the situation, asked them to stay with Gil and Denny, and to take their statements. "Come on," he said to her, then together they crossed the road and into the grass. The further they walked, the taller the grass became.

"Stay on the trail," Gil called.

"Some trail," Ricky said, as he knocked the grass with his forearm. "And what the hell cluster of trees was that guy talking about? They're clustered…"

When he came to an abrupt halt, she rushed to where he stood and quickly spotted three bodies. "This is bad," she said, and slipped the shoe covers over her boots, then the latex gloves onto her hands.

"Yeah, it is," Ricky said, also covering his boots.

Since Ricky had twelve years experience on her, she let him take the lead. When they reached the bodies, which were lined side-by-side in a neat row, she was grateful she'd skipped breakfast. She swallowed hard and stared at the three women who were clearly deceased.

One was young, maybe in her late twenties or early thirties. The second victim was much older, and she guesstimated her as being somewhere around eighty. The other woman was unrecognizable. A large part of her lower body had been badly burned and her face and head looked as if it had been beaten in with a sledgehammer. Based on the Y-shaped suture along her torso, it also looked as if she'd been autopsied. All three vics were naked, their bodies clean of debris and had been cut— horizontally—across their stomachs, then crudely sutured.

Careful where she walked, Beth approached the younger victim. As she moved closer, she breathed through her mouth, hoping to ward off the stench and trying to ignore the flies swarming near the third victim. Thank God it was still early and the temperature was moderate. If it had been later in the day, the smell and flies would have been worse. "Looks like they were dumped here."

"That's what I was thinking." Ricky glanced to the ground. "No sign of a struggle."

When Beth noticed the small set of sutures near the young woman's clavicle and on her abdomen above the horizontal cut, her stomach soured. She'd seen this before, but needing to be sure she was right, she bent down and gently touched the woman's lips. They didn't open.

"Don't touch," Ricky said. "We need to call this in and wait for Forensics and Homicide." Ricky reached toward his shoulder and used the radio to call Dispatch.

"I don't know if this is your classic homicide," Beth said after he ended the call. Staying crouched, she studied the older woman, who also had small sutures near her clavicle and on her abdomen. "These women were embalmed, and the third woman looks like she's been autopsied."

"I agree on the signs of autopsy, but embalmed? How do you know?"

"I grew up with a girl whose family owned a funeral home. One time she snuck me and another friend of ours inside and took us to the embalming room." She'd never forget that night, or the bad dreams during the months that had followed.

"There was a man on a table with tubes protruding here and here," she said, pointing to the small sutures on the dead women. "My friend didn't realize her dad was still working. Before we could leave, he busted us. When he realized how freaked out me and the other girl were, he explained what he was doing."

"I don't think I want to know." He crouched next to her. "Tell me anyway."

"He was draining the blood from the man's veins and fluids from his organs."

"Yep, didn't need to know." He pointed to the horizontal cut on the young woman's stomach. "I've seen autopsied bodies, and this looks nothing like what an ME would do. Is this part of the embalming process?"

She shrugged. "I don't think so." Not wanting to compromise the crime scene before Forensics had a chance to process it, she remained next to the young woman, but stood to gain a better view of the third victim. "She's also decomposing, which means she wasn't embalmed like the others."

"So we have two women who've been embalmed, and this third vic who looks like she was beaten, burned and autopsied. This is messed up."

As she studied the woman's face, Beth had a quick flashback to a horrible traffic accident she'd worked when she had first become a paramedic. "No one beat this woman. The lacerations on her head and face...it looks like her head went through a window."

"Maybe. Could be she was escaping from a fire and a window shattered. Or maybe she knew something about the embalmed women and it got her killed."

"Could be as simple as a car accident," she suggested. "The ME's accident investigation team would've examined her and possibly performed an autopsy before releasing the body to the family."

"If that's the case, and she was examined locally, we should be able to get a quick ID." He took a step back toward the narrow trail. "If she was murdered? I don't want to think about having a killer on the loose who's cold enough to embalm and autopsy his own victims. Come on, let's go wait on Homicide and CSU."

"Okay," she said, but remained still, her focus on the decomposing body. She wasn't a medical examiner or forensics investigator, but as a former paramedic she'd seen plenty of dead bodies. Some had passed on hours or days before her unit had been called to the scene, others had died on the way to the hospital. Based on the rate of decomposition, in her opinion, this one had been dead for at least a few days, maybe longer if she'd been kept out of the heat and stored somewhere cold. But why would someone store dead bodies?

She followed after Ricky. By the time Gil and Denny had finished giving their statements to the other deputies, the Collier County Crime Scene investigators pulled alongside the road, along with an unmarked sedan and two deputy cruisers. When the two CSU investigators stepped out of the van and began to suit up, she was relieved to see they'd be working with Stacy and Keith Rains. The couple had met on the job and had married last year. She and Stacy were good friends, and Keith was a good guy. They were both great at their job, and since she was friends with them, she knew they'd keep her in the loop, should the detectives assigned to the case dismiss her and Ricky from being involved.

But when two men climbed out of the unmarked sedan, she realized she wouldn't have to worry about being dismissed from this investigation. She knew Detectives Nick Wagner and Jerry Tennyson well. If Nick had it his way, he'd know her intimately.

"Morning," Nick greeted them, as he and Jerry approached. "What do you guys have for us?"

"Three dead women," Ricky said. "Looks like the bodies were recently dumped here."

"Three?" Stacy asked, when she and Keith joined them.

"Yeah," Beth began, "it also looks like two of the victims were embalmed and the third one was autopsied."

Jerry, who had Nick by at least twenty years, looked to his partner. "Just when I think I've seen it all." He glanced to Gil and Denny. "Did those two find the bodies?"

Ricky nodded. "Busch and Collins took their statements, but we had them stick around until you showed."

"Good." Nick turned to Stacy and Keith. "Are you ready to get started?"

Keith nodded and met Beth's gaze. "Bring the tape and lead the way."

While Nick and Jerry went to speak with Gil and Denny, she and Ricky led the CSU investigators to where the victims were located. Keith stopped when the women came into view, then had her and Ricky set up a perimeter with the crime scene tape. Just as they'd finished, Nick and Jerry made their way toward them.

"Well?" Nick asked.

"Beth's right," Stacy began, as she examined the youngest victim, "this woman was embalmed." She glanced to the older woman. "Both were, and the third vic was autopsied."

"Got some insect activity." Beth looked to Keith, who was crouched on the opposite side of the row of victims. He raised his camera and began photographing the burned woman.

"How long do you think they've been out here?" Jerry asked.

Keith took another picture. "When I'm done documenting the scene, I'll get samples of the larvae and run tests once I'm back in the lab. Quick guess? Looks like we've got flesh flies making a home on the vic. The female flies don't usually lay eggs, but deposit twenty to forty larvae on their host. Based on the stage the larvae are in, they've been on her for maybe a day or less. But don't quote me until I run the test."

Less than a day? "Question," Beth began. "Does anyone find it strange that she looks like she's been decomposing longer than a day and that, other than the flies, her body is clean? And what do you make of the cuts along all the victims' stomachs?"

"The ME gets to look into that," Keith said. "But I agree. Her body—actually, all of them—look as if they've been washed. If you've seen a decomposing body, there should be more fluids around the orifices. This vic has that, just not the amount I'd expect based on the deterioration of her flesh."

"Let's not forget these two aren't decomposing," Stacy said, and looked to the two detectives. "It's hard to say when they were embalmed. I've seen bodies exhumed after being buried for months that, other than for mold, looked almost as good as they did on display at a funeral home. Since these bodies are outside, they would turn quicker than one in a sealed coffin."

"How quickly?" Nick asked.

"In the heat, maybe a week or less."

Jerry swatted a fly from his face. "Let's get the victims fingerprinted."

Ricky tapped her shoulder and thumbed toward the road. She gave him a nod, then the two of them headed back to the cruiser.

"Beth," Nick called.

She told Ricky she'd catch up with him at the cruiser, then stopped and faced Nick. "What's up?

"We keep missing each other at the office. How've you been?"

Not now. While Nick was an excellent detective and had the case resolutions to prove it, he couldn't catch a clue that she wasn't interested in dating him.

She looked over his shoulder to where the two CSU investigators worked and Jerry stood observing. "I've had better mornings. Do you want Ricky and I to take a head shot of the decomposing woman and check with the ME's accident investigation team to see if she's a match to any recent accidents?"

She caught the disappointment in Nick's dark-brown eyes before he slipped on his sunglasses. "It's always business with you. How about a little fun? Let me take you to dinner."

Maybe some women would find it romantic to be asked out on a date when three dead bodies lay on the ground twenty yards away, but she wasn't one of them. She'd been a cop for nearly four years and had learned to separate the job from her personal life. Right now she wanted to focus on the job and find out what had happened to those women, not have to deal with a relentless detective who couldn't take no for an answer.

"You know how I feel about dating guys I work with, plus school is keeping me busy. So, how about it? What do you need Ricky and I to do?"

"I'm the one who's sorry." He glanced over his shoulder toward the bodies, then faced her again. "I shouldn't have asked after we just viewed the victims." His mouth tilted in a wry smile. "I looked really desperate just now, didn't I?"

If she hadn't worked with Nick, she probably would have gone out with him the first time he'd asked her. He had the dark good looks she was normally attracted to, and was smart and had a great personality. From what she'd heard, he had invested the inheritance he'd received upon his father's death into a popular bar and grill located on Bonita Beach. Between his career with the Collier County Sheriff's Office and his investment, the man was supposedly doing well where his finances were concerned. She liked that in a man, which was one of the reasons she liked Shane. She wanted to be with a guy who had goals and did what he could to attain them. But she did work with Nick. Even after she quit the force, she still probably wouldn't go out with him. He might be good looking, smart, funny and financially stable, but at thirty-five, he'd also been divorced three times. When it came to relationships, he had a lousy track record.

She took a step back, hoping he'd catch the hint that she no longer wanted to have this conversation. "You're fine. What do you want me and Ricky to do?" she repeated.

"We're going to call in more CSUs, deputies and hopefully a cadaver dog. When they get here, you and Ricky can help search the area to make sure our perp didn't leave any more bodies lying around."

With a nod, she walked away. When she reached the road, she saw Busch and Collins sitting in their cruiser, while Ricky leaned against theirs. She walked to him and mimicked his position.

"Did he ask you out again?" Ricky asked, and folded his arms across his chest.

"Yep."

"No wonder he's been divorced three times. Someone needs to teach him the art of *amour*."

"You think?" As she told Ricky about Nick's plans to continue the search, she looked to where the fishermen had parked their truck. Now that the Dodge Ram was no longer obstructing the view, she noticed a patch of grass that looked as if something heavy had been resting on it. "When we got here, Gil and Denny's truck and boat trailer were on the road, right?"

Ricky nodded and followed her gaze. "I see it," he said, and pushed off the car. After they reached the grass in question, Ricky knelt, then looked toward the direction of the bodies. "There's an impression in the grass. No tire tracks, though."

Keeping her eyes to the ground, she moved into the grass. "*Two* impressions. And look at that section of tall grass. See how some of the blades are broken?"

"Yeah, and look where they stop." He glanced from the road to the broken grass. "Gil and Denny's boat trailer had two wheels. These imprints are similar."

"Right, like someone backed a trailer into the grass and angled it toward where the bodies were dumped. *But*, it could be as simple as a boater was backing in and out of this spot."

"We're a mile from the water," Ricky reminded her. "I get what you're saying, but why risk damaging a boat or trailer to turn around here? Why not go the extra mile and make the turn where it's easier?"

"True. So let's say the killer has a boat trailer, or just a small trailer in general, he backs it up here, then what? He's not going to go back onto the road, then find the trail we took."

"I wouldn't." Ricky said. "Too risky. I'd go straight through."

She met his gaze. "Let's walk it."

The two of them kept their distance from the impressions in the grass and began walking at the angle where they'd noticed the last of the broken blades. Within minutes, they met up with the crime scene tape they'd placed around the perimeter of the bodies.

"What're you two up to?" Keith asked, as he placed something into a plastic vial.

Ricky quickly explained what they'd found. When he'd finished, Stacy nodded to her husband. "I'll check it. There's nothing more here."

"What do you mean there's nothing more?" Jerry asked, and glanced at his watch. "We've been here for less than an hour."

Stacy shrugged. "We could be here for three hours and we'd still have the same conclusion—these women were dead before the perpetrator dumped them." She shook her head. "Since that's the obvious, let me rephrase. We think the suturing done to the victims was made postmortem."

"Yeah, but we're both wondering if the perp killed these women then abused their corpses," Keith began, "or if they were dead before he got to them."

"Meaning?" Jerry asked.

"I'm not an ME, but I've seen enough deaths to conclude that the two embalmed vics show no signs of dying of unnatural causes. That's not to say they weren't poisoned, or maybe smothered, obviously a thorough autopsy will be needed to draw that conclusion."

"But," Nick prompted.

"But it could be they were dead before the perp got to them."

Nick took off his sunglasses and rubbed his eyes. "Are you suggesting that these bodies might've been stolen?"

Keith shrugged. "That's for you to find out," he said, and raised a gloved finger. "Either way, Stacy and I agree that the embalming and the autopsy look to have been done by a professional."

"That's not too fucked up," Jerry said, and let out a sigh. "Is the ME coming?"

Stacy shook her head. "No. I called it in and the Chief ME

is going to handle the autopsies. Since he signs off on all the autopsies, he might recognize the one performed on this victim," she said, pointing to the decomposing woman.

Keith stood. "While Stacy checks out the tracks Beth and Ricky found, I'm going to head back to the lab. I've got another van coming to remove the bodies."

As Keith left and Stacy investigated the tracks, more deputies and CSU investigators arrived. Busch and Collins exited their cruiser, and once everyone had been given an area to search for more victims, Beth and Ricky started in the direction they'd been instructed to cover.

"I went flying yesterday and watched the sun set from the sky," she said to her partner as they began the search, and tried to use those memories to blot out the three corpses.

"Bet it was nice."

"It was more than nice, it was beautiful." She waved toward where the bodies had been left. "This isn't. I'd love to be back in the air with my head in the clouds, than down here dealing with reality." She'd rather be with Shane. Enjoying his company and his kisses, and pretending three women weren't dumped along the side of the road like unwanted trash.

"I wouldn't mind joining you," Ricky said. "What do you think about the bodies being stolen?"

"Nick was just talking out loud. Why would anyone steal dead bodies, then abuse them? Besides, even Keith couldn't confirm that those women weren't murdered before they'd been embalmed."

"And the burned vic?" He sighed. "This is going to sound girly, but funeral homes give me the creeps."

"Since I'm a girl, I won't take offense to that comment," she said with a half-smile.

"You know what I mean."

"I do. Where's this coming from?"

"Where else would you steal a dead body from?"

"Good point—if they were stolen. So what creeps you out about funeral homes?" she asked, then stopped to inspect a garbage bag. Thankfully it was filled with only trash.

"Trusting a total stranger to treat a body with respect. Think about it. Your friend showed you what went on in her dad's embalming room, but what happens behind closed doors when it's just the embalmer and the corpse?"

"I don't want to think about that."

"Beth! Ricky!" Nick called.

The two detectives emerged from the area where she and Ricky had found the tire tracks earlier. Nick waved them over. When they met up with him and Jerry, Nick said, "Got a search warrant and an ID."

Thank God. "On which vic?" she asked.

"The decomposing one." Nick looked down at his cell phone. "Charlotte Pallesen, age twenty-seven, was killed in a car accident this past Sunday night around midnight. She was autopsied by a Collier County ME during the night, then released to Williams Funeral Home Tuesday late afternoon. Cause of death was blunt force trauma. Her toxicology report states her blood alcohol level was point two-seven."

Ricky whistled. "That's high for a woman who couldn't have weighed more than one hundred and ten pounds. Did she pass out at the wheel?"

"No tire marks were found at the scene, indicating she never bothered to slam on the breaks before plowing into a cement barrier at sixty miles per hour." Nick shaded his cell phone screen. "Keith said he spoke with the tech who'd released the body to the funeral home. According to him, Pallesen was being cremated."

Despite the rising temperatures, a chill ran over her skin. "Did she have family?" Beth asked, thinking about what Ricky had just said about funeral homes. "Someone had to pay for the cremation."

"Yeah, and if Charlotte Pallesen is lying over there," Jerry began, and thumbed toward the opposite side of the road, "then whose ashes are in the urn the family received?"

"Good question," Nick said, and pocketed his cell phone. "We've got an officer meeting us at the funeral home with the warrant. Once Stacy finishes up here, she's going to meet us there."

"You two follow us." Jerry started for the sedan. "We're going to want to bring the owner in for questioning."

When Jerry and Nick walked away, she climbed into the cruiser, then buckled her seatbelt. "Something is off about this," she said, once Ricky was inside the car. "I can see why Nick and Jerry want to start with the funeral home director, but I have a hard time believing that he, or his employees, had anything to do with the dead women. They have access to a crematory, and Pallesen was supposed to be cremated to begin with, so why dump her body?"

Ricky began following behind the detectives' sedan. "I was just thinking the same thing. Doesn't make sense. They'd have to know the body would lead back to the funeral home."

She called Dispatch to let them know where they were heading, then reached into the door pocket for her cell phone. "I'll be curious to see what's either inside or missing from the bodies. Those cuts along the victims' stomachs remind me of the snake case."

He groaned. "God, I hated that one. It still bugs me that we never caught who killed that girl."

The girl was Kathleen 'Katie' Reed. She'd only been twenty-one when the life had been choked out of her. But her killer hadn't stopped there. He'd cut open Katie's stomach and had sewn a baby rattlesnake inside. Postmortem.

Like today, Beth and Ricky had been the first on the scene. The detectives who'd worked the case had allowed them to stay part of the investigation. Unfortunately, the few leads they'd had dried up quickly, leaving them and Katie's father to wonder who had killed Katie and why.

"It bugs me, too," she said, and checked her phone. When she saw that Shane had sent her a text, some of the tension she'd been carrying since first seeing the three bodies abated. Then she read the text.

Had a great time last night. Sorry can't make it for dinner.

"Airboat guy?" Ricky asked.

"Playing Scrabble."

He chuckled. "Sure you are. Lighten the mood for me. What kind of date does he have planned this time? Is he going to fly you to Miami for dinner?"

Disappointment settled in the pit of her stomach. "He was supposed to come to my place for dinner, but he just cancelled."

"You told him, didn't you?" Ricky asked.

"Yeah, and he was cool with it," she said, remembering the way he'd kissed her. If Shane had a problem with her job, he sure as hell had a funny way of showing it.

"What's the text say?" After she read it to Ricky, he shook his head. "Notice he didn't suggest getting together another time?"

Yes, damn it. "He was cool with it," she repeated, but sent Shane a quick text back, telling him she was free tomorrow night, if that worked better for him. If he didn't want to see her again, she'd know soon enough.

"If I were you, I'd text him back and offer up another day and time."

"I just did." As she was about to put the phone back in the door pocket, Shane responded.

Sunday doesn't work. I'll text you sometime.

"Son of a bitch," she said, and shoved the phone in the pocket.

"*Dios mío.*" Ricky made the sign of the cross. "I don't think I've ever heard anything worse than damn or hell out of your mouth. What did the asshole text back?" After she told him, Ricky shook his head. "He wasn't cool with you being a cop."

"Thanks for pointing out the obvious." She folded her arms across her chest. "Just drop it. I went on two dates with the guy and it wasn't anything special." A total lie. The time she'd spent with Shane had been special. The three airboat rides, two dates and hot, intimate kisses had meant something to her. *He* had started to mean something to her. She liked Shane, could see them dating and their relationship growing. She'd sworn he had been just as into her. How could she have read him so wrong? Better yet, how could he have kissed her the way he had last night, then so easily dismissed her today?

"Want me to kick his ass for you?" Ricky asked.

She grinned and glanced at him. "He's not worth it."

Ricky shrugged. "If you change your mind, I got your back."

Although she knew Ricky was joking, a part of her wouldn't mind doing a little butt kicking. Shane was a jerk. Last night—the way he'd treated her and kissed her—he'd led her to believe he hadn't cared that she was a cop. He'd led her to believe he actually cared about her.

How could he? How could he have led her on that way?

Ricky pulled into the parking lot of Williams Funeral Home. "Got your head on straight?" he asked.

"As always," she said, pushing Shane from her thoughts—for now—and concentrating on the three dead women.

Lola's Rental House, Everglades City, Florida
Friday, 5:45 p.m., Eastern Standard Time

"Everyone is cool with this?" Lola asked, and looked around the newly renovated living room.

Barney nodded and sat next to Harrison on the couch. "I don't like lyin' to Shane, so I'm definitely good with this."

"So am I," Harrison said, never taking his gaze off the laptop perched on his lap. "Maybe he'll finally stop giving me the stink eye."

Vlad furrowed his blond eyebrows. "Vlad no understand this stink eye, Harry say."

Harrison glanced up from the laptop, then across the room to where Mel sat in an oversized chair staring at Vlad with impatience and disdain. "Look at the way Mel is staring at you and you'll have your answer."

Vlad turned to Mel, and grinned. "Ah, now Vlad understand. Shane look at Harry like Shane have constipation."

Mel tossed her long, thick blond curls over her shoulder,

then reached into her leopard print tote bag accented with hot-pink trim and pulled out a switchblade. "Now, honey," she began, in her usual southern accent, "that's not a word you use in a lady's presence."

Vlad's eyes narrowed and his face hardened. "Ice cream lady plan to cut Vlad for talk of bathroom?"

Mel began filing her long nails, which had been painted the same color as the trim on her tote. "It's a nail file, you big goof. If I was gonna cut you, I would've done it weeks ago." She blew on her nail, then slipped the file back into her purse. "And you would've never seen it comin'."

Lola rolled her eyes. "Enough. Mel, are you fine with telling Shane? You two have been friends since you were kids. I don't want him having a problem with you being involved with us."

"Shane knows to stay out of my business," Mel said. "Ain't that right, Barney?"

Barney grinned. "That's right. So why are we tellin' him now?"

"A few reasons. Ian called and gave us our first assignment." Two nights ago, Lola had been sitting on the couch with Ryan and expressing her concerns over the fact that Ian had yet to give them a case. They'd also discussed telling Shane about ATL. While they had planned on letting him in on their operation this morning, that hadn't worked out because not everyone could be present. So they'd moved the meeting to tomorrow morning. Now that Ian had finally given them an assignment, it seemed like a good time to clue him in on what they were doing. "The second reason is," she continued, "Shane is around all of us too much. I'd rather he know up front, than have him snooping around or talking to people outside our crew to get answers. Plus, Ryan and I are tired of lying to him. I also want to bring Shane in on the case."

"Hell, no." Barney shook his head and leaned into the couch. "That boy just got out of prison."

"So what?" Mel asked. "He's not on parole."

"He's got a felony record," Barney argued. "Which means

he can't possess a gun."

Mel shrugged a shoulder. "Who needs a gun if you know how to use a knife."

God, the woman scared her. She was sweet and beautiful, always wore a smile and was great with the customers and kids who visited their ice cream shop. If only those customers knew Mel ran a chop-shop, could dispose of a body without batting her long lashes and had a thing for knives.

Barney sighed. "The girl's gotta point."

"Are you insane?" Harrison asked, and looked to Lola. "Please tell me you don't agree with either of them. Especially Mel."

Harrison had expressed his concern over having Mel part of their team. While Lola agreed that the ice cream lady might be a bit of a loose cannon, Mel had connections they needed and knew how to keep her mouth shut.

Lola held up a hand. "No one needs to worry about Shane carrying a gun or knife. I simply want him to know what we're up to and have him go with me to meet with Dr. Adams."

"The doc who patched up Ian and John?" Barney asked, referring to her future stepfather and John Kain, one of Ian's CORE agents. "He seemed like an all right kinda guy. What's he done?"

"He didn't do anything." When she heard car doors slam, she looked out the window. "Ryan's here with Shane. Let me and Ryan handle telling him."

When Shane entered the room looking pissed off at the world, Lola had second thoughts about telling him anything. She'd take the stink eye Harrison had mentioned earlier over the anger in Shane's narrowed gaze. Lola forced a smile. "Glad you could finally see what we've done at the rental house," she said, and met Ryan's stare.

Her fiancé put a hand on his brother's shoulder. "What do you think?"

"Since you already had a homecoming party, is this an intervention?" Shane asked.

"What Shane mean?" Vlad asked Harrison.

"If someone is on drugs or an alcoholic, or maybe *smokes* too much, friends and family will get them in a room and try to fix them."

Vlad mumbled something in Russian, then crossed his arms and settled his big body on the ottoman near Mel.

"This isn't an intervention," Ryan said. "More like an introduction. Have a seat." After he and Shane sat on the vacant couch in front of the bay window opposite from where Barney and Harrison sat, Ryan looked to her and nodded. "You've got the floor."

"Shane, I'm not an accountant," she said, deciding to be blunt. "When I met Ryan, I was employed by a criminal investigation agency called CORE. Same with Harrison. After he helped CORE bring down a mass murderer, and had spent a few months in prison, he joined the agency and worked closely with CORE's computer forensics analyst."

Shane shifted his gaze from hers to Harrison's. "And Vlad? Is he really a former heavyweight boxer?"

"да." Vlad nodded. "Vlad have fight sixteen match and never lose. If not for mob, Vlad would won Russian heavyweight title."

"I coulda' been a contender," Barney said, mimicking and quoting Marlon Brando's *On the Waterfront* character.

Shane cracked a smile, while confusion crossed Vlad's face.

"Anyway," Lola continued, "as Vlad said, he was a boxer. Unfortunately the Russian mafia forced him to work for them. He was a hitman." She studied Shane's face for a reaction, but the man didn't flinch.

"Go on," Shane said, still looking at Vlad.

"Vlad eventually escaped the mob and fled to the U.S. He ended up working for the mass murderer Harrison helped CORE bring down."

"Y'all realize how farfetched this sounds, right?" Mel asked.

"You're not helping," Barney said, his tone censoring.

Shane leaned forward. "Okay, so Lola's a private investigator, Harrison's an ex-con and computer geek, and Vlad's a former hitman. Yeah, nothing farfetched there," he said with heavy sarcasm, and shifted his gaze to Ryan. "Is this a joke?"

"Nope." Ryan snagged Lola's hand. "Go on, hon. Tell him the scope of our organization."

She gave his hand a squeeze, then explained everything to Shane. She told him about the case that had brought her, Harrison and Vlad to the Everglades six weeks ago, about the hunt and the laws they'd broken to ensure a killer would never kill again, along with how that case had given Ian the idea of taking CORE above the law.

"Why are you telling me this?" Shane asked when she'd finished.

Lola drew in a deep breath and hoped to God she wasn't making a mistake. "Because we want to add you to our team."

CHAPTER 7

Lola's Rental House, Everglades City, Florida
Friday, 6:02 p.m., Eastern Standard Time

SHANE GLANCED AROUND the room, his gaze touching on every person there. "This is your team?"

"We call ourselves Above the Law," Harrison said.

"After an old Steven Seagal movie?" Shane leaned into the couch and laughed. When he realized no one else thought this was the slightest bit funny, he sobered. "You guys are serious."

"About everything," Ryan said, his gaze shifting to Mel.

Furious, Shane shook his head. "I can't believe you and Barney let Mel get rid of a dead body." Mel might be a little crazy, but she had the potential to avoid the high-octane level of crazy the rest of her family possessed. Thanks to Above the Law, it appeared Mel had officially followed in her family's footsteps.

"C'mon, sugar. You know damn well no one tells me what I can and can't do." Mel grinned. "Besides, that little visit to my daddy's swamp earned me ten grand. According to Lola and her rich step-daddy, we get paid cash per job. And I do love me some cash."

"Mel's right," Lola said. "This is under the table and off the books. Whatever the job pays, we split the cash."

"How many jobs have you done?"

"We were just given our first assignment."

The full moon was Monday, so Shane couldn't blame what had happened yesterday, and now today, on that. He wanted to. He wanted to hold someone or something accountable for messing with his life. Before Beth had told him she was a cop, he'd thought that maybe—if she could move past his felony record—he had a shot at a normal relationship. That hadn't happened. Now he was being asked to join some secret operation on their first mission. How could he have a shot at anything normal if he took up with Above the Law? He had a record. If he ended up busted for doing something remotely illegal, he'd wind up back in prison. There was no way in hell he'd allow that to happen.

"Sorry, I can't do it," he said, remembering his prison cell. "I'm not messing with the law."

"We're not doing anything illegal," Lola said.

"So having Mel dump a body in her daddy's swamp isn't illegal?"

Lola held her thumb and index finger an inch apart. "A little. But those were extenuating circumstances and this new case shouldn't be anything like that."

He shook his head. "Not interested. You've got enough people on the payroll. You don't need me. Don't worry, though. I won't tell anyone what I know." He glanced between Harrison and Vlad, who both stared at him with disappointment. "I'm glad I finally found out about you two. I was starting to worry about my paranoia."

"Vlad not glad."

"Lola isn't, either." She gave him a quick smile. "But I understand. Why don't you take Ryan's truck and head home? We'll pick it up after we're finished with our meeting."

"Are you dismissing me?" he asked, and looked to his brother for confirmation.

"Afraid so, man. Lola needs to discuss the case with the

team, and you're not part of it."

"Which is a shame," Lola added. "It's an interesting case and we could've used your expertise."

"Expertise on what?"

"Snakes."

Vlad groaned. "Vlad hate snake."

"Dude," Harrison began, "you said the same thing about alligators and now Polina is the love of your life."

"No, Misty love of Vlad life. Polina like child Vlad never have."

"Anyway," Lola said. "We'd like to get started. So…" She nodded toward the door.

He didn't want to be dismissed and didn't want to be part of their crew. While he knew Lola and Ryan were teasing him with just enough info to intrigue him, he also refused to take the bait. "Fine." He stood and started for the door. Before he opened it, he turned around and met Lola's gaze. "What kind of snake?" he asked, his curiosity getting the best of him.

"We're not sure yet."

Except when he'd been in the Army, he'd had snakes all his life. When he had been sentenced, he'd asked Ryan to keep Harriett, his four-foot ball python, but to find homes for his corn and king snakes. He'd owned Harriett the longest and hadn't been ready to part with her.

"What'd the snake do?" he asked.

"The snake didn't do anything. Someone used the snake to send a message."

"How?"

Lola gave him a patient smile. "Since you're not interested in helping, that's all I'm at liberty to discuss."

At liberty, my ass. "It's not like I'm going to tell anyone."

"Sorry. Doesn't matter."

Son of a bitch. "Whatever," he said, then opened the door and stepped onto the porch. As he headed for Ryan's truck, he slowed his pace. Why in the hell would his brother involve himself with this? He had a good business and was making money. After what he'd been through when he'd been a SEAL, he'd never thought Ryan would pick up a gun again.

"Shane," Ryan called.

He turned. As his brother came down the porch steps, he pictured what had gone on at this house two months ago. The anger and worry he'd been tamping down from the moment Lola had mentioned her organization shot to the surface. "What the hell is wrong with you?" he asked, and walked quickly toward Ryan. "Your fiancée is risking your, Barney's and Mel's safety and freedom. Do you realize you would all go to prison for what you did to that man?" He shoved a hand through his hair to stop himself from punching common sense into Ryan. "Christ, I just got out. I don't want to go back and I don't want you guys heading there with me."

"That jackass would have killed each one of us if he'd had the chance. I don't regret my participation in his death or getting rid of his body."

"You guys could've involved the police." He raised a hand. "I don't want to know why you didn't. I don't want to be an accessory to murder, even if it is after the fact."

Ryan rested his hand on Shane's shoulder. "Since you know, you already are."

He knocked his brother away. "Thanks for giving me a choice in the matter."

"I'm sorry," Ryan began, "I struggled with Lola asking you to join us. I don't want to be the reason you go back to prison. But I also hated keeping what we're doing from you, and honestly, your involvement would be limited."

"Meaning."

"You can't carry a gun, Lola knows this and doesn't want you to. Neither do I. But you own a plane. You could provide us transportation when we need it."

"Is that all I'd do?"

Ryan glanced to the blue sky and let out a breath. "I'd like to be able to talk to you about the assignments we're given," he said, and met his gaze. "I don't always trust my judgment."

"Do you trust Lola?"

"Yes."

"What about Vlad and Harrison?"

"They're good guys. They're loyal to Lola and I think they'd do anything to make this organization work. Right now, it's all they have."

He still wanted no part of Lola's group. He couldn't go back to prison. After tasting freedom, he'd flee the country and become a fugitive before he allowed that to happen.

"I know we dumped a lot on you this morning. Take my truck, go home and give it some thought. If you still want no part of ATL, no hard feelings." Ryan took a couple backward steps. "I'm heading back inside. I'll be by to pick up my truck when we're done here," he said, then turned toward the house.

As he watched his brother walk inside, instinct told him to go home and pretend this had never happened. But he couldn't. Now that he was aware of ATL, of Lola, Vlad and Harrison's history, he didn't like the idea of not knowing what his brother might be involved with, or if Ryan's life could be placed in danger. Same with Barney and Mel. They were his family, and he didn't want anything to happen to them.

Ryan might trust Lola, but he didn't. Before today, he'd had no problem with her. She'd been great to him and treated his brother with love and respect. Only she'd just been given her first assignment, and it hadn't sounded as if she'd had much experience before taking over ATL. *That* concerned him. His stomach filled with unease. Her inexperience could possibly put people he cared about in prison or in a grave. He couldn't allow that to happen. He couldn't care less about whatever Lola's boss was paying them. All he cared about was making sure his family walked away from whatever situation Lola placed them in, and the only way he could do that was to involve himself with ATL.

Shit. He didn't want to risk his freedom, but he couldn't live with the guilt if something ever happened to his brother and he could have stopped it. Decision made—right or wrong—he walked toward the house. When he stepped inside, the room went silent.

Ryan looked at him, and Shane didn't miss the guilt in his

brother's eyes. "Change your mind?"

"Maybe." Shane focused on Lola. "What if I want out?"

"Then you walk away. All we ask is that you don't tell anyone about us."

"I won't carry a gun or get rid of a body," he said, and glanced to Mel. "I'll fly you where you need—within reason—as long as it doesn't interfere with my business."

"That works for us," Lola said. "We were just going over our assignment. Are you in?"

He moved to the couch and sat next to his brother. "Yeah, I'm in."

"Since Shane and I have a meeting with the medical examiner—"

"Why me?" Shane asked. "I'm transportation."

"Right, but I was hoping you'd come with me and take a look at the snake remains that were found."

"Back up," Barney said. "Medical examiner? I thought you were meeting with the doc."

"Dr. Adams *is* the medical examiner. Actually he's Collier County's *Chief* ME. He also teaches forensic pathology at South University," Lola said, then explained to Shane how David Adams had come to the rental house the night CORE agents had killed a killer. Ian Scott, the owner of CORE and Lola's future stepfather, had been donating to Dr. Adams' family foundation, DON (Doctors, Osteopaths and Nursing), a nonprofit company that provided medicine and surgeries to people in third world countries. For his services that night, Ian had paid Dr. Adams for his time and silence.

"Ian made a call to Dr. Adams. He's willing to speak with us about the case," Lola continued. "If we play this right, he could be a valuable asset to ATL."

"Hell, yeah." Harrison nodded. "An ME on the payroll would be more than an asset. He could give us inside info that I might not be able to hack from the Sheriff's Office's operating system."

Hacking was illegal. Hacking into the sheriff's computer system? Good God, that'd put Harrison back in prison for a long time. What had his brother been thinking? Maybe he'd try to talk some sense into Ryan and then they could both walk away. He'd guarantee if Ryan left ATL, Barney and Mel would, too.

"Exactly," Lola said to Harrison, then she looked to Shane. "Are you okay with going with me to meet with the ME?"

Since that didn't sound illegal, he nodded. "I'll go."

She smiled. "Good," she said, and looked down at the notebook she held. "So here's what we have. Florida State Senator, Parker Bryan, contacted Ian around noon. His son-in-law, Thomas Williams, was arrested after three dead bodies were discovered this morning. All three bodies were found alongside Shell Island Road in Collier County, and, according to Dr. Adams, each one either had snake skin shedding or snake eggs sewn inside."

"Why arrest Williams?" Mel asked. "What's his connection?"

"He owns Williams Funeral Home, along with a crematory. Those women were in his care and were supposed to be cremated Tuesday night or Wednesday."

"Do we know how long the bodies were in the woods?" Ryan asked.

Lola shook her head. "No. That's on my list of questions for Dr. Adams."

"That's a huge question," Shane said. "If they were supposed to be cremated Tuesday or Wednesday, what's he been doing with them between then and the time he dumped them?"

"Besides sewing in snake shedding and eggs?" Lola cringed. "This is where it gets twisted. Dr. Adams told Ian the bodies had signs of sexual abuse."

Mel gasped. "A necrophiliac? Sweet baby Jesus. That's disgusting."

Vlad held up a hand. "Hold onto the phone. Why would funeral home man dump body? Why not cremate or bury women to keep hidden the evidence?"

"Vlad has a point," Harrison said. "Having access to a

crematory would be a perfect way to hide his crimes."

"Which is why Senator Bryan hired us to prove his son-in-law didn't do it."

Ryan let out a sigh. "Even if we prove Williams is innocent, we'd still have a necrophiliac running loose. Does Ian want us going after him, too?"

"He said it would depend on if he had a new assignment for us." Lola glanced at her watch. "Shane and I are going to meet with Dr. Adams. Mel, use the extra laptop and look up cases of necrophilia. This is a subject I'm not afraid to admit knowing nothing about. I want to understand the psychology behind it and also see if there are any cases similar to this one. Harrison, start digging into Williams' background. We need to know who works for him, along with any family member who could have access to the bodies." She scooped her car keys off the coffee table and looked to Shane. "Ready?"

"What about me and Ryan?" Barney asked.

Lola smiled. "You get to help Ryan hang the kitchen cabinets that arrived this morning."

Naples, Florida
Friday, 7:16 p.m., Eastern Standard Time

"I'm really glad you decided to join us," Lola said, then made a right turn when the GPS instructed her. "What made you change your mind?"

He'd spent the past forty minutes of their drive grilling her about her past and CORE. Not to avoid explaining why he'd decide to join them, but to find out exactly what he'd just joined. While Lola had given him the basics of the operation, he'd been more interested in CORE. He wasn't disappointed. He was intrigued. From the sounds of it, Ian Scott had a shit-ton of money and connections, and his agency had plenty of clout to go with it. He was impressed with some of the cases CORE had solved, cases that had occurred while he'd been sitting in a cell counting the number of cinderblocks on the wall and cracks along the cement floor. While he'd been on the inside, he'd paid attention to the news—sports and world news mostly. Hell, if he'd wanted to hear crime stories, all he'd have had to do was eavesdrop on conversations from his fellow inmates.

"I'm nosey," he finally answered.

"Seriously? *That's* the only reason?"

"Maybe I didn't like knowing what you guys were up to, then knowing no one would tell me about it because I wasn't in the secret club," he said. As much as he'd like to be honest and tell Lola he didn't trust her, and that he worried about his brother, Barney and Mel following her lead, he'd keep that to himself. For now. He'd see how things went during this first assignment. After all, she was marrying his brother, and he didn't want his honesty causing a problem between him and Ryan.

She chuckled. "Makes sense. I hate when people keep secrets." She adjusted the AC. "So how'd your date go?"

He kept his eyes on the car in front of Lola's Honda Pilot. "If you're implying I was keeping my date secret—"

"I wasn't. I'm just not good at appropriately segueing into a different conversation."

"In that case, it didn't go well."

"I'm sorry. Did you tell her about...you know?"

"Christ, Lola. Less than an hour ago you coerced me into joining your merry band of unofficial private dicks, then handed out orders like an Army sergeant. How is it you have a problem saying incarceration?"

"Incarceration," she said. "See, no problem." She made another turn. "I care about you and I'm trying to be tactful."

"I appreciate your tact, but you can be blunt with me. To answer your tactful question, no, I didn't tell her. We just didn't hit it off like I thought we would."

There was no way in hell he was going to tell Lola or even Ryan the truth about Beth. He doubted that they, or the rest of ATL—God, he was going to have to get used this underground organization—would appreciate knowing he'd been unknowingly dating a cop.

"I'm sorry things didn't work out. Vlad said Kiss Beth was cute."

Anger and resentment settled deep in his chest. Beth wasn't cute. She was beautiful. And she couldn't be his. He loved her expressive eyes and smile. He loved the way she laughed with ease. Her laughter had been genuine and, despite not being able to see her again, he'd never forget the times they'd had on the boat or in the air. Maybe she'd been put in his path to help him overcome some of the uncertainty he'd been carrying with him from the moment he'd walked out of prison. He'd come home with a plan to take back his life, but being around her had him wanting back more than his business. After seven years of being alone, he wanted a woman with him along for the ride.

"Like I said, we just didn't hit it off." The GPS let them know they'd arrived at Collier County's District Twenty Medical Examiner's offices. "How is it okay for us to be here?" he asked.

"Dr. Adams said he'd sneak us in through the employee entrance." She parked behind the building, then pulled out her cell phone. "I'm sending him a text to let him know we're here."

"Yeah, but how's he going to *explain* us being here?"

"Next of kin stopping by to view the body."

"*Are* we viewing a body?"

"I'd rather not, but if what he has for us requires a quick peek, then that's what we'll do." She reached for the door handle. "Are you okay with that?"

When he'd been a Night Stalker, he'd flown the dead and injured out of enemy territory. One of the worst missions he'd piloted—and one he'd never forget—had been in Syria, shortly after 9/11. They'd been under enemy fire when his crew chief had ordered him to touch down. As mortar shells had exploded and gunfire lit up the night, the soldiers they'd been sent to rescue had loaded onto the Black Hawk. Over the noise of the helicopter blades, the explosions and rapid gunshots, a man had wailed. Shane had looked over his shoulder and stared in shock at the soldier missing both of his arms and legs. Before he could fully register the pain and horror the man had experienced, Shane's crew chief had ordered him into the air.

His adrenaline high, he'd lifted the Black Hawk off the ground while their door gunner had opened fire on the Iraqi insurgents below them. Minutes before they'd reached base, the injured soldier had died. He'd been only twenty-two, and had left behind a pregnant wife.

When he'd been in prison, Shane had often thought about Private First Class William 'Billy' Randell. The kid should have died when the mortar shell detonated near him and blew off his limbs, but he'd hung onto life for a short time. As he'd lain in his prison cell, Shane had sometimes imagined what the kid had been thinking about during those final moments—his wife and unborn child, of never being able to hold his baby or caress his wife's skin, the challenge of living life without arms and legs. Had Billy given up the will to live or had it been his time? He'd like to think it had been Billy's time, and that he'd fought just as hard to live as he had on the battlefield, just like many others he'd rescued and couldn't save. They, along with desperately wanting his life back and to make up for the years he'd lost languishing in prison, had inspired him to keep up the fight, and to not give up hope. That seven years was nothing compared to dying or losing limbs. That—

"Should I take that as a no?"

He shook off the memories and thought back to what Lola had said before he'd gone in his head. "Viewing a dead body isn't on my list of must sees," he said, and opened his door. "Don't worry. I can handle it."

As they crossed the parking lot, a man in his late thirties to early forties opened the door and waved them inside. "Good to see you again," he said to Lola. "I wish it were under different circumstances."

"Thanks, Dr. Adams. This is my partner, Shane."

The ME gave him a firm handshake, and said, "Please call

me David. Follow me. Your timing is perfect. My assistant just left for his thirty-minute break, which will give me enough time to show you what I have."

David led them into a stark white room with blinding overhead fluorescent lighting. "This is the Main Autopsy Suite," he said, waving a hand toward the three stainless steel tables parallel to the sinks along one of the walls. Unfortunately, the tables were occupied, but at least white sheets covered the bodies.

"Are these the victims?" Lola asked.

"Only one of them. The other two are in the refrigerated storage area." David approached the table closest to them. "Unless you want to see the victims, which I don't think is necessary, I can quickly explain what I found and show you what was in each of the victims' abdomens."

Either the fluorescent lighting was playing tricks on him, or Lola's face had paled since leaving the car. "We don't need to see the bodies," Shane said, and noticed the relief in Lola's eyes.

"Good, then let me start with this victim." David pointed to the woman on the table. "Darla Hafner was thirty-two when she died of ventricular fibrillation last weekend. The detectives working the case informed me that the family held her funeral services Monday and Tuesday. Her cremation was scheduled for Tuesday evening. Because her body was displayed at the funeral home, Darla had been embalmed."

"Is it possible that the snake remains you found in her stomach were placed there during the embalming?" Lola asked, the color in her face returning.

"In my opinion, no. When a body is embalmed, a trocar is inserted in the abdomen and used to remove fluids, stomach contents and waste. Once this is done, formaldehyde is then pumped back into the abdomen and the embalmer uses a trocar plug to seal the opening. First, there's very little formaldehyde left in her abdomen, which leads me to conclude the cut to her stomach was made *after* she was embalmed. Second, the embalmer who worked on Darla, along with one of the other victims, sutured the opening where the trocar had been used—which is rare. Those sutures differ from the horizontal ones I found along Darla's stomach."

"How so?" Shane asked.

"The material. Under the microscope, I compared the suture string used by the embalmer to the string I pulled from the stomach. I'm going to have the samples sent to a specialist, but I believe the non-absorbable synthetic sutures aren't the same. The embalmer used a coated polybutester suture. Whoever sewed the snake remains into the victims used nylon sutures." David nodded toward one of the metal tables along the opposite wall. "Let me show you what we found in each of the victims' abdomens."

When they reached the table, Shane looked from the three sheddings to the six small oval eggs. "It looks like this guy took one snake shed and cut it in three. With the head missing, it's hard to tell right off if this snake was venomous. There's another way, if you'll let me check something out."

David handed him a pair of latex gloves, then looked at the clock. "I would prefer to not have to explain why you're here to my assistant, so let's make this quick. I can always meet you later or discuss more over the phone."

After putting on the gloves, Shane carefully moved the snake shed until the cuts along the shed lined up, then inspected the scales under the tail.

"What are you looking for?" David asked.

"Venomous snakes have a single row of scales under the tail, non venomous have a double row. This shed has a double row." He located the snake's anal plate, which was a single scale, then set down the snake shed to inspect the piece that had once covered the majority of the snake's body. "The texture of the scales are smooth. I have a ball python and her shed is similar, same with the king snake I used to own. Will you contact a herpetologist?" he asked.

Lola frowned. "What's that?"

"They specialize in snakes," David began, "and I've already been in contact with a professor from South University. I've worked with her on a previous case, which is something else I want to discuss. Come with me." He checked the clock again as he led them to a small writing station. "Two years ago I autopsied a young woman. Katie Reed was discovered in a wooded area similar to where the three victims were found today. She also had a horizontal incision across her stomach. The sutures were made with common fishing line and inside her stomach was a young rattlesnake." He opened a folder and handed it to Lola.

Shane looked over her shoulder and studied the photograph. "Was the snake alive?"

"Barely."

"And the woman, how did she die?" Lola asked.

"Strangulation. Based on the bruising around her neck, I concluded the killer used his hands."

Lola looked at the next photo. "You told Ian that the women were sexually abused, was this victim, too?"

"No, and not all three victims were abused." David nodded toward the woman on the stainless steel table. "Darla was, vaginally and anally. One of the other victims, Martha Garey, the seventy-nine-year-old woman who had also been embalmed, had signs of abuse, but nothing like Darla. It appears as if the perpetrator had used an instrument of some sort to simulate sexual activity."

"What about the third victim?" Shane asked.

"Charlotte Pallesen was autopsied here just this past Tuesday morning after her body was recovered from a traffic accident. Other than the snake shed and eggs sewn into her abdomen, there were no other signs of abuse." He set the file on the desk. "What I find interesting about these victims is the connection to Katie Reed. After I examined her, I'd tried to find cases that were similar to hers." He shook his head. "I didn't find a thing. Now, two years later we have three woman with snake remains sewed into their bodies."

"Do you think it's the same person responsible for Katie Reed's murder, or is someone copycatting?" Shane asked.

"Here's the interesting part," David said. "The information

about the young rattlesnake I found in Katie was never disclosed to the press. So, if someone was copycatting the original murder, they had to have been part of the investigation or have known about the murder."

"Or the killer switched his MO," Lola suggested. "Did you find any trace evidence on the three victims?"

"Nothing. He was very thorough."

"What about the funeral home director? Have you heard anything more about him?" Shane asked.

"Only that he was arrested."

Lola glanced to Darla's body. "Have you dealt with other cases of necrophilia?"

"Fortunately, no." David looked at the clock again. "I'm sorry to cut our meeting short, but I need to get back to work."

"No need to apologize." Lola shook his hand. "Thank you so much for your time."

David smiled. "Allowing you here and showing you evidence from a criminal investigation is beyond unorthodox. But I like Ian and I find your involvement on this investigation intriguing and, for the funeral home director, possibly helpful."

"Why's that?" Shane asked, and also shook David's hand.

"Why would a funeral home director leave bodies in the woods where they could be found? A trip to the crematory would have easily and effectively hidden his crimes."

"You don't think he did it," Lola said.

David gave Lola a small smile and led them out of the autopsy suite. When they reached the exit, he said, "Based on the evidence I've seen so far today, no. But CSU is collecting evidence from the funeral home. They could change my mind."

Lola stopped and stood in the open doorway. "About that additional evidence. If Ian didn't tell you, I'm sure you know by now that the funeral home director is Senator Parker Bryan's son-in-law."

"He did. I've been working on autopsies all day and haven't caught the news. If Thomas Williams' arrest didn't make the six o'clock news, I'm sure his story will be on the nightly report. This is too high profile. Add on the necrophilia angle and I can see this making national headlines."

"So you can understand our sense of urgency on this case. We need to prove he didn't do any of this. Would you be willing to let us know about any new evidence that comes your way?" Lola asked. "If Ian isn't compensating you, I'd be happy to—"

David held up a hand. "Ian's been more than generous to my family's foundation, and to me. As I said, I'm intrigued by your involvement—which I won't share with my counterparts or the Sheriff's Office. I'm assuming you'll hold the same discretion."

Lola flashed him a smile. "Absolutely.

"Good. Then I'll be in touch."

After they said their good-byes to the ME, they walked across the parking lot toward Lola's Honda. A van pulled into the parking lot just as they reached the car. As Shane climbed inside, the lights from the tall lampposts revealed the Collier County CSU logo along the side of the passing van.

"Our timing was good, huh?" Lola started the car, and let out a deep breath. "Wow, did that get me pumped."

"I'm sure my brother would love to know an autopsy room does it for you."

"Don't be gross," she said with a chuckle, and exited the parking lot. "Investigating a crime is what has me pumped. It's been almost two months since I've done anything related to the job and I've missed it." She glanced at him before making a turn. "So what do you think?"

"About the case? Pinning the corpses on Williams is too easy."

Lola hit the Bluetooth button on her steering wheel. As the phone rang over the car's speakers, she said, "I'm heading back to the rental house. We need to move fast on this. If there are other players involved, we need to know who they are. We might be a while. Are you good with this?"

"I said I was in. So, yeah. I'm good."

When Harrison answered the phone, and Lola began speaking to him, Shane looked at the clock on the dash and considered how his evening should have gone. If he hadn't cancelled his date with Beth, he could've had a nice dinner, maybe a beer and a few laughs. They could be sitting on her couch, kissing, talking, kissing some more…

He'd made the right move. A cop dating a murderer was bad. A cop dating a murderer who was involved in an underground organization that skirted the law was even worse. Yeah, he'd made the right move, even if it didn't feel right. At all.

Beth's House, Marco Island, Florida
Friday, 9:36 p.m., Eastern Standard Time

"That son of a bitch," Beth mumbled as she stripped out of her clothes. She was so going to bust Shane's butt. Too busy to get together tonight? No, more like he was too busy working his own investigation. Why else would he have been at the ME's?

She stepped into the shower and let the hot water wash away the disgust she'd been carrying with her throughout the day. Dead bodies, helping CSU at the funeral home, being dumped after two dates by a liar…it was an all-around crappy day.

All day she'd had herself worked up thinking Shane no longer wanted to see her because she was a cop. When Stacy had pulled the van into the District Twenty Medical Examiner's parking lot, and Beth had seen Shane climbing into a Honda Pilot with an Asian woman, her mind had raced in so many directions she'd become dizzy with embarrassment, anger and, yes, curiosity. At least her mind wasn't too muddled to not memorize the Honda's license plate. Still. Why would Shane be at the ME's? Yes, the Medical Examiner's building had frequent guests, but those guests included students, family members who needed to claim next of kin, or law enforcement. As for the Asian woman, the only conclusion she could come to was that she had to be Shane's future sister-in-law. She'd never met the woman, but Shane had told her Vlad liked to refer to her as Asian Lola. None of the dead women they'd found had been Asian. Not even close. So why would Shane and Lola pay a visit to the ME? Was it possible they knew one of the women? Or was it possible they were law enforcement?

She lathered her hair. Who could he and Lola work for? DEA? ATF? Based on Shane's appearance, she doubted he was FBI, but could be wrong. She racked her brain trying to think of current cases she knew about that would require help from the DEA, ATF or the FBI. Not coming up with anything, she considered asking around at work tomorrow, but didn't like that idea. If Shane and Lola worked for a law enforcement agency, he obviously hadn't wanted her to know. Maybe he worked undercover? She let out a sigh and rinsed her hair. No, that sounded like the makings of a TV show or movie.

She was a cop. If Shane Monahan was his real name, she could run a background check on him. But if her superiors discovered she'd run an unlawful search into Shane's background, she could find herself in serious trouble. Although she might be graduating this May, she still needed her job to help pay off her student loans and bills until she passed the Bar and secured a position with a law firm. Besides, she firmly believed rules were put in place for a reason, which was why she'd rarely broke them.

Rarely, not never.

Shower finished, she toweled off and realized there was nothing wrong with surfing the Internet for information. She threw on a tank top and a pair of thin cotton lounge pants, then went into the kitchen and poured a glass of wine. After she settled on the couch with her laptop, she turned on the TV. News vans and reporters from all the local networks had caught wind of Thomas Williams' arrest. By mid-afternoon they'd planted themselves outside the funeral home, and she'd like to see how the media planned to cover the story.

When her computer finally booted up, she took a sip of wine, then set the glass on the end table. Once she logged onto the Internet, she typed in Shane's name. Within seconds a number of links appeared on the screen. The top subject line snagged her attention and had her heart racing.

War Hero Sentenced to Seven Years

NORFOLK, VA.— On Monday, former Army Night Stalker, Shane E. Monahan (29), was convicted of involuntary manslaughter and sentenced to five to seven years for the murder of Theodore Nowak (32).

Last October 2nd, at approximately 11:45 p.m., Monahan was in Chumps Dump Bar & Grille when the murder occurred. Witnesses said Monahan and his brother, Ryan Monahan (28), had been drinking heavily. Monahan claimed his brother was 'coldcocked' by Nowak, after Nowak accused the brother of hitting on his girlfriend. Witnesses from the bar also confirmed this. When Nowak then assaulted Monahan, Monahan hit Nowak with enough force that Nowak fell back and hit a table.

According to the medical examiner, when Nowak fell against a table, subsequently hitting his temple, the temporal artery supplying blood to the brain ruptured, causing his death.

"Oh, my God," Beth gasped, and stared at Shane's mug shot. His hair was short, not a military crew cut, but close enough. His face was clean-shaven, giving him a boyish look.

He'd aged since the picture had been taken. The fine lines along his brow and around his eyes were deeper, and his face was now harder. God, what had he endured during his time in prison? She knew criminals and had arrested repeat offenders. She'd seen what prison could do to a person, and her heart ached for Shane. Despite what she now knew about him, his murder conviction didn't lessen her attraction to him. It should. She was a cop. She arrested bad guys for a living.

But Shane *wasn't* a bad guy. Or was she trying to justify that it was okay that she'd made out with a murderer? No. She needed to stay out of her head and go with her gut, which told her Shane was a decent man.

She went on to read the other articles she'd found on the Internet. All gave the same basic information. Stunned, she leaned back and reached for her wine. Now she knew he wasn't part of any law enforcement agency, and suspected why he'd dumped her, which was a good thing. As a deputy, she couldn't date a felon, let alone a convicted murderer. Only something didn't ring true. One of the articles claimed he'd served the full seven years. She could see a one to maybe three-year sentence for what he'd done, but seven years? That made no sense to her. She'd studied plenty of similar cases and had never seen one person go to prison for longer than four or five years. Clearly, Shane hadn't intended to kill the man, but to defend himself and his brother. Something wasn't right. Even the cop in her knew it.

She typed fast and did a search for the docket sheet that would give her Shane's case number, the charges against him, what he'd been convicted of, along with his sentencing. The articles she'd found might have given her the majority of this information, but she wanted more. The docket sheet could list motions, any plea agreements, and maybe a clue as to why Shane's sentence had been longer than the norm for someone without a prior criminal record.

As she waited for the files to load, she pictured Shane in his Cessna. She knew he'd been twenty-nine when he was sentenced. When she'd met him, she'd placed him in his mid-thirties. How long had it been since his release? It couldn't have been that long. He had an aircraft tour business, yet worked at his brother's airboat company. Shane had claimed he'd been doing airboat tours to help out his brother, now she wondered if it was the other way around.

"Tonight's top story deals with a morose subject."

Beth looked up from her computer and stared at the TV. The anchorman wore a grave expression as he gazed at his audience and explained the discovery of the three dead women, along with their connection to Williams Funeral Home. When the camera panned out to a reporter sitting next to the anchorman, Beth immediately recognized the woman. Vivian

Banks had been at the funeral home this afternoon and had tried to ask her a few questions. Beth had ignored the reporter and had kept her focus on helping CSU and securing the location.

"It's as strange as they come," Vivian told the anchor. "According to my sources, the three women were scheduled to be cremated Tuesday night or early Wednesday morning. What I'm wondering is what is contained in the urns the victims' families now possess?"

That had been something they'd all been wondering, and why Nick and Jerry had collected the urns from the families. Unfortunately, the high heat used during the cremation process destroyed any DNA evidence, making it impossible for technicians to clearly ID who or what had been cremated in the victims' place. Since there were ashes in the urns the detectives recovered, Jerry had expressed concern that the three women were planted as a decoy, and that the ashes could possibly be from other victims.

"More importantly," the reporter continued, "how will Thomas Williams' arrest affect Senator Parker Bryan's reelection campaign?"

What did the senator's campaign or reputation have to do with the three women? The only person whose reputation had been ruined was Thomas Williams. Even if they discovered Williams had nothing to do with the women other than embalming two of them, she could see Williams having a hard time shaking the stigma of these accusations, but not the senator.

"Will Senator Bryan or the Collier County Sheriff hold a press conference?" the anchor asked.

"At this time, Senator Bryan has refused to comment. The Sheriff's Office scheduled a press conference for tomorrow morning at nine." Vivian's mouth tilted in a slight smile. "But *I* have exclusive information to share with you now. My source informed me the three women were found with snakes sewn inside their bodies."

"Oh, no." Beth reached for her wine. Just like they'd done

with Katie Reed's murder investigation, Nick and Jerry had chosen to keep the snake evidence found in the three victims from the public to weed out the crazies who liked to make false confessions. Whoever had leaked the snake evidence had not only screwed with the investigation, but had given the reporter the wrong information.

"That's horrifying," the anchor responded, shock evident on his face.

"What's more horrifying is that this isn't the first time Collier County has had a similar murder. Two years ago, Kathleen Reed was found murdered. All we were told was that she'd been strangled. What detectives hadn't made available was that Kathleen Reed was also found with snakes sewn in her stomach. Coincidence?" The reporter shook her head. "I don't think so."

Beth's cell phone rang. As the reporter wrapped up her segment, Beth checked the caller ID, then answered. "I take it you're watching the news," she said to Ricky.

"Can you believe this?" he asked. "Who in the hell could've talked to her?"

She shoved her damp hair over her shoulder. "I have no idea, but I have a feeling we're all going to have our butts handed to us tomorrow."

"No shit." He let out a sigh. "Since she didn't get the information right, I doubt it was someone from CSU or the ME's division. Those guys love their evidence. If they're going to leak it, they'll be accurate."

"Actually, this might end up being okay because her source wasn't correct. If someone comes forward claiming they put snakes in those three women and say nothing about snake eggs or shedding, they can be ruled out."

"True. Anything else happen after I left?" he asked.

Beth muted the TV. "CSU confiscated the van the funeral home uses to transport the deceased to Williams' crematory. When I left tonight, they were just getting started on it."

"Did anyone find Williams' son?"

Dustin Williams was the only child of Thomas and Audra

PART II

Always carry a flagon of whiskey in case of snakebite and furthermore always carry a small snake.

—W.C. Fields

KRISTINE MASON

CHAPTER 8

Columbia, Alabama
Friday, 10:24 p.m., Central Standard Time

"HE DIDN'T DO it right."

Rage, primitive and ferocious, settled deep in the pit of his stomach and made him want to take a bat to someone's head. Namely, whoever had dared to steal their ritual. "No, he didn't." The Reverend muted the TV and looked at his daddy. "Too bad there ain't nothing to do about it."

"C'mon, boy," Daddy said, his once deep baritone voice now raspy and wheezy. "What'll the congregation think if they hear about this? Whoever did this can't get away with makin' us look like fucking *pree*verts, you hear me? We got a reputation to uphold."

Daddy had a point. During the two years since he'd sent Katie Reed to a better place—after the rattler had eaten the evil from her soul—he and his daddy had left Tennessee for a warmer climate. While they were trying to find a place to settle, a place where Daddy could live out the remaining days of his life, they'd traveled to areas throughout Appalachia where there were pockets of believers stupid enough to hand over their money for a little fire and brimstone.

And snakes.

Always snakes.

He shook his head. Damned fools.

"Remember that Turner boy from North Carolina who got hisself into killin' critters?" Daddy asked. "How you think his folks'll feel 'bout this?"

Daddy had another good point. But Daddy was either slipping or his liking for animals was showing. Cory Turner hadn't just killed critters. The eighteen-year-old jackass had dismembered them. Cory's family's pets, the neighbors'— whatever stray dog, cat, squirrel, rabbit or coon he could find—had been in serious trouble if that crazy-ass boy caught them. That hadn't been the worst of it. Cory had gone after the slow kid who'd lived a quarter mile from his parents' small farm. Not in a perverted way—he had saved that for his younger sister—but he'd hurt that boy badly. Tied him up and had poked him with a rake just to see how sharp the tines were.

Cory's parents, along with a few other families in that small North Carolina town, were staunch believers in his daddy's teachings. As he and his daddy had made their way south, one member of their congregation had contacted them, asking for help.

They'd wanted the Ritual of the Serpents.

On his sickly daddy's behalf, he'd given those folks what they'd wanted. He'd taken a bat to that crazy-ass boy's head, then once he was dead, he'd made it so the baby rattler could eat the evil festering in his soul. Afterward, he'd dumped the Turner boy in Georgia, far away from his hometown, so folks would think he'd simply up and left.

They'd made a solid fifteen grand off of the ritual, too. Thinking about the money and the way that boy's head had split open made him feel a little better. Not much. He didn't like being mocked and that's exactly what had just happened. Someone had taken *their* ritual and mocked it. "I don't know if the Turners will even know about what happened in Florida," the Reverend said, more concerned about finding the pervert than a bunch of hillbillies.

"Come on, boy. Think. Those folks might be stupid enough to believe in our bullshit, but they's the type of people who love their idiot boxes. Ain't like we was watchin' the local news, neither. Nope, God dang CNN had this splashin' 'cross the country. Now you need to fix it."

"Fix it how? It ain't like I'm a detective."

"And it ain't like I'm tellin' you to arrest someone. You're a smart one. You know what needs to be done."

The Reverend had killed out of spite and he'd killed for money. What Daddy implied meant he'd kill to prove a point. While he didn't have a problem with that, heading back to Florida *could* cause a problem. Thanks to the pervert, the law would be on full alert, and he'd have to be careful.

"Maybe you should spell it out for me," the Reverend said. "'Cause once the deal is done, there ain't no goin' back. Plus, it ain't like I'm gettin' paid this time."

Daddy chuckled, which threw him into a major coughing spell. The Reverend rose and rushed to his side. He took the cup of water off the table next to the full-sized bed he'd set up in the living room, then angled the straw toward his daddy's mouth. Once he'd taken a drink and the coughing stopped, Daddy rested a hand on his shoulder.

"Son, this ain't about gettin' paid, it's about makin' sure our congregation *believes*. If they don't believe in our shit, then there ain't no more money. I know you followed Katie's story after you did the ritual on her. I was right there with you. So, you tell me? How is it three dead bodies show up with snakes in 'em, when the police and reporters never said word one about 'em?"

That had been his first thought when he'd seen the newscast. Daddy was right. They *had* followed Katie's story and knew the police had never once mentioned finding his baby rattler in her belly. Surprisingly, they hadn't even told Harlan. "Whoever put the snakes in those women knows exactly what I'd done to Katie," the Reverend answered. Which, to him, meant that someone behind a badge had copied the Ritual of the Serpents.

But did they know about him?

Doubtful. Otherwise he'd already be in custody.

Now that his daddy's coughing fit was over, he went back to his recliner, then picked up his bottle of beer and took a long drink. "I'll call Suzie in the morning, then head down to Florida once she's here." Suzie was a believer and a former Army nurse. Since she lived in a shitty trailer with her equally shitty husband, he knew she'd jump at the chance to stay overnight with Daddy for few days.

"Whatcha gonna do when you get there?" Daddy asked.

He lifted his beer to his lips and took another swallow. "Well, let's think about this. If the police never told those news people about the snakes in Katie, I'm thinking one of them is behind this. After I get you settled for the night, I'll get on the computer and do some checking."

"Checkin' on what?"

"Who knew about the snakes. You know, the detectives and such."

"Whatcha gonna do when you find 'em?" Daddy asked, a wicked gleam in his eyes.

The Reverend drained the last of his beer and grinned. "I'm gonna kill him."

The Rental House, Everglades City, Florida
Friday, 11:40 p.m., Eastern Standard Time

Shane sat on the sofa near the bay window of Lola's rental house reviewing the details of Katie Reed's murder. He had to hand it to Harrison. The man definitely knew how to obtain information. While he and Lola had made the drive from the ME's back to the rental, Harrison had hacked into the Sheriff Office's computer system and had printed off everything he could find related to Reed's murder case. He'd also managed to find information on the current investigation, as well as

Thomas Williams and his family. Although the hacking made Shane edgy, it'd be Harrison's ass, not his, should someone from the Sheriff's Office find out. Still, he didn't like it.

Lola set her stack of papers on the dining room table. "I'm done with my pile, are you guys about ready to brainstorm?" She had been reviewing the files they had on the three dead women, while Harrison and Vlad had been digging into Williams' information.

"I'm ready," Shane said, then looked to Harrison and Vlad, who sat on the other couch, papers scattered in front of them on the coffee table.

Harrison nodded. "Yeah, we're good."

"Vlad hope this brainstorm is not for long."

Lola stood and carried over her file. "We're all tired," she said, then sat on the chair opposite from Vlad and Harrison. "Let's get a plan of action put in place for tomorrow, then we'll call it a night. I'll make sure the rest of the group is aware of what we've found and what we're doing." Since Barney, Ryan and Mel would handle opening up the boat shop in the morning, Lola had told them not to come to the rental house. Knowing Ryan and Barney, if they hadn't finished hanging the kitchen cabinets, they'd work until the job was complete. As for Mel, she'd probably gone back to her chop shop to work on the Camaro that had happened to find its way into her garage.

"Vlad only tired from sitting on couch." He waved to the papers on the coffee table. "This bore Vlad to crying."

"Tears," Harrison said, then picked up a piece of paper. "If we can, I'd like to start with Thomas Williams. I also printed what Mel found on necrophilia, but haven't had the chance to go over it yet."

Lola nodded. "Have at it. I'll look over what Mel has for us later."

"Okay," Harrison began, "Thomas Williams and his wife, Audra, are both forty-nine and have only one son, Dustin. Dustin is twenty-one and has worked for the funeral home since he was sixteen. He's currently getting his degree in mortuary science. He's also certified to operate the crematory."

"Interesting." Lola sifted through her file, then plucked out a sheet of paper. "Dustin picked up Charlotte Pallesen from the ME's Tuesday. His signature is on the release form."

"Then why did they arrest Thomas?" Shane asked. "The son was obviously the last person in possession of Pallesen's body."

"According to a report made by Detective Jerry Tennyson, Thomas claimed that Dustin picked up Charlotte's body from the ME's, then came back to the funeral home for the other two bodies. The son was supposed to take them to the crematory, but came down with a stomach virus. Thomas said that he couldn't make the trip to the crematory because he and his wife were attending a city business owners' function at Naples Country Club. Detectives verified Thomas's alibi."

"Yeah, but who can verify the kid's?"

"Exactly," Lola said. "Which makes me wonder if Thomas and his wife are covering for their son."

"Does Thomas explain how he thinks the bodies ended up in the woods?" Harrison asked.

Lola shifted the papers around, then read, "Thomas Williams claims the bodies were in the van when he left for the business function."

"Wait, they left three bodies in a van?" Harrison asked.

"Thomas didn't think so. He told detectives that his son was supposed to put them in the cooler for the night, then transport them to the crematory in the morning. When he arrived at the funeral home the next day, he said the bodies weren't in the van or the cooler, so he assumed his son must have felt better and decided to take them to the crematory after all. Since that obviously didn't happen, Thomas now assumes his son was too sick to move the bodies and left them in the van. He believes that someone must have broken into the garage and stolen them."

"Vlad smell shit of bull. Do not this funeral home have camera to video?"

"No working cameras, but the place has an alarm." Lola

looked back at the file. "When questioned about this, along with the fact that there were no signs of forced entry, Thomas said his son must have forgotten to set the alarm and lock up properly."

"Pretty convenient," Shane said.

"So let's say the kid's the one who took the bodies, and Dad has nothing to do with it," Harrison began. "Why wouldn't Dustin cremate them once he was finished having his fun?"

Shane shrugged. "Then how would anyone know about the snake shedding and eggs in the victims' bodies?"

Lola raised her brows. "Good point. Maybe this guy is showing off. Let's talk about the snake stuff. Shane, tell us about Katie Reed."

"Vlad have question. Where Dustin?"

"His parents told police that he had tickets for the Miami Heat game. Dustin and a friend left for Miami yesterday afternoon and planned to stay for the weekend. They tried calling his cell phone, but it's been turned off."

"Back up for a second," Shane said. "The last time anyone saw Charlotte Pallesen was at the ME's on Tuesday afternoon. The kid gets sick, the parents go to a function, the bodies are left in the van. On Wednesday morning, did Williams question the kid about the fact that there were no bodies in the cooler or the van?"

Lola went to another page in the file. "Thomas told detectives he didn't ask because he figured Dustin had taken them to the crematory." She looked up. "He did have ashes to pass out to the victims' family."

"The kid knows something," Shane said.

"Detective Tennyson noted the same thing in his report. The detectives also contacted the Miami-Dade police and asked them to check the hotel where Dustin and his friend, Joshua Kidd, were supposed to be staying. No one had booked a room under either of their names, and when the police showed hotel employees their driver's license photos, no one recognized either man." She looked to Harrison. "Has Dustin been in any trouble?"

"No record that I could find. That's not to say he doesn't have sealed juvie files. Want me to check?"

"If you can." She closed the folder. "Okay, on to the snake stuff. Shane?"

After Shane explained to Vlad and Harrison what David had told them about Katie, Vlad shook his head. "Vlad no understand point to this. Why snake?"

"Who knows? Anyway, Katie lived with her father, Harlan Reed, who adopted her when he married her mom, Sally. Sally died six years ago. Katie had one misdemeanor for possession of marijuana. The detectives who'd worked her case noted that when they'd interviewed her friends, they'd discovered that Katie had progressed from weed to crack and heroin. These friends also claimed that she would sometimes trade sex for drugs, but she hadn't gotten into full-blown prostitution."

"If she'd lived she might have," Harrison said, his tone cynical.

"We'll never know. Okay, so the cops interviewed the guys she was getting the drugs from, her friends, her dad and came up empty. They didn't have one viable suspect." Shane pulled out the ME's autopsy report. "David autopsied Katie," he said for Harrison and Vlad's benefit. "According to her toxicology report she had alcohol and an opiate in her system—likely heroin. There were no traces of rape or sexual activity. She was found naked and her killer had washed her body. No fibers, hairs or DNA were discovered, and the police never told the public about the snakes." He set the paper in his lap. "If someone was copycatting Katie's murder, they didn't do it right."

"Thank God, otherwise this would be a murder investigation," Lola said. "What I'm wondering is who knew about the snake in Katie's stomach."

"Thanks to that reporter, everyone does now," Harrison said.

Lola sighed. "Yeah, that's too bad."

"Here's what's really bad," Shane began. "Guess who

handled Katie's funeral?"

"No way," Harrison said, glancing up from his laptop. "That would mean anyone who'd worked for Williams Funeral Home could've known about the snake."

Lola shook her head. "I can't see the police disclosing that information, but I would think whoever handled her body would be able to tell that her killer had made the incision along her stomach."

Shane stifled a yawn. "Either way, it's a piece of incriminating evidence against Thomas Williams. I'm surprised this wasn't in Detective Tennyson's report. He worked Katie's case, too."

"Could be his report is incomplete," Lola suggested. "Harrison was only able to find the initial report Tennyson had written up, but there's nothing here about what had happened during the interview they'd conducted with Thomas, once they were back at the Sheriff's Office."

"Vlad think funeral home son is answer."

"Lola think Vlad right," she said. "I'm concerned Thomas, and maybe even his wife, are covering for their kid. After all, he *is* their only child."

Harrison shook his head. "Man, I don't know. If I found out my kid was having sex with dead bodies, I sure as hell wouldn't want him on the loose."

"But you're not a father. I think you'd be surprised what you might do for your child." Lola stood. "Tomorrow, let's plan on—"

"Hold up," Harrison said, and stared at his laptop. "I didn't find a juvie record, but I did find Dustin's Facebook and Twitter account." He tapped at the keyboard. "Nice. His Facebook profile is public. We could make a list of local friends and start with them."

"Is the guy Dustin went to Miami with one of his Facebook friends?" Shane asked.

"Lemme check." After a few strokes to the keyboard, Harrison smiled. "Not only are they Facebook friends, but Joshua isn't in Miami." He turned the laptop around and set it on the coffee table. "The dumbass posted a selfie twenty minutes ago. See the background? That's Bare Bones strip club in Fort Myers. Vlad and I have been there."

The Russian's cheeks grew red and he looked to the wood floors. "Vlad no remember."

"How could you not? You got a lap dance from a stripper who looks just like your crazy ex."

"Misty love for Vlad what made Misty crazy. Club stripper not pretty like Misty."

Harrison chuckled. "So I guess you *do* remember the strip club after all."

Vlad looked to Lola, apology clear on his face. "Vlad sorry. Vlad no mean to grade women."

"While I find strip clubs a bit degrading, you don't need to apologize," Lola said. "What you can do is go to the strip club and find Joshua. If Dustin isn't with him, maybe Joshua knows where he is. And if we don't find Dustin tonight, we'll look tomorrow. Senator Bryan gave Thomas' attorney's contact info to Ian and said he'd speak with us. Since it's not like we can interview Thomas, I'm going to call his attorney in the morning after he's finished meeting with Thomas."

"Do you want me to go with Vlad and Harrison?" Shane asked, hoping Lola would say no. He had no desire to go to a strip club. They didn't do it for him, and right now the only woman he wanted to see naked was the one woman he couldn't have.

"No, I'll drop you off at home. You might not be on parole or probation, but if Vlad and Harrison run into trouble, I don't want you caught in the middle of it."

"If they run into trouble they might need my help," he said, defending himself. Although Lola was right, he wasn't stupid. If he suspected they'd have an issue, he'd force Vlad and Harrison to pull back.

"Shane, go home. Vlad and Harry promise no problem with Strip Club Boy."

"Yeah, we'll be fine," Harrison said. "Me and Vlad have been itching to get out of Everglades City and start working."

"See? They've got it covered." Lola reached into her purse and pulled out her wallet. "Here," she said, handing Harrison cash. "For the cover charge, parking and *one* drink. No lap dances from the Misty lookalike. Got it?"

Harrison grinned. "Yes, Mom."

"And no guns."

"Vlad have knife. No need for gun."

"You've been hanging around Mel too long," Lola said. "Keep the knife in the car and please stay out of trouble. Make sure you call me if you find Dustin. I don't care how late it is."

He and Lola exited the rental house and walked toward her Honda. "You *were* kind of mothering them."

"Was I? Should I have gone all badass and told them if they fucked up I'd string them up by their balls?"

Shane laughed. In the short time he'd known Lola he'd never heard her talk that way.

"Your reaction is exactly what theirs would've been. Here's a little secret," she said once they were in the car. "I could take them both out without breaking a sweat or using a weapon."

"Is this your way of warning me that I should follow orders and not fuck up?"

"I'd never go after you. We're family." After she backed out of the driveway, she glanced at him. "But I wouldn't have a problem asking Ryan to kick your butt."

He chuckled and shook his head. "I'd like to see him try," he said, then asked her what time she was talking to Thomas Williams' attorney.

"Nine. He's going to see Thomas around eight, so hopefully he'll be able to shed some light on the son."

His mind strayed to the future attorney he'd callously dumped, and he wondered what Beth had ended up doing tonight. *Don't go there, Monahan.* Right. She was too good for him anyway.

He then thought back to his and Lola's visit with the ME, along with the research and brainstorming session at the rental house. Honestly, other than his time with Beth and his first few trips out on the airboat and Cessna, tonight was good.

He'd had an opportunity to work his mind and operate on the other side of a prison cell, which was something he could hone in on and use. He'd spent seven years surrounded by criminals, rapists and murderers. He'd listened to their stories as some of them had bragged about their crimes. Never once had he considered himself one of them, but with what he'd learned during his incarceration, he could definitely think like one of them.

But after Lola dropped him off and he made his way to his bedroom, his mind wasn't on trying to think like a killer, or, in this case, a variation of one since no one was actually murdered. His mind strayed back to Beth. The text he'd sent her had been shitty and he knew it had implied the whole 'don't text me, I'll text you' crap. Still, he hadn't said that he'd never wanted to see her again. He could call her or text her, ask to make plans for another night and apologize for the lame text.

Then what?

He would always have a record. Even if Beth chose to accept that and still wanted to see him, he was now privy to an organization that skirted the law Beth upheld. If he told Lola and Ryan, along with the rest of the crew, he wanted out, he couldn't bring Beth around. The last thing they needed was a cop in their business.

After opening the window, he crawled into bed. As he stared at the rotating ceiling fan and listened to the frogs and insects carry on, he knew that no matter how he sliced it, he was screwed. All his life he'd gone after what he'd wanted and had attained it. He'd joined the Army with the intent to be a Night Stalker. Check. After the Army he'd decided to start his own aircraft tour business. Check. The money had started flowing and he'd achieved other dreams. He'd bought a house, a motorcycle and truck. Check, check, check. He'd had it made. He could still have it made.

Alone.

He rolled on his side and began counting the number of croaking frogs.

Naples, Florida
Saturday, 12:56 a.m. Eastern Standard Time

Sleep eluded him. Careful not to wake Gabriela, he rose from her bed, then headed down the steps to the kitchen. Once there, he poured himself two fingers' worth of scotch, then drank it in one gulp. He poured another, put the cap on the bottle, then walked out onto the lanai. Crickets chirped as the cool breeze moved the wind chimes in the corner of the patio. He took a seat on one of the padded chaise lounge chairs and sipped his drink. While he enjoyed a cocktail or two, this past week he'd needed more than that to fall asleep—like a bottle of Jack.

Last night hadn't been bad. He'd been on top of the world. The bodies were out of his house, and the ring he'd bought Gabriela had been placed onto her finger. Tonight, guilt and worry had taken him down a few notches. Fortunately, Gabriela hadn't wanted to fool around. Although he'd wanted to see if he could still function as he had the past two days, his mind hadn't been on sex, but on what the police had found.

He'd figured the bodies would eventually be discovered, just not this soon. When he'd first concocted his plan, his hope had been that the bodies would have been so badly decomposed by the time they'd been found that there would have been no evidence of sexual abuse. Thank God he'd had the foresight to plant the snake shedding and eggs in their stomachs.

Thank God for the idiot who'd leaked the snake evidence to the press. While the two cases had their major differences, no one could deny the way the snakes tied them together. What surprised him, though, was Thomas Williams' quick arrest. He hadn't meant for that to happen. While he'd figured the man would be questioned, he'd also assumed the police would realize that if a funeral home director had access to a crematory, he wouldn't leave bodies laying out in the open for all to see.

He took another sip of the scotch. Oh, well. He wasn't a

fan of Senator Bryan anyway. The blowhard had been a staunch supporter of the President's ridiculous healthcare plan, which he abhorred. Since many Floridians loved the senator, he doubted his son-in-law's arrest would damage Bryan's campaign. Hell, by November, most people would have already forgotten all about the funeral director, his connection to the senator and the dead women.

He hoped.

What if I need another body?

He drained his glass. Once the police realized they'd had it all wrong about Williams, he wouldn't be surprised if funeral homes across the county, maybe even the state, bolstered their security systems. Families would demand it. No one wanted their loved ones stolen from a funeral home, their bodies abused, mutilated and—

He raised the glass to his lips, remembered it was empty, then let out a sigh. *He* had stolen bodies, abused and mutilated them. All in the quest for a normal sex life.

He snorted, then pushed himself off the chaise. He was pathetic. The lowest of the low.

After he locked up, he went into the kitchen to set the tumbler in the sink. He glanced at the bottle of scotch, tempted to have another shot just for good measure, but decided against it. He was having a celebratory brunch with Gabriela and her family tomorrow and didn't want to be hung over.

He grabbed two water bottles from the fridge, then went back upstairs. When he reached Gabriela's bedroom, he stood in the doorway and stared at his fiancée.

Two years ago, he'd been in charge of the country club's marketing committee and had suggested they revamp their website. He'd received proposals from various web designers, and had loved the concept Gabriela had come up with the most. The first time he'd invited her to the club to discuss the details, he'd been left awestruck and practically mute. She was so beautiful and vibrant, and interested in him. At first he'd thought her interest had been a ruse to gain the job, but even after the contract had been signed and she'd finished the web development, she'd made it clear she had wanted to be with him. Not for his money, not for the job he'd given her, but for *him*.

He loved her so much, and couldn't lose her. Life would be boring and worthless without her smile and laughter. If it weren't for his sexual hang-ups, they'd be the perfect couple.

He pushed off the doorjamb and walked across the room. When he climbed onto the bed, she rolled to her side and snuggled against him. He lightly caressed her soft skin. For now, his sexual hang-ups were a thing of the past. For now, he wouldn't have to worry about her growing restless and wanting a man to fulfill her desires.

For now...

The future frightened him. Based on his past track record, he might need another body to renew his passions. Would he take the risk? Absolutely. Gabriela was the reason he'd taken the bodies in the first place. It had all been for her.

To keep her satisfied and with him, he'd do it again and again.

And they'd never catch him.

CHAPTER 9

Lola's Rental House, Everglades City, Florida
Saturday, 3:14 a.m., Eastern Standard Time

SHANE PARKED BEHIND his brother's Suburban, rushed into the house, then came to an abrupt halt when he reached the gutted kitchen.

You've got to be fucking kidding me.

He slowed his steps and glanced around the room. Ryan looked pissed as hell. Lola had her back turned and her hands on her head. Barney was grinning and Mel was stifling a yawn. His gaze stopped on the funeral home director's son, then drifted to Harrison and Vlad, who looked as if they'd just caught themselves a four hundred pound Goliath Grouper.

"Did we deliver or what?" Harrison asked.

Dustin had been blindfolded, gagged and bound to a chair in the center of the kitchen. His hands were tied behind his back and his ankles were secured to the chair legs.

He grabbed his brother's arm and pulled him aside. "This is seriously fucked up."

"No shit. Everyone, move," Lola ordered, and pointed toward the living room.

He let go of Ryan's arm, then followed everyone out of the

kitchen. Once they met by the bay window, Lola turned on Vlad and Harrison. "You weren't supposed to bring him here," she said, her tone hushed, but filled with anger. "What the hell were you two thinking? This is kidnapping."

"Vlad and Harry no kidnap."

"That's right," Harrison said. "We got to talking to Dustin's buddy, found out our boy here is into dealing, told him we wanted to buy some stuff, and he was fine with coming with us." He shrugged. "So, technically, this wasn't a kidnapping."

Mel let out a soft chuckle, and pulled a switchblade from her purse. "The technicality angle works for me. Here, honey, go use this to get him to talk," she said, and handed the knife to Harrison.

"Hell, no," Lola said. "This wasn't how I wanted things to go down, and this *is* a kidnapping." She cracked her knuckles and looked as if she wanted to punch a wall—or maybe Vlad and Harrison. "Okay, Dustin's here, so let's deal with it." She glared at Mel. "Minus the knife."

"I dunno," Barney said. "Knives are pretty effective. When I was back in 'Nam—"

"Damn it, you're not helping." Lola tightened her long ponytail and looked to Vlad. "Does he know your names?"

"Nope," Harrison answered. "Vlad went by Ivan, and I told him my name was Nico." He grinned. "That was the name of Steven Seagal's character in *Above the Law*."

"How clever," she said with an eye roll. "But at least he doesn't know your *real* names. Let's keep it that way."

"How will…?" The Russian frowned, clearly trying to decide how to refer to himself without doing it in third person. He let out a sigh. "Vlad find this impossible. Vlad will stay with Ivan."

"Or you could refer to yourself as 'I' like normal people," Harrison suggested. "*Or* we could give ourselves names like they did in *Reservoir Dogs*. I can be Mr. Blonde." He nodded to Vlad. "He could be Mr. Brown and—"

"Oh, my God, will you stop?" Lola stepped forward and took the knife from Harrison. "We're not doing that. At all.

Now let's go back in there, question him, then get rid of him."

"I don't know if I can take him to my daddy's swamp tonight," Mel said.

Lola glared at her. "I didn't mean kill him. My God, what is wrong with you? Never mind. Let's just do this." When they reentered the kitchen, Lola said, "Remove his gag."

Vlad shoved the gag under Dustin's chin. "You guys are fucking crazy," he shouted. "You want drugs? I'll give you what I have, but I'm small-time. I *work* for a supplier."

"We're not interested in drugs. We're interested in dead bodies," Lola said.

"Holy fuck. Oh, my God. I can't. You got what you wanted from me the other night. I can't give you any more bodies."

Ryan took a step forward. "What are you talking about?"

"The three dead women, you sick fucks. I saw the news and heard what you did to them. What are you people, a satanic cult or something?"

"Did you *sell* the bodies?" Lola asked.

The kid's forehead creased. "You know damn well I didn't sell anything. One of you *stole* them."

"We didn't," Lola began, "but we're interested in who did. Your signature was on the medical examiner's release form. You were the last person to see Charlotte Pallesen's body. What happened to it?"

Dustin pressed his lips together and remained silent.

"I suggest you answer me."

When he still didn't speak, Lola folded her arms across her chest and nodded to Vlad. "Don't mark up his face. Yet."

"да," he responded in Russian, then punched Dustin in the stomach.

As the kid grunted then coughed, Shane pushed a hand through his hair and wondered just how far Lola would take this. He grabbed his brother's arm again, then leaned close to his ear. "This is wrong," he whispered.

"Lola won't let Vlad hurt him," Ryan whispered back.

Was his brother pussy-whipped, delusional or had he changed that much since Shane had been in prison? If he was back in the Army and Dustin had been the enemy, he'd have had no problem using a little force to gain information. But he wasn't in the Army and, if what Dustin had told them was true, he hadn't mutilated and defiled the three bodies.

Lola ran a shaky hand across her forehead. "I don't want my colleague to have to hit you again. Are you ready to answer my question?"

When Dustin shook his head, Lola sighed. "Hit him again."

As Vlad raised his fist, the kid shouted, "Wait. Just hang on a sec and let me catch my breath."

"We ain't got a sec, boy," Barney said. "Time's a wasting."

"I *did* sign the release form, then I went back to the funeral home for the other two bodies."

"Why didn't you have the bodies with you in the first place?" Shane asked. "Why make two trips?"

"Because the other two weren't ready, and I had plans for the night. I grabbed the woman from the morgue to save time. It's a thirty-minute drive to the crematory, and it takes about two to two and a half hours to cremate a body. My dad was expecting the bodies to be cremated by the end of the day. I knew there was no way I was going to be able to get all the bodies cremated and still hook up with my buds, so I figured I could at least take care of one of the bodies, keep the other two in the cooler at the crematory and finish the job in the morning."

"Your dad claims you came down with the flu," Lola said.

Dustin frowned. "Do you know how my dad is doing? I heard they arrested him."

"You heard right. Thanks to you, people now think he's a necrophiliac. Do you know what that is?" she asked.

"I grew up around dead people and have heard every joke out there. Yeah, I know, and I also know my father isn't capable of doing what that reporter claimed."

"Explain."

"I'd already loaded the other two bodies in the van when I got a call from a buddy of mine."

"Joshua Kidd?" Lola asked.

"How'd you know? Never mind. Yeah. My plans for the night had changed and there was no way I was going to even be able to do one body. So I lied to my dad and told him I was sick. After he left, I was supposed to put the bodies back in the cooler, which I planned to do. Then I got another call."

"My, my, sugar," Mel said. "You're a popular guy. Are you sure you're only a small time dealer?"

Dustin straightened. "I'm telling you the truth."

"We're not interested in the drugs you're dealing," Lola said. "We're interested in what happened to the bodies."

Dustin swore and shook his head. "This'll kill my parents."

"Your dad's in jail and his reputation could possibly be destroyed," Lola said. "What do you think your parents are going to be more concerned about, their drug-dealing son or having necrophilia attached to Williams Funeral Home?"

Dustin's chin trembled slightly and he cleared his throat. "This is all my fault." He let out a breath. "I can supply you with weed, X and shrooms, but I don't mess with anything harder than that. My buddy had two buyers interested in the weed and X. Since I over bought from my supplier, I was short on cash and wanted to move the stuff. But the buyers didn't want to wait, and I didn't want to lose them. So I left the bodies in the van, figuring I'd put them in the cooler after I made the drop. When I tried to start my car, it wouldn't turn over. The frickin' battery was dead. I could've used the van to jump it, but didn't want to waste the time."

"So you took the van with the bodies in it," Lola said, disgust in her voice. "Nice. What happened next?"

"I stopped by my apartment, picked up the drugs, met up with the buyers, made the delivery, then figured what the hell? I might as well get at least one body cremated, that way I could cut out early the next day. I had tickets for Thursday night's Miami Heat game and thought I'd head down there a day early and do a little partying. But things got all fucked up."

"How?" Lola asked.

"I'm a few minutes from the crematory when I realize I'm being followed. I thought I was being paranoid because I still had drugs in the back of the van, until I pulled into the parking lot. The SUV behind me lights up and follows me into the parking lot."

"Lights up?" Harrison asked.

"Police lights. I was freaking out, thinking I've got an undercover cop ready to bust my ass. Turns out, the guy wasn't a cop."

"Someone was impersonating an officer?" Ryan asked with disbelief.

"Fucked up, right? He had on a ski mask and shoved a gun in my face. He forced me out of the van, then ordered me to move the bodies from my van to his car."

"What kind of vehicle?" Shane asked.

"It was an older Chevy Tahoe. Dark-blue or green. Piece of shit, too." Dustin shook his head. "Since it was dark, and the only lights at the crematory are the ones at the entrance and exit, I couldn't tell that it was a piece of shit or that it wasn't a cop car until it was too late. "

Lola took a step toward Dustin. "Describe the man."

"I'm five-eleven, and the guy was a couple of inches taller than me. He was bigger, too."

"Overweight?"

"No, muscular. He had on jeans, black sweatshirt and boots. Like I said, he had on a ski mask, so I couldn't see his face. But he was either white or Hispanic."

"Eye color?"

"Couldn't tell."

"What'd this guy say to you?" Barney asked.

Dustin shrugged. "He told me to put the bodies in his truck, or he'd put a bullet in my head and do it himself. He also said that if I went to the police or told anyone, he'd make an anonymous call to the cops and let them know about the drugs. He said he'd been watching me and knows I'm dealing. Then he leaves and I'm left standing there trying to figure out what to do next."

Shane rubbed the back of his neck. "You obviously cremated someone. Whose ashes are in the urns the police confiscated?"

Dustin clenched his jaw. "My parents are going to kill me."

"Because?"

"Can you take the blindfold off me?"

"No," Lola said. "Answer the question."

"I know a guy who works for a pet cremation service. I called him and asked if he had any animals. He had five dogs and two cats still waiting to be cremated. So I told him he could have the Miami Heat tickets, a quarter bag of weed and a hundred bucks if he'd let me have the animals."

"Wow, dude. That's fucked up," Harrison said.

"It's not like I killed them," Dustin said, his tone defensive. "I don't care what you guys think about me, but I'll tell you this—whether we're talking animals or people, I respect the dead."

"Clearly." Lola raised a brow. "Dealing drugs with corpses in the back of your van was very admirable."

"Why so many animals?" Mel asked.

"There's a kind of check and balance system during cremation. Anytime I turn on the cremation chamber, a third party who monitors it is notified. I have to type in the deceased person's name and weight into the computer. So when I got the animals, I divided them between the three cardboard cremation containers until each container was at the proper weight. Then I cremated them. I ended up staying there all night to finish the job."

Lola rubbed her eyes. "Okay, so you put the animal ashes in containers, then what?"

"I dropped them off at the funeral home, recharged my car battery, then went back to my apartment and slept all day. When I woke up, I sent my dad a text and told him I was heading for Miami and that I'd see him Sunday. I've been hanging out at Josh's place ever since."

"Why'd you shut off your cell phone?" Lola asked.

"Are you kidding me? Man, I was scared. I broke all kinds of laws."

"Right. You broke the law, but your dad is the one sitting in jail. If you would've contacted the police immediately, you could have saved your family and yourself a lot of grief." Lola glanced around the room. "Any more questions for Dustin?" After a unanimous no, she said, "Okay, let's get him out of here."

"Are we makin' him gator bait?" Mel asked, then chuckled when Lola glared at her. "Just jokin', honey. Don't be so sensitive."

"You two." Lola pointed to Vlad and Harrison. "Take him back to his car, then follow him until he's close to the Sheriff's Office. Dustin has a confession to make." As Vlad untied the kid from the chair, Lola added, "I suggest you tell the police guilt and concern for you father is what compelled you to finally come forward, and make no mention of us. We *will* know if you mention this little conversation and we *will* retaliate. A fist to the stomach is nothing compared to what we'll do to you. Understand?"

"Yeah, I got it," Dustin said, then Vlad tossed the man over his shoulder and carried him from the room.

"Now we know what happened, and can confirm Thomas Williams' innocence," Lola said.

Shane pulled his truck keys from his pocket. "How much you want to bet the guy who stole the bodies not only knew that Katie Reed's family used Williams Funeral Home for her service, but that he's been following Dustin around for a while?"

"I agree, and by this time tomorrow I wouldn't be surprised if Thomas is back at home."

"Case closed?"

"I'll need to talk to Ian about it," Lola said. "Personally, I'd like to find out who stole the bodies."

****

Collier County Sheriff's Office, Naples, Florida
Saturday, 7:08 a.m., Eastern Standard Time

Beth rushed from the women's locker room to Nick's desk. When she didn't find him there, she went down the hallway toward the interview rooms. Sean, an officer she'd trained with, stood guard outside one of the closed doors. "Morning," she said. "I heard Thomas Williams' son turned himself in. Is he in there?"

"Yeah, Nick and Jerry have been talking to him for almost two hours."

"Have you heard anything?"

"Nothing yet. The kid's had four bottles of water. I imagine they'll have to break soon." Sean eyed her for a moment. "Ricky said you two were first on the scene. Have any idea who leaked the deal about the snakes?"

"No clue. Has the sheriff said anything?"

"No, but the captain has. He's pretty PO'd and blaming CSU."

"Really?" She knew Stacy and Keith would never say anything. As for the other crime scene investigators, she'd worked with several of them, too, and couldn't see them going to the press. The memory of seeing Shane and possibly Lola leaving the ME's entered her mind. "He's not concerned that the leak came from the ME's office?"

"I haven't heard anything about—"

The door to the interrogation room opened. First Jerry, then Nick stepped into the hallway. Seconds later, an officer escorted Dustin Williams, who she recognized from not only his driver's license photo, but pictures she'd seen in Thomas Williams' office down the hall.

"Is he under arrest?" she asked, once Dustin and the officer had disappeared around the corner.

"Morning," Nick said with a smile.

"Sorry. Good morning. Is he under arrest?"

Jerry chuckled. "You're relentless. No, he's not under arrest. We have to check a few of his alibis, but I think his story is legit."

Nick nodded to Jerry. "Especially because CSU recovered animal hairs in the back of the funeral home van."

"Hello." Beth gave them a slight wave. "I wasn't there during his interview, so I have no idea what you're talking about."

Nick started walking down the hall toward his desk. "Come with me and I'll explain while I get a cup of coffee."

She followed Nick and listened as he told her how Dustin claimed the bodies had been stolen from him. Once they were back at his desk, and half of his coffee had been drained, he leaned back in his chair. "So it makes sense that Thomas Williams had nothing to do with any of this. His kid? Well, if he'd have come forward in the beginning, it would have saved his dad a lot of embarrassment."

"So you're going to let Thomas go."

"Once we confirm the son's story, they'll both be free."

"Except that means there's still someone out there with a weird fetish."

Nick glanced around, then leaned forward. "Look, I'm not saying this crime isn't worth investigating, but Jerry and I have another case we're working that takes precedence."

"The stabbing victim," she said, remembering the man who'd been found a week ago, lying in his bed, knife wounds to his chest.

"Yeah, and I don't want that case to go cold. We have a few leads we want to follow up on today."

"I understand." Collier County didn't see that many murders, and this one had been brutal. There had been no motivation for the murder of the well-liked, middle-aged man, along with no signs of forced entry. "But what about the connection to Katie Reed?"

"Even the ME doesn't think there's a connection." He handed her a file folder. "Jerry's report is in here, along with what the ME and CSU have so far. Look it over if you want, but I think I can sum it up for you. Someone knew about the snake in Katie's stomach and tried to mimic it."

She took the folder and was now glad she'd come to work early. She was anxious to read the report, not only because this case interested her, but to see if there was anything that might connect back to Shane or Lola. As she'd lain in bed last night, her mind kept drifting back to why Shane had been at the ME's. Chances were that he and Lola had gone there to see a family member. Maybe not necessarily one of the victims, but someone else who'd died recently. Since that was the only logical explanation, she ached for him even more. He couldn't have been released from prison that long ago, now he had to deal with a death in his family.

"Thanks," she said. "Mind if I hang here until my shift starts and read through this?"

He grinned. Nick really was a good-looking guy. Too bad he had a bad track record with relationships. Then again, she had been dating a guy who had a prison record, so who was she to judge. Maybe she should finally take Nick up on his past offers and have dinner with him. As she opened the folder, though, she pictured Shane, not Nick, sitting across from her at a restaurant. She started reading before she began imagining more than dinner with Shane—comforting him, holding him, loving his body. With a sigh, she focused on the report.

Thirty minutes and a cup of coffee later, she closed the file and set it on Nick's desk. "Thanks again. I've got to meet up with Ricky and get to work."

"If I clear it with your sergeant, how do you feel about following up on Dustin's alibis for us?" Nick asked. "Like I said, Jerry and I have a few leads we want to check."

Daily patrol grew boring after a while, and she loved when she and Ricky were given these types of assignments. "Sounds great. We'll start with his friend, Joshua Kidd." She jotted down the man's name and last known address, the name and address of the strip bar they'd been at last night, along with the pet cremation service where Dustin claimed to have received the animal remains. "I'm curious…if everything checks out, I would think Dustin would be cited for *something*. I get he was afraid to come forward, but he'd admitted to dealing drugs and to giving those three victims' families urns containing animal remains."

"We were hoping the ADA planned to charge him with something, too. While you were reading the file, I just got a call from her and she said Dustin lawyered up and is willing to give us the name of his drug supplier in exchange for immunity."

Although having information on a dealer was good, she still wanted Dustin to be held accountable. The victims' families deserved to have some justice, especially if they never caught the person who had been behind the abuse of their loved ones.

"Better get used to the BS plea deals. Depending on what type of law you go into after you graduate, you're going to run into this kind of crap all the time."

Lovely. She stood. "I gotta go. We'll call you and Jerry once we have something."

"Sounds good, but don't forget that you two get to write up the report," he said with a smile, and picked up the phone.

Crap. She hated writing reports. They were tedious and boring, even if they were necessary. "I'll write mine in glitter."

As Nick chuckled, she walked off to meet with Ricky. When she caught up with her partner and told him what Nick and Jerry wanted them to do, Ricky was excited. For whatever reason, he loved questioning people. Twenty minutes later, they knocked on the door of Joshua Kidd's condo.

When he didn't answer, Ricky pounded harder. "His car's here," he said. "How much do you want to bet he's sleeping off a night of boozing."

"Dustin said he deals weed, ecstasy and mushrooms. Could be the X that—"

"Comin'," a man shouted, then opened the door. Joshua stood in the threshold wearing nothing but a pair of briefs. He looked at their uniforms, then shook his head. "I didn't do anything wrong."

"Who says you did? Joshua Kidd, right?" Ricky asked.

He nodded. "That's right."

"We just want to ask you a few questions."

Joshua glanced over his shoulder. "I've got someone here."

"So?"

"So I don't want her to know I'm talking to the police."

"Did you at least let her sleep in your bed?" Beth asked. "We'll promise to keep our voices down."

With a sigh and a nod, Joshua let them inside. The condo was modern and clean. It also had the type of tile flooring she'd been considering for her place once she had the extra cash. "What's this about?" he asked, then picked up a can of Mountain Dew off the coffee table.

Ricky glanced around the room. "You're friends with Dustin Williams, correct?"

"Yeah, why?" He shook his head and slumped into a dark-brown leather chair. "Oh, shit. Is he okay? You're not here to tell me something happened to him, are you? He was supposed to come back here last night and never showed."

"Where were you and Dustin last night?" Ricky asked.

He shrugged. "Me and Dustin had wings and beers at Ironwood Grille, then later we went to Bare Bone."

"The strip club?" Ricky asked.

"Yeah." Joshua looked over his shoulder before facing them again. "My girlfriend doesn't know," he whispered.

"As long as you cooperate, she doesn't have to," Beth said. "Dustin was supposed to go to Miami Wednesday afternoon with you. What happened?"

"Don't know. He said he'd scored courtside seats for the Miami Heat game. I didn't get too excited about it because he's fed me the same kind of crap in the past."

"Meaning?"

"Look, I've known Dustin since we were kids. His parents have money. His grandpa has even more. Sometimes he comes through with his promises, other times he doesn't."

"If you didn't go to the game, what happened to the tickets?" Ricky asked.

"Dustin said he had to sell them."

"Because?" Ricky prompted.

"Don't know. He never said. To make up for it, he took me to Bare Bone and paid for everything."

"Did Dustin talk to you about his father's arrest?" she asked.

Joshua ran a hand though his hair. "That's messed-up shit. *I* brought it up when he didn't. But all he said was he didn't want to talk about it."

"What do you know about his side business?" Ricky asked.

"Side business?"

"We know he sells drugs," Beth said. "Dustin claims you had a couple of buyers for him Tuesday night."

"Am I going to get busted for this? I mean, I don't use, I just hook some people up with Dustin now and then."

"I wouldn't encourage you to hook anyone up, but no, we're not here to bust you. We're interested in Tuesday night."

Joshua nodded, then told them about the two drug deals that had taken place that night. His story matched Dustin's. "I thought it was messed up that he brought the body van with him." He shrugged. "But I guess if you hang with the dead enough…"

"So Dustin didn't tell you what happened to him after he took the bodies to the crematory?"

"Nope. I assumed he ended up staying at work, since he was supposed to meet me and a couple of other guys out later that night."

"You said Dustin planned to come back to your condo last night. Why did you two split up?" Ricky asked.

Joshua glanced between the two of them. "Again, I don't deal, Dustin does."

Ricky nodded. "We got it. So what happened?"

"Last night, Dustin ended up BS-ing with a couple of guys. They seemed cool, bought us a couple of drinks and then a lap dance for us and them. When we were getting ready to leave, Dustin tells me the two guys want to buy some weed from him. His stash was back at his apartment and the guys offered to drive him there, then drop him off at my place when the deal was done." Joshua shook his head and let out a sigh. "I was drunk and shouldn't have been driving. Looking back, I should've never let Dustin go with those guys. They were cops, weren't they? Is that how you found out about the drugs?"

She shifted her gaze to her partner, who kept his focus on Joshua. "Can you describe the men?"

"Yeah, one was tall. I'm talking, like, six-five or six-six. Blond with a Russian accent. The other guy was about my height, late twenties or early thirties and had brown hair."

Son of a bitch. Beth didn't flinch, but seethed on the inside. "Did you get their names or see what they were driving?"

"Russian guy's name was Ivan. The other guy went by Nico. I didn't see their car. Dustin walked off with them into the back parking lot and I was parked on the street." Joshua stood. "So were those guys cops?"

"That's all for now," Ricky said. "Thanks for your time."

"Wait," he called as they were walking out the door. "You were asking about Tuesday night. Did Dustin have something to do with those ladies they found in the woods?"

"Thanks again," Ricky said. Once they were in the cruiser and driving out of the condominium complex, he glanced at her. "What'd you make of Ivan and Nico?"

"Not sure," she lied. If she hadn't seen Shane and Lola outside of the ME's last night, she wouldn't have given them much thought. Since she had, and since Dustin had turned himself in at around five this morning, she suspected Vlad and Harry had something to do with Dustin's confession. Granted, Vlad probably wasn't the only gigantic Russian living in the area, but what were the chances of Joshua and Dustin meeting up with a man who fit Vlad's description? Why or how the four of them had anything to do with the investigation, she didn't know. She could tell Ricky her suspicions, but didn't want to until she had a few answers first. Shane had been out of prison for a short time. She might not owe him anything, and they might not be dating, but she hated to draw attention to him and be the reason he ended up back in prison. She could be wrong about Vlad and Harrison. As for Shane and Lola, again, it could be as simple as they had a connection to a family member who'd been brought to the morgue.

Now she was lying to herself. There were too many

coincidences where the four airboat company employees were concerned.

"When we stop at the strip club, we'll ask about Ivan and Nico," Ricky said, and made a turn. "Maybe they were looking to score, or maybe they knew who Dustin was and encouraged him to step forward."

"Dustin made no mention of the Russian and his friend during his interview with Nick and Jerry. But I agree. It wouldn't hurt to ask about them." Then she'd discourage Ricky from following up on the two men until she found out whether Ivan and Nico were really Vlad and Harrison.

And she knew exactly who to go to for answers.

Shane's House, Everglades City, Florida
Saturday, 5:22 p.m., Eastern Standard Time

Beth pulled her SUV into Shane's gravel driveway, then parked and killed the ignition. Her belly filled with a swarm of nervous butterflies. She couldn't help it. Yesterday morning, they were—in her mind—still dating, and she'd been foolishly hoping they'd continue to date and maybe take their relationship to a more physical level. His text had changed that. Finding out he'd murdered a man obviously hadn't helped, either. Now she needed to discover what he and the others were up to.

Except a part of her didn't want to know. After reading through Shane's docket sheet and learning more about his case and conviction, along with the man he'd killed, she still didn't think he was a bad person. Just a man in the wrong place at the wrong time. That, of course, didn't negate the fact that he had served seven years in prison and had a record. It also didn't refute her feelings for him.

She rubbed a hand along her forehead. Maybe she should have called him first to give him a heads-up that she needed to talk with him. The memory of him exiting the ME's had her opening the car door. No, this was the right move. Besides, this wasn't about them.

Or was it?

She'd withheld information about the Russian going by the name of Ivan, along with his counterpart, Nico, from her report. She hadn't mentioned her suspicions to Nick or even Ricky, who she trusted with her life. She wanted to believe Shane and Lola were next of kin, and that Ivan and Nico weren't Vlad and Harrison. Damn it. She wanted Shane to be a normal guy so she could still date him.

With a sigh, she continued up the driveway. As she walked past Shane's truck, she heard chains clanking, along with a male grunt. Curious, she followed the sounds and made her way into the carport. As she rounded the corner toward the back of the house, she came to an abrupt stop and sucked in a breath. Shane, shirtless, a sheen of sweat glistening along his tanned skin, was beating the hell out of a long boxing bag hanging from the ceiling. His chest was better than what she'd fantasized it would be. Smooth and toned, he had a set of pecs she'd love to hang onto as she rode him. She drifted her gaze to his abs. My God, they were ridiculous. Maybe it was a good thing they'd never ended up in bed together. He was so hard and lean, he made her regret skipping her daily run—for the past three days—and eating one of the brownies Ricky's wife had packed in today's lunch. And his arms…each punch he delivered revealed every single muscle, and had her imagining running her hands along his thick biceps or holding onto them as he filled her.

She cleared her throat before her fantasies took over, or he caught her gawking at him. He stopped punching and grabbed the bag before it hit him. His gaze drifted from her running shoes, to her black capri leggings, then over her tank top before meeting her eyes.

"Evenin', officer," he said, his eyes holding a strange combination of hunger and suspicion.

"As you can see, I'm off duty."

He glanced to her breasts. "I can definitely see that," he

said, let go of the bag, then removed his boxing gloves. "How did you know where to find me?"

"I used the plates from your truck to get your address." Now she really did look like a stalker. "We need to talk, and I didn't want to do it over the phone."

He picked up a towel and began wiping the sweat from his hard body. "About?"

She swallowed and took a step forward. "Not us. Your text was perfectly clear."

He grabbed a water bottle. As he unscrewed the cap, he moved toward her. "All I said was that I couldn't make it for dinner."

She glanced around the carport. "Right. Because you had plans last night and tonight. I can see you're very busy."

He took a couple more steps, until only a foot or so separated them. "I thought you said this visit wasn't about us," he said, taking a drink from the bottle.

"It's not. You don't want to date me. I get it."

"I never said that in my text."

"You might as well have." Before the conversation completely derailed, she added, "I know why you don't want to see me."

He drained the rest of the water bottle, then crushed the plastic in his hand. "What do you know?" he asked, his eyes filling with curiosity and maybe shame.

Her mind and heart raced with indecision. It didn't help that he stood too close. That she could easily reach out and run her hands along his chest.

Focus, Beth.

Right. What did she know? Too much and not enough. She didn't want to dredge up his past or hurt him, but she wanted answers. She needed him to stay out of trouble. If he was doing something illegal, he could wind up back in prison. She couldn't imagine being incarcerated in the first place. But to have a short taste of freedom, only to be locked away again, would be a miserable fate.

Hoping to slow her heart rate, she drew in a deep breath. "I know you spent the past seven years in prison. What I don't know is why you and Lola were at the Medical Examiner's last night, or why Vlad and Harrison left a strip club with the son of a man accused of abusing three corpses. Any chance you can enlighten me?"

CHAPTER 10

SHANE WANTED TO punch the hell out of the bag again. He'd ended their relationship because Beth was a cop and he was an ex-con. He'd done it in a way so she wouldn't have to know about his time in prison or what had put him there. Having Beth think of him as the dick who'd dumped her had been more appealing to him than her knowing he was a murderer.

Damn it. He wanted to ignore her question, throw her over his shoulder, put her back in her car and tell her to never come around again. He wanted to be an asshole and treat her like shit. But he couldn't. He didn't want to hurt her more than he already had. Then again, she'd have to care about him to feel any kind of hurt. Had she? He'd like to think so because he sure as hell cared.

And how in the hell was he supposed to focus on her question when all he wanted to do was drag her inside, strip her clothes from her sexy body and sink himself inside her? "I think you should leave," he said before he made good on what he wanted, and wound up with a broken nose or a knee to the groin. He'd noticed the way she'd stared at his chest, and he'd been turned on by the heat in her gaze. But she wasn't here looking to hook up with him. No matter how hot and sweet she was, or that her perfume drove him crazy with the need to taste her, she was a cop, and he'd do well to remember that.

"No answer?" Beth asked.

He and the rest of ATL could be screwed if he didn't rein this in and keep Beth in the dark. Unfortunately, she was dead on and already knew more than she should. He'd have to play dumb and find a way to make her leave.

He stepped away from her tempting body. As he walked toward the door leading into the house, he tossed the water bottle into the recycling can. "Sorry. What was the question?"

She folded her arms across her chest, which only drew his attention to her breasts. He'd touched them, had rubbed his thumb across her hard nipples. "Cut the crap," she said. "You know exactly what I asked you. And stop staring at my boobs."

"I wasn't." He leaned against the door. "Even if I was, it'd only be fair."

"Because?"

"You were staring at my chest."

Her face flushed. "No, I wasn't."

"Sure you were. I'm not complaining, and you shouldn't complain about me staring at your boobs. They're nice."

"You're such a jerk," she said, dropped her arms and walked toward him. "I don't want to talk about your chest or my boobs. I want to know why you and Lola were at the ME's."

"First, you brought up your boobs, not me."

"Would you stop?"

He held up a hand. "Second, I don't know what you're talking about. I was at my brother's helping him hang kitchen cabinets and Lola was there bossing us around."

"Interesting, because the Honda Pilot I saw had a license plate registered to Lola Tam. I don't know how many Asian women named Lola are living in the area, but I find it rather coincidental that *you* happen to be connected to one."

"One what?"

"You're a smart guy. Playing stupid isn't working for you. If you'd rather not tell me, then I'll go ask Lola."

Before she turned away, he snagged her arm. "We weren't there. Even if we were, what would it matter? Or is this *harassment* what you do whenever a guy breaks up with you?"

"You're a jerk for even suggesting something so stupid." She yanked her arm free, then shoved him in the chest. "We'd have to be in a relationship to have a break-up, and you're the first guy I've…never mind. This is a waste of time."

He stepped in front of her, blocking her path. "I'm the first guy you've what?" he asked, dying to know. Cared about? Why did he want to know? Why torture himself over a woman he couldn't have?

"You're the first guy I've gone on a second date with in years. Damn it, Shane. I like you. I get why you didn't want to see me again and, as bad as this sounds, at least you have a valid excuse for not wanting to date a cop."

"Wait, guys wouldn't date you when they found out what you do for a living?" What a bunch of dumbasses. If circumstances had been different, he'd be proud to be with Beth. She was smart, had goals and he bet she even looked hot in an ugly cop uniform.

She nodded. "And for the record, I didn't use my badge to find out about your background. When I saw you last night, I thought you might be DEA, ATF or work for some other agency. After I got home, I did a quick Internet search and saw articles about your trial. I looked up your docket sheet and read through the case file. It's crap that you were sentenced to seven years and served every one of them."

He grabbed her by the upper arms and hauled her closer. "Ever kill anyone?" he asked, not sure if she was playing him to gain answers to her questions or if she actually held sympathy for him.

She blinked. "No. Thankfully I've never had to discharge my weapon in the line of duty."

"I have."

"That was an obvious accident. You didn't go into that bar with murder on you mind."

"No, I didn't. But when I was in the Army, there were

missions that hadn't gone well and I was forced to do what was necessary. I killed men—don't know how many, who they were or if they had families who would miss them. I know there's a difference between killing in combat and what I did to that man in the bar, but either way I feel guilty about it. Every single day."

"If you didn't feel remorse, then I'd think there was something wrong with you," she said, and gripped his biceps. "The man you killed, do you know about his background?"

He knew all about Theodore 'Ted' Nowak. In a way, he might've done the world a favor by ending his life. At the rate Nowak was going, it was only a matter of time before his violent behavior led to someone's death. "I know enough."

"Did you know he was carrying a concealed weapon that night? A knife was strapped to his ankle, and a gun was found hooked to his belt. He'd also been arrested for domestic violence and had served four years for rape."

"I know all of that, but it doesn't make what I did right, even if he took the first swing." He let go of her and moved back to the door. "Look, I appreciate that you're not judging me for what I've done, but it doesn't change the fact that you're a cop and I'm an ex-con. For whatever it's worth, I had a great time with you and I'm sorry you had to find out about me the way you did." With a final glance, he turned and headed inside. She pushed through the door before he could close it. He quickly crowded her in the narrow hallway and used his size to try to intimidate her. "Go home, Beth. If you don't leave, maybe I'll call the cops and have you arrested for trespassing and harassment."

"I dare you," she said, her eyes holding challenge as a small smug smile tilted her mouth. "While they're here taking your statement, I'll be sure to have them ask why you were outside the ME's with Lola last night. Then I'll call the detectives who are working the investigation you and your friends seem so interested in, and have them look into Vlad and Harrison's backgrounds. While they're at it, Lola's, too."

He pushed her against the door, slamming it shut. "That

would be a really bitchy thing to do. And a serious mistake."

Her breath hitched and her gaze drifted to his mouth, then his chest. "Are you threatening me?"

The hunger and desire in her eyes drove him crazy and had his dick hardening. Damn, she smelled good and it amazed him how much he wanted her. She was nosing around in his business and trying to bully him into telling her something that could cost Harrison and Vlad their freedom. Harrison had a felony record, too. If his participation in last night's kidnapping and hacking into the Sheriff's Office's computer system were discovered, he'd go back to prison. During the drive to the ME's, Lola had given him more information on Vlad. The man was wanted by the Russian government, Interpol and practically every U.S. government agency out there. If caught, Vlad wouldn't just go to prison, he'd go to Death Row.

Not wanting to think about what could happen to Vlad or Harrison, or even himself, he ignored the way her scent turned him on and inched closer. "Yeah, I'm threatening you. Stay out of my business. If you don't, you could hurt a lot of people." Like his brother, Barney and Mel. Since they were all present during Dustin's questioning, they could all be screwed.

"Fine. Then I'll back off."

He slid his hand into her hair, and messed up her ponytail when he gripped the back of her head. "Liar." Aching to kiss her, he inched closer. "You should have never come here, and when you had the chance, you should've left. You know about me and that should have had you running scared."

"You know about me. That should have you wanting to be honest. I haven't told anyone I saw you last night or about Vlad or Harrison." She cupped his jaw and ran her thumb along his beard. "I don't want to see you go back to prison. Please. Just tell me the truth."

God, when she looked at him like that, her hazel eyes imploring, understanding and sympathetic, he wanted to tell her everything. It wasn't his call, though, it was Lola's. Only Lola wasn't here.

He didn't know what to do. Part of him wanted to tell her

the truth, the other part wanted to wait until he had the okay from the rest of the group. He liked and trusted Beth. If she'd wanted to cause trouble for him, she would have already let someone she worked with know that he and Lola weren't where they were supposed to be last night. Same went for Vlad and Harrison.

"Just tell me," she repeated.

He loved the way she was touching his face. Their bodies were only inches apart. If he moved a little closer, her breasts would be against his chest. A little closer still, and she'd definitely know she had him hot for her.

He slid his gaze to her mouth, remembered the feel of her lips against his. How hungry she'd been for him the other night. How he'd gone home alone and wallowed in what couldn't be. But she was here now and he wanted her. Badly.

"It'll cost you," he said, and inched closer.

Her sexy mouth curved in a small smile. "You really are a jerk."

He took another step forward, caging her against the door. "And I really did want to come over for dinner last night."

She slid her hand from his face and into his hair. "I really wanted you to come over, too."

"Until you found out about me," he said, tossing cold water on a hot moment to give her time to push away from him. He didn't want her to, but he also wasn't a total bastard.

"Of course I was upset. You lost so many years."

He fisted her ponytail. "I murdered a man. You're a cop. *That's* what should upset you."

"No, what upsets me is that I found the man I want and I can't have him."

Want, not wanted. That Beth could still want him after what she knew about him was humbling. She was too good for him. He should do the right thing, stop touching her and kick her out of his house. He didn't want to. He angled his head closer to hers, close enough her breath touched his lips. "If you don't leave, I'm going to kiss you."

"Is that another threat?"

"One I plan to make good on."

"Then we have a problem. I'm not leaving until you answer my questions."

He pressed his body against hers, forcing her back to the door. "I warned you," he said, then crushed his mouth against hers. She immediately parted her lip and he took advantage. Fuck going slow. This time around he needed to leave little doubt in her mind as to what he wanted from her. He wanted her to be his. He needed to matter to her.

As he deepened the kiss, he knocked her ponytail free. He loved her hair and wanted it down. He'd love to see all those brown waves spread out on his pillow, but wouldn't push his luck. He would take advantage of having her here and in his arms, though. The opportunity to hold her again might not happen after today, and he wasn't one to waste a tempting opportunity.

He moved his hands down her body, along her breasts and waist, then over her hips. Grabbing her ass with both hands, he lifted her. When she twined her arms around his neck, he stepped away from the door. Keeping his lips seared to hers, he carried her into the living room and lay her on the couch. Her running shoe dug into his rear when she wrapped a leg around him. He didn't care, but for what he planned to do to her, she'd have to lose them.

As he trailed open-mouthed kisses along her throat, he began sliding her tank top up her stomach. "You can still leave," he murmured against her soft skin.

"Not until you tell me the truth," she said, her voice breathless.

Using his arm to brace himself above her, he pushed her tank top higher, revealing her lacy bra. He ran his hand over her breasts and down her bare stomach. "Still time," he said when he reached the waistband of her pants.

She ran her hand along his arm and shoulder, then into his hair. "Not leaving," she said, then she sucked in a breath when he slipped his hand beneath her panties and dipped his fingers into her heat. Warm, soft and wet, she made him so damned hard. As much as he'd love to shove her pants down and replace his fingers with his dick, he wouldn't. Beth deserved better than a quick fuck. He did, too. He might be able to make her his right now, but what about tomorrow or the next day? He was tired of living in his head, tired of fantasizing. He wanted his fantasies to become reality.

Her breath quickened as he pressed his fingers deeper, moved them faster. He looked to her exposed bra and wished he'd taken the time to move the lace aside so he could see her nipples, then he met her gaze. The desire in her eyes made his chest ache. If only he could see that desire every day.

Loving the pleasure crossing her pretty face, yet wanting more, he removed his hand from her sex and rested his knee on the area rug. After brushing his lips against hers, he kissed his way down her body, and tugged her pants and panties over her hips. With her clothes around her ankles, her shoes stopping them from coming off completely, he ducked his head until the material locked him between her legs. He ran his hands along her legs and lifted her rear slightly.

"I'm going to taste you." He kissed her inner thigh. "You could tell me to stop, and then leave."

She moved to one elbow and sifted her hand through is hair. "I'm not going anywhere," she said, then directed his head to her sex.

He loved a woman who knew what she wanted. If he wasn't careful, he could end up loving this woman. As it was, he was already crazy about her.

Keeping his gaze locked on hers, he refused to consider the emotional impact that would likely ensue once Beth left his house, and ran his tongue along her smooth labia. Her shoes dug into his back as she shifted and arched her body. When he spread her lips and kissed her like he'd kissed her mouth, she groaned, shoved both hands in his hair, pulling it away from his face. It had been so damned long since he'd tasted a woman. But Beth wasn't just any woman to him.

In his mind, she wasn't a cop and he wasn't an ex-con. Strip away the labels, and they could be good together. He'd deal with that impossibility after she left him. Right now, her pleasure was his only concern.

He drew her clit between his lips and slipped two fingers inside her. Her inner thighs trembled as he pumped his fingers and licked and sucked her clit. Her breath came in rapid pants. Her grip on his head, tighter. "Don't stop," she said between breaths, then dug her heels into his back and let out a harsh moan.

As she came, he tasted heaven. Now that he'd had a taste, he wasn't sure he could let her walk away without a fight. But it wasn't his fight. He wasn't the one who had a job that frowned upon dating murderers.

He eased his fingers from her, then kissed her inner thighs.

"Oh, my God," she said with a smile, and closed her eyes. "That was—oh, my God." She opened her eyes and pushed herself upright, then swung her legs off the couch, knocking him to the floor. "I'm sorry." She helped him remove his head out from under her pants, then quickly stood, hiking the material up her sexy legs.

"What's the problem?" he asked, rubbing his shoulder where it had connected with the coffee table.

Beth tugged her tank top back in place. "You," she said. What the hell had she been thinking? She hadn't, she'd let her body do the thinking and now she had to deal with the repercussions. "All you had to do was tell me what you and Lola were doing at the ME's and then I would have left."

"I gave you plenty of opportunities to leave. You're the one who stuck around. I didn't hear you complaining between moans."

"It was a little hard to leave when you were touching me and...you know."

"Going down on you? Yeah, I do know. I'm still more than a little hard."

Guilt gave her a little shove. He'd given her a fantastic orgasm and ended up with nothing in return. "Sorry I'm the only one who came out ahead."

"No pun intended," he said, and cracked a smile. "Don't

worry about it. I wouldn't have had sex with you anyway."

"Why not?" If she hadn't gained control of her body, they *would* be having sex.

He shrugged. "I need to shower."

"Right. Well, thank you for being hygienically thoughtful." She fixed her ponytail. "So, do you plan on answering my questions?"

"No," he said, and stood.

His athletic shorts did little to hide his erection, and she now wished she hadn't come to her senses. She might have just had an orgasm, but she wanted another.

"Then I'll go talk to Lola and ask her."

"No, you won't. I told you to stay out of our business."

"Okay, then I won't." She took a few steps toward the hallway leading to the carport. "Thanks for…" She cleared her throat. "Bye, Shane."

He stopped her before she could reach the hallway. "Thanks and bye? That's all you have to say? If I didn't know any better, I'd think you were a guy." He took her hand and drew her close to him. "Am I going to see you again?"

"Only if I find out what you're doing is illegal."

The disappointment in his eyes made her heart speed up a notch. She didn't want this to be a permanent good-bye, but as long as she was a cop, she couldn't date him.

"Then maybe I'll rob a bank." He lifted her hand. "Feel what you do to me."

Oh, God. "Shane, stop. I already know. Your shorts gave me quite the view."

"I wouldn't complain if you wanted to touch me there." He smiled and pressed her hand against his chest. "But this is what I want you to feel."

Beneath her palm, his heart raced as fast as hers. She met his gaze. The longing in his eyes had her throat tightening. Sweet, smart and sexy, she could fall even harder for this man and didn't want to walk away. But what choice did she have? Even though she wouldn't be a cop forever, she would soon be an attorney, and she suspected that any law firm she applied to would frown over one of their attorneys dating a murderer.

"We just met," she said, and blinked back the tears misting her eyes.

"I don't care."

"A month from now you won't even remember my name."

He cupped her face. "What if I want to be with you a month from now?"

"We can't."

After kissing her forehead, he took a step back. "I know, and it wasn't fair to suggest dating. I don't want you to lose your job because of me."

"It has nothing to do with my job. Yeah, it would be a problem, but who I date is my business." She moved forward and pressed a finger against his chest. "I can't be with a man who doesn't trust me. And I'm not—is that your snake?" she asked, and moved her finger from his chest to point it across the room.

"Yes. She's a ball python. Her name's Henrietta. Okay, so you're telling me that if I answer your questions, you'll date me."

"No," she said, still staring at the snake. "I said I wouldn't date a man who doesn't trust me." She met his gaze. "Are you an expert on snakes? Is that why you were at the ME's?"

"I don't know what you're talking about."

"Would you stop lying to me? You had to have heard about the three bodies we found yesterday, and how the ME found snakes in the women," she said, sticking with the misinformation the reporter had given viewers. If Shane and Lola hadn't been up to anything illegal or covert, she wasn't about to reveal information kept from the public.

"Yeah, I heard about it. Sick stuff."

"Did you know one of the victims?"

"No."

"Were you at the ME's as a consultant?"

"No."

"Here's another reason why we wouldn't work—I don't date liars."

As she turned away, he grabbed her arm. "I'm not lying. I don't know the victims and I wasn't there as a consultant."

"So you *do* admit to being there."

"Yeah, just to get you to stop interrogating me."

"Why were you there?"

"Is Thomas Williams still in custody?" he asked.

"No. His son came in early this morning and…oh, my God. Vlad and Harrison forced him to confess, didn't they?"

"Does it matter? An innocent man is free."

Dumbfounded she stared at him. "Do you work for a private investigator? Did someone hire you to prove he was innocent?"

"Something like that."

"And Lola, Vlad and Harrison work for this same investigation agency?"

He nodded. "We didn't do anything illegal."

Although relieved, she still had a hard time believing that any investigation agency would hire a man with a felony record. Shane couldn't even carry a gun, and how was it that he'd been hired on so quickly after his release from prison?

"What's the name of the agency?"

"That's confidential."

She rolled her eyes. "No, that's bull." She shook her arm free. "I'm leaving. One more thing. You guys helped set an innocent man free, do you plan on finding out who abused those corpses?"

"I'm done with the interrogation." He crossed his arms over his chest. "If you don't like it, you know your way out."

"Nice. So much for the crap about how you want to be with me."

"It's not crap," he said, his tone filling with irritation. "You're the one who threatened to not date me if I didn't tell you the truth. I told you what you wanted to know, but it's still not enough. You're probably going to leave here and go talk to Lola anyway, aren't you?" When she didn't answer, he swore under his breath. "So much for the trust factor." He dropped his arms. "See you around, Beth. I'll text you some time."

"Don't bother," she said, then rushed down the hall. He was dead right. She *was* going to talk to Lola, not because she didn't believe him, and not because there were holes in his story. Nick and Jerry were making their murder investigation top priority, and she'd worried that what had happened to the dead women would turn into a cold case now that Senator Bryan's name was no longer attached to it. She didn't want that to happen, and she didn't like the similarity between this case and Katie Reed's. If Lola, Shane or anyone else involved with this agency had leads she and Ricky could work with, maybe Nick and Jerry would change their priorities, or, at the very least, let her and Ricky take a stab at the case.

"Beth, wait," Shane called.

She stopped a few feet from her car, but didn't turn around. He was right and she didn't want to face him. She'd thrown the trust card at him, then had gone against her own convictions by planning to pay a visit to Lola anyway.

"If you want to see Lola, I'll take you."

"Why?"

"Just trust me on this." He sighed. "Come back inside. Let me take a quick shower, then we'll head over."

She finally turned around. "Should I be afraid of Lola?" she asked, and followed him inside.

"No, she's sweet."

"Okay, so she's sweet. But does she have an issue with cops?"

He shrugged and started down the hallway where she assumed the bedrooms and bathrooms were located. "There's water and soda in the fridge. Help yourself."

"Wait, you didn't answer my question," she said, just as he stepped in a room and closed the door. She was growing tired of having her questions ignored, but was happy Shane had offered to go with her to see Lola. If the woman did have an issue with cops, he'd be there to smooth things over. She couldn't see there being a problem, though. After all, they were on the same side of the law.

Ryan and Lola's House, Everglades City, Florida
Saturday, 6:52 p.m., Eastern Standard Time

Lola stood near the canal running along the back of their house and watched as the sun slowly dipped below the horizon. She dragged in a deep breath, then shivered slightly. Ten minutes ago, she'd been hot and sweaty from her daily workout. Now that the sun had gone down and the breeze had kicked up, she was chilled and could use a warm shower. Preferably with Ryan.

As she walked back into the house, she finished draining her water bottle. When she entered, Sadie greeted her at the door. She gave the dog some love, then asked, "How're you doing, sweetie?"

"I'm just fine, thanks for asking," Ryan said, and wiped his hands on a rag.

She gave Sadie a quick scratch behind the ears, then approached her fiancé. "You're not jealous of the dog, are you?"

"Since her only job is to look cute, and I've been working hard on your backsplash, I think I deserve more attention than Sadie."

She eyed the glass subway tiles. "Wow, this looks great. I was worried it might not work with the countertop." She leaned toward him and ran her fingers into his hair. "What a good boy you are."

Chuckling, he grabbed her hand and pinned her against the counter. "I also think I deserve more than a pat on the head."

She twined her arms around his neck. "I agree. Why don't you call it a night and come take a shower with me?"

"I love that idea," he said, and kissed her.

A knock came at the door just as he deepened the kiss. When he showed no intention of allowing them to be interrupted, she tapped his back.

"They'll go away," he said, and ran his hand over her breast.

The knock came harder. "Are you sure about that?"

He sighed and took a step back. "We're finishing this."

"Absolutely. See if you can get rid of whoever it is and meet me in the shower." As she walked toward their bedroom, Shane's voice carried down the hall, then Ryan called her. Damn it. She wanted shower sex, then snuggle-time on the couch. "Coming," she answered, then headed back toward the living room.

Shane was in their small foyer, patting Sadie's head, a pretty woman standing next to him. "Hi, Shane," she said.

"Hey, Lola. Sorry to drop by like this."

"No problem. We were just hanging out."

"Good." He placed his hand on the woman's lower back. "This is Beth Price."

Kiss Beth. Happy Shane and Beth had worked out after all, Lola smiled and shook Beth's hand. "Nice to meet you," she said. "Did you meet Ryan?"

"I did." Beth grinned. "I loved the airboat tours I went on at your place."

"Glad to hear," Ryan said. "So, what are you guys up to tonight?"

Shane pushed a hand through his hair. "I tried calling your phones to let you know we were coming over."

"My phone is on the charger in my room, and Ryan accidentally left his at the boat shop. And I told you it's no big deal. Can I get you two something to drink?"

"You should have a house phone," Shane began, "that way you wouldn't miss calls and I wouldn't be dropping by unexpectedly. What if there was an emergency?"

Lola grinned. "Is this an emergency?"

"Not really."

Beth cleared her throat. "I'm a Collier County deputy."

Lola's stomach soured. Son of a bitch, Shane was dating a cop. "Really? I bet you have some interesting stories to tell."

"Yeah, I also see plenty of interesting things." She glanced to Shane. "Don't be upset with Shane for bringing me to your house."

Lola shrugged. "Why would we be upset?" She looked toward their unfinished kitchen. "So, about that drink."

"Let me start by saying that I want what you want," Beth said.

"Which is?"

"To find out who dumped the corpses in the woods, and if the corpses are linked to Katie Reed's murder."

"I just moved down here a couple of months, but I do remember hearing something on the news about her. She was killed a couple of years ago, right?" It took everything in Lola's power to not look at Shane, and to stay polite. Had he told Beth about them? "I also heard they let Senator Bryan's son-in-law go."

"Lola, I saw you and Shane leaving the ME's last night," Beth said, then raised her hand, and quickly added, "I looked up the plates on your Honda Pilot, and know it was you there with Shane."

All of those years of acting classes and Lola's theater degree were about to pay off. She gave Beth a look of confusion. "That's not possible. I was here last night."

"Have you ever gone online and looked yourself up?"

"Why would I do that?" she asked, knowing as soon as they left she'd do just that. Technology played a major role in solving cases, but could be a problem when it came to personal information.

"I know your mom is Cami Carlyle, and that your dad was a stuntman. I also know that you majored in theater and even starred in small roles as a child. What I want to know is what *you* know about the three dead women we found yesterday."

Lola raised her brows. "I'm sorry, but accusing me of doing something I didn't do, looking up my plates, finding my info on the Internet…it's not only rude, but I can see this leading toward police harassment." She turned to Ryan. "Shane's right. We need to get a home phone. Nice meeting you, Beth," she said, then turned away.

"I *know* you were at the ME's."

She stopped and faced Beth. Today Ian had given her the go-ahead to continue their investigation and find the necrophiliac. This deputy was not going to screw with their first assignment.

"And I don't like having an uninvited guest coming into *my* house slinging false accusations," she said, taking a few steps toward the woman.

"I didn't want to resort to this, but would you rather meet at the Sheriff's Office and discuss this there? I could arrange to have the detectives working the case present. I'm sure they'd be interested in—"

"Hold up." Shane grabbed Beth by the elbow. "I didn't agree to any of this."

"Oh, my God," Lola gasped. "You didn't agree to what? Never mind. I want to talk to you privately."

"Screw that," he said. "You know, when I was in prison—"

"You told her?" she and Ryan asked at the same time.

"Internet," Beth responded.

"Beth knows all about it," Shane said. "She also knows we were at the ME's last night, and that Ivan and Nico were the last two people to be seen with Dustin before he turned himself into the police."

"Ivan and Nico?" Lola asked, and fought hard to hide her panic. "I don't know what you're talking about?"

"I know Ivan and Nico are Vlad and Harrison," Beth said. "I don't know how they got Dustin to talk, and I honestly don't care. An innocent man is free. But here's my concern— this case is going to go cold. This wasn't a murder, and while abuse of a corpse is nothing any cop would take lightly, murder, sexual assault and armed robbery will take precedence. I don't want that happening. Shane told me you work for a private investigator, but wouldn't give me the name of the agency." She held up a hand. "That's fine, and I don't care who you work for. But if you have information you could share to help make sure this case doesn't go cold, I would appreciate it."

How dare Shane tell this woman about them? "If I worked for an agency, I would be happy to offer up any information I could. But I don't. I'd like you to leave," she said, and turned away.

"Please don't blow me off," Beth said, and grabbed her arm.

Out of instinct, Lola quickly flipped her wrist, and latched onto Beth's forearm.

Beth smiled and let go of her arm. "Don't bother with the *jiu jitsu*. Unless you plan on hiding my body in a swamp, I suggest you let go of me and hear me out. I don't want to blow whatever cover you guys have, I just want help."

Oh, God. Had Shane told her what Mel had done? Yeah, they were going to have a *serious* talk. She released Beth. "If your detectives aren't making those women a priority, why are you?"

"Because my partner and I were the first on the scene for both Katie Reed's murder and the women found yesterday."

Damn it. She did not want to sympathize with this woman, but couldn't help herself. After viewing the photos taken at Katie Reed's crime scene, then her and Shane's visit with David, she imagined seeing the bodies had been tough.

"There has to be a connection," Beth continued. "We kept the information about the snake found inside Katie's stomach from the press."

"The reporter gave the wrong information," Lola said, then wished she'd kept her mouth shut, especially when Beth smiled.

"So the ME told you what he'd found sewn inside the women." She shrugged. "If you don't want to admit you were there, then don't. I already got the confirmation from Shane." She pulled out a business card. "My cell phone number is on the back. If you're interested in sharing info, give me a call." She turned to Shane. "I'm ready to go."

"What makes you think the necrophiliac is connected to Katie Reed's murder?" Lola asked, interested to hear what Beth knew. "Maybe you have a copycat."

Beth faced her. "A copycat who didn't do a very good job of copying. He went through the effort to try and make those women look similar to Katie, so why not use a live snake instead of shedding and eggs?"

"Or at least the shedding of a rattlesnake," Shane suggested.

Lola glared at Shane and willed him to keep his mouth shut until they could talk in private. She wanted to continue to be able to go to David for help on future cases. If Beth blabbed that the ME had given them pertinent information about an investigation, he could be in trouble. She didn't want trouble for him, or for them. She didn't want to see ATL dissolve after only one assignment.

"Maybe he couldn't get a rattler," Ryan said. "Florida requires a permit to own a venomous snake."

Beth nodded. "According to the Florida Fish and Wildlife Commission, to get a permit you're obligated to one thousand hours of verified experience with a venomous snake. Not that it could matter to the investigation. I doubt a murderer or necrophiliac would care if he's keeping a rattlesnake without the proper permit."

"During Katie's investigation, had detectives looked into people with those permits?" Lola asked.

"Florida Fish and Wildlife Commission gave us a short list of people who had permits to own rattlesnakes. We ran a background check on every one of them and found nothing that would suggest they'd been involved in Katie's murder."

"What kind of leads did you have?"

"After interviewing friends and family, none. If Dr. Adams didn't tell you, there were no fibers, hairs, fingerprints or DNA found on or near Katie's body."

"Who do you think leaked the snake evidence to the press?" Lola asked.

Beth shook her head. "You're asking a lot of questions, yet won't answer one of mine. If you'd like to continue this conversation, it needs to be two-sided."

Lola held up Beth's business card. "I'll call you sometime."

Beth rolled her eyes. "Right. I've heard that before. Thanks for your time. It was nice meeting you."

When Beth walked out the door, Shane lingered at the threshold. "I think we can trust her."

"Really?" Lola asked. "And what exactly were you thinking

with? Your brain or your—"

"Enough," Ryan said. "Maybe Shane's right. Beth could've told the people she works with about you and Shane being at the ME's, and about Vlad and Harrison being at the strip club, but she didn't." Ryan stepped over to her, and ran a hand along Lola's arm. "She could be an added source. It might not be a bad thing to have a deputy working with us."

Lola glanced to Shane. "Beth's waiting for you. I'll give this some thought. Be at the rental house at nine and we'll finish discussing this."

"Yes, ma'am," he said, then left.

Once the headlights of Shane's truck were no longer visible, she turned to Ryan. "How can we even consider working with Beth? Think about it. She might be throwing the whole 'we're on the same side' crap now, but what will happen when things go bad between her and Shane?" She rubbed the back of her neck where the tension was building. "I thought those two weren't seeing each other."

"That's what I thought, too."

She slumped on the sofa. "How am I going to handle this?"

Ryan sat next to her, then wrapped an arm around her shoulder. "Look, I know Shane and Beth took you by surprise, but I didn't like the way you talked to my brother."

"I'm sorry. I didn't mean to snap at him. You know I care about Shane."

"I do know that." He squeezed her close. "So, let's talk this out, and come up with a solution."

"Over a glass of wine?"

"Whatever it takes." He smiled. "I'll get us something to drink."

She stopped him. "That's okay. I'll take care of it. Beer or wine?"

"Beer works," he said, and gave her a kiss before she stood. "Lola, we'll figure out a plan, okay?"

She forced a smile and nodded, then went into the kitchen. She loved how rational and patient Ryan was, and how he could calm her down with a simple kiss. Unfortunately, what they now had to deal with wasn't so simple.

Ian had put her in charge, and she couldn't let her organization fall apart over a lovers quarrel. Barney, Mel, Ryan and her, they'd be okay. Her main concern was Vlad and Harrison. Beth could ruin them. If she opened her mouth and ATL wasn't prepared, Shane and Harrison could end up back in prison. As for Vlad, given how many government agencies wanted him, he wouldn't be looking at hard time, he'd be facing an executioner.

That wasn't going to happen on her watch.

CHAPTER 11

Everglades City, Florida
Saturday, 7:17 p.m., Eastern Standard Time

"I THOUGHT THAT went well," Shane said, as he drove them back to his place.

Beth glanced away from the passenger window and looked at him. "Absolutely. You're right about Lola. She's a *real* sweetie."

He grinned. "You just caught her on a bad night."

"I think I almost caught a fist to the face. You were right. It's definitely a good thing you went there with me, and I honestly don't blame her for the way she reacted. I'm a cop, and she doesn't know or trust me." She studied him for a second. "What did she say to you after I left?"

"That we'd discuss you tomorrow."

"That's it?"

"She might have mentioned that I wasn't thinking with my head, but something else."

Her cheeks grew warm as she remembered how he'd looked between her thighs, and then later, how evident his erection had been. "Again, how sweet."

His grin grew. "I don't care what Lola thinks about me or

you. You shouldn't either."

"Oh, I don't." If Lola didn't want to share information, then so be it. As a deputy, Beth could guarantee she had more resources available to her than any private investigation firm. "Is she your boss?"

"I don't work for anyone but paying customers."

"How is it that you have paying customers when you were just released?" she asked, then immediately regretted the question. She didn't want to keep going back and forth with the cop and ex-con issue. Plus, they were already on Shane's street, and she needed to go home and mull over everything that had gone on from the moment she'd seen Shane knocking the crap out of the punching bag. "Never mind. It's none of my business."

"It's a legit question that I don't mind answering. I might've avoided some truths, but I never lied to you. You've been in my plane—which I own outright—so you know I'm a pilot. Before prison, it's like I told you. I had my own business and would take people on tours over the Glades, or fly them to Miami or the Keys. I plan to do it again, and am just waiting on the rest of my permits to come in so I can get the business back up and running. I didn't lie about what I did in the Army, either."

"I never said I didn't believe you, and I didn't mean to put you on the defensive."

"You didn't. I just want to be clear." He pulled into his driveway, then parked the truck. "I had it going on before Norfolk," he said when he faced her. "Business was good. I had a nice house, a sweet motorcycle, money in the bank."

"You don't have to tell me this."

He reached over and touched her face. "Maybe I want you to know that at one point I was more than an ex-con. I worked hard and was proud of who I was. Maybe I want you to think of me as more than just a felon."

Her throat tightened. She cleared it and laid her hand over his. "I already do, and I'm proud of you for going full force to do what it takes to get your life back on track. After seven years away, I imagine you had and still have a lot of adjusting to do."

He gave her a smile that bordered on boyish. "I was nervous during our first date. Getting used to being in public, using regular utensils and plates…I was afraid I was going to make a fool of myself. But you made it easy to forget."

God, she hadn't considered the things she took for granted, like metal forks and steak knives, or being able to drink from a cup made of glass. "Did you have trouble driving or flying?"

"Driving wasn't too bad, flying wasn't either. I had a moment or two of panic when I first got in my plane, but I also hired an instructor to be with me just in case my memory wasn't all there. Bet you're glad you're hearing this now, and not before I took you flying."

She smiled. "I trusted you then, and I honestly trust you now. I doubt you would have put either of us in danger, if you weren't confident you could fly."

His grin faded. The muted lights on the dashboard did little to reveal any emotion in his eyes. "Other than being released from prison, the evening I spent with you flying, then going to dinner, was the best day I'd had in over seven years. I'm sorry I wasn't upfront with you."

Before she could respond, he moved away, then opened the truck's door. She did the same, climbed out and met him by her car. "Do you want to come in?" he asked. "I'm not much of a cook, but I have a stocked refrigerator if you're hungry, or I can order a pizza."

She wanted to stay. She wanted to finish what they'd started on the couch. She wanted to raid his refrigerator and spend hours talking to Shane and learning more about him. What would be the point? She already liked him too much. Spending more time with him, becoming physically involved would only make it harder for her to walk away from him. And she would walk away from him. Her future career and her current job were important to her. Shane could become important to her, too, and she never wanted to be placed in a position where she had to choose between what she'd worked so hard for and him.

"Thanks, but I should get home. It's been a long day."

The porch light cast shadows along his face as he stared at her. "So is this when you tell me you'll text me sometime?"

She looked to the gravel. "Thanks again for taking me to see Lola. If she changes her mind, maybe we'll see each other again soon."

"We don't need Lola for that. If *you* change your mind, you know how to reach me," he said, then ran his hand along her arm.

She stepped back and dug into her purse for her keys. She wasn't a mind reader, but they'd had two serious make-out sessions against her car. While she'd love another, it would only make walking away that much harder. "I'm sorry. I really need to get going."

He held up his hands, then leaned in and kissed her cheek. As he lingered there for a few seconds, she closed her eyes, inhaled his masculine scent, and relished the warmth of his breath and the softness of his beard. She could turn her head a fraction and kiss him the way she wanted. Just one more kiss.

He stepped back before she could decide. "Good night, Beth," he said, and gave her distance to open the car and slide inside.

Her eyes filled with tears. She didn't want to say good night or good-bye. She didn't want to leave things between them so final. Clenching her jaw to keep her chin from trembling, she closed the door, then put the keys in the ignition. As she backed out of the driveway, the headlights put Shane on display. Every touch, kiss and word spoken between them rushed through her mind as if she were fast-forwarding a movie. Once she'd backed onto the street, then drove off, she let out a long breath and let the tears fall.

How was this fair? For once she'd met a man she liked and wanted to be with, but couldn't. She might have told him that no one dictated who she dated, only she didn't have the nerve to risk everything she'd worked for to be with him.

God, she was such a hypocrite. After years of being

dumped after the first date because men couldn't handle that she was in law enforcement, she had no business rejecting Shane because of his record. Then again, being an ex-con wasn't exactly the same as being a cop. She picked up her cell phone, then tossed it back in the center console. She'd love to pick Erin's brain and find out what she thought about all of this. While she knew she could trust Erin to not say anything to her husband, or anyone else, how she felt about Shane was too personal. He was supposed to be a fun distraction between work and school, but had become more than that.

Despite his past, she trusted him. He might have kept his conviction from her—which she understood—but he'd been open about himself. Although it had taken coercion, he'd been somewhat honest about his involvement in the case they were investigating, and had taken her to see Lola.

Feel what you do to me...What if I want to be with you a month from now?

She pulled her SUV to a stop at the red light and remembered how hard his heart had beat beneath her palm. She wanted to be with him a month from now, too. But what about the months after that? What if she took the risk, continued to see him, then her co-workers found out she was dating a felon? If she lost her job, she could find another. Rumors could spread, though, and follow her as she moved on to another job, then later to law firms.

The light changed to green, but she didn't take her foot off the brake. Or, she could tell anyone who passed judgment on her and Shane to kiss her butt.

With no traffic on the road, she lifted her foot, placed it on the gas, then made a quick and illegal U-turn. In minutes, she was back on Shane's street and pulling into his driveway. After grabbing her purse, she rushed to the front door.

Her heart raced as she gave the door a quick knock. Maybe she was being presumptuous. Yes, he'd offered to feed her, but maybe he—

The door opened. Shane stood there for a second, his eyes widening slightly—with shock, or maybe relief—then they sizzled with the same heat she'd seen when he'd been between her thighs. He didn't smile. He didn't say anything. He let her inside.

When he closed the door behind her, he took her purse, then set it on the floor. "Why'd you come back?" he asked, and made no move to touch her.

"You said your fridge is stocked. Mine isn't."

"Is that the only reason?" he asked, the heat and uncertainty in his eyes had her taking a step forward.

"No," she said, and touched his jaw. "I want to be with you."

He drew in a breath. "Now?"

She pulled her tank top over her head. "Now."

He grabbed her by the hips and hauled her against him. "The shoes are coming off this time," he said, and instead of kissing her, he walked backward, taking her with him. "I want you in my bed."

As he led her down the hall, she dropped her tank top, then grabbed the hem of his shirt. By the time they reached the bedroom, she had it off and was running her hands along his chest. When she reached his jeans, he grabbed her hand, stopping her. She met his gaze, the intense hunger in his eyes making her nipples hard and her knees weak. "Not yet," he said, his knuckles grazing her stomach. He then slid her pants over her hips, but didn't touch her panties. Instead, he edged her to the bed, sat her down, then bent and removed her shoes and socks. Once he was finished, he slid his rough hands up her legs.

He hadn't kissed her and now avoided touching her sex, and she wanted him kissing and touching her. She reached out and ran her hand along his face, then tilted his chin. "I'm in your bed."

He skimmed his hand along her stomach, then gripped the side of her waist. "I haven't had sex in over seven years." Although the hunger remained in his eyes, there was also hesitation. "I don't want to disappoint you."

"It's been three years for me," she said. "So it sounds like we both have a lot of making up to do. But we can't do anything until you lose those jeans."

He grinned and stood, then began unbuttoning and unzipping his jeans. Anticipation curled through her belly as his jeans dropped to the floor. Now that he wore nothing but a pair of dark-gray boxer briefs, she looked at the thick length of his erection, at his tight abs and muscular chest until she met his gaze. Anxious for them to both be naked, his hard body on top of hers, she pushed off the bed and went to him. When she settled her hand on his erection, gripped him through the cotton, he sucked in a breath, snagged the side of her panties, then tugged them down her hips. As she kicked them aside, he unhooked her bra. He moved the straps down her arms, cupped her breasts and brushed his thumbs along her nipples. "You're beautiful," he said, then finally kissed her.

She opened her mouth and slid her tongue along his. As he deepened the kiss, took possession of her mouth, she hung on to his broad shoulders for support. Never before had anyone kissed her with so much passion. His hands were everywhere. Her breasts, her stomach, her back and rear. When he pressed a couple fingers inside her heat, she moved her hands inside the waistband of his briefs, then shoved them down. With his erection pressed against her stomach, he pumped his fingers and walked her backward toward the bed.

He released her lips. "I can't stop touching you," he said, his voice husky, sexy. "There's a condom in the drawer."

As she reached to open the nightstand drawer, he rubbed her clit, then dipped his fingers back inside. Distracted, turned on, she managed to find the unopened box, tore into it and pulled out a condom.

"Open it," he said, still working his hand. "I can't stop." He gently pinched her nipple. First one, then the other, back and forth, driving her crazy with need as she tried to tear the package.

Once she had the condom out, she gripped his erection and sheathed it. Before she could stroke him the way she'd been aching to, he released her breasts, ran his hand through her hair and tugged. "First time's going to be hot and fast," he said against her neck, his beard, warm breath and words causing goose bumps to skid along her skin. He sat her on the edge of the bed, then pressed her back. "Then I'm going to take my time and taste every inch of your body."

Flashbacks to earlier, when he'd pleasured her with his lips and tongue, had her imagination going wild. She couldn't wait to take him into her mouth and give him the same pleasure.

Thoughts of what she'd do to him scattered when he moved her legs apart, withdrew his fingers and pressed the tip of his erection against her sex. He ran his hand along her outer thigh, then beneath it, raised her leg and looked to where they were almost joined.

He shifted his penetrating gaze to hers. His eyes had darkened with desire, and glittered with emotions she couldn't identify. "I want to fuck you," he said. His crude words didn't offend her, instead they had her stimulated sex clenching with the need to be filled. "You deserve better than that."

She reached between their bodies and gripped his length. "Fuck me now, make love to me later."

The corner of his mouth tilted in a small, almost triumphant smile. Holding her gaze, with one quick thrust, he entered her. She gasped, and quickly gripped his bicep. His breath came out on a hiss as he closed his eyes, pulled out, then slammed into her again. Undeniable pleasure crossed his face as he moved over her. "You feel so damned good," he said, then bent his head and captured a nipple between his lips. After a quick suck, he tongued the taut peak, then leaned back, and thrust, over and over.

Unable to resist his body, she reached up and touched him everywhere she could reach. His chest, his abs, his arms. Keeping one hand on his shoulder, she slid the other up around the back of his neck and urged his head down. He gave one of her nipples a quick lick before capturing her lips. Sagging to his elbows he drove deep. One. Twice. Then he let out a harsh groan.

Breathing hard, he gave her cheek a kiss. "Don't move," he

said, slipped out of her body, then out of the bed.

She moved to her elbows and stared at his bare butt as he left the room. Unfulfilled, her sex still convulsed. She reached down and touched herself to ease the ache. If he couldn't have sex for a little while, she'd understand. She couldn't be too disappointed since he'd given her an orgasm hours ago. Rubbing her clit, she fell back against the mattress. Oh, but she'd love another orgasm now. He'd warned her their first time would be hot and fast, and he'd been right. It had been hot, but way too fast.

"You are so sexy."

She stilled her hand, and moved back to one elbow. Shane stood in the doorway, his gaze on her sex. His erection—now condom free—hadn't changed, giving her hope for that orgasm her body demanded.

"Don't stop." He stepped into the room and walked toward the bed. "Keep touching yourself." After she rubbed her clit, she slid a finger between her labia. "More," he said, and climbed onto the mattress. After he shifted her body until she lay on the center of the bed, he skimmed his knuckles along her inner thighs, then joined her fingers with his.

He gave her nipple a tug as he pressed their fingers deeper. "You're so wet."

"And you're still hard." She sucked in a breath when he rubbed her fingers along her clit. "We should do something about that."

"I plan to." He moved their hands from her sex and replaced them with his mouth.

She let out a moan and cupped her breasts. He licked her, sucked her clit, used his lips to give her labia a gentle tug, then he speared his tongue inside her. Kissed her sex the way he'd kissed her mouth. She shoved her hands through his hair to keep his head in place. "So close," she said, as her stomach tightened with the first signs of an impending orgasm. He moved his tongue faster, lashed it against her clit. Her inner thighs trembled. Ripples of desire began to radiate from her sex, then she let out a moan as her orgasm hit her hard and fast, moving throughout her body. She cupped her breasts, then flinched when he ran his tongue along her over-sensitized sex. With a slight chuckle, she raised her head and stared at him. Damn, he looked so sexy between her legs. As much as she'd like to keep him there for the rest of the night, she wanted him inside her again.

She pushed upright, he did the same. She touched his jaw and ran her tongue along his lips. He opened his mouth and kissed her. Slow, like he had during their first kiss. As they kissed, he smoothed his palms along her breasts and nipples. Now that his hard length was no longer out of her reach, and dying to touch him, she took him in her hand and stroked him.

His low moan, which bordered on a growl, made her smile. She kissed the corner of his mouth. "I want to taste you."

"Later." He eased her back, quickly put on a condom, then covered her with his body. "I want to make love to you," he said, kissing her lips, her temple, as he eased himself inside her.

She hugged him and twined her legs through his. Skin to skin, no space between their bodies, they kissed and caressed each other as he slowly rocked his hips. She had no idea how much time had passed. She didn't care. She loved being with Shane, being one with him. Right now it was just the two of them. No labels. No investigation. No worries. Tomorrow…she didn't want to think about tomorrow. For now, for tonight, they belonged to each other. They belonged together.

As they came together, he kissed her. Once their breathing returned to normal, he rolled to his side and drew her close to him. "Will you stay the night?"

She shifted until they were breast to chest. "Will you let me raid your fridge?"

He grinned. "Will you take a shower with me after the raid is over and let me wash your body?"

She let out a sigh, as if being naked with Shane was a horrible and an excruciatingly boring ordeal. "The things I'll do for free food."

Chuckling he quickly shifted and pinned her beneath him.

"All of that just for a ham sandwich? I can't wait to see what you'll do when I break out the ice cream."

Naples Beach Hotel, Naples, Florida
Saturday, 8:49 p.m., Eastern Standard Time

The Reverend stood on the third floor balcony of his beach view suite. Although too dark to see the beach, the crashing waves let him know he'd arrived in Paradise. He inhaled deeply and took in the salty air, then went back into the suite to finish unpacking.

He might be here to set the record straight and make sure his congregation would never doubt the power of the Ritual of the Serpents, but he looked on this as a working vacation. While he worked to find out who had copied what he'd done to Katie, he planned to make sure he had himself some beach time. Too bad the nearest strip club was in Fort Myers, a fifty-minute drive from the hotel. Since he hadn't been laid in a while, catching a view of tits and ass would be mighty nice. He supposed he could go to the club and not drink. The last thing he needed was a DUI. He shook his head. He'd catch so much hell from Daddy if that happened.

He finished placing his clothes in the drawers, then inspected the minibar. Daddy had his rules, and he understood them. At the age of eight, just before they'd planned his mama's death, his daddy had told him he was a con-artist, and had said, "I take people's money, and I want to keep takin' my congregation's money." Daddy had also told him that he'd wanted his boy by his side as he grew their congregation and duped people from their hard-earned cash.

Over the years, Daddy had taken those fools who believed in the nonsense he spewed for every penny he could. But Daddy had been smart. He'd forced them to live modestly. Vacations were a different thing, though. His daddy would make sure his congregation thought father and son were going on a camping trip to take time for reflection, and to be one with nature and God. The reality was, instead of camping in a shitty tent, they'd taken trips to Hawaii, Costa Rica and the Bahamas. When he'd been old enough to enjoy Sin City, Daddy had taken him to Vegas for his twenty-first birthday and had bought him a woman for the night.

Smiling, he cracked open a tiny bottle of gin, then poured it into a glass. Yep, he and Daddy'd had some good times together. If only Daddy wasn't so damned old and sick. Losing him was going to be hard. They'd had a good gig going for many years. On the flip side, once Daddy was gone, he could disappear right along with him. His inheritance had grown to around three-quarters of a million. He'd no longer need to live like a monk and could finally enjoy the money they'd amassed.

He glanced around the luxury suite and envisioned a naked woman, maybe two, on his bed. When his cell phone rang, the vision vanished and he answered the call.

"Well?" Daddy asked. "Make it there okay?"

"In my suite and unpacked." He glanced to the container on the floor. "I just gotta take care of the rattlers."

"Leave 'em for tonight. They might be spooked after all that traveling." The TV playing in the background quieted. "What's your plan?"

If Harlan hadn't kicked the bucket eight months ago, he would've paid the man a visit to find out if he'd opened up his big mouth to anyone. He and Daddy both doubted he had, otherwise he'd only cause trouble for himself. Not just with the police, but him. The night he and Harlan disposed of Katie's body, he'd warned the old man that the wrath of God would come down upon him if so much as breathed a word about Katie's death.

"Where's Suzie?" the Reverend asked. He didn't want Daddy talking freely in front of the nurse. He liked the woman and didn't want to have to kill her. Not all of their congregation knew about the Ritual of the Serpents, but many did.

Some had witnessed the ritual firsthand, others knew about

it by rumor. But only a few of the rituals had begun with murder. Six to be exact. The rest had been performed the way they'd taken care of Mama—after the person had already died. His concern was over the six killings they'd done. Daddy's, too. Last night, after they'd caught the news and decided he needed to drive to Florida, they had tallied up how many people knew about the killings, and had counted to nineteen. The Reverend had suggested that he should go find those nineteen people and make sure they don't talk. But Daddy had said that killing nineteen people would raise too much suspicion on them, and that those God-fearing folks wouldn't talk anyway. The Reverend and Daddy might've done the killing, but those people had paid for it. They'd go to prison just the same.

"Suzie-Q is snorin' away on the recliner," Daddy said. "Now I know why her and her no-good husband sleep in separate rooms."

Suzie chose to sleep in a separate room—door locked—to avoid when her husband took to drinking. Now that was a man he'd have no problem killing, if Daddy would let him. The Reverend had no tolerance for men who beat women, even if they'd deserved it. Plus, he liked Suzie. The woman sure knew how to cook.

"So, how 'bout it?" Daddy asked. "Whatcha gonna do tomorrow?"

He opened his laptop. "After you conked out on me last night, I went through what I had on Katie's murder." He took a swallow of gin, then flipped open a notebook, which he planned to burn before he left Naples. "I've got the names of the detectives, the deputies who found the body, the medical examiner, CSU people, three more deputies I saw in a newspaper picture, assistant district attorney and sheriff. Some are women, so I'm ruling them out seein' as how he fiddled with the bodies."

"If that ain't plain nasty, I don't know what is." Daddy sighed. "Okay, that's a big list you got there. How're you gonna narrow it down?"

He took a sip of the gin. "I was thinkin' on that during my drive here. Now, I could be wrong, but my gut is tellin' me the reporter got her info from someone who's worked Katie's murder and these three bodies."

"Makes sense to me, but my gut's thinkin' that with what you'd done to Katie, that rattler would be hard to keep secret from folks outside of her case. Every person who works for the sheriff could know. They could've gone on and then told their wives about it. Getting' the picture?"

"I'm makin' too much work for myself."

"Got that right." Daddy chuckled. "'Member what that dang raccoon did to our house in Tennessee?"

The Reverend laughed. "Hell, yeah. What I remember most was how spittin' mad you were when we came home from church and found the house wrecked." That raccoon had found its way into the pantry and trash, and scattered shit all over the house. But they couldn't figure out how it had found a way inside or where it had been hiding.

"And do you remember how I caught that little bastard?"

Daddy was of the *you catch more flies with honey* mindset. Now that he'd brought up the raccoon, he knew exactly what needed to be done. "I remember." His daddy had set food on the table, then hid in the closet with a baseball bat. The man had told him later that the coon had kept him waiting for nearly an hour before it'd showed itself. Then he'd pounced on it and sent it to raccoon heaven.

"Good. So tell me again, you got yourself a big list, how're you gonna narrow it down?"

The Reverend smiled and helped himself to another bottle from the minibar. "I'm going to send them a message, then watch everyone on my list."

****

KRISTINE MASON

Tic Toc Bar, East Naples, Florida
Saturday, 10:56 p.m., Eastern Standard Time

The Reverend sat at the bar, nursing his second beer and using the mirror behind the rows of liquor bottles to watch the crowd behind him. Since he was average looking, he knew he wouldn't stand out in the crowd, and this bar had a hell of a crowd. The classic rock cover band had people dancing to their shitty sound. Man, had they destroyed Van Morrison in their last set. But folks liked them. The only reason he tolerated the music was because of the small blonde he'd had his eyes on from the moment he'd walked through the door.

She was perfect. Maybe five-one and one hundred pounds, he could kill her and move her dead body with ease. Plus she was alone. When he'd first arrived, she'd been sitting with a group of men and women, couples he'd assumed. One by one, those couples had left, but she'd remained. She hadn't acted as if she'd been hard up for company, though. With the way she'd moved from table to table, hugging some folks, laughing and joking with others, he'd assumed she was a regular. A regular who felt safe here. A regular who'd probably been in the bar dozens of times and had no worries about going into the parking lot alone.

When the cover band ended their song, she let out a holler and raised her beer bottle. Smiling, she walked off the dance floor, shook her head when offered a shot from a group of guys at a nearby table, then made her way to the bar. She stood about four feet from him, but now that the band had stopped, he could clearly hear her ask the bartender for a glass of water, then tell him she was ready to call it a night.

That was his cue. He finished his warm beer, placed money on the bar, then left. When he exited, he nodded to the smokers standing outside and kept on walking. When he reached his car, he unlocked it and climbed inside. Then waited. And waited.

It'd been a long day and he'd spent too much time in his Impala. Eight and a half hours if he added on stops for food,

242

gas and bathroom breaks. He checked his phone for the time. He'd give the blonde another twenty minutes, then head back to his hotel suite. Tomorrow might be a better day to do this anyway. Tired, he worried about being sloppy, and there was no room for sloppiness when it came to killing.

Minutes passed, his eyes grew droopy. Worried someone might come by and catch him dozing, he decided the hell with it and started the car. As he was about to back out of the parking spot, he spotted the blonde in his side view mirror. She teetered as she walked, passed his car without noticing him, her lips moving as if she was singing, a half-smile on her face. He'd watched her put down three beers and a shot in the hour he had been at the bar. Since she'd been there when he'd arrived, he assumed she'd had even more than that to drink. Given her size and the way she swayed as she walked, she had to be good and buzzed. Perfect.

He let the Chevy idle. Once the blonde backed her white late model Toyota Corolla out of her parking spot, he shifted his sedan in reverse, then followed her out of the parking lot. He kept his distance, though. Even if the woman was as drunk as he suspected, that could make her more alert to the cars around her. She could be watching for the police, and instead notice he was following.

She drove for about a mile before her right turn signal began blinking. He slowed and kept driving, but used his rearview mirror to watch her pull into a gas station and park in front of the convenience store. He quickly turned right onto a side street, made a U-turn, then waited for her. Minutes later, the white Toyota passed the side street and he began following her car again. She veered a bit, her car's tires flirting with the yellow lines on the road, and lit a cigarette. He smothered a yawn and wondered how far away the blonde lived, or if she lived alone.

Her turn signal went on again, this time the left one. He followed her down a street, past a row of older ranch-style homes, then into the Sunshine Bay apartment complex. Fortunately, the complex wasn't gated and there were very few cars in the parking lot. So as not to raise her suspicions, he drove past the complex entrance, found another one further down, and entered the parking lot there. As he neared where the woman had parked, he saw her exiting her car, a cigarette dangling from her mouth. She stumbled back, used the opened door to right herself, then plucked the cigarette from her mouth and let out of stream of smoke.

He slowed to a stop behind her car and rolled down his window. She hadn't noticed him yet because she had her back to him and was reaching into her car for something.

"Excuse me, ma'am," he called, and shifted the Chevy into PARK.

The blonde fell back against the door again, dropped her cigarette onto the asphalt and clutched her purse to her chest.

He smiled. "Sorry, ma'am. Didn't mean to startle ya. I'm trying to find building D. Can you point me in the right direction?"

She frowned and slowly blinked. "There's no building D in this complex," she said, with a slight slur.

"This is just what I need." Rubbing his eyes, he shook his head. "I've already been in the car for eight hours and all I wanna to do is see my girlfriend. She moved here for a job two months ago and this is my first time visitin' her."

The blonde relaxed and pulled another cigarette from her purse. "What's the name of her apartment building?" she asked, then lit the cigarette.

"Sun Bay."

She blew out smoke and giggled. "Oh, hon, these apartments are part of Sun*shine* Bay."

"You're kidding." He let out a sigh. "Well, can you tell me how to get to Sun Bay?"

"Never heard of it." She took a drag. "What's the address?"

"Don't know. All she told me was Sun Bay apartments, Naples, Florida, building D, room two-oh-two."

The blonde flicked an ash. "Sorry I can't help. You better call your girl."

"My cell phone died and I left my dang charger at home—

in Alabama." As she giggled, he asked, "Do you know if there's a gas station nearby? One that might have a pay phone?"

"Do they even have pay phones anymore?" Swaying, she took another hit off the cigarette and pulled her cell phone from her purse. "Here, you can use my cell," she said, and neared his car.

He opened the car door, then stepped out, but left the Impala running. "I really appreciate the help. I'm hoping she'll answer. She's funny about takin' calls from folks she don't know."

"I'm with your girlfriend," the blonde said, and handed him the phone.

She stood arms' length from him, smoking her cigarette and humming one of the songs he'd heard earlier at the bar. So far he'd earned her trust, but he wanted her to move a little closer and give her no chance to run or scream for help.

He pretended to punch numbers into the phone, then placed it near his ear. "Hey, honey," he said to the pretend girlfriend. "I think I'm lost. I wrote down Sun Bay, but my GPS took me to Sunshine Bay." He acted as if he was listening to the pretend girlfriend talk and glanced to the blonde. Her eyes had become droopy. She ashed on herself, then dropped the cigarette and snuffed it with her shoe. "Got it. I'll see you in about ten minutes. Love you, too."

He let out a chuckle, which drew the blonde's attention to him. "Did you get an address?" she asked, and lurched forward a step.

"I got it all screwed up. I was supposed to go to Sun Bayside apartments."

Her face screwed up in confusion, then she shook her head. "Never heard of it." She yawned and held out her hand.

"Thanks again for the help," he said, and before he gave her back the phone, he quickly glanced around the parking lot, then to the apartment windows. There were a few with lights on, but no one peeking outside. Now was his chance. Anticipation suddenly rushed through his belly. It's been a while since he'd killed and he had forgotten how much he'd missed the power he held over life and death. "You're a Good Samaritan."

As he handed her the phone, he dropped it before it touched her fingers. "I'm so sorry," he said, and bent to the ground. He picked up the phone and looked at it. "Shoot, I accidentally cracked your screen."

She knelt and took the phone from him. "What? Oh, no. I just got this a few weeks ago."

"I'm really sorry," he said, and stood. He glanced from the back of her head to the side of his car and wondered how much of a dent she'd leave. There was only one way to find out, and he was about due for a new car anyway.

"Wait. I don't see a crack," she said, squinting at the phone. "You will."

She looked up at him. "What are you—?"

He kicked the woman in the throat. She fell to the ground, gasping and writhing as she clutched the front of her neck. He grabbed her by the hair and the back of her jeans, then slammed her head into the Impala's wheel well until she went limp. Yeah, he'd been right. She couldn't have weighed more than one hundred pounds.

He opened the rear driver's side door, then tossed her on top of the garbage bag he'd laid on the backseat before going to the bar. After he'd retrieved her phone, he climbed inside the Chevy, then drove out of the parking lot.

He glanced at his rearview mirror and noticed the Toyota's car door was still open. Good. Someone would notice that, and her purse, and look for her. He wanted someone to alert the police. He wanted her found, and the pervert who'd thought it was okay to copy the Ritual of the Serpents to make a move.

Thirty-five minutes later, he pulled onto Shell Island Road, drove another half mile, then parked. Although the boat ramp at the end of the road closed at dusk, and he didn't expect any traffic, he wanted to make this quick. Since three corpses had been found here, deputies might make a point of patrolling the area.

The Reverend climbed out of the car, then opened the

trunk. He pulled out two pairs of latex gloves from his bag, retrieved the knife and threaded fishing line, along with the container of snakes. After setting the items onto the pavement next to the left back tire, he slipped on one set of gloves, then opened the rear passenger door. He wrapped the blonde in the garbage bag, and pulled her from the sedan. Damn, it was dark, but the trunk light would have to do.

He checked the blonde's pulse. Still alive. Shit. He picked up the knife and slit her throat, then cut her shirt from her body. When he'd disposed of Katie, she'd been naked and washed. There'd be no time for that, but that was okay. Whoever was copying him would get the message.

He plunged the knife into the left side of her stomach and sliced right. After making sure he'd made a deep enough cavity, he stripped off the gloves, put on the other pair, then slid the container closer to the trunk. He needed to be able to see the rattlers and make sure one of them didn't bite him. With care, he quickly grabbed one of the young rattlesnakes by the back of the head, slammed the container shut and moved back to the blonde. He skimmed his hand along her torso until his fingers sank into her stomach. Using his fingers to pry the opening wider, he shoved the snake inside her and covered a hand over her stomach to keep the snake from escaping. With his free hand, he felt around for the needle and fishing line, found it, then made quick work of stitching the snake inside the woman's stomach. Once he'd tied off a knot, he cut the fishing line with his knife.

Satisfied, he grabbed the ends of the garbage bag and pulled it out from beneath her. After tossing both pairs of gloves onto the bag, he rolled it into a ball, then placed it, along with the bloodied knife, fishing line and snake container back into the trunk. He'd deal with the blood on the knife and needle later. Right now, he needed to leave the area and head back to the hotel.

He climbed into the car and started the engine. Despite the rush of killing the blonde, he yawned. Man, oh, man had it been a long day. Tomorrow would likely be just as long, and he needed his sleep. After all, *the early bird catches the worm*. Fishermen would be traveling down Shell Island Road by the ass crack of dawn to use the free boat ramp. One of them was bound to find the blonde. Which reminded him…

He slowed the car to a stop, picked up the blonde's cell phone, then used the front of his shirt to wipe his prints from it. He opened the car door and, still using his shirt, dropped it on the road, then he continued driving.

Yep, by this time tomorrow Collier County wouldn't know what the hell had hit them, but the pervert who'd copycatted him would. And when he found out who that pervert was, he'd show him exactly how the Ritual of the Serpents worked.

In great detail.

CHAPTER 12

Shane's House, Everglades City, Florida
Sunday, 6:40 a.m., Eastern Standard Time

THE CESSNA SOARED above the Glades. He glanced to the right and smiled at Beth. Damn, she looked sexy sitting there in a tiny red bikini, her breasts spilling from the top. When she unbuckled her seat belt. He tensed. "Keep it on, if something happened—"

She pressed a finger to his lips. "Just keep flying," she said, as she undid his shorts. "Hot and fast, remember?"

Memories of taking her hot and fast in his bed ran through his head as she leaned over and took him into her mouth. He sucked in a breath. Holy hell, it'd been so damned long since he'd experience anything like this. They shouldn't be...she shouldn't be...

The Cessna's controls went haywire. Gauges flipped back and forth. "You need to stop," he said, gripping the wheel. "I'm not good enough for you."

She looked up at him, then ran her tongue along his dick.

"I'm a murderer."

Without responding, she took his entire length in her mouth.

"Didn't you hear me?" He stared at the way the gauges continued to move out of sync and gripped her by the hair. "I'm not good enough."

"Shane, it's just a dream."

Beth's voice woke him. Purplish-pink light from the rising sun filtered through the slats of the window blinds and stretched across the bed. He came alert and glanced down the length of his body. Christ, he'd never seen anything sexier in his life. The light touched on Beth's face, on her mouth, on the way she held his hard dick against her lips.

"Sorry if I woke you up," she said, not looking sorry at all, and stroked him.

He loosened his hold on her hair. "Did I hurt you?"

She kissed his erection. "Nope. Tell me what you were dreaming about."

"You." He touched her cheek. "We were in my Cessna. You were wearing a red bikini and doing what you're doing right now."

She smiled. "Reality is so much better," she said, then took him in her mouth.

He drew in a breath and pushed her hair aside so he could watch her. She licked, stroked and sucked him. Drove him crazy with the way she swirled her tongue over the head of his erection. When she lightly grazed her nails along his sac, it took everything in him to keep his head from falling back against the pillow. He wanted to watch, sear this image onto his brain. He wasn't good enough for her, and knew in his gut that what they had going wouldn't last. Last night, this morning, she was his. Tomorrow? The next day? He didn't want to think about the days ahead, not with what she was doing to him now.

As she simultaneously sucked and stroked him, his balls tightened. He didn't want to come yet, not without being inside her first. He reached over his head for the box of condoms on the nightstand, grabbed one before accidentally knocking the rest to the floor.

She held his gaze as she ran her tongue along him, then glanced to the condom. After giving the head of his erection a hot, open-mouthed kiss, she took the packet and tore it open, then rolled the condom over him. "Stay like you are," she said. She dragged her breasts along his torso and up his chest, then straddled him. Without a word, she took his erection by the base, guided it inside her heat, and sank down. Using his chest for support, she rode him.

Her breasts swayed near his face. He leaned up, captured a nipple and sucked. Between the dream, then reality, he wasn't going to last long. Still tonguing her nipples, he gripped her hips, then raised and lowered her. Faster, harder. Her breath came in quick, short bursts. She dug her fingers into his chest and came on a groan.

His stomach tightened as her sex convulsed around him. He moved her hips faster, then he came right along with her. While his orgasm shot through his body, he sank her down on him and tensed. Let the brief moment of euphoria wash over him as he released himself. Closing his eyes, he dropped his head against the pillow and drew in a deep breath. Damn, he wanted to wake up like this every day.

Her hair tickled his chest as she ground her pelvis against him. He opened his eyes and moved her hair from her face. She met his gaze and gave him a small, sexy smile. He smiled back, then drew her close for a kiss.

"Morning," he said.

"Morning." She let out a sigh of satisfaction, then lay against him. "I could fall back asleep just like this."

He could, too. He loved the way she fit against his body. Hell, he loved being with her. "It's still early. Why don't you sleep for a little longer and I'll make us breakfast?"

"I'd rather sleep with you." She raised her head and looked at the clock on the nightstand. "What time are you meeting Lola?"

He didn't want to think about Lola or the bitch session she'd likely give him when they met. "Nine."

"Since it's almost seven, we should probably get up," she said, then shifted off of him.

The loss of her warmth had him curling her next to him again. "We have time. If I'm a few minutes late, Lola will get over it."

"She already doesn't like me, and she's probably mad at

you. I think it's a good idea for you to make it on time. I need to get home anyway and start studying."

"When you're done studying, do you want to go flying later?" he asked. After they'd made love last night, they'd raided his refrigerator and had a couple of beers. They'd talked, not about them, Lola or the investigation, and not about his incarceration. Instead, he'd told her about his childhood, a little about his time with the Army and his plans for his business. He'd also asked Beth dozens of questions about herself, her family and her time as a paramedic. She amazed him. She was barely thirty and had accomplished so much in a short time. She had her career mapped out, goals in place, and with her go get 'em attitude he had no doubt she'd succeed.

"Can I let you know later? Sunday's are my big studying day and I need to make sure I get as much done as possible."

"Sure," he said, keeping the disappointment from his voice. He understood that school was important, he just hoped this wasn't her way of ditching his ass.

"If I do run late and can't make it here before sunset, maybe you'd like to come to my place."

He kissed the top of her head and ran his hand along her arm. "Works for me," he said, relieved she wasn't blowing him off. Yet. Knowing the inevitable outcome of his relationship with Beth, he should let her continue with her busy life, rather than allow himself to become more attached to her. If he wanted to be ready for the peak tourist season, his concentration should be on setting up his business, not Beth or when she'd drop the hammer and choose her career over him.

Moving a little fast, Monahan.

He looked to the ceiling. So what? He liked her and wanted to be with her. He didn't care that he hadn't known her for long. Why the hell should he question his need to be with her?

Because she didn't need him screwing up her life.

She lifted her head and leaned in for a kiss. "Come on, lazy bones. I'll help you make breakfast." After she climbed out of bed, he stared at her naked body and watched her dress. He'd like to undress her again before she left. He'd like to—

"I think my phone is ringing," she said, and pulled her shirt over her head.

He'd been too busy eyeing her curves and thinking about what he'd like to do to her, and hadn't heard anything. When she left the room, he rose from the bed and grabbed his underwear off the floor. Once he'd stepped into a pair of shorts, he grabbed a t-shirt, then headed into the living room.

Beth sat on the couch, concern in her eyes. She held up a finger. "Thanks for letting me know. Call me after you leave." She ended the call and pushed a hand through her hair. "That was my partner, Ricky." She blew out a breath, and stared at the snake terrarium. "Another woman was found along Shell Island Road. From what Ricky's heard, she was murdered and there's a cut along her stomach. Let me rephrase," she said, and looked at him. "Her stomach was cut, then sewn shut."

He lost his appetite. "Like Katie Reed?"

"Sounds like it. Ricky's heading there now, and said he'd call me later with the details." She stood and hugged herself. "I'm worried that whoever dumped the three corpses gave Katie's murderer a reason to resurface."

"You don't think this could be the same guy?"

"It could, but the only thing connecting the three women to Katie is snakes. What was found in the stomachs of the dead women wasn't the same as the rattlesnake in Katie's."

He nodded. "The sutures were different, too." When she cocked a brow, he said, "I'm assuming I can trust that you won't tell anyone the ME gave us information."

"Of course. Dr. Adams is good and I don't want him getting in trouble. Can you tell me how you know him and why he gave you access to confidential information? Is he connected to the private agency you work for?"

He could, but if Lola found out she'd have a frickin' fit. "Lola told me David helped her with another case. Since I was still in prison, I don't know the details. When we were hired to prove Thomas Williams' innocence, she called David and asked if he'd be willing to help her out again. I think David was game because he thought the police arrested the wrong person."

"Did he tell you that?"

"In so many words," he said, then added, "It'll be interesting to see what, if anything, is in this new victim's stomach."

"Along with what was used to sew her back up, since fishing line had been used on Katie and suture string was used on the dead women." She dropped her arms, then grabbed her phone off the couch. "I'm sorry, but I'm going to have to skip breakfast. I want to get as much studying done as I can."

"So you can go into work?"

She walked to him and wrapped her arms around his waist. "So I can see you later." She gave him a wry smile. "And maybe have a chat with one of the detectives working the case."

"Good, then we'll have plenty to talk about when I come over. Unless you just want to use my body again."

She gave his rear a light swat. "I didn't hear you complaining," she said, and kissed him. "I'm going to get dressed."

Ten minutes later, she stood at the front door. "Is seven or eight too late for you?" she asked.

He hooked his finger in the top of her shorts and tugged her close. "Not at all. Text me and let me know which it is."

"I'm glad I came back last night. Thanks for the sandwiches and beers."

"What about the orgasms?" he asked, then grinned when her face flushed. He kissed her. "Sorry, I couldn't resist."

"That's okay." She smiled and cupped his crotch. "I faked half of them."

Laughing, he squeezed her rear. "Head home and I'll talk to you later."

After Beth left, he went into the kitchen. As he poured a cup of coffee, he considered calling his brother to talk about last night, then decided the hell with it. He'd see him and Lola soon enough. He truly hoped she would be open to working with Beth on this investigation, otherwise she'd place him in an uncomfortable position. As long as he and Beth were together, he refused to work behind her back. He wasn't about to blow a good thing just when it was starting.

The Rental House, Everglades City, Florida
Sunday, 8:59 a.m., Eastern Standard Time

Shane stepped inside the rental house and immediately saw Lola sitting on the sofa with Ryan. "Good morning," she said with a smile.

Since he'd expected her to be furious with him, he immediately grew uneasy. "Morning." He nodded to his brother.

"How's Beth?" Lola asked.

He kept all thoughts of being with Beth last night and this morning out of his head. Lola was acting too friendly, and he needed to keep his guard up because he had a feeling this light conversation was going to turn dark. Fast. "Good."

"That's nice. I'm glad to see you two worked things out, considering you hadn't meshed."

"Me, too." He cleared his throat and stepped into the living room. "You're not mad about last night?"

Still smiling, she said, "Why would I be mad that you brought a cop to our house, or worried that you told Beth about us?"

"Vlad no worry," the Russian called from the kitchen. "Kiss Beth nice."

Shane let out a sigh. "Who else is here?"

"Harrison," Lola said. "Guys, would you please come in here."

"Dude, I gotta say, I never pegged Beth for a cop," Harrison said, as he and Vlad made their way into the living room.

"I honestly thought she was a law student."

"Is she?" Lola asked.

He nodded. "She graduates in May, so she won't be a cop forever. Look, I told you I tried to call."

Lola leaned into the cushions. "I wish you would have tried harder. Do you realize the position you put us in? I get you like Beth, but you also took it upon yourself to let a *cop* know about our business."

"But she could help us."

She pushed off the sofa. "She could also hurt us. Don't you see that? I'm certainly not going to tell you who you can and can't date, but if you continue to see her, it could risk our operation. We need to—"

"Then maybe I should be out." Shane moved toward the door, and placed his hand on the doorknob. He wasn't about to walk away from Beth for ATL. "I'll be honest, there were two reasons I'd decided to join you."

Lola moved toward him. "Would you let me finish?"

"No. I need to say this."

She threw a hand in the air. "Fine."

"It's like I told you, I'm nosey. But the main reason is that I don't know you, or these guys," he said, thumbing toward Harrison and Vlad. "The three of you roped my brother, Mel and Barney into your secret club after you hunted down a man and killed him."

"I explained the circumstances. It wasn't as if we wanted to kill him. He'd left us no choice."

He considered the fateful swing he'd taken at Ted Nowak. "There's always a choice, and when those choices are made, there are always consequences. I don't like the idea of my brother being involved in something that could get him killed or put him in prison. So far, Harrison is looking at time for hacking into the Sheriff's Office's computer system. Bringing Dustin here to interrogate him?" He glanced at Vlad and Harrison. "You two can justify it all you want, but blindfolding, gagging and tying him to a chair is kidnapping. If the cops find out, we're in trouble because we *all* knew about it, and we didn't stop it from happening."

"I told you there'd be risks," Lola said.

"You did. But I honestly didn't take what you're running here as something serious. Your first assignment was to prove a funeral home director wasn't a necrophiliac. It wasn't as if you guys were going after drug lords, arms dealers or serial killers. I mean, how many cases do you think you're actually going to get working out of Everglades City?"

Lola folded her arms across her chest. He couldn't be sure, but he swore there was hurt in her eyes before she narrowed them. "You don't think what we're doing is serious?"

"I think it's seriously messed up that you'd risk your fiancé's life and freedom."

"I agreed to be part of this." Ryan stood, then moved next to Lola. "I knew what I was getting into when Lola's boss asked me to join her," he said, and took Lola's hand in his. "After what went down here, and how Ian and his CORE agents handled business, I wanted to be involved."

"No, you wanted to be the hero."

"Screw you."

That might have been a low blow, but Shane knew his brother, and knew that Ryan needed to matter. When they were kids, he had always been looking for ways to shine. "It's true. I know you and I know what you went through in Pakistan. You don't need to chase bad guys to feel like a better man. What's wrong with running a business, getting married and giving me nieces and nephews? What's wrong with having a *normal* life?"

Ryan grinned and shook his head. "When have either of us had a normal life?"

Shane couldn't answer that. Neither of them had been interested in following in their father's footsteps and going into a trade, and neither of them had been college material. They'd grown up exploring the Everglades and dreaming about adventure. Looking for excitement he couldn't find here, Ryan had joined the Navy, then had applied to be a SEAL. Shane had joined the Army for the same reason, but had tied in his love for flying by applying to be a special operations pilot, then later a Night Stalker. There was nothing normal about either of their decisions. But after losing seven years of his life, he needed normalcy. He wanted to run his business, settle down with a good woman and live his life without looking over his shoulder and wondering when the law might catch up with him.

"I get where you're coming from," Ryan said. "I also told you I struggled with Lola asking you to join us. The reason I agreed is because you own a plane. I figured the only time you'd really be involved is when one of us might need a lift or when we were talking about a case."

"Ryan's right. Each one of us has a certain skill set that will help our operation. Yours is transportation. You can't carry a weapon, and I'd never ask you to. But you can fly us in and out of places." She drew in a breath. "What bothers me is that you're not taking what we're doing seriously. Shane, your brother and I hunted a man who was hunting my *mother*. I cleaned his blood and brain matter off that floor." She pointed toward the gutted kitchen. "Right in that room I watched as David removed bullets from Ian and John. I was there when the decision was made to use Mel to get rid of a killer's body. And I'll be honest. It stripped me of my innocence and made me realize that if given the chance, I can make a difference. We all can." She let go of Ryan's hand and stepped toward Shane. "In comparison, our first ATL assignment was definitely easy, but they won't all be. I don't want to have to ask David to come here and remove bullets from anyone, and I don't want anyone going to prison. Again, I'm not trying to tell you who you can and can't see, but I need to ensure that we are a solid group, and that each one of us can trust the other to have their back. I need to make sure Beth isn't going to disrupt that."

Jesus, she'd cleaned brain matter off the kitchen floor?

"Lola's right," Ryan said. "But I trust you and your judgment."

"Ryan thinks we should work with Beth. My concern is that if you two don't work out, she could become vindictive and out us. Do you want that to happen?" Lola asked. "I mean, you two just met, how well do you really know her?"

"She doesn't want me going back to prison, so I'm not worried about her telling anyone what we're doing. And if she wanted to cause problems for us, she could have already done it."

"I'm not going to dispute that, but I also don't trust so easily. Especially when I'm not only looking out for the welfare of ATL, but for it's crew."

He stepped away from the door. "Again, she's not going to be a cop forever, and I didn't tell her anything except admitting to belonging to a private investigative agency. She already knew too much and planned to come talk to you with or without me. I tried to diffuse the situation the best I could."

Lola held up a hand. "And you did. I'm glad you were there, otherwise I don't know how I would've reacted. That being said, Ryan and I talked and I'm going to tell Ian about this and suggest that we don't pursue the necrophiliac case."

"Why?"

"Beth knows we were involved, and I think it's best that we let the detectives handle the case. It's not worth exposing ourselves."

"I think Beth might want to change your mind about giving up on this case."

"Why's that?"

"Deputies found another body on Shell Island Road."

"Another corpse?" she asked.

"No. The woman was murdered and it sounds like the MO is the same as Katie Reed's. Beth will know more later."

"Thanks for telling us." Lola looked to Ryan. "I'll talk to Ian about this, but I'm still concerned about working with Beth."

Harrison cleared his throat. "If I may," he began. "Me and Vlad are the only two who have everything riding on this. If anyone should be concerned about what happens to ATL, it should be us. Lola could find a job, or work for Ryan. Mel and Barney already have jobs and Shane has the flying gig. Me and Vlad, this is all we've got. Shane, dude, I was locked away for a couple of years, and I think it's great you're dating. I wish I was. But would a cop be my first choice? Hell, no."

"Vlad agree. But Vlad like Kiss Beth."

"You don't even know her."

"Vlad know Kiss Beth like Polina. That good enough for Vlad."

Harrison stared at Vlad for a moment, then said, "Anyway, Lola, I also get where you're coming from on this. But we have a prime opportunity to align ourselves *with* the law. If we have Beth in our corner, she could feed us info so I don't have to run the risk of hacking into the sheriff's computer system. If she hears that the law is suspecting we're out there doing something we shouldn't, she could give us the 411. Think about it. If you decide to stick with the necrophilia case—which I'm *not* okay with dropping—and we find the guy, what would you do with him? We can't make him swamp bait."

"It's one thing to defend ourselves against a killer," Ryan said. "But we're not murderers or vigilantes."

"No, we're not." Lola looked to Shane. "We *would* need a cop we could trust."

"Exactly," Harrison said. "Let's say we find the necrophiliac. We can't arrest him, but we could hand him over to Beth and let her take care of the legal end of things."

"Harrison is right." With a nod, Lola approached Shane. "The only family I have is my mom, and she's in Chicago. Ryan is my family now, so are these guys. I'm sorry if I popped off on you last night, and I'm sure Beth thinks I'm a real sweetheart."

Shane grinned, and finally relaxed. "She thought you were going to hit her."

Her eyes widened. "God, no. When she grabbed my arm, I reacted." She shook her head and sighed. "Please understand that while you might not think much of what we're doing, it's important to me, Vlad and Harrison."

"Me, too," Ryan said, and looked at him. "After working with Lola and going after the jackass who'd kidnapped her mom and Ian, I realized I missed the rush and adrenaline I used to get when I was with the SEALs." He shrugged.

"There's also nothing wrong with wanting to be a hero every now and then."

"I know, and I'm sorry for what I said about that."

"So," Lola began, "are we okay? We could still use a pilot, and apparently a cop."

Looking at the situation from Lola's point of view, he could understand her reaction last night, along with her struggle to allow Beth access to ATL. Before he'd found out about ATL, he'd liked Lola, and still did, even if he was on the fence about ATL. Plus, it was clear that she and his brother were not only in love with each other, but they both believed in what they were doing. Now they were willing to believe in him—and Beth. "I'll talk to Beth."

"Let us know what she says," Lola said. "If she wants to talk with me about it, I'm here."

Guilt settled on his shoulders as he looked to Lola. "I'm sorry I didn't take you guys seriously. The killer who was hunting your mom...what you dealt with had to have been hard. I give you credit for taking on this organization after that."

She smiled. "Thanks, Shane. That means a lot to me."

He started for the door. "I'll call you later."

"Hold up," Harrison said. "Anyone want to comment on the dead body they found on Shell Island Road?"

Shane turned. "I told you what Beth knows. Which wasn't much."

"Yeah, but don't you find it strange that a body matching Katie Reed's murder showed up at the same place where the three dead women were found?"

Lola nodded. "The MO is the same as Katie's, not the corpses', correct?"

"That's the way Beth understood it. She also said she was worried that whoever dumped the women, might have given Katie's murderer a reason to resurface."

"Did she say why?" Ryan asked.

"No."

"Vlad will take knife to the darkness."

"You mean stab at the dark," Harrison corrected.

"That what Vlad say. Knife, stab, all same to Vlad."

"Go ahead, Vlad," Ryan said. "Knife to the darkness works for me."

The Russian gave Harrison a smug smile. "As Vlad was to say, if Vlad kill man—this all hypocritical, of course—Vlad would not like for another killer to copy Vlad in way that make Vlad look like sick-job."

"Katie's killer doesn't want to be associated with a necrophiliac," Shane said, liking Vlad's suggestion.

"So after two years he comes out of hiding to prove a point," Lola said. "I'm wondering how many women he'll kill to make sure he gets his point across."

"Does this mean we're still working the necrophiliac case?" Harrison asked.

She met Shane's gaze. "Absolutely. Hopefully with a little help from the law."

Naples, Florida
Sunday, 9:24 a.m., Eastern Standard Time

He pulled into his driveway and hit the switch to open the garage door. He glanced next door. His neighbor, Ned, stood next to his golf cart. George and Marty, two scratch golfers who'd taken more of his money than he cared to admit, sat in the golf cart next to Ned's. Since he hadn't played golf in over a week, he envied the men. If he didn't need to be back at Gabriela's by eleven to take her to meet her parents for brunch, he would have tried to play a round this morning. Maybe later he'd head to the driving range and hit a couple of buckets of balls.

After he exited the car, he waved to the men. "When's tee time?" he asked.

"We're set for ten. These two mooches came by for a Bloody Mary. Want one?" Ned asked, and raised his glass.

He'd love one, or three. "I'm good, thanks."

"We can use a fourth," Marty said.

He walked across the lawn. "And let you take my money?"

"C'mon," George began, "last time it was only twenty bucks."

"Twenty bucks, and then I had to buy you a couple of beers after."

Ned laughed. "I told you not to make any extra side bets with the rat bastard."

"So what do you say?" George asked. "Can you make the tee time?"

"Can't. I'm having brunch with Gabriela and her parents to celebrate our engagement."

"Hey-ho." Ned set his drink in the golf cart cup holder, then reached over to shake his hand. "Congratulations. Gabriela's a great gal."

"Does this mean you got rid of the snakes?" Marty asked after he and George also offered their congratulations.

"One of them. Gabriela's planning on moving in with me in May, so I've got a few months before I have to get rid of him."

"Speaking of snakes, did you hear about the woman they found on Shell Island Road?" George asked.

Women. "Yeah, that's horrible and disgusting. I feel bad for the families of those three women," he said, wishing he could go back in time and be with his dead lover. While he still had no problem satisfying Gabriela, he'd come to realize how much he missed his dead lover, being able to touch her and do what ever he wanted without complaint. "Now that they let the senator's son-in-law go, I wonder if they'll catch the guy."

"Disgusting doesn't even cover it," Marty said, and cringed. "Makes you wonder what's wrong with people. What would possess a man to want to have sex with a corpse?"

If only Marty knew.

"I'm not talking about the three women they found Friday," George said. "I'm talking about the woman they found *today*."

Blood rushed to his head and gave him a brief moment of vertigo. He leaned against Ned's golf cart, and did his best to act casual. "Today?"

"Yeah, I caught it on the news just before I went to pick up Marty. Deputies found another woman on Shell Island Road."

"No shit?" Ned asked. "Interesting that they let that funeral director go free and another body shows up, huh?"

"It wasn't another corpse, and that guy left for Jacksonville to stay with family right after he was released," George said. "That reporter on Channel Five. You know, the sexy brunette? She was going on about how the Sheriff's Office isn't handling the investigation right and that her source thinks there're two bad guys out there."

Marty chuckled. "Did she use the term 'bad guys'?"

"Don't know. I had to paraphrase because I was too busy checking out her cleavage."

As the other men laughed, he forced a smile while his mind raced and his stomach rolled with nausea. *Two* bad guys?

"Did the sexy brunette say if the woman was murdered?" Ned asked.

"Yep. Don't know how." George checked his watch. "I want to practice my putting. Are you guys ready to head to the club house?"

He wished the men luck, then hurried into his house. After turning on the TV, and finding nothing about the murder on any of the local channels, he opened his laptop and did a search for breaking news in Naples, Florida. Within seconds, the page loaded. The top headline read: *Murdered Woman Found on Shell Island Road.* He clicked on the link, and read the short article.

NAPLES, FL.— Early this morning, Collier County deputies were called to Shell Island Road when a local fisherman discovered the body of a woman. Cause of death and the victim's identity are unknown. The fisherman, Lyle Lewis, said he saw the body on his way to the boat ramp and described the grisly scene as something from a horror movie. Lewis claims the woman had her throat slit and a long gash along her stomach. He also said that it looked as if her killer had sewed the gash.

This latest victim, the three corpses that were found Friday on Shell Island Road, and the murder of Kathleen Reed are eerily similar. Police have yet to comment on whether the cases are linked.

He closed the laptop and ran a hand through his hair. *What have I done?* His chest tightened and his stomach cramped with guilt. A woman had been murdered because of him.

He couldn't panic. Not yet. The article mentioned nothing about snakes. Whoever had killed this woman could have decided to do a little copying of his own.

Even as the thought entered his mind, he knew it was ridiculous. By mimicking a cold case, he'd poked at a hornet's nest. He'd given a murderer a reason to come out from hiding. Would the man kill again, or was this victim his way of making it clear that he didn't like being associated with a necrophiliac? If that was the case, he received the message loud and clear. There would be no more dead lovers. No hot intimate nights where he could freely use and abuse his lover's body. All he would have from here out were his fantasies.

But would his fantasies be enough?

He pictured the dead woman. Her throat slit. Her stomach slashed.

Damn it, they had to be.

CHAPTER 13

Beth's Townhouse, Marco Island, Florida
Sunday, 7:40 p.m., Eastern Standard Time

MURDER WAS DISTRACTING. Shane was, too. Beth pushed aside her textbook. Contract law couldn't hold her interest, not when her mind was on Shane, the private agency he worked for, and the woman found this morning.

When her cell phone rang, she checked the caller ID, and debated whether or not she should answer. She loved Erin, and had been dying to tell her what had happened with Shane, but he should be by any minute, and for what she wanted to tell Erin she'd need more than a few minutes. Friday had been the last time she'd spoken to Erin. As far as her friend knew, she and Shane were through.

As the call went to voicemail, she realized so much had happened in the past two days. Sex, murder, private investigators...

A knock came at the door. Anxious to see Shane, as well as a little nervous, she pressed a hand to her stomach and hurried to the door. When she opened it, Shane greeted her with a smile, flowers and a pizza. She grinned. She couldn't remember the last time a man, other than her dad, had brought her flowers.

"Hi." When he stepped inside, she rose to her tiptoes and gave him a kiss. She hoped that she wasn't being presumptuous. They weren't exactly a couple, and might never be. In the meantime, she'd take advantage of every kiss and touch she could. "Did you have any trouble finding my place?" she asked, leading him into the kitchen.

"Not at all. This is a nice area." He set the pizza box on the counter, then handed her the flowers, which were a mixture of white and purple lilies, lavender daisies, dark-purple button poms and small white roses. "For you."

She inhaled the fragrant bouquet. "Thank you, they're beautiful," she said, then kissed him again. "I love them."

"You're welcome." He touched her cheek. "Did you finish studying?"

"For the most part," she said, and pulled a glass pitcher from the cabinet. "I was trucking along all morning and early afternoon, but after I met with a detective I work with, I had a hard time focusing."

"Is he working the murder investigation?"

She filled the pitcher with water. "Yeah, he and his partner are also handling the necrophilia case, too."

He leaned against the counter. "Can you talk about it?"

"To you?" She glanced at him, and didn't understand the uncertainty in his eyes. "Why wouldn't I?" she asked, and set down the pitcher and flowers. "I thought we established a line of trust. You've been somewhat honest with me, and I've been completely honest with you."

He grinned. "Somewhat?"

"Am I wrong?"

"No, you're right. I haven't been totally honest, but it doesn't mean I don't trust you."

She walked over to him, then wrapped her arms around his waist. "*That* I believe," she said, then kissed him. When his stomach rumbled, she tapped his flat abs and laughed. "Let's get you fed."

"I haven't eaten much today." He opened a couple of

cabinets. "Where are your…never mind, found them." He set the plates on the counter, then looked at the flower arrangement. "Don't you own a vase?"

"Do you?"

"I'm a guy."

"And I don't get enough flowers to have a reason to buy a vase. By the way, gender shouldn't matter when it comes to owning a vase."

"You're right. Tomorrow I'm going to buy two. One for each of us. I'm also going to make sure your vase is always filled."

Damn, the man was hot, sexy and sweet. "What are you going to put in your vase?"

"Since it sounds like you won't be buying me any flowers, I'll dump a bag of M & M's or jelly beans in it."

She handed him napkins. "Since you're so sweet, *I'll* buy the candy for your vase."

He raised a brow. "I'm too badass to be sweet."

"Well, then you're a sweet badass, who has a nice ass," she said, and gave his rear a little squeeze. "Beer?"

Shane carried the plates, silverware and napkins to her small table. "Depends."

"On?"

"If I'm staying the night."

She reached into the fridge and grabbed a couple of beers, then set the bottle in front of him. "Does this answer your question?"

He pulled her onto his lap. "You're sure?"

"Why wouldn't I be?"

"Maybe we should talk first. You might change your mind."

"Lola?"

He nodded. "We hashed it out this morning, but I think we're good now." He tucked a lock of hair behind her ear. "I want us to be, too."

Us. That tiny word said so much.

She opened his beer. She could care less what Lola thought of her, or if she disapproved of her and Shane. She wanted him to stay the night. "I won't change my mind." She kissed his cheek, then moved to the seat next to his. "Let's eat and talk."

"I wasn't exactly honest about the private agency," he said, opened the pizza box, then placed a slice on her plate. "We're not regular investigators."

She reached for her beer. "Are you licensed?" she asked, and took a sip.

"Lola is, but she'd lose her license if her activities were discovered." He took a slice for himself. "She used to work for a legit private investigation agency. A couple months ago, her boss asked her to start an operation in Florida that's not so legit. My brother, Vlad, Harrison and a couple of other people I don't think you've met are a part of this operation."

"Other than not having properly licensed investigators, what makes this not so legit?"

"You were right about Vlad and Harrison having everything to do with Dustin Williams turning himself in. They might have kidnapped him, and we might have coerced him into telling us what happened to the bodies."

"Might have?"

He took a bite of his pizza, and nodded. After he swallowed, he said, "Harrison might have also hacked into the Sheriff's Office's computer system to find out what detectives knew about Dustin and his dad."

She took a long drink of her beer. "Do you realize how much trouble you guys could get in to if that was discovered? Oh, my God, Shane. What are you thinking? You just got out of prison, do you want to go back?"

"Of course not."

"Then why are you aligning yourself with these people?"

"Because I don't know Lola, Vlad or Harrison, and I want to make sure none of them get my brother into any trouble." He picked up his pizza. "Aren't you going to eat?"

"I noticed you haven't had a sip of your beer."

He glanced at the bottle. "I'm still waiting for you to ask me to leave," he said, then took another a bite of his pizza.

"Why would I ask you to leave? Because I'm now

associating with a criminal?"

"I'm not a criminal."

"No? Were you there for Dustin's *coercion*?" When he nodded, she drew in a breath. "If Dustin told the detectives this, they would have come after whoever took part in the kidnapping. Including you."

"The kid was blindfolded. The only people he could ID are Vlad and Harrison."

Blindfolded? "Did you gag him and tie him to a chair, too."

"Maybe," he said, and finished his pizza. After he used his napkin to wipe his mouth, he reached for his beer. "I'm thirsty."

"There's water in the fridge." She shoved her chair back, and stood. "You also know where the door is."

He snagged her hand before she could walk away. "Do you trust me?"

"This isn't about whether I trust you or not. Shane, I can't be with a man who is flirting with the law. What happened to you in Norfolk is different. You didn't mean to kill that man. But you've now chosen, knowing damn well the risk, to willingly involve yourself with a criminal organization."

"They're not criminals, at least not all of them are, and we want what you want, remember?" He rubbed his hand along her arm. "Please sit down and eat. Let me finish saying what I have to say, and then make up your mind about it. Okay?"

She didn't want him to leave and wanted to trust him. Still, she worried about his future, should he continue to associate with Lola and her people. She worried about hers, as well. If it became known that she knew about this operation, and they did something major—like murder a man—she could be in serious trouble.

She sat back down, and picked up her pizza, which had grown cold. "Fine," she said, curious what he had to say. "I'll listen, but I can't promise to be open-minded."

"Thank you." Shane took a water bottle from the fridge. "The purpose of the organization is to help clients who can't get what they need through proper legal channels. For example, Senator Bryan hired us to prove his son-in-law was innocent."

"We would have proven that without your help."

"Eventually. In the meantime, you guys were pretty quick to arrest Williams."

"I'll give you that, and thought the same thing. Tell me about another case you've worked, or was this your first?" she asked, then took a bite of pizza.

"Mine and theirs."

"You're telling me the necrophilia case was the operation's very first one? Tell Lola to close the doors before one of you gets hurt or convicted."

"She's not going to do that. The agency she used to work for has deep pockets and is backing her on this. The owner *wants* ATL to be successful."

"ATL?"

"It's an acronym for our operation."

She half-smiled. "I get that, just not what it stands for."

He cleared his throat, picked up his beer, then put it back in the fridge. "Above the Law."

Chuckling, she tossed her napkin on the plate. "You're screwing with me, right?"

"No, and I didn't come up with the name. I guess Harrison did." He leaned against the counter. "The man backing ATL has more than just money, he's very well connected. His legit agency is well known and his agents have been called in to assist police and sheriff's departments, state agencies and even the FBI."

"Did Senator Bryan call this man and ask for help?"

"Yes."

"What about Dr. Adams? Does he know this man, too?"

"That's my understanding."

"You won't tell me this man's name or the name of his agency?"

"Do you have a flashlight?"

"Yes, why?"

"I thought maybe you might want to shine it in my eyes

while you continued to interrogate me."

She chuckled. "Sorry, but you have to admit that you'd be asking a lot of questions, too."

"And I did. I grilled Lola, just like you're grilling me." He sat back down. "I can't tell you the name of the man Lola works for or the name of his agency. Lola asked me to keep him out of the conversation."

She let out a sigh. "Lola knows we're having this little talk. Why is that?"

"Because she has a proposition for you."

"Am I going to want to hear this?"

"Hear me out, and if you're not interested, just say so and it'll never be brought up again."

Except if she continued to see Shane, she'd constantly wonder and worry if he was up to something illegal. She cared about him. Last night had made her realize how much, and not just because he was great in bed. She'd loved talking with him, learning about his past, present and what he wanted from the future. But they couldn't have a future if he wound up back in prison. Or dead. "Okay, go on," Beth finally said.

"Since we obviously don't have the authority to arrest anyone, and we don't want the police or any other agency to know we exist, Lola would like you to be our local liaison. We can lead you to the evidence you need to make an arrest, bad guy goes to jail, our client is happy and you get the credit for keeping the streets clean."

He made it sound too easy. "If we're working on the same case, would Lola be willing to share information with me?"

"Yes."

"Let's say I had a case that you weren't involved in, would ATL be willing to help?"

"I suppose it would depend, but I don't see why not. We're on the same side, we just have a different way of getting the job done."

She was tempted to jump at his offer. She liked rules, but there'd been times when she hadn't wanted to follow them.

With a sigh she toyed with her napkin, folding it over itself and remembering one of those times. "About a year after I became a deputy, a man called 911 and reported his son was missing. Ricky and I were sent to the house, and found out the son was four. The boy's mother was there, crying and carrying on as I would expect. But there were no tears. The father was also frantic, but it came off as rehearsed. I thought it was me being overly suspicious, but even Ricky agreed. We searched their house, their yard, the neighbors'. We called in detectives, additional deputies and CSU." She shook her head. "We found nothing. No evidence that anyone but the parents had been at the house, no forced entry, nothing that indicated a kidnapping. It was as if that little boy simply vanished."

She tossed the napkin on the table, then reached for her beer and finished it. "Detectives interviewed the hell out of the mom and dad," she continued, and stood to grab another bottle. While she had the fridge open, she pulled out Shane's untouched beer, as well. "They ran background checks, conferred with CSU, interviewed family, friends and neighbors, then ended up releasing the couple because not one thing indicated that they had anything to do with their son's disappearance." She set his beer in front of him. "In my gut, I knew they did something to him. A part of me didn't want to know, but damn if I didn't want justice for that boy."

"What did you do, Beth?" he asked, as he reached across, and gave her hand a gentle squeeze.

She sipped her beer, and gathered the nerve to tell him. "I followed them whenever I had the chance, even when I was off duty. I pulled them over several times, and each time I did I came up with excuses to search their vehicles. Ricky ended up so mad at me, he threatened to request a different partner, especially when the couple went to my superiors and complained that I was harassing them. My captain gave me a warning and told me to back off. I did, but didn't want to. The thing is, he, Ricky and every person who worked that case, believed the parents had something to do with that child's disappearance, but legally, we did everything we could until our hands were tied."

"You never found the boy."

"No. I think they killed him and tossed him somewhere in the Everglades or in the Gulf. The dad happened to own a boat." She met his gaze. "If you guys were around then, offering me this same proposition, I would've had you go after that mother and father, and *coerce* them into confessing."

"How would you want us to do that?"

She brought to mind the photographs she'd seen of the little boy. He'd been adorable. Dark hair, big blue eyes, precious smile. And the same people who had brought him into this world had murdered him. She'd had no proof, still had none, but gut instinct blamed the parents. "Whatever was necessary."

"What was the boy's name?"

She held his gaze. "Hunter."

"Do you want ATL to investigate the parents and try to find Hunter?"

Yes. She wanted those people to pay for whatever they'd done to their son. "Right now, I'm only interested in finding the man who just murdered Elizabeth Neal."

"Is she the woman they found this morning?"

She nodded. "Are you finished eating? If not, I'll wait to tell you the details."

"Before you get into it, what are your thoughts on ATL?"

"I think you guys need to be careful."

"And?"

She liked the idea of having an additional 'crime fighting' resource at her disposal, and would have seriously used ATL to find the missing boy. There'd been many times over the years where she'd wanted to break rules to make an arrest, but had been too afraid of losing her job. ATL could possibly break those rules for her, and by affiliating herself with them, Shane wouldn't have to keep his activities from her. At least she hoped he wouldn't. Between yesterday and today, 'trust' had been brought up many times, and she trusted her instinct. Shane wouldn't screw her over. Lola? Time would tell.

"As long as I can walk away with my name never being

associated with your group," she began, "I'd be willing to occasionally work with you. Keep in mind, I'm not going to be a cop forever. You're eventually going to have to find someone else to help with any arrests."

He smiled and gave her hand another squeeze. "We'll worry about that when it's necessary." He let go of her, picked up the pizza box, then went to the refrigerator. "Other than being murdered, what happened to Elizabeth Neal?" he asked, and put the pizza away. "Lola called the ME this afternoon, but he said he couldn't talk with her."

"That doesn't surprise me. We found out that the person who leaked the information about the snakes worked for Dr. Adams. The woman was a part-time autopsy tech, and had only been on the job for a few months. She's been let go, and I heard the reporter who she leaked the info to is making a big stink over her firing. So I'm sure Dr. Adams is exercising extreme caution right now." She stood and picked up their beers. "Let's go sit in the living room and talk." After they made their way into the living room, and Shane took a seat on the couch, she sat next to him. "Like I said earlier," she continued. "I met with the detective who's working the investigation. Nick—"

"The detective?"

She nodded. "Nick told me that the last time anyone saw Elizabeth Neal alive was yesterday night around eleven. She was at the Tic Toc bar in the east Naples area. The bartender said she was buzzed when she left alone. No one remembers seeing anyone leave right after her, and we know she drove herself home. We also know she stopped at a gas station minutes after she left the bar to buy cigarettes. Video surveillance and the store clerk back up this. From there, what happened to her becomes questionable. Her car was parked in front of her apartment building, the driver's door open, and her purse was lying in the middle of the parking lot. Someone who lives in the complex saw this at around one in the morning and reported it to police."

Shane rested his arm along the couch cushions and inched

her closer to him. "Doesn't sound like the killer was trying to hide her abduction."

"Nick and his partner, Jerry, thought the same thing. The deputies who were called to the apartment complex early this morning, also treated this as a possible abduction and had immediately called in CSU. They found a couple of cigarette butts—that were Elizabeth's brand—one by her car, the other near her purse. Nick and Jerry talked with CSU, and they all think someone—likely the killer—drove through the parking lot, parked behind her car and called her over. For whatever reason, she left her car door open, walked to where the car must have been parked, then talked with the killer long enough to smoke two-thirds of a cigarette. CSU did find tiny drops of blood on and near her purse. They're waiting on DNA results, but considering how badly her head had been beaten, everyone is assuming the blood belongs to Elizabeth."

"No one heard anything?"

"Nothing." She rested her head against his arm. "Nick said this particular apartment complex had issues with mold. One of the buildings is vacant while they clean it up, so there's not a lot of people currently living there."

"Or it could be she never had the chance to make a sound."

She rolled her head to the side and lay her hand on his thigh. "After I finish telling you about Elizabeth, do you want to play Scrabble? I have Yahtzee, Boggle, Life, or we could play cards instead."

He grinned. "Where's this coming from?"

"You've been here for an hour and our conversations have centered around a lot of heavy subjects. I don't want it to always be that way."

"It won't, because we won't let it." He kissed her forehead. "Finish telling me about Elizabeth, then I'm going to kick your sexy butt in Strip Scrabble."

"And how does one play Strip Scrabble?"

"I'll let you know as I make up the rules." He squeezed her close. "If you don't want to talk about the murder now, we can do it in the morning."

"No, it's okay. I think what's bothering me is how random and violent this killing was. He took her to Shell Island Road, not the exact spot where Ricky and I found the three corpses, but close enough."

"How close?"

"A tenth of a mile, and instead of trying to hide the body in the woods, he left her where he'd killed her, right along the side of the road."

"Katie Reed was killed somewhere else, then her body was dumped, right?"

"Right. There're plenty of differences between Katie and Elizabeth's murders, but Nick and Jerry still think it's the same guy. Let me tick off the differences," she said. "Katie was killed somewhere else, her body was nude and cleaned. Elizabeth was killed on the side of the road, she was fully clothed. Katie was strangled, Elizabeth suffered blunt force trauma to the head, but that wasn't what killed her. He'd slit her throat. The similarities? Dr. Adams said the cut along Patricia's stomach, as well as the fishing line used to sew her up, were the same as what he'd found on Katie. And, of course, there's the baby rattlesnake he'd found inside her. The question is, how many killers are we looking for, and did one or both of these men leave the corpses in the woods?"

"What do the detectives think?"

"The man who killed Katie also killed Elizabeth, but had nothing to do with the corpses. I think they're right."

"Vlad suggested that the killer is back to make a statement, that maybe this guy doesn't want to be associated with a necrophiliac."

In between sips of coffee, and sneaking peeks at her chest, Nick had mentioned the same thing. "Nick's words were, 'Murder is okay, but having sex with a dead body is worse.'"

Shane raised his brows. "I don't even know what to do with that."

"I know. What's scary is will this guy kill again? If he wants to make it clear that he didn't abuse the corpses, will he keep killing until the necrophiliac is arrested?"

He kissed her forehead again. "I'm just a pilot. Do you want me to tell Lola about Elizabeth and have her see what she can find?"

"Yes," she said, and stared at him. "You're more than a pilot. If you weren't, Lola wouldn't have asked you to join her operation."

"She made it clear, they wanted me because I could fly them in and out of places when necessary."

This, she preferred. She'd rather have him flying members of ATL than taking part in illegal activities like hacking and kidnapping, or worse. "Are you okay with that?"

"Oh, yeah. I get to know what they're up to and I get to make sure my brother's okay without having to play secret spy." He touched her chin. "I haven't shot a gun since I was in the Army. After I got out, I didn't even enjoy hunting anymore because holding a gun reminded me of war, and killing. Before that one punch I threw in Norfolk, I hadn't been in a fight since high school. Prison was different. If I took a swing, it was to protect myself when guards weren't around." He caressed her cheek. "ATL? I'm still struggling with this. I can understand why Ryan wants to be part of it, and not just because of Lola. When we were kids, we both wanted to lead these exciting and adventurous lives. I think he still wants that. But I've had enough excitement and adventure." He stared at her for a few heartbeats. "I went off on a tangent, didn't I?"

She smiled, then kissed him. "No way. I feel like I do most of the talking and I love it when you let me in here," she said, ran her hand through his hair, then held the back of his head. "If you don't want excitement and adventure, what do you want?"

"To spend the evening doing what normal couples do."

"Strip Scrabble is normal?" she asked, ignoring the disappointment suddenly settling on her shoulders. She refused to allow it to ruin the evening. She hadn't expected him to say that he'd wanted a relationship with her, but after everything they'd discussed and the trust they'd placed in each other, the romantic inside her had hoped for something more than a butt

kid had reminded him of how much power and control he had. How he could decide whether someone deserved to live or die. He'd admit, he had gone a little high and mighty after taking a bat to Cory Turner, and he probably shouldn't have killed that couple camping about a mile from where he'd dumped Cory's body deep in the Georgia woods. But it sure had been fun.

Under the light of the moon, he'd stumbled upon their campsite. Their fire had been nothing more than red glowing embers, and he'd watched as they screwed in their tent.

Then he'd killed them. As the man had been pumping himself into his gal, he'd entered the tent and had smashed his head in, then he'd done the same to the screaming woman.

He'd confessed to Daddy, only because he'd come home bloodier than he should have been, and Daddy had asked him why. He hadn't had any reason except that he could. He could kill and get away with it. Hell, between himself and Daddy, they'd taken the lives of over a dozen people and they were still free. He planned for things to stay that way.

"Don't worry about it, Daddy. I won't do any unnecessary killin'." He glanced to the newspaper. "I do have some good news. I think I know where to start looking for the pervert."

"Because of the woman you killed."

"No," he answered honestly. "It's a little too soon to tell if that made a difference or not. I tried to get close to the crime scene by hanging around reporters and pretending I was one of them, but couldn't see much of anything. I did notice the detective who worked Katie's case was there, but I've already ruled him out. He looked too shook up."

"Don't mean nothing. If you act the part, people will believe anything."

After years of preaching bullshit, Daddy would know. "I hear you, but I still don't think it's him. After what I just read in the paper, I'm going to start with the Medical Examiner's office," he said, then told Daddy about the article.

"You think a doc diddled with the corpses?"

The Reverend stood and walked toward the balcony. "I'm more interested in the doc's employees. I went on the county website and saw a postin' for a part-time autopsy assistant. Under education and experience, it said they'd *prefer* one year's experience in the field and a high school diploma. Maybe our copycat wasn't even working for the ME when I killed Katie. Could be we're dealing with some pervert who gets his rocks off hangin' out with the dead, he decides to take it a step further and snatches the bodies, then pins it on us."

"Could be. Check it out and check on the ME, too."

"I will," he said as two pelicans flew past his suite. "Since you're a little bent about what I did to the woman last night, are you still okay with me killin' whoever mocked us?"

"Son, he took what you and me done to your mama and made a mockery of it. No one but us knows we'd sliced up her belly 'cause it was the next best thing to guttin' her. Not even the members of our church who watched us. I don't know about you, but that means a little something to me."

Of course it meant something to him. That had been the day he'd become a man and a reverend. All while having his first taste of revenge. His mama might've already been dead, but watching as Daddy cut her open, then helping him hold her stomach together as Daddy had sewed the snake inside her had symbolized freedom. From her wrath. From the chains of the Bible she'd forced him to read. From having to follow a moral code of right and wrong.

"Think about Katie," Daddy continued. "Harlan believed in what you'd done. Knowing his daughter went to God's arms free of sin allowed him to die a happy man. Same goes for anyone else who's asked us to perform the ritual. It don't matter that me and you don't believe in what we preach, what matters is making sure the people who line our pockets believe. I'm old and won't be 'round much longer. But you're young. The money I've got saved will only last you so long. How'd you feel about havin' to get yourself a real job? 'Cause without our congregation, that's what you'll have to do."

Being forced to actually work, and possibly have some asshole boss him around didn't work for him. He looked to the waves lapping at the shore. He wanted *this* lifestyle, and to be able to freely fly off to a tropical paradise without having to worry about punching a timecard.

"Now," Daddy began, "you've gone and killed a woman to ferret this man out. I get where your mind was, but no more killin' unless it's the *pree*vert, understand?"

"Yes, sir."

"What's done is done. We can't expect our copycat to rush to the police and confess 'cause he's feelin' all guilty, but you gotta figure he's stewin' on this."

"The pervert should be wondering what we know about him." He should kill another, just to make it clear.

"That's what I'm sayin'. So, you follow up on that medical examiner deal. It looks like a promisin' start."

Sitting, watching and waiting for someone from the Medical Examiner's office to act out of the ordinary sounded boring as hell. But he'd do as Daddy had asked. He'd stick to playing detective instead of killer. For now. He did have five more snakes, and wouldn't mind putting them to use before they upped and died on him.

"You're a good son," Daddy said. "God knows I love you, and if I weren't a shell of a man, I'd be right by your side."

"I know you would. Don't worry, Daddy. One way or the other, I'll find him, and I'll take care of him."

By any means.

Lola's Rental House, Everglades City, Florida
Monday, 9:47 a.m., Eastern Standard Time

Lola finished reading through everything Mel had printed off on necrophilia. "Well, that was entertaining."

Harrison looked up from his laptop. "Do I get to decide whether I want to hear about it or not?"

She wrinkled her nose. "Don't worry, I'm not going to subject you to any of it. Honestly, it pretty much confirms what we, and the detectives, believe. We have two perps. One who's a murderer and one who is a regular necrophiliac."

He leaned back in the dining room chair. "As opposed to an irregular necrophilliac? To me, any way you slice it, there's nothing normal or regular about it."

"Obviously. But according to this study I just read, there is also necrophillic homicide, which is killing someone with the intent to have sex with the body, and necrophillic fantasy, which is fantasizing about having sex with the dead, but not following through with it. If the same man who abused the corpses killed Katie and Elizabeth, or even only Elizabeth, why wouldn't he have abused her body, too? He had the opportunity."

"Maybe she was too warm," Harrison suggested.

"If you don't change the subject, me and Vlad are walking off the job," Barney called from the kitchen where he and Vlad were tiling the floor.

"Turn on the radio," she said.

"Vlad broke it yesterday."

Harrison rolled his eyes. "You can't trust him with electronics. Do you know how many cell phones he's gone through?"

"Vlad hear Harry loud and crystal clear."

"Good. Then maybe you'll be more careful with your stuff." He looked at her. "Back to what I was saying."

She held up a hand. "I agree with Barney, we don't need to discuss body temperature. The detectives think whoever killed Elizabeth might have done it to disassociate himself from the necrophiliac."

"Vlad say that before," the Russian shouted. "Why no one listen to Vlad?"

"Stop your damned shouting," Barney said, then stepped out of the kitchen. "What the detectives should be looking for is the snake connection."

Harrison pulled out a file. "They have. I have the herpetologist's report right here."

"I saw that report, and fell asleep while I was reading it," Barney said. "All she talked about was the type of snakes these two guys used."

"Could be three guys," Harrison said.

"I don't think so. The only thing leaked to that reporter was the use of snakes, not how he'd sewed them into the bodies. The cops never told the public fishing line was used on the Reed girl."

"So what's your thought on the snake connection?" Lola asked.

He pulled out one of the dining room chairs and sat. "When I was back in 'Nam, I met a kid from West Virginia. Don't remember where from exactly, I do remember thinking he was a strange one. He had a thing for snakes. Not like Shane or Ryan. Those boys had always been curious about nature, and snakes are curious creatures."

"Vlad do not want to be lying with tile until tiny hour of night. Barney need to make story quick."

Barney glared at Vlad for a second. "Anyhow, so this kid catches a snake when we were out on patrol, hides it in his sack, and brings it back to camp. Sarge catches the kid outside one of the tents, on his knees and rubbing the dang snake over his head and face."

Lola cringed. "That's so gross."

"Ain't it though? So Sarge asks the kid what the hell he's doing, and that boy tells him he's getting in touch with God and the Holy Spirit. That's when Sarge tells him to get rid of the snake and go see the chaplain. But that kid didn't want to get rid of the snake, and when Sarge caught him with it again, he lopped its head off with a machete." Barney shook his head. "You shoulda seen that boy go nuts. It took three men to hold him down. He kept shouting about his salvation, and that God worked through that snake and protected him from harm or some such nonsense."

"Are you suggesting this is religious?" Lola asked.

"No. Snake handling is illegal. They don't have churches anymore."

Harrison's fingers moved along the keyboard. "Uh, no it's not. I mean it's illegal to have live snakes, but it doesn't mean people still aren't practicing. According to Wikipedia there are churches in the Appalachian Mountains, Alabama, Georgia, Kentucky, Tennessee, the Carolinas and West Virginia. Just last year, a pastor from Kentucky died after he was bitten by a rattlesnake." Harrison looked up at Barney. "Holy shit. Dude, you're a genius. Why didn't you say something earlier?"

"Don't know, I guess I didn't think about it."

A fire ignited in Lola's belly. Finally, they had something they could use to connect the two murdered women. "Harrison, see if you could gather a list of towns where people are still holding these religious services."

"Okay. What do you want me to do from there?"

"Check each town and see if there's been a similar murder during the last two years." She stood and grabbed her purse. "Call Rachel and ask her to access NCIC. Tell her we're looking for any case that relates to a snake, or murder victims who had their abdomen sliced." Due to Ian's connections with the FBI, CORE had been granted access to the FBI's National Crime Information Center, something ATL would never have. She could mention the religious angle to Beth and have her people do the search, but wanted to have more information before she approached her. Honestly, she wanted to prove to Beth that ATL wasn't a crackpot organization. Although Shane had told her that Beth was willing to occasionally work with ATL, Lola suspected the deputy had her reservations, which she understood. They had no track record, and no way of showing her what they were capable of doing.

"What do you want me and Vlad to do?" Barney asked.

"Finish tiling the kitchen."

"And what Asian Lola do?"

"I'm going to go home and take a crash course in snake handling."

PART III

Never wound a snake; kill it.

—Harriet Tubman

KRISTINE MASON

CHAPTER 14

Two days later...

Fort Myers, Florida
Wednesday, 3:48 p.m., Eastern Standard Time

THE REVEREND'S CELL phone rang. He glanced at the screen, then decided to ignore it. Daddy had become a fucking nag. The man just wouldn't quit. For the past two days, he'd practically called him every hour on the hour for a damned update. If he'd had news, Daddy would have been the first to know. But he had nothing. Not a fucking thing. He'd watched and tailed any male who had anything to do with autopsying bodies, which included two techs and one medical examiner. When his efforts hadn't panned out, he moved on to the Chief ME. Since yesterday afternoon, he'd been following Dr. David Adams. He hated it and couldn't understand why anyone would want to be a cop or a private dick. Sitting in a car, staring at closed doors waiting for someone to come out was about as much fun as watching Suzie clip Daddy's nasty-ass toenails.

But Daddy had insisted he follow the man, then move on to the detectives. He didn't want to do either. He wanted to send another message.

The only bright side about the doc was his woman. Hot damn, she was a mighty fine piece of ass. Long dark hair, breasts that would fill his hands perfectly and a curvy ass that he'd like to bang all night long. If Daddy saw the woman, he'd change his mind about the doc. A man wouldn't need to fuck the dead when he had a woman like that.

The car behind him honked when the Reverend made a quick, sharp turn. Damn, he needed to stop thinking about the woman's body and focus on the doc's car. He'd been trailing behind Adams ever since he'd left the ME's offices forty-five minutes ago. They'd just hit Fort Myers, and he hoped this was about as far north as they'd be going. He was tired of being in the car and following the man. Here he was in Paradise, staying at a swanky hotel and he couldn't enjoy any of it. He should have never listened to Daddy.

The phone rang again. He swore, then answered it. "Yeah?"

"Is that how you answer the phone?" Daddy asked.

"Sorry, but all these calls are making me edgy."

"Get over it. What's the doc doin' now?"

"Driving."

"To where?"

"Don't know. We're in Fort Myers now and I feel like he's driving in circles. Like he's killin' time."

Daddy let out a breath. "Pull back, boy. He knows you're followin' him."

How would Daddy know anything? He was lying in a bed eight hours away. "The doc don't know squat. I guarantee his mind is on his woman. But I do think I should call it quits on tailin' him."

"Boy, I told you. No more killin' unless it's the *pree*vert."

"I heard you the first half dozen times you told me," the Reverend snapped, tired of doing nothing, tired of Daddy's nagging.

"After all I done for you, and that's the way you talk to your daddy?"

Guilt suddenly replaced his irritation. Daddy was a good

man and had always done right by him. "Sorry, Daddy. I didn't mean to disrespect you. I'm just frustrated is all and…wait," he said, his gaze locked on the doc's Mercedes. "Holy hell." He slowed his Chevy.

"What is it?"

"The doc just pulled into a fucking funeral home and I gotta piss." He glanced across the street and saw a Burger King, that would work, plus he could grab a sandwich, too. "Daddy, I'm gonna let you go. I'll—"

"Hold up, boy. If you gotta piss, do it in the funeral home. Go inside and see what the doc's doin'."

"He sure as hell ain't stealin' a body. There's got to be fifty-something cars in the parking lot."

"Maybe he's not gonna steal it now. Maybe he's scopin' the place to see if he can get it later."

Daddy was off on this one. Doc Adams had it all. Big ass-house, fancy car, beautiful woman. He wasn't here scoping out anything. He was here to pay his respects. Since he had to take a leak, he'd go inside anyway. If he didn't, that might mean more nagging calls from Daddy.

"Fine," the Reverend said. "I'll go inside, but after today, I'm done following this guy."

"That's fine. Call me when you're finished there."

He ended the call. After he parked, he checked his reflection in the review mirror, then glanced down at his blue golf shirt and khaki pants. Once he'd realized that the doc lived in a country club community, he'd made sure he dressed like a golfer. If anyone had stopped and asked him what he was doing in the area, he could lie and say he was there to golf. Now, he could go into a funeral home without looking like a bum.

When the Reverend left the car, he sucked in a breath. He'd been in air conditioning all day, and hadn't realized how hot it'd become. Before his pits started to sweat and stain his shirt, he quickly made his way inside the funeral home. Once there, he realized why the parking lot was so full. There were two signs indicating either Patricia Oakley's showing or Margaret

Donaghue's. He wasn't sure if the doc had gone into door number one or two, so he peeked around the corner of Margaret Donaghue's room, saw there was hardly anyone inside and nodded to one of the funeral home staff. Then he made his way into the next room. Jam packed with people, he knew he wouldn't have to worry about anyone questioning why he was there. Hell, there were so many teary eyes they wouldn't even notice him. But he noticed the doc. He stood in the receiving line, his hands in his pockets, his gaze on the woman in the coffin.

Curious who the dead woman was, he stepped back into the hallway and picked up one of the morbid funeral trading cards located on a stand near the entrance to where the wake was held. He glanced at the dead woman's picture, then her stats. Patricia Oakley had died at the age of thirty-five, and would be missed by her parents, Lawrence and Barbara Oakley and her sister, Holly Samuels, and a shit-ton of nieces and nephews. He slipped the trading card into his pocket, then looked to the address book. When he didn't find the doc's name, he wondered why the man hadn't signed in like the rest of the folks. Maybe the doc was having an affair with Patricia and hadn't wanted anyone to know he'd come to pay his respects to his mistress.

He picked up the pen, thought about signing the doc's name just to screw with him, but then a sniveling woman approached him from the side. In case he was wrong about the doc and these people knew him, he made up a fake name and address for himself, and quickly scribbled in the book. After he handed the pen to the woman, he made his way back into the room and pretended to be interested in the dozens of bouquets lining every inch of wall space.

As he looked at the cards attached to the flower arrangements, he'd periodically checked on the doc. The receiving line was still long, but the doc was now nearing Patricia's family. He shook the father's, then the mother's hand. He probably told them how sorry he was for their loss, before moving on to the sister, who would have been hot if her nose wasn't red and raw, and her eyes weren't puffy. Once the doc had done his duty, he approached the casket, then knelt. Thank God Daddy wanted to be cremated. The idea of kneeling next to his dead body and staring at a bad makeup job was fucked up.

He shifted his gaze to the clock. Jesus, how the hell much longer was the doc going to pray? He was holding up the receiving train. If he didn't move along, people might grow impatient and start rioting for their turn to take an up-close view of the dead woman.

The doc finally stood. Thank Christ, because he still had to use the bathroom. The Reverend stood, too, then watched with curiosity as the doc touched the dead woman's hand. Interesting. The man hadn't signed the address book in the hall, but had been comfortable enough to touch the woman. Then again, the doc touched dead people for a living. Still, the Reverend thought the doc's actions were odd.

Keeping his head down, the doc walked away from the casket and bee-lined for the exit. The Reverend followed him. Instead of leaving the funeral home, though, the doc walked down the hall, opened a door and disappeared inside. As he trailed behind, he hoped the doc was leading him to a bathroom. When he reached the door and saw the men's room sign, he let out a sigh of relief and quietly entered.

The room reeked of flowers, bleach and old people's farts. He should know, since that's how his Daddy's bathroom smelled. He approached the privacy wall, then hesitated at the corner. He had balls, but he wasn't stupid. The doc had yet to see his face, and he needed to keep it that way. As it was, thanks to a well-oiled door, the man probably hadn't heard him enter. He'd do what he should've done early. Go to Burger King, use their bathroom and buy a burger. Then he'd forget about the doc, go back to his hotel and enjoy the beach. While he sunned himself, he'd plan how he would send another message to their pervert.

As he turned to leave, a quick intake of breath—not his—made him freeze. The Reverend edged around the corner. The mirror above the sinks reflected two empty urinals and two bathroom stalls. One of the stalls was closed. Holding his breath and keeping his steps light, he crept a little closer inside, then crouched.

The doc's shoes faced the toilet. The small amount of pant leg he could see moved slightly, as if the doc was plucking at the front of his pants. Maybe his zipper was stuck. The doc let out a breath, then another. He grinned. Damn, did the man need pliers to undo his fucking pants? Talk about a pisser. He turned to leave again, then stopped. The sudden, quick, smacking sound coming from the stall was too familiar. The doc's breathing had changed and had become faster, harsher. Son of a fucking bitch. The man was masturbating in the bathroom of a funeral home *after* he'd prayed in front of a dead woman. Damn, Daddy had been right to have him follow the doc, but before he killed the man, he needed to be one hundred percent positive.

He snuck closer to the stall, then peeked through the small slit of the door. The doc had his left hand against the wall and stroked himself with his right. The Reverend carefully slipped his hand into his pocket and pulled out his cell phone. He opened up the camera app, held the phone to the slit in the door and took the picture.

Gotcha.

Shane's House, Everglades City, Florida
Wednesday, 5:12 p.m., Eastern Standard Time

Beth's excitement deflated as she pulled into Shane's driveway and parked alongside Lola's Honda. She'd had a great day and didn't want it ruined by the woman's bad attitude. To be fair, she hadn't seen or spoken with Lola since the night she and Shane had dropped by her and Ryan's house. Over the past couple of days, she'd tried to consider her relationship with Shane from Lola's point of view. Lola had been given the opportunity to run her own organization, and, days into their first case, Shane had brought a cop into the mix.

She exited her car, then grabbed her overnight bag from the back, along with the tote bag she'd filled with the container of tossed salad she'd made, rolls and store bought brownies. As she lugged the bags to Shane's front door, she made a promise to herself to play nice, put on a smile and give Lola another chance. Before she knocked on the door, it opened. Shane stood in the threshold wearing loose khaki shorts, a worn t-shirt and flip flops. Today he had his hair pulled back. While she liked the look, if they were going to dinner or meeting her parents—which was a subject she wanted to touch on tonight—when they were just hanging out, she loved it loose. She loved running her hands through his hair, and the way the soft strands tickled her breasts when he kissed a path from her neck to—

He cleared his throat. Her cheeks heated and she quickly shifted her gaze from his smiling mouth to his eyes. He stepped onto the small porch and took her bags. "Whatever you were thinking about," he began, whispering in her ear, "hang onto that thought until Lola leaves."

She kissed his cheek. "How long is she going to be here?" she whispered back.

He held open the door for her. "Not long, and I think you'll like what she has to say."

She hoped so. She didn't want her and Shane's evening spoiled by Lola. "Smells good in here," she said, and walked inside his house.

"I promised you lasagna, and I keep my promises."

"Who made it?" she asked with a smile.

He peeked into the tote bag. "Who made the brownies?"

"Hi, Beth," Lola said, and stepped out of the kitchen carrying a water bottle. Her long, straight dark hair draped along her bare shoulders. Her pale pink sundress hugged her slim figure in all the right places, showing off her toned arms and reminding Beth that she really needed to be more diligent about working out.

"You look nice. I love your shoes," Beth said, and glance to Lola's dark-pink heeled sandals. She had shoe and leg envy, but even if she bought the same pair of sandals she'd never have legs as long as Lola's.

Lola glanced to Beth's cut off denim shorts. "I like your shorts and your hair looks nice."

"How long is this going to go on for?" Shane asked with a chuckle.

Lola tossed her hair over her shoulder and narrowed her eyes at Shane. "I know you and Shane have plans." She walked to the coffee table and pulled a folder out of her over-sized purse. "I'm only going to stay long enough to give you this," she said, and offered Beth the folder.

"What is it?"

"Hopefully a lead."

"For the snake case?" Beth asked, and took the folder.

"Yes. Harrison and I compiled a report for you. I'm afraid this will be all the help you'll get from us on this case. Which is too bad. I really wanted to help you stop this guy."

She looked from her to Shane. "Is it because of us?"

"Not at all. I'm glad you agreed to work with us. I told my boss about you and, while he's okay with us working with you, too, he's worried this case will end up involving the FBI."

"Nick and Jerry haven't said anything about calling in the Feds."

"For obvious reasons, Senator Bryan is following this case very closely. My boss told me he spoke with him yesterday, and the senator has been pushing the FBI to investigate. I don't know if they will, neither does my boss, but ATL can't be close to this."

"I understand the risk, and I appreciate this," she said, opening the folder. The title page of the report read: *Snake Handling 101.* She moved to the next page and skimmed a few paragraphs. "You think this is motivated by religion?"

"Possibly, on some strange level. The people who believe and practice the snake handling ritual do it as a sign of their faith in God. The threat of being poisoned by the snake is what tests their faith. Some of these believers don't stop at snakes. I've read that some have drunk poison." Lola moved next to her. "Flip to the next page. There's a Bible quote they use to justify their practices."

Beth skimmed until she came across a passage from Mark 16:17-18. "Shane, have you seen this?"

"Some of it. Read the quote."

"And these signs will follow those who believe: in My name they will cast out demons; they will speak with new tongues; they will take up serpents; and if they drink anything deadly, it will by no means hurt them; they will lay their hands on the sick, and they will recover," Beth finished quoting Mark, and looked to Lola. "What made you think to look into snake handling? And why do you think this could be a lead to our case?"

"Have you met Barney yet?"

"Older guy with an eye patch?"

"That's him."

"We haven't officially met. Is he part of ATL, too?"

"Yes, and he's the one who insisted the snakes were the key. We started checking into snake handling, noticed a lot of these churches specifically use rattlesnakes, and then we dug deeper. In that report is a list of all the known places where we've confirmed that snake handling is still being practiced. We took that list and ran it against what we received from NCIC."

"Please tell me you didn't have Harrison hack into the FBI."

Lola raised a hand and smiled. "No worries. This was done legitimately, and we found one case we think is worth pursuing. Seven months ago, the skeletal remains of a male were found in the woods near Ivy Log, Georgia. His skull had been shattered, and the ME concluded he'd died of blunt force trauma. What the ME wasn't sure about were the nicks at the top of the pelvic bone. He'd indicated in his report that it appeared as if the victim has also been stabbed and the knife had caused the nicks."

"Or his stomach had been cut open," Beth said, flipping

the pages until she found the ME's report. "No ID on the victim?"

"None. Here's the best part, the skeleton was on top of the bones of a small snake."

Beth snapped the folder shut and stared at Lola. "And?"

"Unfortunately the bones weren't kept. But there are two photographs, taken before the skeleton had been moved where you can see the snake bones."

"Are there one of these snake handling churches near Ivy Log, Georgia?"

"No, but we found rumors of a church that dabbles in snake handling only about fifteen miles away in Murphy, North Carolina." Lola walked to the coffee table and picked up her purse. "I know the snake handling info is a long shot, the skeletal remains are, too. Especially because the victims here have been female, but it might be something to consider."

"No, Lola. This is good. I really appreciate the effort you and Harrison have put in to this. Thank you."

"I wish we could do more." Lola pulled her keys from her purse. "I've got to run. Ryan and I are going to dinner." She hesitated at the door. "Thanks again for keeping ATL to yourself."

"Of course," Beth said, and after Lola left, she shoved the file into her overnight bag.

"You don't want to look through it?" Shane asked.

"Lola gave us the gist of it. I'm also glad to see she's more accepting of me," she said, then went to him and twined her arms around his neck. "I don't want to talk about the case, Lola or ATL tonight."

He slid his hand up the back of her shirt. "We didn't last night."

"That's because we were too busy kissing." After her class, Shane had met her at her place. By the time he'd made it over, it had been past ten-thirty. They'd both worked all day, and she had been too exhausted to think about anything but making love to Shane. "Not that I'm complaining," she added.

"We should kiss now."

"We should. But I want to hear about your news first."

His eyes lit with excitement. "My last permit came in the mail today. I'm meeting with an attorney on Monday, my insurance agent on Tuesday, and Harrison did a mockup for my website last night."

She hugged him. "That's fantastic. I'm so happy for you. It sounds like you'll be making your grand opening weeks before you'd planned."

"I don't know how grand it will be. But the first time I started the business I did it on such a tight budget I was living on bologna sandwiches and mac and cheese. This time around I have money in the bank. One of the other reasons Lola stopped by was so I could sign over my part of the airboat business to her." He released her, then picked up the bag filled with the food she'd brought and started for the kitchen.

"Are you pulling out of the rental properties, too?" she asked, as she followed him.

"Since I'm living in one of them, I don't know what I'm going to do yet. Which isn't fair to Ryan. In peak season, we can get anywhere from fifteen hundred to two thousand a week."

She unpacked the bag, while he took the lasagna out of the oven. "If Ryan doesn't care, come up with an amount you can both agree on and pay him by the month. Once the business is bringing in money you could think about moving."

"Or I could buy Ryan out of this house." He glanced around the kitchen. "It needs some updating, though."

From the kitchen, she glanced into the living room. The carpeting was in decent shape for a vacation rental, and would be fine if it was still 1985. The kitchen and bathrooms were also dated, but livable. "You don't have to do it all at once." She turned and took plates from the cabinet, then set them on the table. "I have a brilliant idea. After we eat, we can watch home improvement shows and get ideas for the house."

He stared at her as if she'd lost her mind. "I have an even better idea. After we eat we can watch basketball."

She set out the silverware and napkins, while he opened a

bottle of wine. "Do you have any board games?"

"No, and even if I did I wouldn't play with you. You cheat."

Monday night, she'd kicked Shane's butt in Strip Scrabble. He'd ended up naked, while she'd still had on her bra, underwear and shorts. "I do not cheat."

"Then how did you know perianth was a word?" he asked, and scooped the lasagna from the tray. "That cost me my underwear."

She laughed. "I told you, my mom has been taking gardening classes since we moved down here. I picked it up from her. If you don't believe me, you can ask her yourself."

Shane sat across from her, and pretended to be interested in what was on his plate. While he knew she was joking, the reality was, he didn't want to meet her parents. He didn't want them asking him questions and finding out that their daughter was seeing a convicted murderer.

"Is something wrong?" she asked.

"Not at all," he said, and took a roll.

"This lasagna is delicious. Where'd you get it from?"

"Mel made it for me."

"I wish I could cook like her. Is she the blonde who works at the ice cream shop?"

And a chop shop, and for ATL. "That's her. Did you find out what you got on the paper you turned in last week?"

"Yes, my professor posted it this morning, and I got an A."

"That's great."

"I know my schedule is light this semester, but I'm ready for school to be over. My parents want to throw me a graduation party this summer and invite my brothers and their families down." She split a roll and buttered it, swiping her knife across it four times. "I told them they were crazy and I didn't want that. I'd love to see my brothers and nieces and nephews, but including spouses and kids, we're talking twenty-three people."

More people he didn't want to meet. "Yeah, that's a lot. When are your parents coming home from vacation?" he asked, to avoid counting the number of tiles along the backsplash behind her. God, what the hell was wrong with him? He'd slowed down on the counting, and hadn't added anything up since Saturday when Beth had showed up and he'd been beating the crap out of the boxing bag.

"They came home this morning. Because I knew I wouldn't see them after work, Ricky and I did a quick drive-by. They had a great time on their cruise. My mom said she's going to make a slide show of all the pictures she took, and have me come over to view them with her and my dad." She half-laughed. "As soon as my mom told me this, my dad said, 'Jesus H. Christ, Irene, I took the damned pictures. Why the hell would I want to watch a slide show?'"

Fuck. Her father was going to hate him. He was going to sic her four brothers on him and make him disappear. "Your dad sounds like a character."

"He comes off like a grouch, but he's really a softy."

Beth was the youngest of five and the only girl. There was no way in hell her father was going to be a 'softy' when it came to who his daughter dated.

Shane reached for his glass of wine. Why the hell hadn't he considered her family's reaction? Because he'd never imagined that a week after their first date and first kiss that she'd still be sitting across from him. He'd never planned to go past a date or two. He had asked her to dinner because, yes, he'd been fantasizing about her for a week, but the main reason had been because he'd wanted to be a normal guy. A normal guy dating a normal girl. Only there wasn't anything normal about him, or her. She was exceptional, not normal. She deserved better than him. His past might not bother her now, but one day it will.

As they finished dinner and cleaned up the dishes, she chattered away about the rest of her day. When they brought their glasses and the bottle of wine with them into the living room, and took a seat on the couch that had been used by the dozens of tourists who rented the house, he wanted to tell her to leave and not look back. For fuck's sake, what did he have to offer her? He didn't even own his own couch.

"I'm sorry," she said, when she snuggled next to him. "I've been talking your ear off. I think I had too much caffeine."

Despite what was going through his head, he wrapped an arm around her. Because deep down, he *didn't* want her to leave. He wanted her around tomorrow, and tomorrow he'd want the same. While he'd been in prison, he had been taught plenty of harsh lessons. The harshest—life was too damned short.

The other lesson he'd been taught? You can't always have what you want.

"Go ahead and talk my ear off, I've got another."

She kissed his cheek, then leaned forward and glanced around the room. "Where's your laptop? I want to see the website Harrison's designing for you."

"It's on the end table next to Harriet." When she looked at the terrarium, and he considered the snake case, he said, "I'll get it."

"I'm not afraid of your snake." She stood and walked to the end table, then bent and inspected Harriet. "How do you know she's alive? Never mind, she just moved a quarter of an inch. Look at that, I think she moved an eighth of an inch." She turned and carried the laptop over. "I can see how Harriet provides you with hours of entertainment."

He chuckled and pulled her in for a kiss. "Smartass."

She gave his beard a little tug. "There's the smile I've been missing tonight. Are you sure there's nothing wrong?"

"I'm good." He took the laptop from her. As he opened it up and found the file of the website mockup, she rubbed his back. "What do you think?" he asked.

She leaned against him and stared at the screen. "I love it. Where did you get these aerial shots from? They look professional."

"Barney took those pictures from up in my Cessna. Because he ended up with so many great shots, Harrison is going to set up a photo gallery page," he said, his mood lightening. Rather than dwelling on if and when he'd meet her family, he'd focus on the fact he had something positive to show her, something that was his, not rented and not on loan. Before prison, his business had been successful and one of the most important accomplishments of his life. He could tell her about his success, and he had mentioned it, but he needed for her to see that she hadn't made a mistake with him. He wanted her to be proud of him.

"That's a great idea. People need to be enticed to pay you to give them the real deal." She wrapped her arm around him and continued to comment on the different pages Harrison had designed. When her cell phone rang, she gave his shoulder a squeeze, then stood.

While she pulled her phone from her purse, he closed the laptop. "I don't know if I want to answer this," she said, and stared at the screen. "It's Nick."

The detective. Damn. He would rather sit through a marathon of home improvement shows than hear about the discovery of another dead body. "Then don't answer. You're off the clock."

"You don't want to know?"

"I wouldn't mind hearing about it on the news."

"Sometimes I feel the same way," she said, then answered the call like he figured she would. She was invested in the case, and because he was invested in her, he supported whatever choices she made even if it ruined their night together.

Eight to ten years ago, the thought of being devoted to a woman, of wanting to prove his worth would have never entered his mind. He hadn't been selfish. He'd been focused on making money to secure his future. Back then, dating and sex were a distraction from the stress of running his business and adjusting to civilian life. While he still had plenty of adjusting to do, at least this time he didn't have to do it alone. And Beth wasn't a distraction, she'd become important to him, more than he'd ever imagined.

"That's great," she said to Nick. "But I can't tonight."

He shouldn't be listening to her side of the conversation. He refilled their wine glasses, and emptied the bottle. To give her privacy, he stood to take the bottle into the kitchen, then lingered when she said, "Tomorrow I have school, and plans for Friday."

Was the detective asking her out? He stepped into the kitchen, set the bottle on the counter and tried his damnedest to tamp down the jealousy creeping through his chest like a bad case of heartburn. He shouldn't jump to conclusions. The guy could be calling about something else. He could also be old and ugly.

"No dead bodies," she called.

"That's always a positive," he said, as he made his way into the living room. "What'd Nick want?"

She sat and reached for her wine. "It was nothing."

Let it go and don't be a jealous dick. "Didn't sound like nothing. Was he asking you out?" Fuck it. He'd never played games with women before, and wouldn't be played now. He wanted to belong to her, just as much as he needed her to belong to him. He didn't know what this was…love? Maybe. He supposed some people, would say one week was too soon for that. Those people could spend seven years in prison, locked in their heads, and then go ahead and tell him the proper way to control the array of emotions bottled inside him.

She set down her wine glass. "Nick is part owner of a bar on Bonita Beach. He invited me to go see a band they've booked for the week."

"Did he invite your partner, too?"

"I didn't ask." She leaned into the couch. "So what do you want to do? It's nice out, we could go for a walk."

"Is Nick old?" He didn't want jealousy messing up their night, but he couldn't let it go.

"Thirty-five."

"Is he ugly?"

"Why are you doing this? I'm not interested in dating Nick."

"Is he ugly?" he asked again.

She crossed her arms. "No. Anything else you want to know?"

Insecurity kicked him in the balls. Nick was a detective, not a felon. He wasn't ugly and also had his own business. Why the hell wouldn't she choose Nick over him? He'd bet his Cessna her parents would prefer she date a cop over a murderer.

"Nope," he finally said.

"Please don't tell me you're upset Nick asked me to come watch a band."

"Sounded like he was persistent about it. Why didn't you tell him you were seeing someone?" Was he moving too fast and expecting too much? So the hell what.

She let out a breath, and stood. "We've been seeing each other for a week. I didn't want to be presumptuous with you eavesdropping on my conversation."

"If you didn't want me to hear, then you should have stepped outside or gone in another room."

"Right, like that would make this ridiculous conversation better. Then you'd think I was keeping something from you, which I'm not." She pressed a hand to her stomach. "Don't let Nick be an issue. I'm here with you, which is where I want to be."

He leaned against the wall. "Why? The sex is great, so I get that, but—"

She narrowed her eyes and fisted her hand. "You think I'm only here for sex?"

"I didn't say that."

"Yes, you did."

"I was going to add that you could be with a guy who has a good job, owns a business and won't embarrass you when you introduce him to your family and friends."

"For a smart guy, that's a dumb thing to say. You have a good job, and your own business. And unless you plan to entertain my parents with potty jokes, I doubt you'll embarrass me."

"My prison record should."

She took a step forward. "If it bothered me, I wouldn't be here."

"Then why are you here?" He pushed off the wall and held up a hand. "Forget I asked. I don't want to argue with you.

You're right. It's a nice evening, we should go for a walk."

"No. I want to finish this." She walked across the room until she stood in front of him. "Do you remember how I woke you up Monday morning?"

He'd never forget opening his eyes and seeing the way Beth had rubbed his erection along her lips. "I remember."

"When you were still dreaming, you talked in your sleep. You told me what you were dreaming about, but do you remember what you were saying?"

He looked away. "Let's drop this. I've got a lot on my mind and didn't mean to blow Nick's call out of proportion."

She touched his jaw, and forced him to meet her gaze. "Do you remember?"

"I said I'm not good enough for you."

"It hurt to hear you say that. You might have been dreaming when you said it, but I think you feel that way. And you're so wrong."

He gripped her by the upper arms. "I'm not wrong. I don't think I'm good enough for you. Jesus, Beth, during the seven years you've been serving the community as either a paramedic or cop, I was sitting in prison for murder. You follow rules, you hardly swear."

"What the fuck does swearing have to do with anything?" She fisted the hem of his shirt. "I'm sick of the way you keep throwing your record in my face."

"Sorry, but it's kind of big deal to me."

"And it doesn't change the way I feel about you. You're a good man, who made a bad choice. You need to stop allowing your past to define who you are now. You've already lost too many years. Haven't you served enough time?"

He gave her a slight shake. "I count."

"Of course you do." Tears filled her eyes and she drew in a breath. "You count to me."

God, he didn't give a shit if it was too soon or not, he fucking loved this woman. "I meant that I count things. In my head, I'm always adding things up. I started doing it about two weeks into my sentence to keep my mind active. The only time

I've stopped counting is when I'm with you. But when we were eating dinner, the habit came back the moment you brought up your parents. Being sent away…I disappointed my family, friends and myself. I don't want to be a disappointment to you, and I don't want you to disappoint your parents by being with me."

He let go of her arms and used his thumbs to wipe her tears. "Don't cry for me. I deserved what I got. It doesn't matter that Ted Nowak wasn't a good man, or that it was an accident. I took a person's life."

She hit him in the chest with both hands. "I'm not crying for you." He took a step back when she hit him again. "I'm upset because you've set us up to fail and you're using your record as a shield. If I hadn't come here to confront you about being at the ME's, would you have ever called me?"

"I'd want to."

"But you wouldn't. You wouldn't have given *me* the chance to decide if your record mattered or not."

"I was trying to save you from having to make a choice."

"No, you were rejecting me before I rejected you. Is that what your trying to do now?" she asked, her eyes holding so much hurt, it made his chest ache.

"No." He gripped her hips and hauled her close. "I need to be with you."

"You're a strong man, you don't need me. You need to stop being so hard on yourself."

When she tried to pull away, he turned her so she was against the wall, and unable to run from him. "Wrong." He took her hands in his. "When I'm not with you, kissing you, tasting you, making love to you feels like it was nothing but another made-up fantasy." He pinned her hands against her hips. "Until I see you again. But I need more than your body," he said, running his hands over her breasts until he cupped her cheeks. "I need your trust."

"I do trust you."

"With what?"

She searched his eyes. "I don't understand what you mean."

He should shut the hell up and kiss her. Rip off her clothes and end this entire conversation. But she thought he was using his record as a shield, that he would try to reject her before she could come to her senses and walk away from him. He couldn't have her thinking any of that, not when it was far from the truth. "My felony will follow me to the grave. You stay with me and it'll follow you, too. I'm not pushing you away. I'm making it clear what you're getting into by being with me. This, you and me, isn't like ATL."

Her eyes widened a fraction before she looked over his shoulder. "You won't walk away from me when it's not working for you."

"I don't do anything by half. I'll work harder to prove you're supposed to be with me. What I want to know is if you'll do the same."

CHAPTER 15

SHE HAD TRUSTED him with her body, and had trusted him enough to take a risk with ATL. Now he wanted to know if she trusted him with her heart. He hadn't come out and said as much, but the implication was there. Would she walk away when things became too hard, or would she stick it out and work on their relationship? Her parents had been married for forty-five years. She understood the ups and downs, and that love wasn't always easy.

Did she love Shane?

They'd met almost two weeks ago and had been seeing each other for only a week. Love wasn't supposed to happen that fast, but grow with time. That's how it had been for her parents, and her brothers and their wives. A slow process of learning their partner's likes and dislikes, of developing a trusting bond that would stay with them a lifetime. She'd based her ideology of love and marriage on those relationships. During her first year of college, she'd fallen in love with Tyler—or so she'd thought. He'd been sweet and fun. They'd dated for three months before she'd slept with him, another three before they'd admitted they loved each other. But that love hadn't been strong. Tyler had been immature. The goals he'd once claimed he would achieve had been shoved on the backburner when he'd joined a fraternity. Partying had become his mistress, and she hadn't been willing to work hard enough at their relationship to accept his new friends, or the person he'd become.

Older, wiser, she had to pat her younger self on the back for walking away from a man who would have sucked the energy out of her and distracted her from school and her goals. Yes, she'd loved Tyler, but when she compared that young love to the emotions Shane stirred, there *was* no comparison.

So was this love? Was she willing to trust him with her heart and to fight to be with him?

"I'm going to take your silence as a no," Shane said, and dropped his hands from her face.

She gripped the front of his shirt to keep him from walking away. "Shane, give me a second to think."

His mouth curved into a mocking, half-smile. "If you have to think about it, then you already have your answer. It's not the one I want, but it's the right one."

"You're being totally unreasonable. This all started over Nick's phone call. I told you I don't want him, I want you."

"No, this started before that. When you started talking about your parents I realized how selfish I'm being."

"Stop worrying about whether my parents will be disappointed in me because I'm seeing you. They treat me like the adult that I am and don't interfere in my life. They've always been supportive of my choices."

"What parent would be disappointed in a daughter like you? But let me ask you this, if your daughter brought home a murderer, would you pull her aside and ask her what the hell she was thinking? Do you really think your mom and dad would be okay with this? How about your brothers? I can just see the holidays. Uncle Shane sitting in the corner by himself, your nieces and nephews keeping their distance because their mommies and daddies told them he's a bad man."

She hadn't thought about that. Would her family give her a hard time? Did she care? Of course. She loved them and wanted them to be proud of her and the man she loved.

Her chest tightened. "Oh, my God."

"Clicking into place, huh? You're the baby of the family and the only girl. Your dad didn't want to tolerate watching a slide show from his recent vacation, so do you really think he's going to tolerate me?"

Her dad would be furious. Her mom would soothe him, then take her aside and tell her this wasn't love, but her way of trying to break free of her good-girl mold. Oh, God. She'd fallen for a man her parents could hate on principle and she didn't know what to do. Her heart said go with it, her head told her to take a step back and put together a neat and tidy bullet point list of the pros and cons.

He tilted her chin with the back of his finger. When she met his gaze, her eyes stung with fresh tears. The patience, agony and longing in his gaze made her legs grow weak. She tugged at his shirt, and gripped the base of his neck to keep him from pushing her away and to keep herself from sagging to the floor. Knowing someone for one week shouldn't have this effect on her, but Shane wasn't just someone. He was something special. Prison hadn't damaged him, and his record hadn't made him less of a man in her eyes. Most men would walk away from what he'd endured broken. Not Shane. He'd walked away ready to reclaim life, and he wanted her with him while he fought his way back into society. She respected and admired him, and she was grateful their paths had crossed. He made *her* feel special, and cherished. He had showed her that breaking rules and taking risks had its rewards. He'd showed her that there were no rules when it came to falling in love.

"Go home, Beth," he said, and caressed her lips with the pad of his thumb.

"I don't want to."

"We're only a week in to this. You'll forget about it."

At the beginning, she'd wanted a wild and fun distraction, and if something more had come from their relationship, she'd welcome it, enjoy it and hang on to it for as long as she could. Something more had happened. It didn't matter that they hadn't know each other long. She knew enough. Shane was good, and he was solid. In a matter of days they'd developed a bond she'd never experienced before, and she wasn't ready to lose it. She didn't want to lose him.

"What happened to proving you're supposed to be with me?"

His eyes darkened with the hunger she'd grown familiar with and loved. He ran his hand along her thigh, then pressed it between her legs and rubbed her through her denim shorts.

She shoved him. "This isn't about sex."

He stilled his fingers. "I never said it was. I just wanted to cop a feel before you left."

"No pun intended, right? You're being a jerk."

He looked to the wall, and moved his hand away.

She let go of his shirt, grabbed his hand put it back where it belonged. "I'm not leaving. This isn't about sex, ATL, my job or my family. Just you and me." She tugged at his hair. "Look at me." When he did, she saw the regret and apology in his eyes. "You don't want me to leave, and I don't want to go. You're right, if I had a daughter and she told me she was dating an ex-con, I'd have a problem with it. My mom and dad will no doubt have a problem with it. But I don't, because I know you."

"After one week?"

"You didn't have a problem with wanting to be with me after only a couple of days."

"Because I know how short life is, but I don't want to screw up yours."

"The only way you'll screw it up is if you make me leave."

He pressed her against the wall and applied pressure to her sex. The friction of the denim had desire rushing through her body. "Don't fuck with me, Beth. I don't want only tonight. I want tomorrow and the day after that."

He wanted a commitment. "What do you want me to say? What will it take to convince you that I want that, too?"

He stilled his hand. The intensity, the unabashed devotion in his eyes humbled her and filled her with hope. They could make this work. Against the odds, despite what anyone else might think of their relationship, together, standing side by side, they could prove that labels, mistakes and tarnished pasts meant nothing.

"Say that I'm yours," he said, the raw emotion, the need and uncertainty in his voice making her ache for him. She never wanted him uncertain about them.

"You're mine." She tugged his head closer. "And I'm yours."

He let out a ragged breath, then kissed her. Primal, passionate, as if he was branding her and sealing her words to his lips. She kissed him back with the same need and desire, and reached for the hem of his shirt. She needed his body, she needed to be one with him, feel his skin and his heart beating against hers.

She broke the kiss long enough to pull his shirt over his head. He did the same, stripped her of her shirt and bra, then pressed her back against the wall. Her nipples rubbed against his chest as he held her close and kissed her. Anxious to have him completely naked and inside her, she undid his shorts, slid them and his boxers over his hips and stroked his hard length. He groaned against her mouth.

"I love the way you touch me," he murmured, then bent and kissed a path from her lips down to her chest. As he took a nipple into his mouth, teased it with his tongue before drawing it between his lips and sucking, he unbuttoned and unzipped her denim shorts and slipped his hand inside.

When his fingers grazed her, then dipped between her labia, she wrapped an arm around his shoulder and clung to him. While he pumped his fingers, he ran his other hand along the small of her back, then over her rear, shoving her shorts to the floor.

He dragged his lips from her nipple, then down her stomach. Kneeling in front of her, he spread her labia and tongued her. She sagged against the wall, and ran her hands through his hair. His fingers and tongue drove her crazy. Teased and tantalized. She loved the way he worked his mouth along her, sucked her swollen lips, licked her clit, but wanted him filling her with his hard length. She wanted him buried deep, needed that connection, that bond she didn't want to ever lose.

She tugged at his hair and looked down at him. He met her gaze. The dark desire in his eyes matched her own. "What do you want?" he asked, then swept his tongue along her sex.

"I need you inside me."

Never taking his eyes from hers, he stood. He erection brushed her stomach as he lifted her leg and pressed her against the wall. "It's where I want to be," he said, then shifted his hips, and thrust.

She sucked in a breath and hung onto his broad shoulders. Leaning into her, he kissed her neck. As he moved, driving himself deep, dragging his erection along her clit, he lifted her. "Wrap your legs around me."

When she did, he pressed her against the wall. She sifted her hands through the back of his hair, and crushed her mouth against his. Kissed him with the same possessiveness as he'd shown her. He was hers. She wanted no other woman to know this man the way she did. She wanted his touch, his mouth and body to be hers alone. She would break every rule out there and fight to keep him.

Greedy for more, for the orgasm that had been flirting with her body from the moment he'd touched her sex through her shorts, she sucked in his lip, then broke the kiss. "Take me from behind."

He stilled, and stared at her. Then he slowly let her feet touch the floor. A small, sexy smile curved the corner of his mouth as he slipped from her. "Turn around."

When she did, she pressed her palms against the wall, tossed her hair over her shoulder and looked at him. Watched as he took his length in his hand, then groaned when he slid it between her wet folds. Slowly, inch by inch, he entered her. Once he was fully seated, he took a fistful of her hair in one hand and gripped her hip with the other. He leaned in, his warm breath caressing her neck and sending goose bumps along her skin. "Now what do you want?" he asked, his voice low, husky.

"Make us come."

With something in between a harsh growl and groan he nipped her shoulder, then kissed it. "You want me to fuck you?"

She wanted rough, she wanted him to possess her and make it clear she was his. "Yes," she hissed, and pressed her rear back for emphasis.

The grip along her hip became almost painful, but only increased her pleasure, especially when he began to move. Slow at first, pulling his length all the way out, then plunging back in, taking her hard and deep. Over and over, he teased her body. Frustrated, and hungry for more of what she knew he could give her, she slid her hands down the wall, then bent her body and raised her rear higher. "More," she said.

He let go of her hair. Now gripping both of her hips, he moved faster, harder. She looked over her shoulder again. God, he was so sexy. She loved the pleasure and determination crossing his face, the way the muscles along his chest, arms and shoulders bunched as he moved her over his erection. Their gazes met. His expressive eyes held more than lust and desire. Tenderness? Love?

He slowed his pace, then stopped and slid from her body. Confused, she turned. "What's wrong?"

He pressed her back against the wall, then raised her leg again. "I want face to face." He entered her. "I want to watch you come."

She shoved her hands through his hair and kissed him. But as he increased the tempo, rocked her body with each thrust of her hips, her breath quickened. She moved her lips from his, and held his face in her hands. His breath fanned against her mouth. She leaned in to taste him again, but as the pressure that had building suddenly burst she tilted her head back and let go.

"That's it, baby," he said, as her orgasm took over her body, tightened her muscles, sent waves of pleasure through her. Then he quickly pulled out, and with a catch to his breath, he released himself on her stomach. She reached down, gently rubbed his testicles until he let out a deep breath and rested his forehead against hers. "No condom."

"I'll go on the pill." She kissed his temple, his cheek, his lips.

He let go of her leg, set it on the floor, and kissed her. Hot, open-mouthed, he kissed her as if they hadn't made love, as if he hadn't had enough. When he ended the kiss, he tilted her chin. "That first time you came on my boat, I couldn't stop thinking about you after you left."

"I couldn't stop thinking about you. That's why I came back." She grinned. "Twice."

His eyes softened. "I left prison feeling like half the man I was when I went in. You make me whole again. I know I went a little caveman on you, but where you're concerned, I can't help myself. I know what I want and what I need."

Her throat tightened and fresh tears moistened her eyes. "I know what I want and what I need, too. When we were, you know, I thought about another woman even trying to take my place. In my head, I might have gotten a little cavewoman."

He grinned. "Did the claws come out?"

"I own a gun."

Chuckling, he cupped her cheek. "You're something special."

"I was thinking the same about you."

He ran his hand along the side of her body, then settled it on her rear. "Beth, I…" He gave her a quick kiss. "Let's clean up and go for that walk. When we're done, I'll watch as many hours of home improvement shows as you want. As long as you feed me the brownies you brought."

He was going to say something else. She knew it in her gut, but wouldn't press him. They'd already said enough, and, in her mind, had showed each other how they feel. "Deal," she said, and kissed him.

****

Naples, Florida
Wednesday, 9:06 p.m., Eastern Standard Time

The Reverend sat in the corner of Holly and Christopher Samuels' darkened garage sweating off his balls. He'd followed the couple from the funeral home where the good doc had gotten his rocks off in in the men's bathroom, watched as they'd stopped by a house to pick up their three kids, then had followed them to their two-story Mediterranean-styled home. When the husband had walked down to the mailbox, leaving the garage door open, he'd taken advantage of the opportunity, and had rushed from behind the shrubs along the side of the house, then slipped inside. Now he sat in the far corner of the garage, behind the two smelly trashcans next to the couple's minivan. He'd taken a risk coming here, and had considered killing the dead woman's mother or father instead. But they lived in a gated community, so Holly would have to do. The risk was higher, but the reward would be well worth it. Once the doc received this latest message, he'd damn well know his secret wasn't so secret anymore.

He still couldn't believe the man—with all that he had—would resort to screwing dead bodies. He preferred his women warm and willing, liked when they panted and moaned, and let him know he was fucking them just right. He'd like to fuck Dr. Adams' woman. Maybe he should. She'd be warm, but she wouldn't be willing, though, and Daddy didn't approve of rape.

The door to the house opened, spilling light into the garage. Then the motor for the garage door began to hum, as the door started to rise. His heart rate kicked up, and he hoped like hell whoever was coming into the garage wasn't planning on using the minivan. He hadn't planned on a confrontation in the garage, but a sneak attack inside the house.

He wanted to strike the fear of God into the doc. He wanted the man to know that he had the ability to kill anytime and anywhere, even in a house filled with five people.

"How long are you going to be?" Holly asked, her voice tired and raspy, likely from crying all day.

"Just half an hour," her husband said. "If you want me to stay, I don't have to go."

"No, you're fine. It's been a long day and you need to blow off steam." He heard the sound of a kiss. "Go for your run. Since the kids are asleep, I'm going to pour a glass of wine and take a bath. Don't be surprised if I'm in bed when you get back. I don't think I've ever been this exhausted." She let out a long sigh. "And we have to do this all over again tomorrow."

Another kiss. "I'm so sorry, baby. I loved your sister, too. With your dad's heart condition, I'm worried about your parents. Maybe we should have them stay in our in-law suite for a few days and keep an eye on them."

"I already asked them and they refused. My mom said they're thinking about going to the Keys. That was my sister's favorite place to vacation," she said, her voice cracking. "We had wonderful family vacations there."

"I can take time off work, and we can go with your parents. It might be good for us, and the kids. The girls don't understand what's going on and I think they could use the extra time with us."

"That's a great idea. Since Patty died, I feel like I've been neglecting them. I feel guilty."

"They're young, and they won't remember," Christopher said. "You're a good mom, and you need to allow yourself time to grieve."

"Thank you," she said, and the Reverend rolled his eyes when he heard them kiss again. "I love you. I'll try to stay up until you come back."

"Love you, too," Christopher said, then his sneakered feet moved across the concrete floor. Seconds later, the garage door, along with the door to the house closed.

The Reverend waited a few heartbeats, then rose from his hiding spot. He squeezed around the minivan, then the sedan next to it, and made his way to the door. When he reached it, he tried the handle with his gloved hand. It turned with ease.

The lights were off in the small utility room, and the door to the main part of the quiet house had been left open. He neared the doorway, then peered around the corner of the short hallway. He had less than thirty minutes to do the deed, and no time to waste. As he crept along the hallway, he noticed a light on in the kitchen. It would be convenient if the woman was in there pouring the wine she'd mention to her husband. He didn't want to have to search the house and risk waking up a kid. He wasn't opposed to killing, but had a soft spot for little ones.

He thought about Mama. Even after all of these years, he still wondered why she'd been so damned cruel to him. He'd been her only child. He'd been a good kid, and had never gotten into any trouble, yet she'd hated him. She'd never had a kind word for him, hugged or kissed him. Instead, she'd beaten and verbally abused him.

A squeak came from the foyer near the kitchen. He forgot about Mama and took a few steps. Some sort of caged rodent—a hamster or gerbil, he figured—let out another tiny squeak, then hopped on a wheel and ran. He stepped away from the cage, then went in search of the woman.

After checking the downstairs, and not finding her, he stopped in the kitchen. Rather than opting for a knife, he snagged a large frying pan and grinned as he remembered how he'd once pictured bashing Mama in the head. He gripped the handle tight. Although not cast iron, tonight the frying pan would do.

The Reverend left the kitchen and made his way to the second level. When he reached the landing, he stopped and looked around. Well, hell. There were five doors, four of them closed. The opened door had the light on, and was the kids' bathroom. The shower curtain was decorated with cartoony starfish and seahorses, bath toys sat on the corner of the tub and a potty training seat was on the floor in front of the regular toilet. He glanced away from the bathroom and looked at the closed doors. None of them had light seeping out from under the bottom of the doors, so he had no choice but to check each one of them.

He started with the one on the end, and hoped it was the

master bedroom. He didn't want to wake a kid and alert the mother, and would rather take her by surprise on his own. Turning the doorknob, he slowly pushed open the door. A nightlight glowed on a crib, where a toddler lay sound asleep. The Reverend crept back out, then opened the next door. A set of twin beds paralleled each other from opposite walls. He glanced at the kids, who were both sleeping, then closed the door.

Two down, two to go. He stopped at the next door, found a guest bedroom, then moved to the end of the hallway. When he pressed his ear to the door, and heard water running, he turned the knob. He stepped inside the bedroom, light from the partially opened bathroom door touching on a king-sized bed.

He tightened his grip on the handle of the frying pan. Then peeked through the crack in the door. The large mirror over the double sinks and vanity reflected a shower, water spilling into the garden tub, and Holly. She sat on the closed toilet lid, wearing a light blue bathrobe. Her face was in her hands and her shoulders shook. On a sob, she reached for the toilet paper, pulled off a chunk, then blew her nose. With the way she'd been crying earlier today, he was surprised she had any tears left in her.

In a minute or so, there wouldn't be any more tears.

He looked over his shoulder to where he'd left the master bedroom door open, and gave the hallway a final check. Kids were stealthy, and he didn't want one sneaking up on him. With the coast clear, he returned his attention to the mirror. Holly took another wad of toilet paper, wiped her eyes, then stood. She lifted the lid of the toilet, dropped the used tissue inside, then flushed. As she stepped away, she removed her robe. Damn, for having three kids, the woman had a nice figure. She walked to the tub and tested the water with her hand, then adjusted the faucet knob, turning it to cold. With her back to him, she sat on the marble surrounding the tub, absently moving the water around with her hand.

Inching the door open, he stepped inside. The lighting

above the bathroom mirror cast his shadow along the tile floor. Before she noticed, he raised the frying pan, rushed toward the tub, then smashed the metal against the back of her head. With a grunt, she fell forward and hit the tile with a loud thud. Groaning, her fingers shaking, she raised her hand to her head. He hit her with the pan again, then once more for good measure.

He grabbed her by the shoulder, flipped her over and checked her pulse. When he found one, her wrapped his hands around her neck, then squeezed as hard as he could. After a minute or so, he checked her pulse again. Satisfied she was finally dead, he tossed her bathrobe over his shoulder, took her by the arms and dragged her body out of the bathroom, through the bedroom and into the hall. The kids' doors were still closed as he moved her down the steps. Once he reached the first floor, he hefted her over his shoulder, picked up a set of car keys from the kitchen counter and headed into the garage. He pressed one of the buttons on the key fob, unlocking the sedan. Once he opened the rear passenger door, he tossed the woman inside, then placed the bathrobe on top of her.

He checked his watch. The husband would be back within the next ten minutes, maybe less. He opened the garage door, rushed to the driver's side, climbed in and started the car. After backing out, he drove toward where he'd parked his Impala three streets away in the part of the development that was vacant and still under construction.

Keeping to the speed limit, he watched for the husband, but never saw him. He could still be running, or he could have already returned to the house. If that were the case, he wouldn't have much time before the man notified the police.

When he pulled alongside the Impala, he double checked to make sure no one was around, then pulled Holly's body from the car and placed her on the garbage bag he'd spread across the Impala's backseat earlier. Leaving her sedan in the middle of the street, he slid into his Chevy, and started it. As he began to drive, he decided against going back to Shell Island Road.

With the amount of bodies that had been found there, the police would definitely be patrolling the area more diligently. He always had a Plan B, and knew the perfect place to leave the woman.

He only wished he could see the good doc's face once the dead woman was discovered. Dr. David Adams would shit his pants, and he was pretty sure his hot girlfriend would, too.

Ryan and Lola's House, Everglades City, Florida
Wednesday, 9:42 p.m., Eastern Standard Time

When the patio door slid open, Lola turned away from the deck rail. Sadie padded onto the deck and came to her. She gave the dog some love, and glanced to Ryan. The sconces on either side of the glass slider framed his body, a body she should be loving right now.

"You disappeared on me," he said, and moved toward her. "I came out of the shower expecting to find you in bed. Nekkid."

After they'd returned home from dinner, Ryan had decided to take an hour to finish adding the baseboards along the kitchen walls, which required breaking out the giant manly saw—for three pieces of wood—and a shower. While Ryan had become in touch with his inner builder, she'd called her mom. She missed her, and had hoped her mom would come down for a visit. But the rehearsal schedule for Cami's latest play had been moved up by several weeks. If she wanted to see her mom, she would have to make a trip to Chicago. According to Ian, that wasn't going to happen any time soon.

She grinned and ran her hands up his chest. "Nekkid?"

"Yep, maybe on your hands and knees ready to reward me for installing your woodwork."

"You do deserve a reward for that, don't you?"

"I think so, but I have a feeling your mind isn't on my reward. Let me guess, Ian stole the phone from your mom."

She sighed. "I'm going to have to start calling her during the day when he's not home."

"Bad talk?"

"No, it was fine. He wants us to start working on another assignment."

He rubbed the small of her back. "That's great. Two cases within a week. It'll keep Harrison and Vlad away from the boat shop. What's the assignment?"

"Ian wants us to go after Smitty, the drug dealer who was supplying the two guys who put Ian and my mom through hell." When Ian and her mom were being hunted, they'd stumbled upon a trailer that had been used by the two men to store their cocaine. Since their bodies were rotting deep in the Everglades, the men were no longer an issue, but Smitty was. Ian wanted him found and his operation stopped.

"Smitty's working out of Siesta Key, right?"

She nodded. "I'll have Harrison get on his computer tomorrow to see what he can find about the man. I don't want to send him and Vlad there without knowing what this guy's reach is and how many people he has working for him. Ian had done a little digging, too. He wanted to make sure the DEA or the FBI didn't already have agents after Smitty. The last thing we need is to screw up an investigation in progress."

"I take it he didn't find anything."

"No, it sounds like Smitty has been running under the radar."

"So, what's the problem?"

"There isn't one."

He pressed her close to him. "Liar. What are you worried about?"

"I don't want anything to happen to Harrison or Vlad. If they ended up hurt or…I don't think I could handle that."

"Then I guess you should've thought about that responsibility before you agreed to run ATL."

"Thanks for the reassurance." She pushed away from him, but he tightened his hold and kept her in place. "Let go. I don't want to talk about this."

"I do. If you're afraid someone will get hurt every time we're given a new assignment, it's going to show. How do you expect any of us to feel confident about you or our missions, if you don't have confidence in yourself or us? Do you think Harrison and Vlad can handle going to Siesta Key to deal with a drug dealer?"

Harrison and Vlad had helped bring down a mass murderer responsible for the deaths of over two hundred people. Harrison had been raised on the streets, had spent time in prison and understood street justice. Vlad had spent the past ten years avoiding captivity by outwitting the Russian mob, the Russian government, Interpol and several U.S. agencies. They might joke and fool around, but when it came to business, they were dependable. They'd also become the brothers she'd never had.

"Of course I think they can handle it," she said.

"Then the problem is?"

"Maybe it's Shane and Beth."

"You said everything went fine when you saw Beth today."

"It did. But I'm not talking about how she and I interacted. I'm talking about Beth and Shane as a couple." She looked down. "I didn't tell you this, but I had Harrison dig into Beth's background before I spoke to Ian about her. She's squeaky-clean and has nothing but high commendations from her superiors."

He tilted her chin, forcing her to look at him. "Are you worried about causing problems for her?"

"Not just her, but Shane, too. I tried to justify his involvement with ATL by simply making him our ride when we need one. But the bottom line is that if we're caught doing something we shouldn't be, he's associated with us. I don't want him going back to prison because I coerced him into joining ATL."

Ryan grinned. "No one coerces Shane. He and I talked about you and ATL before he met with Beth about helping us out now and then."

She tensed. This was news to her. "And?"

"Shane joined for the exact reasons he told you. He was looking out for me, and he's nosey. I made it clear that I don't need a babysitter, and that if he didn't believe in what we're doing, he should cut bait and walk. I think the only reason he didn't is because of Beth."

"He wants to make sure we don't screw her over."

He nodded. "He didn't say as much, but I know my brother. He's got it bad for Beth."

"I could tell. When she showed up at his house, the temperature in the room rose. I've only seen one other man look at a woman the way he had."

"Yeah, and how was that?"

The love and longing in Shane's eyes had been hard to miss. And Beth, her pretty hazel eyes had sparkled with much of the same. "Like a man in love."

"Who's the other man?" he asked.

"You."

He brushed his knuckle along her cheek. "Who was I looking at?"

Grinning, she pinched him. "Sadie." The dog moved to her side and wagged her tail. She reached down and stroked her soft head. "Joking aside, I now get why Ian had protected me when I was in Chicago and working for CORE. If I ended up hurt, he could lose my mom."

"So you think that if something happens to Shane I'm going to blame you?"

She nodded and met his gaze. "Would you?"

"No. You of all people know how much I blame myself for his conviction."

"Ryan, we've been over this and I—"

"I don't care. The guilt is still there. I'm still moving on with my life and not letting it stop me from being with you, or making sure my business is successful, but it still weighs on me. Honey, you can't predict the future, all you can do is make smart choices, trust your gut and the people who work for you. Deal with the what ifs, if and when they happen. If you want to question yourself, do it with me, not in front of the rest of the crew. They need a strong leader."

"I know, but how can I not think of the what ifs? Beth and Shane had me thinking. What if Harrison or Vlad end up with girlfriends? How do they explain their jobs? They can't live in the rental house forever, and with all the high-tech equipment and weapons we have stored away, they can't bring women back there. And what about us? We're going to get married, but we've never discussed having kids. If I was pregnant or we had a baby, there's no way I'd want you chasing after a drug dealer."

"Don't the agents who work for CORE have kids?"

"Yes, but that's different."

"Why, because CORE is a legit agency?"

"Maybe." She blew out a breath. "I don't know."

"Lola, there are risks with every job. A bank teller could be shot during a robbery, a school teacher could be killed by a student, a factory worker could die from an equipment failure."

"That's different. Those hypothetical people aren't working a job they know could kill them."

"You don't think a bank teller doesn't consider the possibility of being robbed, or that a school teacher hasn't made sure she's trained and prepared for the unthinkable, or that the factory worker hasn't learned every safety step to avoid accidents and injuries? You can't protect your crew all the time. Have faith that they can protect themselves. You mother Harrison and Vlad."

"Shane said the same thing."

"And that's okay, when we're not dealing with ATL. Those two love being here and part of a team. I overheard Vlad tell Harrison that this was the first time he felt like he belonged. You know what Harrison said? He told Vlad this was the first time he felt like he had a family since his brother died."

Her throat tightened. She'd come to love those two, along with Barney and Mel, even if the woman still scared her.

"We're all in this together and we know the risks. Are there a few dents that'll need to be hammered out? Absolutely. But we'll work through them." He kissed her forehead.

"Remember, stay out of your head, and talk to me when you need to."

"Thank you. I needed to hear this."

"Between my advice and carpentry skills, I think you should double up on my reward."

"I'm sure you do," she said, and grinned. "Let's go inside and get nekkid."

Later, after they'd made love and they'd both been rewarded, Ryan curled her next to his body. "I was wondering, how is Beth going to explain the evidence you gave her to the detectives working the snake case?"

"She didn't say and I didn't think to ask. I am a little bummed Ian kicked us off the case."

"Me, too. I would've liked to help stop this guy."

She also wanted to help stop the killer, but Ian had made it clear that the case was no longer their problem to solve. She snuggled closer to Ryan and closed her eyes. There would be other cases. Going forward, she'd take her fiancé's advice, stay out of her head and lead ATL.

With confidence.

CHAPTER 16

District Twenty Medical Examiner, Naples, Florida
Thursday, 11:24 a.m., Easter Standard Time

DR. DAVID ADAMS stood next to the stainless steel table and stared at the sheet covering Collier County's latest murder victim. Guilt pulled at his heart and twisted his stomach with self-loathing. She was dead because of the sickness inside him. She was murdered because he couldn't keep his fantasies locked in his mind.

"Detectives Wagner and Tennyson are here," his assistant said, as he entered the autopsy suite. "They want to confirm there's a snake in the woman's stomach."

He used to love snakes. He used to love life. But after he'd autopsied Elizabeth Neal, that had changed. Instead of doing the right thing and putting a bullet in his head, what had he done? He'd gone to a random woman's funeral to fantasize about her dead body.

"Sir?"

Then he'd masturbated in the bathroom stall of the funeral home. With thoughts and imaginings of taking the dead woman in the most forbidden ways, he'd stood over a public toilet and had stoked himself. He'd had an orgasm with dozens of grieving people milling around in the rooms just outside the bathroom.

He was a piece of shit. He didn't deserve to live. This should be him on the table.

His assistant cleared his throat. "Dr. Adams, what do you want me to tell the detectives?"

That this was his fault. "Tell them to get a cup of coffee," he snapped. "I haven't even removed the goddamn sheet."

"Yes, sir."

"Wait," he said, realizing he needed to remain calm and professional. He might have set these murders in motion, but as the chief medical examiner, his skills could help stop the bastard from killing another innocent victim. "Tell the detectives I should be ready for them in about twenty or thirty minutes."

"Yes, sir," his assistant said, then left the room.

An average autopsy took two to four hours to perform, depending on the complexity of the case. Considering the killer's MO, he would begin with the woman's stomach and would, at the very least, give the detectives the confirmation they needed. Collier County had a serial killer preying on innocent women.

He adjusted the protective mask he wore over his mouth and nose, then glanced at the woman's chart. Holly Samuels, age thirty-eight. He took a quick look at her medical history, read that other than having three children, she'd never had surgery or had been hospitalized. He set the chart aside, then drew in a deep breath. He gripped the edge of the white sheet draping over her head, then pulled it off her.

He stumbled back, knocking into the moveable tray carrying his medical instruments.

Oh my God. Oh my God.

His breath quickened. His heart pounded so damned hard his chest ached. Behind his mask, sweat coated his upper lip.

This had to be a mistake. It *had* to be. His guilty conscience was distorting reality, making him see things that weren't there. He glanced around the empty room, saw that he was still alone, then quickly approached the woman.

He stared at her face, recognized her finely arched brows, long dark hair, the smattering of freckles along the bridge of her nose and cheeks, along with the deep cleft in her chin. He pulled the sheet down to her waist and lifted her hand. He'd held her hand yesterday. He had gently squeezed her hand and had offered her his condolences over the loss of her beloved sister.

Then he'd gone into the men's room and jacked off to her dead sister's image.

Now Holly was dead.

Dizziness suddenly made the room spin. He dropped the woman's hand and braced himself against the surgical table. He fought the panic, the fear.

He knows.

Impossible.

He'd been careful. He'd been watchful. If anyone were to know, it would be the detectives sipping coffee down the hall.

This had to be a coincidence. It *had* to be.

He glanced at the clock. The detectives wanted answers. He did, too.

Honing in on years of practice and experience, he did what he trained his students and assistants to do—he disassociated himself from the body. Holly became an object. He was a mechanic looking under the hood of a car. Instead of nuts, bolts and wiring, he dealt with flesh, bone and organs. He dealt with the mechanics of the human body.

He looked to the incision along the woman's stomach. Just like Katie, just like Elizabeth, the cut was from left to right, from one edge of the pubic bone to the other. And sewn shut with fishing line.

Since his assistant—thankfully—hadn't returned, he used the camera to photograph her. He took pictures of her mutilated stomach, the purple marks along her neck, then her head where it looked as if she'd been hit several times with a heavy object. When he was through, he took his time untwining the fishing line from the woman's stomach, making sure he had it in one piece should investigators be able to match it to a spool. Once he'd bagged the fishing line to study and compare later, he picked up a scalpel and made an incision from the cut, up to her chest. He pulled the skin apart, then sucked in a breath.

With his hands in the woman's stomach, he looked over his shoulder toward the door.

Still alone.

He turned back to the woman, moved aside the dead rattlesnake and plucked the small sandwich bag from her abdomen. His hands shook as he stared at it, at the folded paper inside.

Evidence.

Against him?

It couldn't be. How could anyone know what he'd done? The young, drug-dealing punk he'd stolen his dead lover from couldn't identify him. The kid had gone to the police and had told them his story. If something he'd said had linked back to him, he'd have been arrested by now.

The killer? But how? How could he know? He'd been so damned careful. He'd covered his tracks. Gabriela, his coworkers, his neighbors, the guys he played golf with at the club would never suspect that Dr. David Adams would go against the Hippocratic oath and human moral code. His family's legacy was known around the world. He'd followed in his family's footsteps, had dedicated his life to medicine and was the great-grandson to the founder of charity foundation, DON. He was also the next in line to oversee the nonprofit organization.

His record was impeccable. He'd helped police solve more cases than he could count, and had given victims' families closure.

And yet, the sister of the woman he'd masturbated over now lay on his table, a snake in her belly.

He took the plastic bag from the woman's stomach, wiped it clean with a paper towel, then lifted the waterproof apron he wore, and tucked it in his pants pocket. If the note said nothing about him, then he'd add it to the evidence. If not…he didn't want to consider that possibility.

After he changed his gloves out for a new pair, he used the camera to photograph the snake, then he removed it and placed it on the tray. As he continued to dissect the woman, his assistant entered the room.

"Sorry it took me so long to get back here."

"Not a problem," David said, grateful for whatever distraction had kept the man away. "If the detectives are still here, they can come in and see the snake."

"Another one? Scary." The assistant shook his head. "CSU arrived with the victim's car. The detectives went to check it out and will be back in a bit. But, if you want, I can tell them you're ready."

"That's okay. Let's keep going," he said, and continued to work on the woman's abdominal area. Within minutes, a chill ran through him and he stopped the autopsy.

"Is something wrong?" his assistant asked.

Everything was wrong. "Get the clamp and hold the skin apart."

Once his assistant had done what he'd been told, and David further investigated, he drew in a sharp breath. *Oh my God, she was pregnant.*

"What is that?" his assistant asked. The man was young, and his experience had been limited to performing animal necropsies.

"A placenta," David said with disgust as he used his scalpel to remove the damaged sac, then the microphone suspended from the ceiling to record his remarks. "Note that the incision along the victim's stomach had been approximately four inches deep. The knife penetrated the placenta." He held the small sac in his gloved hand. "Age of the fetus is unknown at this time, and will need to be analyzed, but the fetus appears to be around eight to nine weeks."

He'd been raised to believe that, no matter the age, a fetus was a living human being. The man who had murdered Holly, had also murdered her unborn child. The man was monster.

No, *he* was the monster. This was *his* fault.

How many others would there be? When would the killer stop? Had he been so offended that David had used his MO to cover what he'd done to the three dead women that he had needed to retaliate with murder? Did the bastard expect him to turn himself over to the police and confess? Would his confession stop the killing?

So many questions. So many unknown answers.

After placing the damaged placenta into a plastic container filled with saline solution, he had his assistant seal it. "See if the detectives are ready to come in now," he said, and continued to work on the victim. While his assistant did as he'd asked, he worked out of his normal routine and examined the victim's head and neck. The detectives would want to know her exact cause of death. While he wouldn't have his report finalized for several hours, he could at least give them his opinion.

Detectives Wagner and Tennyson entered the autopsy suite, suited up in hairnets, masks and borrowed lab coats. Due to the recent leak in his department, David asked his assistant to wait outside.

"Thanks for letting us see the victim," Detective Jerry Tennyson said. He'd known Jerry for over ten years, and had helped the detective with evidence that had led to the incarceration of dozens of murderers. If he were to turn himself over to the police, what would happen to those murder convictions? Would those cases now be scrutinized and re-opened? The cluster-fuck that would ensue could lead to new trials, and the possibility that those killers might see freedom long before their time.

"No problem, Jerry. Anything I can do to help stop this from happening to another woman," he said, and thought about the note tucked in his pocket. He couldn't wait to take a moment alone in his office and read it.

Nick Wagner, Jerry's partner, glanced to the table that held the placenta, rattlesnake and fishing line. "What is this?" he asked pointing to the placenta.

"The victim was pregnant. I'm guessing eight to nine

weeks."

Jerry let out a low whistle. "She had three kids. What's sad is that yesterday, she spent the day at her sister's wake. She was supposed to bury her sister today."

"Now her parents have to bury both of their daughters," Nick said, his tone low, angry.

The dead woman in the casket filled David's mind, along with Holly's and her parents' tear-filled eyes, and the grief etched on their faces. "A parent should never have to bury their child," he said, surprised he could talk around the lump in his throat.

"No, they shouldn't." Jerry walked around the table and studied the woman's head. "We found a skillet in Mrs. Samuels' master bathroom with blood on it. Is that how she died?"

"I don't believe so," David said. "I still have to x-ray her skull, but I think she died of asphyxiation." He pointed to her neck, then hovered his gloved hands over it. "See how the bruising lines up with my fingers?"

Jerry nodded. "He choked her to death."

"Just like Katie Reed," Nick added. "My gut is telling me these murders all go back to her."

His did, too. He'd offended Katie's killer. Now women were paying for his sickness and his grave mistake. "Also like Katie Reed and Elizabeth Neal, the incision along Holly's stomach had been made postmortem, and, as you can see, with fishing line."

Jerry glanced to the tray with the fishing line. "CSU found blood evidence in the sand, not at her home. If the cut was made after she died, and he had to drive over forty-five minutes—probably longer—with her in his car, she was likely dead before he took her from her house."

"Jesus," Nick said. "That means she was murdered with her three kids sleeping down the hall."

He wanted to cry. He wanted scream and shout, to flip the fucking autopsy table over and fling the medical instruments across the room. The anger, the remorse, ate at his soul. What this man had done went beyond atrocious. He was pure evil.

"Did she have a husband?" He knew damned well she was married, and had shaken her husband's hand at the funeral home.

"Yes," Jerry said. "He went for a run. Said he was gone for about thirty minutes, came home and found his wife missing."

"A witness walking his dog saw Christopher Samuels running away from his house at nine-fifteen. Twenty-five minutes later, someone called the police to report the Samuels' sedan idling near a vacant lot, three streets from their home."

"Is the husband a suspect?"

"No, we ruled him out. There was no way he could have killed her and dumped her body, then made it back home in time to call 911 at nine thirty-five."

"You mentioned CSU found blood evidence in the sand. I did notice this victim has what looks like sand along her heels. Was she found closer to the boat ramp on Shell Island Road? Is there something in particular that you found at the crime scene that I should be aware of or looking for during the autopsy?"

"She wasn't found on Shell Island Road," Nick said. "Gardeners discovered her body along a recently added, man-made beach inside the Driftwood Bay development."

Dread crawled along his skin. "Driftwood Bay? Near Vanderbilt Beach Road and Goodlette?"

"Yeah, why?"

"My fiancée lives there." Thank God he'd talked Gabriela into staying at his place last night. He'd had to lock the room where he housed his snake in order to convince her, and would continue to do so because there was no way in hell he wanted her staying in her townhouse alone. Where Holly's body had been found was too much of a coincidence for his liking.

Jerry's eyes held sympathy. "Don't panic. We've talked to the community's builder and they're going to have security cameras installed at the entrance."

"Eventually gates, too," Nick said.

How could he *not* panic? If the killer somehow knew he'd

abused the dead women, he could also know about Gabriela. "Did the Samuels live in Driftwood Bay?" The housing community was a mix of single-family homes and townhouses. With the number of residences in the community, it was possible they'd lived there. He hoped that was the case, he wanted the placement of her body to be a coincidence.

Nick shook his head. "She lived in Iona, just outside Fort Myers."

"We're thinking the killer took Mrs. Samuels from her home with the intent to take her to Shell Island Road, saw that we'd beefed up patrol there, then he cruised around the area until he found a location private enough to finish this," Jerry said, motioning toward the woman's stomach. With a sigh, the detective took a step back. "Thanks again for seeing us. When do you think you'll have your report finished?"

He glanced at the clock. "I should have something for you by four."

After the detectives left, David's assistant came back into the room. "Sorry to exclude you," David said. "After how Lori talked to that reporter, I'm paranoid."

Paranoid didn't cover the emotions running through him. Scared, angry and very worried, he needed to come up with a plan. As he worked on Holly's body, he considered his beautiful fiancée, his expensive home and car, his position as Chief Medical Examiner and the teaching job he had at South University where he taught forensic pathology. He didn't want to give up Gabriela, or anything else. He loved living in Naples and his job. Most of all, he loved Gabriela and his freedom.

But what if he left? What if he sold everything, told his family he needed a break from dealing with death and that he wanted to work for the foundation? DON had doctors and nurses stationed in poverty stricken countries all over the world. Until the murders stopped, he and Gabriela could disappear for a while—a year, two at most. If the killer knew about him, and realized he wasn't around to taunt, maybe he'd stop murdering innocent women.

Or maybe the bastard would make an anonymous call to

the police?

But what did the man have on him? He'd covered his tracks. Again, if the funeral home director's son could have identified him, he'd already be in jail. Since he worked closely with the detectives and CSU techs, he knew the trailer, along with the SUV he'd rented to haul it, hadn't been examined for evidence. Not one person from the Sheriff's Office, or his, suspected him or knew his dark secret. Then how? How did the bastard know to pin the corpses on him?

He was moving ahead of himself. He didn't know anything for sure. Where Holly's body had been dumped last night could be a coincidence. If he wasn't careful, his paranoia could give him away.

Hours later, the autopsy complete, his report almost finished, he finally made his way to his private office. He hadn't signed off on the report yet, because he wasn't sure if the note he'd confiscated would make it into the report or not. Now that he was alone, he could make that determination.

He locked the door, put on a pair of latex gloves, then opened the bag. After carefully pulling the note free he unfolded the paper, drew in a deep breath, and read it.

Dear Dr. Sick Fuck Adams,

Whoever conceals his transgressions will not prosper, but he who confesses and forsakes them will obtain mercy. Confess what you did to the dead women, or I will kill again. You have twenty-four hours.

The paper shook in his hands. With his heart beating rapidly, he folded the paper and slipped it back into the bag, then into his pocket. The bastard wouldn't stop. He would keep killing innocent victims and keep taunting him. Even if he managed to talk Gabriela into running away with him, the man might continue with his murder spree. And what if Gabriela wouldn't move to a third world country with him? He couldn't leave her here, vulnerable and alone.

He had taken the corpses to find a way to deal with his sexual anxiety issues. He'd had sex with his dead lover in order to be able to perform properly and to please Gabriela. He'd broken laws and moral codes for the woman he loved. Now she could die because of him. He couldn't allow that to happen, and should pick up the phone and contact Jerry and confess. But he couldn't go to prison. He couldn't sully his family's name. Why should they, or any other innocents, pay for his crimes?

A bullet in the head sounded more appealing by the second, but he wasn't brave enough to kill himself. Damn it, he didn't know what to do.

Wait. Yes, he did. He knew exactly who could help him, and he also knew she would keep his secrets to herself. While he didn't have enough evidence to put Ian and CORE out of business, he could place suspicion on the agency and its founder, enough so that the police would likely launch an investigation.

He picked up his cell phone and dialed Lola Tam's number.

Irene and Ed Price's House, Naples, Florida
Thursday, 4:38 p.m., Easter Standard Time

Beth hugged her mom tight. "I missed you two," she said, then after kissing her mom's cheek, she embraced her dad.

He squeezed her tight. "You, too, honey. How about having a beer with your old man?"

After the day she was having, she could use more than one. "I can't. I have class at six."

"That's right. I keep forgetting it's Thursday. I think I'm still on vacation time."

"How about some iced tea or lemonade?" her mom asked. "Have you eaten? Dad and I were going to grill burgers."

"No, but I'm not hungry. I'll take a lemonade, though."

"She's too skinny, Irene. Make her eat."

"She's a grown woman. If she doesn't want to eat and would prefer to look emaciated, that's her business."

"I love when you two pretend I can't hear you," Beth said with a chuckle. "And I'm far from emaciated."

"Oh, we're not pretending," her mom said, and pulled a jug of lemonade from the fridge. "We're practicing our passive aggressive skills."

"Call one of my brothers and practice on them."

"We took care of that this morning." While the fridge was still open, her dad grabbed himself a beer. "We called Phil before he went to work and tried to guilt him into bringing the family down for a vacation."

"They were just here for Christmas," Beth said.

"I miss my grandbabies." Her mom handed her a glass of lemonade. "Since you haven't given us any, how else are we supposed to get our baby fix?"

"Beth would need to have a husband to have a baby," her dad said.

"Technically, she doesn't. She could go to a clinic and get artificially inseminated."

Her dad cringed. "Why would she want to do that? The whole fun of having a baby is making one."

"Okay." Beth raised her hand, done with this subject. "I don't want to hear anything else about artificial insemination or making babies. You guys are grossing me out."

Her mom laughed and met her dad's gaze. "Does she think we've only had sex five times?"

"Oh, my God, Mom." Beth laughed, too. "Will you please stop? And enough with the passive aggressive stuff. Just be your normal aggressive selves."

Her dad lifted his beer in a toast. "Amen. You know me, I prefer to tell it like it is."

"Then where did this passive aggressive idea come from?"

"During the cruise, we met a lovely psychologist and his wife. He was quite interesting to talk to, and gave your dad and I different ways to approach people to get what we want."

"In other words," her dad began, "we want more grandchildren."

"Because fourteen isn't enough?" Beth asked. Her parents were something else. Since they'd brought up the subject of marriage and children, now would be a good time to mention

Shane. Not that they were planning on marrying, but she would like to eventually introduce Shane to them. She loved him, and wanted her parents to love him, too.

Her stomach did a nervous flip. But she wasn't ready to discuss Shane with them, and hadn't come here for that anyway. Other than their brief visit yesterday morning, she hadn't seen her mom and dad in over a week, and wanted to catch up with them. Plus, after finding out about the latest murder, and how the woman had been killed with her three babies down the hall, she'd needed to be somewhere comfortable. Because Shane was working and she had to go to class, if she couldn't be in his arms, she could be with her mom and dad for a little while.

"Eight more grandkids and we could have one hell of a football game," her dad said.

"Oh, dear Lord." Her mom kissed his cheek. "All you think about is sports."

"Better than the other shit on the news." He looked at Beth. "Are you part of this murder investigation?"

"Unfortunately."

"It's just awful," her mom said, then carrying her drink, walked into the living room. Beth and her dad followed behind. "Thank God you carry a gun."

"So what's going on with these murders?" her dad asked. "Do the detectives have any suspects?"

"Not yet."

Her mom sat on the sofa. "Is that handsome young man, Nick, working on the case?"

Ten months ago, when Nick had first invested in the bar business, he'd invited her, Ricky and a dozen other coworkers to come by for drinks. Since mostly couples were going, she'd asked her parents to tag along. She hadn't wanted Nick to take advantage of her being alone and give her any reason to date him.

"Yes, he and Jerry are the leads."

"He's very handsome," her mom repeated.

"You mentioned that."

"He'd make a nice catch."

"Mom, I told you I'm not interested."

"For cryin' out loud, Irene. The man's been married five times. I don't want my daughter mixed up with that nonsense."

"Three times," Beth corrected. "But thank you for coming to my defense."

"What you need," her dad continued as if she hadn't spoken, "is to give Isaac a chance. The man's got money and he's not ugly."

She stared at her father in utter disbelief. Isaac was his fishing buddy's son, and one of the most obnoxious men she'd ever met. "I don't care how much money he has, he's pompous and arrogant."

"He also chews food with his mouth open," her mom added.

"Teach him to chew the right way then."

"Anyway," Beth said, hoping to redirect the conversation. "We weren't able to talk long yesterday. Tell me more about your cruise."

As her mom and dad talked about their trip, she listened and sipped her lemonade. Her parents made her laugh. Why would they think she needed to know what time they woke, ate or napped, or how the bathroom was too small for her dad to do his business comfortably?

"We went on every excursion we could," her dad said. "You would have loved swimming with the dolphins."

"You two swam with dolphins?"

"No, we watched. You know your father doesn't like going in the water past his knees."

"That's not true. I just don't like going in water filled with things that can bite and sting me."

"Well," her mom began, her blue eyes twinkling, "while we were watching our shipmates swim with the dolphins, we ended up talking to a nice young man who lives in Fort Myers. Ed, wasn't he a handsome devil?"

Her dad looked at Beth and shook his head. "I'll let you be the judge of that."

"Trust me, he was very good looking. I told him all about you and showed him your picture. He gave me his number and wants to meet you. I thought we could invite him for dinner and let you two get acquainted." Her mom stood. "Let me get my camera. I have pictures of him."

"Mom, please sit down. I don't want to see what he looks like, and I don't want to meet him."

"I told you she wouldn't go for it," her dad said, as her mom sat back on the sofa.

"I don't see why not. She needs to see there's more to life than work and school."

Beth let out a sigh. "*She* knows that, and she's already seeing someone."

Her parents stared at her expectantly. "What's his name?" her mom asked.

"Shane Monahan."

"Where did you meet him?"

"When I went on an airboat tour with Erin. He was the captain."

"What the hell kind of job is that?" her dad asked. "You're better off going out with the guy your mom wants to fix you up with, he's a banker."

After Beth explained that Shane was a pilot, had his own plane and business, and only gave airboat tours when his brother needed the extra help, her dad changed his attitude. He turned to her mother, and said, "There, now you can stop nagging Bethie."

Her mom smiled. "I can see that. When do we get to meet him?"

"I'll talk to Shane. I'm sure we can set up something soon."

"How soon?"

Beth shrugged and regretted opening her big mouth. Although she and Shane had a major heart-to-heart last night, they'd never discussed if and when he'd meet her parents. "I don't know. He's busy, I'm busy."

"If you're too busy for dinner, then maybe your dad and I will take one of his tours. I've never seen the Everglades from the air."

She panicked and almost preferred her parent's passive aggressive approach to this full-out aggressive one. They couldn't meet Shane. Not yet and certainly not without her being there. Her parents could be nosey, especially where their daughter was concerned. They were also very intelligent people. If they realized Shane's business was only recently re-opened, they would wonder why, ask questions and piece together that Shane's timeline since leaving the Army had several unexplained years missing. Seven of them to be exact.

I can just see the holidays. Uncle Shane sitting in the corner by himself, your nieces and nephews keeping their distance because their mommies and daddies told them he's a bad man.

Shane's words came back at her in a rush. He'd been right to worry about her family's reaction to him. They could freak out over his past and she didn't want that. She wanted them to accept him, along with her decision to be with him. She wanted their approval, too. No matter how old she was, she loved going to her mom and dad for advice. On this matter she didn't need their advice, she would need them to be open-minded.

"If you want to go on a tour, just let me know and I'll make the arrangements for you," she said.

"Why can't we do it ourselves?" her mom asked.

"Please, just be patient. Shane and I haven't been dating for long, and I don't want to scare him off with the whole meet the parents deal."

"Leave her alone, Irene. Bethie's right. I can still remember the Sunday dinner at your folks' house. It was God-awful." Her dad looked at her. "Your grandparents had me so nervous I couldn't eat. I found out later that was a good thing. Your grandma couldn't cook for sh—"

Her mother gasped. "My mother was an excellent cook."

As they argued about her grandmother's cooking—which really was awful—Beth relaxed. For now, she was off the hook. Eventually the subject would come up again, and she'd have to tell her parents the truth. When her cell phone rang, her parents stopped talking and turned their attention on her. She stood, then retrieved the phone from her purse and checked the caller ID.

"Is it Shane?" her mom asked, hopeful.

"No, it's Nick. I need to take this," she said, then stepped onto her parents' lanai.

"I went through the report you emailed me," Nick said after she'd answered. "What made you think to look into Harlan Reed's background?"

Once she'd read through the file Lola had given her, she realized she would need to come up with a way to make it look like she'd gathered the information on her own. While she'd done plenty of gathering, she wouldn't have thought to look into Harlan's religious beliefs if it hadn't been for Lola and Harrison.

"Desperation," she said. "I kept thinking maybe there was something missed during Katie's investigation. Harlan's alibi for the night Katie went missing couldn't be confirmed because he claimed to be home alone."

"Harlan offered up a sample of his DNA and passed the polygraph," Nick countered.

"If he had anything to do with Katie's murder, he would know her body had been washed and the chance of his DNA being found would be slim. And we both know polygraph tests are unreliable."

"But Harlan's dead."

"You read about how he was originally from Easterville, Tennessee, right?"

"Yeah, which came up during Katie's murder investigation."

"Nick, I'm going to assume the report is in front of you. If you've read through the whole thing, you saw that he'd belonged to the Church of the Living God, which was rumored to conduct snake handling rituals."

"I saw it."

"And, what? Don't you think that's an angle worth considering? In my report is the name of the church's pastor who made local headlines in the seventies for his radical beliefs, and his use of snakes during his private sermons. Based on the timestamp of the headlines, Malachi Rhodes is probably now in his eighties. I'm not suggesting he had anything to do with Katie's murder, but maybe he knows of a parishioner who was off, or who'd taken the snake handling rituals too far." When he didn't say anything, she added, "I know it's a stretch, but it could be worth checking."

"Which is why I tried to find the man. I came up with the same last known address as you did."

"Unless he's been dodging the IRS, they might know where to find him," she suggested.

"True."

"Nick, is something wrong? You sound distracted," she said. Or maybe she was paranoid. Then again, she shouldn't be. She'd been the one who'd spent the time looking into Harlan's religious background, which had led to the discovery of the church he used to attend, along with its pastor. In her report, she also hadn't included the information Lola had obtained from the NCIC regarding the unidentified male victim found in Georgia, with the snake skeleton under his remains. Since she wasn't authorized to use the National Crime Information Center's database, she hadn't wanted to send out any red flags. She absolutely *did not* want her superiors questioning how she'd obtained information that was limited to only certain personnel within the Sheriff's Office.

When he didn't answer, she asked, "Are you still there?"

"Yeah. Did you hear Holly Samuels was pregnant?"

She momentarily closed her eyes, and fought the urge to cry. "No, I didn't know." Now she understood why Nick hadn't been acting like himself.

"Her youngest child is eighteen months, her oldest only five. They'll never remember their mother. What's worse, Holly's sister's funeral was today. Her parents lost their only two children in a matter of days."

Her throat tightened and she rubbed her chin to stop it from trembling. Oh, God. Holly's poor family. She couldn't imagine the grief, shock and horror.

"Since we don't have jack to go on, I'm willing to try just about anything." He paused for a few seconds. "The FBI is stepping in, and might be able to help us locate the pastor."

Lola's boss had been right to pull ATL from the case. While she was still unsure about Lola and her organization, she didn't want to see them busted for their involvement on this, and the necrophiliac case, or disbanded before they had the chance to prove their worth. Like Shane had said, they wanted what she wanted—to give victims and their families justice.

She glanced over her shoulder and saw her parents talking. Shane was part of ATL. If the organization ended up being a focal point for the Feds, he could face prison again. God, why couldn't she have fallen for a regular guy?

"Have you thought about checking NCIC?" she asked, knowing Nick could access the database. "It's been two years since Katie's murder. It's possible a similar case has surfaced somewhere else."

He let out a sigh. "I haven't thought about anything but *our* murder vics, and what I could be missing," he said, weariness in his voice. "Thanks for the suggestion. I still have a long night ahead of me and it's only what? Five-thirty?"

Five-thirty? Crap. "I need to run to class. If you want Ricky and me to work on anything for you, our shift starts at eight. I can be there sooner, though."

"Jerry and I will probably take you up on the offer."

"Then I'll call Ricky and let him know. We'll meet you at your desk before our shift. Before I go," she began, and closed her eyes, hoping she wasn't giving too much away, "when you run the search through NCIC, I wouldn't limit it to female victims only. The murders haven't been sexually motivated, so it's possible he's killed men, too."

"I was actually just jotting down the same thing."

She stood and turned toward the sliding glass doors. Her parents were no longer in the living room, but she could see them in the kitchen, likely preparing the burgers they planned to grill.

"Good, then I'll see you in the morning."

"Thanks again for your help on this," he said. "I also want to apologize about last night. I shouldn't have pushed so hard about going to the bar."

Damn it. Despite Nick's horrible record with women, he was a nice guy. A good guy. She watched as her parents stole a quick kiss. The kind of guy you take home to mom and dad.

But Nick wasn't Shane. He didn't make her legs weak, he didn't make her heart beat out of control. She didn't crave Nick's touch, didn't long to be with him minutes after walking away.

"It's okay," she said. "You're excited about the bar and I don't blame you. It's a fun place."

"Yeah, it's a good time," he said, and she didn't miss the disappointment in his voice. "I'll see you in the morning."

She said good-bye, then hung up the phone. Thank God she had her class as an excuse and could make a quick escape. She didn't want to discuss Shane or the case with her parents. Shane...she'd have to think long and hard about how she would approach her mom and dad about his past. The murder investigation...she didn't want to think about that. She didn't want to imagine what Holly Samuels' family was going through right now.

All she wanted was the killer stopped before he destroyed another life.

CHAPTER 17

Naples Beach Hotel, Naples, Florida
Thursday, 6:02 p.m., Eastern Standard Time

"HOW YOU DOIN', boy?" Daddy asked, with a hint of concern. "I haven't heard from you all day."

The Reverend had spent the day at the beach, enjoying the sun, the sound of the waves, scoping out the tourists and thinking about his next kill. Now that he had the doc where he wanted him, he could keep screwing with the man, keep killing until the pervert confessed.

It had been so damned easy to kill Holly Samuels and the little blonde, he wouldn't mind taking out a couple more people before he dealt with the doc. Not just to torture the doc, but because there wasn't anything like deciding who lived and who died. Hell, when he'd been sitting on the beach, there had been a few people he'd considered killing. As he'd sat on his beach chair picturing how he'd do it, he had also wondered how those people would feel if they'd found out that he'd thought about taking their lives, but had ended up choosing another. Would they be happy? Relieved and grateful some other poor sucker bit the bullet instead of them? Would they have a coming-to-Jesus moment and believe that an angel had stepped in and saved them?

He'd love to find out, but didn't have that kind of time. Sure, he could probably get away with a few more murders, but Daddy would have a fit. The law had no clue who he was, and the good citizens of southwest Florida were terrified by him. The boo-hooing he'd heard all over the news about the Samuels woman had fed his ego, though, and had made him want to continue taunting the doc. They'd called him a monster. An evil murderer. He wasn't either. He was just a messenger.

"Been unwinding is all," the Reverend finally said. "How are things with you?"

"Boy, I ain't the mailman you wave to and chit-chat with on occasion. I saw the news. Why didn't you tell me you was plannin' on killin' another woman?"

"Sorry, Daddy. I thought I made it clear. I told you I was gonna send the doc another message."

"And I figured you meant to kill the doc. Christ, son." Daddy let out a shaky breath. "Did you know she was pregnant?"

He remembered the woman's slim, naked body. "Nope."

"Would it have made a difference?"

Memories from last night filtered through his mind. The baby in the crib, the two little ones in their twin beds. The husband and wife's final kiss in the garage. "Yep," he replied, because he suspected that'd be what Daddy would want to hear. "I would've killed her husband instead."

Daddy let out a tired sigh. "Son, are you...ah, are you gettin' the urge again?"

The urge. Daddy was referring to the couple he'd come upon after dumping the Turner boy's body in the woods. Was he getting the urge to be bad? Hell, yeah. He might've been fantasizing about killing a few more people, but he was also smart enough to know when it was time to move on and head home. "Don't worry about me, Daddy. I'm just fine. I'm sure the doc's gotten the message I sent. I told him he had twenty-four hours to confess, or I'd kill another. What he don't know is that the next person I plan to kill is him."

"That's good. Real good. But you need to end it tonight, and come home."

The urgency in Daddy's voice had him alarmed. "What's wrong, Daddy? Ain't you feeling well?"

"The usual. I'm just a little worried, is all. I need my boy home. I need to know you're not gonna cross paths with the law. You can't kill no more. Understand? Other than the doc, this is over. We made our point."

He supposed Daddy was right. He'd made his point clear, but he planned on making it crystal clear. "We sure did."

"You promise you're gonna take care of him tonight?"

"If that's what you want me to do."

"It is. I wanna know how, and I wanna know when you'll be home."

While he missed Daddy, he would miss his hotel suite and views of the beach, too. Damn, and the room service. "I'll be home tomorrow by suppertime," he said.

"And the doc?"

"I promise to make it quick and clean so I can be back in time for room service," he lied, and grinned. What he planned to do would not be quick and far from clean.

Daddy chuckled. "You do that, boy. Enjoy your last night. Find yourself a woman if you can. Lord knows the pickings are mighty slim around here. You give me a call when you're done."

"I will." After he'd said good-bye to his daddy, he moved onto the balcony and looked at the beach. As always, Daddy was right. His time here was done. He'd proved his point and needed to take care of the doc, and make him his last kill. Maybe it was better this way. He'd stop while he was ahead. The murders would go unsolved and remain cold cases forever. He'd be legendary here. People would talk about him for years to come.

But they'd spit on the doc's grave. He'd make sure of it. He'd make the doc confess to what he'd done to those corpses, then he'd show him the true meaning behind the Ritual of the Serpents.

Revenge.

He thought about Mama again. He'd helped his daddy slice open her stomach and shove a rattler inside of her as a symbolic fuck-you for all that she'd put them through. That had satisfied Daddy, maybe because he'd been the one to use a venomous snake as his weapon to kill the bitch. For him, the ritual they'd performed on Mama hadn't satisfied him. At all. She'd already been dead. She couldn't see what they were doing to her. She couldn't scream and beg for them to stop like he had when she'd whooped his ass.

He never had the opportunity to watch the life drain from her spiteful eyes.

Tonight he'd have that opportunity. For the first time, he would perform the ritual the way he'd always dreamed it should be.

He smiled, then pushed away from the balcony rail to call room service for a snack.

Lola's Rental House, Everglades City, Florida
Thursday, 7:32 p.m., Eastern Standard Time

Lola parked her SUV behind Shane's truck, then rushed inside the rental house. Her entire team was there, gathered around the dining room table and talking. When they saw her, the room went silent.

"What's going on?" Ryan asked, as he stood and walked to her. "Where were you?"

"I met with David Adams at his house." When she caught the worry in his eyes, she gripped his hand. "We have a big problem," she said, and joined the others in the dining room. "David is the necrophiliac."

"The Medical Examiner?" Harrison asked, frowning. "I don't believe it."

She let go of Ryan's hand, then set her purse on the table. "I didn't either." She dug into her purse, then pulled out a copy of the note David had found in Holly Samuels' body, in her hand writing, since David had burned the original in his kitchen sink. "Until he told me how he stole the corpses, how he'd tried to mimic Katie Reed's murder in case the bodies were found before they'd decomposed and how he dumped them."

"Did he say why?" Mel asked.

She shook her head. "I asked, but he told me it was none of my business. What he wants from us is to keep him protected until he can leave the country. What he doesn't realize is we're not going to let him go anywhere until he helps us track down the killer."

"I still don't believe it." Harrison said. "I met the guy. He's normal."

"Maybe sex with dead bodies *is* normal to him," Barney suggested, and looked at Lola. "Why'd he tell you?"

"Because the killer sent him a message. During the autopsy of Holly Samuels, he found this." She opened her copy of the note and read it to the group.

"He quoted Proverbs 28:13," Mel said. When everyone stared at her, she shrugged. "My daddy found Jesus six years ago. Daddy lost Him about a year later, but I remember some of the quotes he liked to preach."

"Preach," Harrison echoed, and looked to Lola. "Maybe we were on to something with the snake handler angle."

"You're welcome," Barney said, and tipped the bill of his ball cap.

Lola ignored Barney. "Shane, did Beth do anything with the information we gave her?"

"When I talked to her earlier today she said she was working on it, but she hadn't gotten far. She finishes her class around ten. I could call her and—"

"No. I don't want Beth to know about this."

"What exactly is *this*?" Barney asked.

"Yeah, I'm still trying to wrap my head around David being

the necrophiliac," Harrison said. "And why there'd be a note in Holly Samuels' body."

"Think about it," Mel began, "Holly's sister's wake was yesterday, she winds up dead today. After researching this gross necrophilia stuff, my guess is when David realized he couldn't steal any more bodies he decided to keep the fantasy going by becoming a funeral home groupie. The killer catches him and decides to send him a message." She tapped her manicured nails along the table. "I'm right, aren't I?"

"Sound's like a big ol' coincidence to me," Barney said.

"David wouldn't admit to knowing Holly Samuels or her sister," Lola said. "Coincidence or not, I think Mel's right. Which also means the killer has been following David around and why we can't bring him here."

"Why would we bring him here? Hell, why are we even having this conversation?" Shane asked. "David's the reason two women are dead. He shouldn't have called you, he should have called the detectives working the case and put an end to this."

Lola pulled a chair out, and sat. "It's not that easy. David obviously doesn't want to confess. If he does, he'll lose his medical license and go to prison."

Shane shrugged. "Not our problem."

"If David turns himself in," she continued, "and the killer disappears again, then detectives are going to be left with a series of unsolved murders. Elizabeth Neal and Holly Samuels' families need justice, so does Katie. The man who murdered them needs to pay. Severely." She met Ryan's gaze. "Plus, David threatened me."

Ryan's face hardened. He leaned back in his chair and folded his arms. "How?"

She drew in a breath. "David knows about this house. He also knows we work for Ian. He said that if he's forced to confess his crimes, and we don't help him until he can leave the country, he'd take down Ian, CORE and us with him. So, we can do one of a few of things. Remove anything in the house that would back up his story and lay low for a while, relocate our operation, or keep David protected until he and his fiancée leave the country."

"I don't like any of those options," Harrison said. "Screw David. What we need to do is go straight to Beth and tell her what we know."

Shane nodded. "I'm with Harrison."

"Agreed," Ryan said. "We don't owe David anything. Besides, what could he say against us? He didn't see us remove bodies from the house. All he did was pull bullets from Ian and John."

"He'd also get in trouble for not reporting their gunshot wounds," Barney added. "So in telling on us, he'd be screwing himself."

"I don't think he could hurt us, CORE or Ian, either. But he's desperate, and I'm not willing to take the chance. Again, this isn't just about David, it's about stopping a murderer."

"And keeping other murderers in prison," Mel added. "If y'all think about it, David's confession could ruin his credibility as a medical examiner and possibly the integrity of the Collier County Sheriff's Office."

Shane scratched his beard. "Shit. I didn't think about that."

"Vlad not follow," the Russian said, and looked to Harrison.

"Let's say you have a dude sitting in prison for murder. He's there because the ME's autopsy helped put him away for life. The dude finds out the ME is a whack job, calls his lawyer and has him ask to have a new trial. That's what I would do, even if I was guilty. Because if this same dude gets a new trial, all his attorney needs to do is put doubt in jurors' minds."

Vlad frowned. "Dude go free."

"Possibly."

"That possibility worries me and Ian," Lola said, remembering her conversation with him. One thing she could say about Ian, as manipulating as he could sometimes be, justice was his number one priority. "I spoke with him after I left David's. He also doesn't think David could hurt us, and he wants the killer caught."

"What about David?" Ryan asked.

"Once it's over, Ian wants him gone."

The Russian sighed. "Vlad will kill David."

"I haven't seen my daddy in a few days," Mel said. "We can use a little daddy-daughter time."

Lola leaned back in the chair and glanced between Vlad and Mel. Two months ago she'd never envisioned herself running a secret organization, let alone having a conversation with a hitman and a knife-wielding sociopath. "We are *not* killing David. What I meant was we will make sure David leaves the country and doesn't return."

Mel shrugged. "What about the killer? I don't suppose you plan to put him on a plane and set him free, too."

"Of course not. We're going to use David as bait and draw out the killer. It's worked before, hopefully it'll work again."

"We need Beth for this," Shane said.

"And tell her what?" Lola asked. "That we're setting up the necrophilliac medical examiner with the hope that we can catch a killer? If we tell her, it'll put her in a bad position."

"Let her decide. Or don't you trust her?"

She leaned forward. "Shane, this isn't a matter of trust. I'm keeping Beth out of this because I don't want her to have to decide where her loyalty lies."

"In other words, honey," Mel began, "Lola doesn't want Beth to dump your butt."

"I'm with Lola on this," Ryan said. "Beth stays out unless we're desperate. She's going to be torn between going to the detectives she works with, and helping you. Not ATL." He looked to her. "So what's the plan?"

Lola took David's house key from her purse, then slid it toward Harrison. "You and Vlad are going to stay with David. Here's a key to his house." She remembered the passcode for the gated entrance of David's golf course community. "You'll also need this to get through the gate," she said, handing Harrison the note.

"Are there surveillance cameras at the gate?" he asked.

"Yes, but they're not operational yet. Which works in our

favor."

"And the killer's," Harrison said, and stuffed the key and passcode in the front pocket of his jeans.

"Unfortunately," Lola said. "Anyway, if David leaves, you follow him. If he has to go to work, you sit in the car and wait for him to finish. Other than when he's working or using the bathroom, I don't want him out of your sight. If he runs, we could lose a shot at finding out who the killer is."

"I dunno," Barney said. "Sounds like that guy isn't going to stop killing until David fesses up."

"David is his audience. If David isn't around to squirm, he might stop, then vanish." God, she hoped she was right, and she wasn't jeopardizing another innocent victim's life. She pushed back her chair. "Vlad, take what you need to protect yourselves and David. Harrison, take your laptop. While you're keeping an eye on David, dig deeper into the preacher angle."

"Beth did tell me she was planning on checking into Harlan Reed's background," Shane said. "Since his daughter was the first victim, maybe you should start with him, too."

"Good idea. See if he was linked to any churches that performed the snake handling ritual." Lola turned her attention to Barney and Mel. "You two will continue to go to work as usual. Same with myself, Ryan and Shane. Remember, we run an airboat business."

After everyone nodded, she stood. "It's a fifty-minute drive to David's," she said to Harrison. "I never confirmed we'd help him."

"Why not?" Harrison asked.

"Because I don't like being threatened. Besides, if David does plan to run instead of helping us draw out the killer—and I think he will run—I'd rather surprise him at his house. That being said, I still want you there tonight. How long before you two will be ready to leave?"

"Fifteen or twenty minutes."

"Thirty. Vlad must feed Polina." The Russian frowned. "Polina will need to feed tomorrow, too."

"I'll feed your dang gator," Barney said. "She'll be fine."

"Barney, good man."

Ryan also stood. "Call us when you get to David's."

She touched Harrison's arm. "I don't trust David. He's desperate and scared. Holly's body was found in the community where his fiancée lives. Don't be surprised if she's there, too." David had been beyond scared. He'd been frantic, manic.

"Vlad no understand. David have woman yet have sex with dead body?"

Barney slapped him on the back. "Maybe it took a stiff to give him a stiffy?"

"Stiff?" Vlad asked.

"I'll explain on the drive over," Harrison said. "Thanks for complicating my night, Barney."

The older man grinned. "Any time."

As everyone left, she pulled Harrison aside. "Call me the moment you get there."

"I will."

She gripped his shoulders and thought about how Ryan had accused her of mothering Harrison and Vlad. She didn't care. "What David did was bad, but what the killer is doing is even worse. I feel like he has a point to prove and I'm worried he'll do whatever it takes to prove it. If you and Vlad get in his way, he—"

"Stop," he said with a patient grin. "We've got this. Me and Vlad, we're a good team. We won't let you down."

She tightened her grip on his shoulder. She loved Harrison. He was like the younger brother she'd never had, even if they were the same age. "I'm not worried about you letting me down." She knocked his bangs aside. "You know how you said that this is all you and Vlad have? It's not. You have me, too." She pulled him in for a hug. "Be safe."

When Ryan cleared his throat, Harrison raised his hands and stepped away. "Brotherly love, man."

"Why not Vlad have this brother love from Asian Lola?"

Lola hugged the Russian, then sniffed. "I thought you quit smoking."

Vlad hung his head after she stepped away. "Nicotine bandage no help Vlad."

She tapped his chest. "You'll quit when you're ready. Take care of each other and call me."

She followed Ryan and Shane outside. Mel and Barney waved as they backed out of the driveway in Barney's station wagon. She waved back, then turned to Shane when they neared his truck. "You know I'm looking out for Beth on this, right?" she asked.

Shane pulled his keys from his pocket, and nodded. "I get it."

"But are you okay with it?"

Ryan took her by the elbow. "He's fine. Let's go."

She wanted to protest and hear Shane's answer, but she had to trust Ryan on this. She had to trust Shane. As she climbed into her Honda and followed Ryan home, she put herself in Shane's position. Whether he'd admit it or not, he was in love with Beth, and she'd forced him into a corner. Who was he loyal to? She wasn't playing games or trying to manipulate him, she was honestly looking out for Beth. In this case, Shane should, too. Because if they had an opportunity to stop a killer, they would take it. By any means necessary.

Dr. David Adams' House, Naples, Florida
Thursday, 8:48 p.m., Eastern Standard Time

"What are you talking about?" Gabriela stood in his bedroom, her hand on her hips, her forehead creased in confusion. "I've never even heard of Burundi and you want me to move there?"

"It's in Africa," David said, and hauled a suitcase from the closet. Still unsure whether Lola planned to help him or not, he wanted to be prepared to leave should the situation grow worse and he had to catch a flight immediately.

"Africa? You want me to move to *Africa?*"

"Only for a year or two." He walked to her, and placed his

hands on her shoulders. "We'll vacation before we go. I'll take you to France, Spain, Greece. Wherever you want. We can spend two weeks relaxing on the beach before I start my work."

She dropped her arms to her sides. "Sounds like you have it all planned out. Question, while you're playing doctor, what am I supposed to do? What about my clients?"

"Your business is web based. You can work anywhere," he said, trying his damnedest to convince her. "This could be good for you. You could network, meet new people and maybe gain new clients."

"In a tiny village filled with sick and starving people? What language do they speak in Burundi?"

"French and Kirundi."

"You're out of your mind. I love you, but I'm sorry I can't do this."

Before he'd met Lola at his house, he'd called his father. He'd explained to his dad that he needed to take a break from his job as medical examiner, and wanted to help the family foundation. His father had been thrilled to have him join them. It had been fifteen years since David had offered his medical assistance to the foundation and had worked side-by-side with his parents. Unfortunately, his folks were in Burundi, rather than South America. Columbia, Peru, Ecuador…Gabriela might have been more open-minded to one of those locations. He needed her to be open-minded now. He couldn't stay in the States, not with a killer taunting him, and not with the threat of his crimes being exposed. He couldn't leave Gabriela, either. If the killer knew about her she would be vulnerable, and the bastard could retaliate against him and use Gabriela to send another message.

"Please, honey. At least think about it. My parents aren't getting any younger and it's important to me to work with them again."

"I can understand that, but what about my parents? You're asking me to leave my family."

"It's not forever and you can visit them anytime you want."

She shook her head and looked over his shoulder. "What about our wedding?" She met his gaze. The disappointment in her dark-brown eyes made his chest ache. "If I don't go with you, what will happen to us?"

"Don't make this so black and white. If you don't want to go, it doesn't mean we can't still stay together."

Her eyes filled with tears. "I'm not sure I can do a two-year long distance relationship. I'm sorry, but if you go, I don't think I'll be here when you return."

He quickly embraced her. "Please don't say that," he said, and rubbed a hand along her back.

She held him tight, and let out a quiet sob. "Why do you have to go now? What about your job as Medical Examiner or teaching at the university? What will you do when you come home?"

He leaned back and ran his finger along her cheek. "I'm burned out," he lied. "Maybe I'm tired of dealing with the dead and want to help the living. When I come home, I don't have to go back to forensic pathology, I could work for the foundation. If it's money you're worried about, I have plenty."

Anger simmered in her eyes. "Is that why you think I'm with you? For your money?" she asked, and swiped a tear from her cheek.

"I've never thought that. I only meant that I wouldn't have to start over once I'm home. Once *we're* home."

She stepped away from him and pushed her long dark hair away from her face. "This is too sudden. I need time to think about it."

"I know I'm asking a lot from you. Why don't we take that two-week vacation? We'll leave tomorrow, and while we're gone you can take that time to decide what you want to do." He approached her again. "Name the place and I'll take you. France?" He kissed her shoulder. "Italy?" He kissed her again.

She smiled, and took his face in her hands. "I don't want to lose you."

"Then fly off with me."

"It's not that easy, and I think it's unfair that you didn't talk to me about this first. We're a couple. Your choices affect me."

His choices had affected too many people. His need to please Gabriela, to keep her happy had ended lives and devastated families. Bitterness sickened his stomach as the irony of his situation—a situation he'd brought on himself—came to full realization. Despite what he'd done for Gabriela, if she didn't join him on the trip to Africa, he could still lose her. Not to another man, but his own monstrous creation. He might not have created the monster who now preyed on the innocent, but by mimicking what the bastard had done to Katie Reed, he'd unleashed him.

"I need a drink," she said. "And I need to think. The vacation I can do, but I can't decide the next year or two of my life in a matter of minutes."

"Again, you don't have to be gone that long. Maybe you could give Burundi a few months. If you can't stand it, you can go home. I'll fly home to see you when I can, or you can visit me." He kissed her. "We *can* make this work. I don't want to lose you, but this is also very important to me. Not just because I want to work with my parents again before they're forced to retire, but to give back to people who are less fortunate. Money, this house, my car doesn't make me a good man. I want you to be proud of me. I want to be proud of myself." He knew he was laying it on thick, but ninety percent of what he'd said was the truth. He did want to work with his parents, and he did want Gabriela proud of him, but he would miss the prestige that went along with his job, as well as the comforts money gave him.

She feathered her fingers through his hair. "I'm already proud of you. You're such an admirable and self-sacrificing man. I couldn't imagine dealing with the stress of your job. Every day you're surrounded by death, and I could understand wanting to help the living. Keep in mind, what you do, how you help detectives, you *do* help the living. You give families closure when they don't understand why their loved one has died. You give detectives what they need to help solve an investigation. You're kind and generous, and give me so much love, there are times I wonder if I deserve you." She gave him a slow, lingering kiss. "Let me get that drink and think."

"I'll join you in a few. While you're in the kitchen, open up my laptop. I pulled up information on Burundi, along with a few vacation spots I thought you might like."

"I like that idea. Want me to make you your usual scotch on the rocks?"

After his day, he wanted the whole damned bottle. "That'd be great."

When she left the room, he stared at the empty suitcase and slumped on his bed. Gabriela was so wrong about him. He wasn't admirable or self-sacrificing. He was despicable and selfish. He'd made a mess of his life, and was trying to salvage what he could by fleeing the country. Lola would be furious once she realized he planned to leave, but he no longer cared. She, Ian and whatever operation they were running could deal with the bastard. He needed to take care of Gabriela, keep her safe, keep her with him.

He needed to do everything he could to talk her into coming with him to Africa. He rose from the bed, and made his way down the steps. When he reached the kitchen, terror gripped him and squeezed. He staggered back and fell against the stair rail. His heart thudded hard. His head grew dizzy as horror shocked his body.

A man dressed in all black stood behind Gabriela. Bound to his kitchen chair, silver duct tape covering her mouth, her eyes wild with fear and confusion, she stared at David. His throat tightened. Tears filled his eyes.

"What's up, doc?" the man asked with a heavy drawl. "You sure have a nice place. What's something like this go for?"

"Leave her out of this."

"And have her miss out on all the fun?" The bastard shook his head. "No can do, doc. See you didn't do it right."

"I didn't do what right?" he asked, and tried to consider his options. Tried to figure out a way to free Gabriela.

"Those dead women. Some killers might get off on being copied. An ego boost, I suppose." His eyes hardened. "I don't take kindly to being mocked or copied. You did both."

"I don't know what you're talking about."

"You didn't fuck those corpses?"

David glanced to Gabriela. Tears streamed down her face as she stared at him with disbelief.

"No. That's disgusting and immoral."

The bastard nodded. "About as disgusting and immoral as masturbating at a funeral home, don't you think?"

A chill washed over him, yet his underarms grew damp with sweat. How had the man known? He'd been alone in the bathroom. Had made sure no one had been inside, and hadn't heard anyone enter.

"I don't know what you're talking about," he repeated, hoping to put doubt in the man's mind.

David flinched when the bastard reached into his pocket, then relaxed when he withdrew a cell phone. "I saw you. I saw you walk up to Patricia Oakley's family, shake their hands and offer your condolences. I watched you go to the dead woman's casket and kneel before her. You were there for quite a while, doc. What were you thinking about? How much you'd like to strip her clothes off and fuck her?"

"That's vile," he snapped, anger—for himself, for the bastard—rising to the surface. "I never did any such thing."

"Really? Who's this then?" he asked, then shoved the cell phone in Gabriela's face.

As her gaze drifted to the screen, her eyes widened. "Is that the doc?" he asked.

With a muffled sob, she turned away.

"See? A woman knows her man. But I'm thinking *your* woman don't know you at all." He put the phone back in his pocket. "I gotta ask you, why? Why would you wanna fuck a dead woman when you have this?" He ran a hand along Gabriela's shoulder, then cupped her breast.

David fisted his hands and lunged. The bastard quickly produced a knife—his kitchen knife—and pressed it against Gabriela's throat. "It's a good idea if you stay right where you are."

David stilled. "What do you want?"

"Didn't you get my note?"

"The detectives have it."

"If that were the case, you'd be in county lock up, not in your fancy home with your hot girlfriend. Whadya do with it? Burn it?"

"It's evidence. I gave it to the authorities, because *I* didn't do anything wrong."

"Hmm." The man rubbed his chin with the back of a gloved hand. "Well I'll be damned. I've made a terrible mistake and had you pegged all wrong."

David didn't relax, and he didn't believe one word that came from the man's mouth. "Leave now and I won't call the police."

"Sure thing."

David flinched when the man tore the tape from Gabriela's mouth. She gasped, then drew in several ragged breaths. "Please. David's right. We won't call the police."

"What's your name, pretty lady?"

"Gabriela."

"Gabriela, you can call me Reverend. I gotta ask you, aren't you curious about all this? Don't you want to know if I'm right about the good doc? You saw the picture of him in the bathroom, don't you want to know the truth?"

"I saw the back of a man's head. I can't be sure he's David."

"I can. I saw him go in, heard him strokin' his dick. You're just in denial. But I'm gonna change all that for you. Where's your cell phone?"

"My purse, on the kitchen counter."

The Reverend leaned over, grabbed the purse, then dumped its contents on the counter. He picked up the phone, and forced Gabriela to give him the password. "Okie-dokie, here's how we're going to do this. Doc, you stay right where you are." He bent and held the phone in front of Gabriela. "Me and Gabriela are going to make a little video. Gabriela's gonna do the questioning."

"I have nothing to hide," David said, his fear and dread compounding. He had to find a way to save Gabriela from the bastard. His phone was in his bedroom, so was his gun.

Gabriela held David's gaze. "What do you want me to ask him?"

"If he fucked those corpses."

She closed her eyes. "Did you?"

The Reverend stroked her hair. "Uh-uh, honey. Open your eyes and wait until I start video taping. And when you ask him, ask him the way I told you." He looked at him. "And if you lie, I'm going to take this knife and slice off her toes." He nudged Gabriela. "Go ahead and ask."

Gabriela met his gaze again. "Did you fuck those corpses?"

He shifted his attention to the knife the Reverend held. "No."

The reverend dropped the phone in Gabriela's lap. "Wrong answer," he said, then moved next to the chair and crouched. He held the blade over her foot. "Which one should I take? This little piggy went to the market—"

"Stop," David shouted. "I gave you my answer."

"You lied to me, and you're lying to your girl. I want to know the truth, and I want her to hear it. I want her to know how sick you are." He pressed the tip of the knife between her toes. "Should we try again or should I start takin' off some of her little piggies."

David stared into Gabriela's eyes. Saw her fear, along with her faith and love for him. The tears he'd been holding back finally fell. In his heart, he knew this would be the last time she'd ever look at him with love.

"Don't," he said, with a catch to his breath. "Please don't hurt her."

"Confession is good for the soul, doc." The Reverend stood and picked up the phone from Gabriela's lap. "Let's try this again. Go ahead, Gabriela. Ask him."

Her chin trembled as she frowned. "Is it true? Did you fuck those corpses?"

He looked away and wiped his eyes. Oh, my God. How

could he say out loud what he'd done? How could he look at his beautiful fiancée and destroy all that was good between them?

"Answer me, damn it," she yelled.

He faced her. "Yes."

"*Dios mío. Oh, Dios mío,*" Gabriela shouted, her voice shaking. "*Hijo de puta asquerosa.* You sick fuck. *¿Cómo pudiste? ¿Cómo pudiste hacer algo tan asqueroso?*"

The Reverend turned off the video recording. He whistled, then chuckled. "Gotta love that fiery Latin temper. The only thing I got outta that was what a sick fuck you are. What else did you say, honey?"

David knew, and didn't want to answer.

"I told him he was a disgusting bastard," she said, her cheeks flushed, her eyes filled with hatred and anger. "And I want to know why. Why would you do something so foul?"

"Wait before you answer, I gotta get this on film," the Reverend said, and started the video again.

"Answer me, David. You owe me that much. Look at me. You got me in this situation, you better tell me why."

"I did it for you," he admitted, his stomach nauseous, his head pounding. "I wanted to keep you happy…physically."

"This was about *sex*?" she asked, disbelief in her tone.

"I tried everything. Viagra, sex therapy, watching porn. I could have an erection, but I couldn't maintain one. I was always so nervous about pleasing you and I needed to find a way to get over my performance anxiety issues."

The Reverend turned off the video recording, then set the phone on the counter. "That's one fucked up reason, doc. Why not buy a blow-up doll?"

"When?" Gabriela asked, as if the Reverend hadn't spoken or was in the room. "When did you have sex with the bodies? Was it the day we went to dinner and you bought me those shoes?" Her eyes widened. "The same day you gave me the expensive lingerie?"

He pictured his dead lover in the red bra and panties, then looked away and nodded. "I'm so sorry."

She laughed without humor. "I should have known something was wrong. I'm sorry for being so stupid. What's funny is that night, for a split second, I'd almost wondered if you were having an affair. That the expensive gifts were your way of dealing with the guilt. But then I thought, no, not David. He's a good man. He loves *me*. Only you *were* having an affair. With a dead fucking body," she said, hatred lacing her voice. "Because of you I'm tied to this damned chair." She turned her head and looked at the Reverend. "You killed those women and put the snakes in their stomachs, didn't you?"

"Don't talk to him," David said, worried what the Reverend might do next. "Be mad at me, hate me, but don't—"

"Don't kid yourself. I *do* hate you. I hate everything about you. You took something good and twisted it into something sickening and bizarre."

"I know it was wrong, but I wanted you happy. I wanted to be normal and to be able to pleasure you when we made love. I love you, Gabriela. Everything I did was for you."

"Doc, you should write greetin' cards for necrophiliacs, 'cause that sure was touching."

"You abused those corpses for me?" Gabriela shook her head. "Did you masturbate at the funeral home for me, too? Was I who you were thinking about, or were you fantasizing about the woman in the casket?"

God, he hated himself. He hadn't thought of Gabriela, he'd fantasized about the control he'd have over his dead lover, of being able to do anything he wanted to her body. "Gabriela, honey, please—"

"Oh, God." Her face crumpled, and fresh tears streaked down her cheeks. "Don't answer. I already know. The past few times we had sex, you wanted me to stay perfectly still and not move or make a sound. I thought you were trying something mildly kinky. Instead, you wanted me to play one of your corpses."

The sadness and revulsion in her eyes weakened his knees. "That's not true. I—"

"Liar," she sobbed. "You're such a liar. I loved you. I

wanted to marry you and have your children. I didn't care that you couldn't always get it up. All I cared about was being with *you*."

"Look, y'all," the Reverend began, "this is very touching and breakin' my heart, but this conversation is a little too disturbing. Even for me."

Gabriela glanced at the Reverend. "Did you kill those women and put snakes in their stomachs?" she asked again.

"Afraid so. In my defense, the doc forced me to. I can't have people thinking I like to diddle with dead bodies."

"Are you going to kill me?" she asked, her voice surprisingly strong. Although she hated him, and rightfully so, he still loved her and took pride in her strength.

"No. I ain't gonna kill you," the Reverend said, then looked at him and grinned. "Doc's gonna do that for me."

CHAPTER 18

SHOCK ROCKED DAVID to the core. He quickly look to Gabriela, the love of his life, the woman he wanted to marry, to have children and grow old with, and nearly fell to his knees. He gripped the stair rail. "I won't touch her. Kill me."

"That'd be too easy," the Reverend said, then moved his leg and pushed a plastic container toward him.

"Please," Gabriela begged. "Don't do this. You don't *have* to do this."

The Reverend used his leg to kick a small duffle bag forward. "But I do. I *really* need this." Never taking his eyes off him, the Reverend picked up the roll of duct tape sitting on top of the bag. "Doc, you asked for this."

David stared at the container, hoping to God it didn't hold what he thought it did. "I confessed. I told the truth. I'll tell the detective, reporters, anyone. Just let Gabriela go."

The Reverend cut a piece of tape with the knife. "Can't do that."

"Why?" he asked, and stepped forward. The Reverend quickly moved the knife and rested it along Gabriela's cheek. "Don't hurt her." David held up his hands and came to an abrupt halt. "Please listen to me. The detectives working the murder investigation do *not* believe the person who dumped the corpses—"

"Meaning you."

"Yes, me. They don't think I'm the one who killed the two women, or Katie. So if this is about taking credit for those murders, I'm not their number one suspect. You are. That's what you want, right? You want credit where credit is due."

The Reverend tilted his head. "Nope." He slapped the duct tape over Gabriela's gaping mouth. "This ain't about credit. At the beginning, it was. I can't tell you how much it pissed me off that you used Katie's killing to cover up your weirdo fetish." He smiled. "Then I smashed that little blonde's head into the wheel well of my car. Ever do anything like that, doc?"

"God, no."

"Well, lemme tell you, it's a rush. Hearing her thick skull smacking against metal." He shivered. "It's almost better than sex." He winced. "Maybe I shouldn't bring up sex, seein' as how your lady here just found out you've been cheatin' on her with dead chicks."

His face hot, his temper spiking, David held the man's gaze. "Go to hell."

The Reverend laughed. "Take a look around, doc, you're already here in the hell *I've* created especially for you." He reached behind and pulled out a gun. "I'm gonna give you the knife. The only person you're gonna use it on is your gal. If you try to use it on me, I'll shoot you in the dick."

He stared at the gun. "I don't care what you do to me."

The Reverend shrugged and, keeping the gun trained on Gabriela's head, he made his way around the kitchen island and opened a drawer. The knife drawer. "Then I guess I'll up the incentives." He set the steak knife on the counter, then held up the razor sharp seven-inch santoku knife. "I've got me one of these big-ass knives at home. It chops, slices and dices, and even cuts through a can." He chuckled. "I'm wonderin' if it'll cut through cartilage." He moved near Gabriela, and pressed the blade against her ear. "Should I find out?"

Gabriela grunted and drew in deep breaths through her

nose. David met her gaze and tried his damnedest to be strong for her. The fear in her eyes, the way they begged him to do something, made him want to risk it all and rush the bastard. But with the sharp blade against her ear, he didn't want to take the chance. Then again, a nick to the ear was nothing in comparison to what the Reverend wanted him to do to Gabriela's stomach.

Concentrating on the hatred, on the rage simmering beneath the surface, he sprang forward only to come to a sudden stop when Gabriela released a muffled scream and a stream of blood suddenly oozed down her cheek. She moaned and cried, as the Reverend pointed the gun at him and stilled the knife.

"I wouldn't do that again," he said. "Next time, it comes off, understand? Now, I want you to pick up the steak knife. It's time you learn exactly how the Ritual of the Serpents works."

When David didn't move, the Reverend pressed the blade into the cut he'd made along Gabriela's ear. As her muffled screams filled his head, he rushed to the counter and picked up the steak knife. Envisioned plunging it into the man's heart or slitting his throat. "I have the knife," he said, gripping the handle tight. "Take that one off Gabriela's ear."

"Can't do that. It's obvious to me that you need a little incentive."

He'd been raised by a family of doctors. He'd never met his great-grandparents, who had created DON, but knew of their legacy. A legacy his grandparents and parents had continued. While he'd gone a different route, choosing forensic pathology to help fellow doctors and law enforcement understand why a person died, he was still a doctor and it had been instilled in him to value human life. He wanted to take the Reverend's life. He wanted him dead, wanted to do to him everything and anything he'd witnessed over the years. For a brief moment, he envisioned the Reverend keeling back, a knife to his chest. Or blood spatter coating the walls as he took a chair and bludgeoned the man to death. He envisioned slicing his throat or, better yet, cutting into his stomach just as the Reverend had cut those women.

Just as the Reverend expected him to cut Gabriela.

"No," he finally said. "I don't need an incentive, but if I refuse, then what?"

"After I take off her ear, I'll do the ritual myself." The Reverend cocked his head. "I've never done one on a living person, but I've always wanted to." He nodded. "Forget it, I'll do it myself."

As the bastard moved the knife from Gabriela's ear to her stomach, David staggered forward. "Stop. I'll do it," he shouted, and not wanting to see the accusation in Gabriela's eyes, he kept his focus on the knife the Reverend held. He could give the Reverend what he wanted, and maybe still save Gabriela. He knew the human anatomy, knew where to cut, how to avoid internal organs and major arteries. He didn't want to hurt Gabriela—he'd hurt her enough—but better he make the incision than the Reverend.

"Smart choice," the Reverend said. "Now cut her."

With the tape covering her mouth, Gabriela inhaled and exhaled through her nose with quick short bursts. He looked to her tear-soaked face, then met her gaze. Humbled by the trust in her eyes, saddened by the fear that was there, too, he took a few steps, then knelt in front of her.

"It would be easier if Gabriela was on the table or floor," he said, hoping to buy time. He had no idea if or when Lola would send her men to his house. When she'd left, she had been angry that he'd threatened her and Ian. He hadn't wanted to, but he'd been desperate. Now he wished he'd placed more pressure on her, and had forced her to commit to helping him. He needed her men. He needed to find a way to save Gabriela.

"The chair is fine." The Reverend placed the knife against Gabriela's ear again. "You've got the count of three to start cutting. If you don't, I'm taking her ear as a souvenir. One."

He shifted his gaze to Gabriela's stomach, then glanced to the floor. He should ram the steak knife into the Reverend's foot. But what if he missed?

"Two."

If the blade connected with his foot, he might be able to overpower him. Or the Reverend could react by slicing Gabriela anyway or putting a bullet in her head. Oh, God. He didn't know what to do. He couldn't bear to hurt her. He couldn't—

"Three. Time's up."

"I'll do it," he shouted, Gabriela's scream forcing him to quickly raise her shirt and expose her stomach. Blood trickled from the fresh cut to her ear. "Please, I'll do it."

"Better hurry up. If you don't, after I take this ear, I'll lop off the other. After that, I'll take her nose. Understand?"

David nodded. He unbuttoned the front of Gabriela's shorts, then skimmed his fingers along her stomach. Based on the autopsies he'd performed, he knew the Reverend had zero surgical skills. His cuts had been crude and he'd gouged rather than sliced. He'd damaged his victims' intestines, uterus and ovaries. Considering David was forced to use a steak knife over a scalpel, his incision wouldn't be any better, but if he could make them shallow, he could avoid piercing major organs.

"Get movin', doc."

David looked up at Gabriela. This should be her choice. He could cut her, and she could still die. Slow and painful. Or the Reverend could prolong the torture by slicing off various body parts. "Do you want him to do this?" David asked.

Since the knife still rested against her ear, she gave her head a slight shake.

Tears filled his eyes. "I love you," he said, then punctured her skin.

Gabriela cried out and arched. Even with the tape covering her mouth, her scream echoed through the kitchen. The knife slipped, and cut deeper than he'd intended.

"Don't move," he ordered, and pressed her chest until her back was flush against the chair. "Please, you'll only make this worse."

"It's gonna get worse anyway. Just cut the bitch."

David wanted to cut him. Slice his throat, stab him in the chest, the stomach, the groin. Never in his life had he hated someone as much as he hated the Reverend. David had known impotency, but not like this. He'd never experienced such helplessness. Powerless against the man, weakened by his own fear he dug deep into the depths of his soul and prayed for strength. He prayed Gabriela would pass out from the pain so that he would no longer have to hear her cries or see her tears.

"Be strong," David said, told himself to do the same, and sliced into her abdomen. As Gabriela cried, and the Reverend chuckled, he made an approximately four-inch incision below her belly button at a depth of about two inches. Blood coated his hands and her stomach. He wiped his palms and the knife handle along his shirt, then rested his rear on his heels. "Done."

The Reverend peered over Gabriela's shoulder. "Spread the skin. I think you're gonna have to go deeper. Don't forget, about making room for the rattler."

David set the knife on the floor, looked up at Gabriela and gently spread open the wound. Gabriela's eyes rolled back, then her head slumped forward. With the knife still in his hand, and the gun trained on David, the Reverend grabbed Gabriela by the hair, and tugged. "Looks like we caught a break, doc. Now we don't have to listen to hear bellyachin' no more," he said with a grin. "Hurry on up and finish the job. I want to be back to my hotel before room service shuts down for the night."

Bastard. The sick fucking bastard. How could he think about room service? How could he have such utter disregard for Gabriela's life? But the Reverend was right. He'd rather finish what he'd been forced to start while Gabriela was out cold, than hear her painful, heart-wrenching cries. With his fingers coated in blood, he continued to move the skin, and he swore. Based on the autopsies of the Reverend's other victims, he knew there wasn't enough room to shove the snake inside the wound. He wrapped his bloodied hand around the knife handle and made the incision another inch deeper.

"Good job, doc." The Reverend stepped away from Gabriela and set the knife on the counter. Keeping the gun pointed on him, he bent and opened the plastic container. Four small snakes lay motionless along the bottom of the container. The Reverend picked one up and gave it a shake. When the snake didn't move, he did the same with the others. "Shoot. Looks like the little fuckers died on us." He sighed. "That's okay. It ain't like they're really gonna eat the evil from her soul."

Confused, David stared at him. "This is really a ritual?"

"Yep, that's what I said. Ritual of the Serpents. Which is why we'll need to pray." The Reverend tossed a snake at him. "Hold onto that rattler and bow your head. *Behold, I give unto you the power to tread*...the hell with it." The Reverend sighed. "It's gettin' late. Just shove it in her."

Anxious to close Gabriela's wound and hopefully stop the bleeding, he worked fast. Pressed the snake inside the incision until only its tail hung from the wound.

"That ain't right, but it'll do. Use the fishing line and needle to sew it inside. I got my mind set on a steak dinner."

Disgusting prick. David wiped his hand on his shirt again, then quickly used the threaded needle to seal the gash along Gabriela's stomach. If she survived this, she would carry the scars of their ordeal for the rest of her life, and they would serve as a horrifying reminder of all that he'd done to her. He hated himself almost as much as he hated the Reverend. He'd wronged Gabriela in so many ways. Because of him, she was a bloody mess and could die. Because of him, two other women were dead.

All because he couldn't have sex like a normal man.

He used the knife to cut the fishing line, then quickly knotted it near the snake's tail. "Can I wash her stomach?" he asked, needing to see the damage to reassure himself that Gabriela could walk away from this—if the Reverend let her.

"No time. Grab the knife, stand up and work on yourself."

David stood and tightened his grip on the knife. "You want me to cut open my stomach?"

"Did I stutter?" He picked up the knife from the counter and hovered it over Gabriela's ear. "Or do you need some incentive?"

He ran the back of his trembling hand along his forehead. Bile rose in his throat, then he saw the blood coating his knuckles and fingers.

Gabriela's blood.

He deserved to die for what he had done to her, and should have killed himself the moment he'd read the note from the Reverend. If he had, Gabriela wouldn't be bound to a chair, a snake sticking out of her abdomen. He looked to the knife, then to the Reverend. "Once I do it, will you leave?"

"I told you I wanted room service."

"Will you leave Gabriela alone?"

The Reverend smiled, then glanced at her. "Yep, I got what I came for."

He focused on the bloodstained knife again. He could slit his own throat, stab his heart, or severe a main artery and kill himself.

"Oh, by the by, doc. If you don't cut yourself properly, I'll finish off your girl. So don't get any ideas about takin' the easy way out, understand?"

If he killed himself, he wouldn't be able to free Gabriela and call for help. If he didn't kill himself, then what? Could he still follow through with his plans and leave for Africa once his wounds healed? Or would Gabriela use the video confession saved to her phone to tell the authorities what he'd done?

He had a gun in his room. He could cut himself— properly—and after the bastard left, call for 911. While he waited on paramedics, he could go to his room, find his gun and kill himself. His death would devastate his family. But what he'd done to his dead lover, and the murders that had followed because of his actions, would destroy them.

"I understand," he finally said.

"Then whatcha waitin' for?" The Reverend grazed the knife against Gabriela's ear lobe. "Do it."

David drew his bloodied shirt over his head, then tossed it

on the floor. Dragging in deep breaths, he pressed the tip of the blade in the same area along his abdomen where he'd cut Gabriela. He glared at the Reverend, who nodded and smiled, then, with hatred for himself and the man in front of him, he tensed his body, and imagined plunging the knife into the Reverend. Holding the man's amused gaze, he sucked in another breath, then thrust.

David grunted and gritted his teeth. He dropped to his knees and panted. The pain, so fucking excruciating, made him dizzy, made him want to scream. But he wouldn't give the Reverend the satisfaction.

"Holy shit," the Reverend half-laughed. "You did it. I can't believe you did it. Damn, Doc, you have a serious set of balls on you. I'll be honest. I couldn't do it. I would've let the bitch lose her ears before I gutted myself." He shook his head and moved the knife away from Gabriela's ear. "Now, c'mon, cut some more."

Pressing his lips together to keep from crying out, he quickly jerked the knife to the right, then dropped it and fell forward. Before he planted his head into the tiled floor, he slammed his hand down and used his arm to brace himself.

Oh, God. It hurt so badly.

He deserved this. He deserved the agony, the humiliation. By dishonoring his dead lover and mutilating the other women, he'd disgraced himself, Gabriela and his family.

"Almost there, doc." The Reverend bent and pulled a dead snake from his container. "Damn, you're one tough son of a bitch."

The Reverend tossed the snake at him. It skidded across the floor and stopped in front of his face. David stared at the small rattlesnake. Acid rose in his throat. He quickly turned his head and vomited on the tile.

"Well, that's just nasty. I suppose I'd puke, too, if I just stabbed the shit out of myself," the Reverend said. "Now, go on and put it in you. And be glad the little fuckers died. They might be young, but they do like to bite."

He inched his bloodied hand along the tile floor and

grabbed the snake. He needed this to be over and done. At this point, he'd take the humiliation of being sent to prison for his crimes and ruining his family's name, so long as the pain stopped.

But the pain would never stop. He knew it in his mutilated gut. If he survived this, nothing would matter. He'd lost everything.

He'd lost the woman he loved.

Determined to save Gabriela, and not caring what the bastard thought of him, David cried out as he rolled onto his back. "You want the fucking snake inside me?" He craned his neck forward, stared at the gash along his stomach, then spread the flesh. "You've got it," he said, then planted his heels against the floor and shoved the rattlesnake into his wound.

He arched his back. Saw stars as pain radiated throughout his body. Caught a brief glimpse of the Reverend, who moved away from Gabriela, his gaze locked on David's stomach and hands, before his vision blurred.

"That's it," the Reverend encouraged. "Hurry up and—" Pounding came at the front door. The Reverend pointed the gun at Gabriela's head. "Don't make a sound." He glanced at his watch. "A little late for company. Are you expecting someone?"

Hope revived David. His heart beat fast and hard, he fought the sluggishness, the disorientation. With his stomach burning, and his mind suddenly racing, he rested his head on the floor and dropped his hands to his sides. "No," he managed, his mouth dry.

More banging rattled the front door. "It's Harry from next door," a man shouted, his voice frantic. "Oh, God, David, I need a doctor. Please, it's my wife." The doorbell rang, followed by another round of persistent knocking.

David didn't know anyone named Harry, and prayed he was one of Lola's men.

The Reverend looked from Gabriela, to him, then down the hall toward the foyer and front door. David rolled his head to the side and followed the Reverend's gaze. While the leaded glass panels on either side of the solid wood door offered privacy, they revealed the silhouette of a man pacing beneath the porch light.

"Should I kill your neighbor?" the Reverend whispered.

David shook his head. "His wife has epilepsy. He'll go away once paramedics—"

"Please," the man shouted. "I need help."

The Reverend muttered under his breath, then turned away from the door. He set his gun on the counter in exchange for the knife. "Gotta go, doc," he said, and kicked the knife David had used on himself and Gabriela across the floor. He bent down next to David and placed the blade against his throat. "I was really lookin' forward to watching you sew that snake in your belly."

"Wait, please," David begged, and noticed a large shadow along the wall across from the laundry room off the garage. A heartbeat later, a huge blond man crept into the hallway. David immediately recognized the man as one of Lola's. He didn't know his name, but remembered seeing him the night he'd gone to Ian's Everglades City house to remove bullets from Ian and one of his agents.

"I won't tell anyone about you," he continued, hoping for more time. To die now, seconds from possible rescue, would be the ultimate punishment. He wasn't ready to die. Not yet. Not until he was certain Gabriela would survive. "Please, let us go." Tears streamed down the side of his face. "I'm sorry I used your ritual to cover my crimes. I'll confess to the police. I swear, I'll tell them everything I did."

"I don't need you to do that now, not when I've got your confession on your girl's phone." The Reverend quietly chuckled as he applied pressure to David's throat. His neck stung as the skin began to split. "What's funny is that me and my daddy made up that ritual."

"You said it was special to you," David said, keeping his focus on the Reverend and not on the large man sneaking up behind him.

"It is."

"Why?"

"Mama hated the rattlesnakes Daddy used during his sermons about as much as she hated me and Daddy. So tearing open her stomach after she was good and dead, and putting a rattlesnake in her belly, seemed like a fitting way to send her off to God."

"You killed your own mother?"

"Nope, rattlesnake bit her." He grinned. "With a little help from Daddy," he said, then sighed. "Time to go, doc. But I want you to know that if weren't for screwing dead chicks, you'd be an okay kinda guy. You definitely have a set of balls, and I respect that. So much so, I'm going to make this quick and—"

The Reverend took a booted foot to the head, knocking him to the floor, and nicking David's throat with the knife. His eyes wide with shock, the bastard quickly scrambled to his feet and reached for the gun on the counter. The blond man kicked the Reverend again, hitting him in the stomach. The bastard grunted, clutched his waist and raised the knife. He glanced at the gun the blond pointed at him, then to Gabriela and lunged.

The blond man sprang forward, then swept his foot under the Reverend's legs. The bastard cracked his head against the chair Gabriela was bound to, then he slammed against the floor, the knife slipping from his grip and sliding across the tile. The Reverend used his hands and knees to push himself up, but the blond man grabbed him by the shirt and tossed him back.

"Don't move," the man said in a heavy Russian accent, raised his gun and aimed it at the Reverend's head.

"Holy…"

David turned his head just as another man walked into the kitchen, and pulled a cell phone from his pocket.

"Don't move is right," the man said. "Vlad, careful you don't step in any blood. We can't leave footprints behind. Understand?"

"да," the Russian grunted.

"Shoot him," David demanded, and tried to pull himself to

his feet. Pain shot from his abdomen and kept him on the floor.

The man with the cell phone looked at David's stomach and flinched. "Holy shit, man, is that thing alive?" His eyes wide and filled with alarm, he took a step forward, then stopped and shifted his focus to the blood on the tiles. "I can't get to you without screwing with the crime scene. Just hang tight."

David moved his hands to his stomach. "Can't. Got to help Gabriela."

"We'll help her," he said, then placed the phone to his ear. "Lola, we're at Dr. Adams'. No, nothing is okay. Bad guy is here, Vlad has a gun on him. Got a female tied to a chair. Her stomach's been sewed up like the other vics."

When the man paused, David ripped the snake from his stomach. He yelled out, and watched in horror as blood poured from the wound. Panting, struggling against the pain, he grabbed his soiled shirt and applied pressure to the crude incision.

"That was Dr. Adams," the man said. "Uh, he just pulled a snake out of the cut on his stomach. Yes, that's what I said. A snake. He and the woman need an ambulance. What do you want us to do?"

Breathing hard, and using one arm, and his knees, David crawled toward Gabriela. "Reverend needs to be dead." When he reached Gabriela, he leaned against the chair and fought a wave of dizziness. "Shoot him," he repeated.

"Got it," the man said, then slid the phone back in his pocket. "Lola's on her way. She wants us to tie up the bad guy and wait for her."

"Good luck," the Reverend said, his tone low, menacing.

"Please just kill him." David coughed, and gave Gabriela's leg a shake. "He's a monster. Look what he made me do. He's—"

"We wait. Vlad, need help?"

"He's gonna," the Reverend taunted.

The Russian sighed, and set the gun on the counter, then

slid it backward. "Harry, take Vlad gun."

Harry grabbed the gun before it slid off the smooth quartz. "Lola said not to mess up his face."

The hint of a smile curved the corner of the Russian's mouth. "Can Vlad break bone?"

"All she said was not the face. Interpret that the way you want," Harry said, and aimed the gun at the Reverend.

"For God's sake, just kill him," David shouted. "Who cares about his face or bones?"

Harry looked at him, sympathy in his eyes. "You should if you want to stay out of prison."

"You can all fuck yourselves," the Reverend said, with a snarl and quickly stood. "This ain't none of your business. It's between me and the doc. Y'all know he likes screwin' dead women, right?"

Vlad rushed the bastard. He released a double jab to the Reverend's torso before the man could react, then the Russian swept his legs again. The Reverend fell to the floor. Vlad pounced onto his back, grabbed both of the bastard's arms and pulled until the Reverend let out a guttural scream.

"Harry, hurry."

Harry pulled handcuffs from his back pocket, then, after tucking the gun in the waistband of his jeans, cuffed the Reverend's wrists. "Stay on him," Harry said, and gingerly stepped over the blood on the tile. He picked up the duct tape the Reverend had left on the table, then went to work. Once he had the Reverend's ankles bound, he took a step back. "We're good."

Vlad grabbed the Reverend's hair, and tugged, forcing the man's neck to arch. "Snake man dead as doorknob."

Harry grinned. "I don't care if you got that one wrong. It was totally badass." He glanced to Gabriela. His smile fell as he met David's gaze. "Sorry, man. I have to wait on Lola before we can call the police."

David sucked in a deep breath as he reached up and touched Gabriela's chest. Her heart beat slowly beneath his palm.

"Where's your gun?" Harry asked. "You used a gun on Dustin Williams, right?"

Memories of the night he'd stolen the bodies flashed through his mind, while regret pierced him harder than the knife he'd impaled into his stomach. "Yes."

"Do you still have it?"

"Yes."

"Do you want this man dead, along with your secrets?"

He closed his eyes and pictured the future that should have been. Gabriela in a wedding dress, hugging and kissing him, making love, her belly swollen with his child. He shifted his gaze to where he'd sewn Gabriela's stomach shut, and imagined life in prison. How his actions would destroy his family, along with what he'd accomplished as chief medical examiner. Too many people had been affected by his selfishness and perverted needs. If he went to prison, that number would rise. Past cases he'd worked on could be reopened. Murderers could walk away. He didn't care if he died. He was already dead inside. There was no future for him. He'd never be free. No matter where he lived or what he did with his life, he'd be imprisoned in his own hell. Alone. The woman he loved would be gone, along with his career, and everything he'd worked so damned hard for—the house, the car, the country club membership, the status, the prestige.

Whether the Reverend survived or not, he was screwed. But this wasn't about him, it was about Gabriela, Katie, Elizabeth and Holly, along with however many others the Reverend—and maybe his *daddy*—had hurt.

He looked to the Reverend, whose mouth was now duct-taped like Gabriela's, then stared into his hateful eyes. "I want him dead."

****

Marco Island, Florida
Thursday, 10:38 p.m., Eastern Standard Time

Shane dropped his cell phone on his lap, then veered off the exit toward Beth's house.

"Son of a bitch," he muttered, and gripped the steering wheel tight. This was such a screwed-up mess. As he turned into Beth's development, he pictured David and his woman, their stomachs cut. Imagined Vlad and Harrison there, holding a murderer prisoner while they waited for help. The situation mirrored what Lola and Ryan, along with the rest of ATL and even the CORE team, had gone through months ago. Only this was different. They *would* call the police. They would do this in a legit way without staining their hands with blood.

He just hoped to God Beth would help them. He hoped to God the man who'd murdered those women and tortured David and his fiancée received the death penalty.

As for David, he deserved to be punished for his crimes. Not by a killer, but by the legal system. He'd brought them into his autopsy suite, had given them information on the necrophilia case, then had stood there acting professional and concerned, when *he* had been the one who'd abused the corpses. If David had come clean after Elizabeth Neal had been found, Holly would still be alive, and the ME would be in jail where he belonged.

He pulled into Beth's driveway. As he climbed out of the truck, then hurried to Beth's front door, he ignored the anxiety bouncing through his stomach and seeping into his chest. What he was about to tell Beth could affect their relationship. He didn't want to lose her or her trust, but he'd rather she hate him, than allow his brother and Lola to go to prison.

Beth opened the door and greeted him with a smile. "Hi," she said, and gave him a kiss. "Perfect timing. I just got home." Her smile fell, and she touched his face. "What's wrong?"

He took her hand and led her to the kitchen table.

"Shane, you're scaring me. What happened?"

Once she was seated, he pulled a chair next to her, and took both of her hands in his. "David Adams is the necrophiliac."

She let out a nervous half-laugh. "Come on. That's—" She stared at him, searched his eyes, then shook her head. "You're serious."

"It gets worse," he said, then quickly explained how Lola had met with him, how the killer had targeted his last victim, and that David had kept the note he'd found in Holly's stomach out of his report.

"When did you find this out?"

"A few hours ago, while you were in class."

"And you didn't think to call me? Never mind. Let me guess, Lola told you to keep me out of this, right?" she asked, disappointment clear in her eyes.

"I'm telling you now. I didn't want to disturb you while you were in class," he said, trying to save his ass. He should have called Beth the moment he'd left the rental house and told her what ATL had discovered. He should have trusted his instincts, because his actions would now have Beth questioning the trust between them.

"How considerate and convenient," she said with heavy sarcasm and started to rise. "I have to call Nick."

Tightening his hold on her hands, he kept her seated. "There's more, and I have to make this quick," he said, and told her what Harrison and Vlad had found when they'd arrived at David's. "Lola and Ryan are on their way to David's right now."

"To do what?" She pulled her hands free from his. "Execute a killer."

"God, no. They're not vigilantes."

"Then what am I supposed to think?" she shouted, and stood. "If Lola had called the police from the start—or me—none of this would have happened. Now there are two severely injured people and a killer sitting in Dr. Adams' house. How does Lola plan to explain that?" She rubbed her temple. "This is *wrong*."

"I know. Look, we need your help. Vlad and Harrison can't get caught up in this, not with their pasts. Lola's sending them home, and she and Ryan are going to take their place. I need to know how much you trust Nick."

"Right now, more than I trust you. At least I know where his loyalties lie."

He leaned back in the chair, her words stinging like a slap to the face. But he deserved her anger. He hadn't necessarily lied, but he'd held back important information from her, information that had led to David and his woman's dire situation. Had he told Beth the moment he'd learned the truth about the ME, David's fiancée would be at home, maybe sleeping, while he was in custody. Then again, they also wouldn't have caught a killer.

"Leave us out of this and hear me out."

Tears filled her eyes. "Talk."

"We have to make it look like David called for help. He's in bad shape, so the evidence will prove there was no way he could have detained the snake guy on his own. Nick could make the arrest and make it look like we were never there. He could make sure my brother and Lola don't go down for this."

"So now you want me to ask a detective and his partner to lie to help save your butts." She shook her head. "In the process, Nick and Jerry will find out that I know about you guys."

"What you know is minor in comparison to what's happening at David's, and ATL didn't do anything illegal. So I can't see you losing your job over this."

"Are you delusional? I know you guys kidnapped a man and I did nothing about it. And in case you weren't aware, kidnapping *is* illegal." She pushed a hand through her long hair. "Why did Lola protect Dr. Adams?"

"Because he threatened to expose us, and if he went to prison all of the cases he'd worked as an ME could be questioned. But the main reason is because Lola wanted to use him to draw out the killer." He stood, and approached her. When she stepped back and shook her head, he halted. "We have to act fast. David and his fiancée need medical treatment before they become the latest victims."

She swiped the tears from her face, then left the kitchen. He followed her into the living room, where she picked up her cell phone and placed a call. She held the phone to her ear and met his gaze. "After tonight, I want nothing to do with ATL." She turned her back. "Nick, it's Beth. I need your help."

As Beth told Nick what had happened, he wondered if her words held a double meaning. She wanted nothing to do with ATL. He was part of ATL. Would what was happening tonight ruin what they had together? When she faced him again, the answer was in her eyes. She glared at him with anger and resentment. As she should. He had placed her in a precarious position, one that could jeopardize everything she'd worked so damned hard for.

"I'll meet you there," Beth said, and ended the call. She looked to him and held out her hand. "I need to call Lola." After he clicked on Lola's number, he gave Beth the phone. "Lola, it's Beth. Get your people out of David's house. I'm meeting two detectives there." Beth's face reddened as she listened to Lola. "Don't screw with me on this." She handed him the phone.

Shane checked the screen, saw that Lola had hung up and looked to Beth, who was sliding her foot into a running shoe. "Is she going to leave?" he asked.

"I hope so. Nick isn't happy. At all." She put on the other shoe, then began tying it. "Neither am I. Thanks to Lola, not only am I risking my career, but I've just dragged two seasoned detectives into this mess." She moved into the kitchen and grabbed her car keys off the counter, along with her purse. "If I were you, I'd bail on ATL. Lola is reckless and has no clue what she's doing. She's going to get you arrested or killed."

While he disagreed, he wouldn't argue with Beth. Later, if she was still speaking to him, he'd plead his case.

He followed Beth into her garage. After she opened the garage door, she made her way to the driver's side of her Toyota. "I'll let you know how it goes," she said, opening the car door.

"I'm going with you."

"No way. You're a felon. I don't want Nick and Jerry to know about you." The overhead light caused the tears in her eyes to shimmer. "I should have gone with my first instinct and walked away the moment I found out who you really are. Instead I let sex warp my judgment. I wanted to be fucked, and thanks to you and Lola, it looks like I'm good and fucked now."

Hurt, angry, he gripped her arm before she slid into the driver's seat. "You don't mean that."

"I saw my parents before class and mentioned you. When they asked to meet you, I panicked, and realized there's no way I can tell them about your record." She looked away. "I don't want to disappoint them or myself."

"You're embarrassed by me," he said, letting her go. Everything they'd said to each other, the emotional, intimate moments, had been real for him. He'd fallen for Beth. He wanted her in his life, and she'd acted as if she had wanted the same thing. His own resentment surfaced. "I told you I wasn't good enough for you, now I'm starting to think it's the other way around. You could have walked away, but you chose to stay, then made promises you had no intention of keeping. I should have called you as soon as I found out about David. I can't take back that choice, but I can tell you this—I've been honest with you about everything else. It's pretty clear you can't say the same."

She pulled on the door handle. "Go home. I'm not doing this now."

He let go of the car door. As she slammed it shut, he hurried to his truck. After he backed out of the driveway, and Beth had done the same, he followed her out of the development.

When they reached the highway, he watched as she turned left, heading north for Naples. Beth was wrong about him and about Lola. He didn't disagree that Lola needed more experience, and that she could have handled this case differently, but he also couldn't deny that she had leadership skills. She looked out for her crew, and had their best interests in mind.

He pulled his cell phone from his pocket, and let the truck idle at the intersection. When Lola answered, he said, "Beth's on the way."

"You're not with her?"

"No. She told me to go home, but I'll head to David's. Are you there yet?"

She let out a shaky breath. "Yeah, it's bad. I think you should do what Beth said and go home."

"What are you going to do?"

"Send Ryan home with Vlad and Harrison. I'm going to wait for the detectives and Beth. I need to fix this," she said, then ended the call.

He made a left turn and drove north. He'd go to David's, not with the hope of mending his relationship with Beth, but to make sure Lola and his brother didn't do anything foolish. Knowing Ryan, there was no way in hell he'd leave Lola to deal with the detectives by herself. He wasn't cool with that idea, either. They all agreed to help David. They should all stand behind Lola.

As for Beth, he didn't believe sex was the reason she'd been with him, not after seeing the hope and love in her eyes, or after the way she'd committed to them. He did believe she was embarrassed by him and his past. He might love her, and he could fight to try to make things right between them, but he wouldn't.

He gripped the steering wheel tight, as anger replaced some of the hurt. He'd spent seven years in prison and had paid for his crime. He was a free man and refused to allow Beth to extend his punishment by locking him away and keeping him hidden from her family and friends. He refused to be with a woman who couldn't love him enough to look past his mistakes. He refused to be with a woman who was ashamed of him.

CHAPTER 19

Naples, Florida
Thursday, 11:06 p.m., Eastern Standard Time

BETH WIPED THE tears from her face. She'd spent the past fifteen minutes chastising herself for being a total bitch, and glancing in the rearview mirror for any sign of Shane. Telling him she wanted him to go home had been the only honest thing she'd said to him tonight. Shane didn't embarrass her, with the way she'd treated him, she had embarrassed herself.

She was in love with him, and she hated herself for the hurtful things she'd said. But he'd taken her by surprise, and had disappointed and angered her. She'd wanted to lash out at him for choosing ATL and Lola over her. If things hadn't gone down the way they had at Dr. Adams' house tonight, would he have told her that the ME was the necrophiliac, or that the killer had contacted him? Would Shane have made love to her, slept next to her, had a morning cup of coffee with her and kept his mouth shut about what he knew? *That* bothered her, because now she would always wonder if he was keeping secrets. She would always wonder how much he trusted her.

She'd wanted to lash out at him, and she definitely had, in a mean and immature way. God, to tell him she'd let sex warp her judgment? That was so far from the truth. She'd taken all of her worries about their relationship and had purposefully tried to hurt him. Earlier, while she'd sat in her contracts class, her mind hadn't been on the subject matter her professor had taught, or even the case, but on Shane. She wanted her parents to meet him. She wanted them to look past the label he carried and see him for what he was—a good, solid, strong man. But as she'd sat there, thinking, contemplating how she'd even tell her parents that Shane had been in prison for murder, she'd also imagined their reaction. It would probably be the same as Erin's had been.

During her drive home from class, curious to hear her best friend's thoughts about Shane, she'd called Erin. When she'd told her friend about Shane's past, Erin had said, "Out of all the men in the world and you've decided you're in love with an ex-con?" She'd then gone on to say that Shane was nothing but a well-needed distraction, that it was the hot sex that had her thinking she was in love with him. Then Erin had reminded her of the same important realities Shane had. Dating an ex-con could result in losing her job as a deputy. Being with him could affect her future career as an attorney, how her clients and coworkers could question her judgment. Even if her family ended up accepting Shane and her decision to be with him, if she and Shane had decided to have children, the stigma of their father's incarceration would follow them.

But did anyone need to know the truth? They didn't. But did she want to treat him like her dirty little secret? Never. Shane had done more to better himself in a week, then most men would do in months or years. He'd set goals for himself, followed through with them, and was a hard worker who expected no handouts. He was her ideal man. He'd been successful once, and she had no doubt—based on his determination—that he'd be successful again. He was loyal, fun, sexy and had an adventurous streak she loved and envied. He wasn't a big talker, but his body language spoke volumes. When he did have something to say, despite his hard, rugged exterior, he said it with his heart. And he cared about her.

She'd seen it in his eyes, felt it in his touch.

She ran a hand along her forehead, then made another turn, taking her closer to Dr. Adams' house. She'd thrown Shane's felony in his face. In her defense, she'd done it because she had worried his record and affiliation to ATL could possibly make a bad situation even worse. Bottom line, she'd needed him to stay away from Nick and Jerry. Once this case was closed, if Nick and Jerry decided to look into ATL, she didn't want them to find out about Shane's involvement. She didn't want him to go back to prison.

Nick. She'd also lied to Shane about his reaction. Instead of being angered that he and Jerry would have to fabricate a story that would fit the crime scene and how the killer had been caught, Nick had been curious, his tone excited. Their investigation would be closed. The victims and their families would receive justice, and a murderer would hopefully be sent to Death Row. Regardless of Nick's positive response, she still hadn't wanted Shane, or any member of ATL at Dr. Adams' house. Their exposure meant hers, as well, and she wasn't sure how Nick or Jerry would react.

Nervous anticipation rushed through her when she reached the gate to the country club community. She rolled down the window, then punched in the code Lola had given her into the keypad. She'd called Nick and had given him the same code during her drive here and hoped she'd beat him to Dr. Adams' house. She needed to make sure Lola and her crew had left. When she drove down the ME's street, she tensed when she saw both Nick and Lola's vehicles. If she'd arrived earlier, even if she couldn't talk Lola into leaving, she could have at least made it clear that ATL was on their side.

She parked, then rushed to the front door. Without knocking, she entered.

Nick stood at the end of the hallway, near the kitchen. He turned, then shook his head. "Finally. Maybe you could tell us what the hell is going on here."

Beth hurried down the hall, then froze when she reached the kitchen. A woman lay on the floor, her bloodied stomach cut and stitched like Katie, Elizabeth and Holly's had been. More blood coated the floor. She shifted her gaze. Dr. Adams sat on the floor next to the woman, a bloodstained shirt covering his stomach. A chill ran through her as she took in the rest of the scene. The small snakes on the floor. The bloody knives. The gun on the counter. The man cuffed and bound against the far kitchen wall.

Ryan and Lola stood near the kitchen island, but there was no sign of Vlad and Harrison. She met Lola's gaze, gave her a slight nod then turned her attention to Nick and Jerry. "How are you going to handle this?" she asked.

"We just got here," Jerry said. "How do you know these people?"

"Does it matter?" Dr. Adams asked, he speech slurred. "We need to get Gabriela to the hospital."

"Hell, yeah, it matters," Jerry said, and pointed to the bound man. "Nothing about this is legit. If we're going to make sure that asshole gets the death penalty, this has to be done right."

Beth relaxed. Barely. Jerry was ready to move around the law, but was Nick? "I know them through an acquaintance. They run a private investigation agency and have been following this case. Lola runs the agency. Dr. Adams had confessed to her that he was the one responsible for the three corpses."

Nick and Jerry both looked at the ME. "David, is this true?" Jerry asked.

The doctor hung his head. "Yes."

"The killer left David a note in Holly Samuels' stomach," Lola began, "stating that if David didn't confess, he'd keep killing. David asked us for help. He didn't want to turn to you, because he worried his work as a medical examiner would be questioned." Lola then quickly explained what Harrison and Vlad had discovered when they'd arrived, and how they'd detained the killer.

Jerry puffed his cheeks and blew out a breath. "Where are your men now?"

"I sent them home. There was no need for them to be here."

The front door opened. Beth turned just as Shane stepped into the foyer.

"Who are you?" Nick asked, reaching for his weapon and stepping out of the kitchen.

Beth touched Nick's arm, stopping him from pulling his gun free of its holster. "He's with Lola," she said.

Without looking at her, Shane walked down the hall. When he entered the kitchen, he glanced around the room, then closed his eyes and turned away.

"I take it you aren't one of the two men that cuffed the suspect," Nick said.

Shane shook his head. "They need to get to a hospital."

"Why is he here?" Nick asked Lola.

"It doesn't matter," Lola said. "He's right, David and Gabriela need medical treatment, so let's not waste any more time." She stepped away from the island and looked over the crime scene. "When we arrived, David told us he'd been up in his room, while Gabriela was in the kitchen. He came downstairs, found Gabriela bound to the chair, the Reverend behind her."

"Reverend?" Jerry asked.

"That's what he's calling himself," Lola said, and nodded toward the man on the floor, who lay there humming, a smug grin on his face.

"What's your name?" Nick asked the Reverend.

"Go fuck yourself."

"He's charming," Lola said. "He also forced David to cut Gabriela, then himself after he confessed to being responsible for abusing the three corpses. When my men arrived, the Reverend was about to slit David's throat."

Nick folded his arms across his chest. "Your men should have called this in immediately."

"I told them to wait. Personally, I think what David did to those dead women is disgusting and perverse. But my opinion doesn't matter. Our objective was to keep David's crimes from being exposed. I'd think you might want to do the same and pin everything on the Reverend."

"Go fuck yourself," the Reverend shouted.

"We got your name the first time," Nick said. "No need to repeat it."

"Kiss my ass." The Reverend spat on the floor. "You ain't got nothing on me. The doc is the one you should be cuffing. He killed those women, *and* done those dead bodies. He lured me here for some sex games with his gal, then threatened me with a gun and forced me to watch him cut the woman."

"Shut up," Jerry said. "The only way I might buy that story is if David hadn't cut himself."

"Well, I don't know how anyone is gonna buy the story you dumbasses are gonna tell. Look at the doc. Ain't no way in hell he could overpower me in his condition. Which means you all gotta produce those two assholes who cuffed me as witnesses. Then you gotta explain why it took hours before y'all called an ambulance."

"Unfortunately, he's right," Lola said, and looked to Jerry and Nick. "But I won't allow my men to come forward as witnesses. So here's how we'll handle this."

Jerry held up a hand. "No, here's how *we're* going to handle this."

"Stop," Dr. Adams yelled, his face frighteningly pale, his eyes glassy and droopy. "Let Lola talk. Please. Gabriela needs help."

When Lola arched a brow, Jerry nodded. "Go ahead."

"Let's keep it simple. After David is forced to cut himself, the Reverend is confident he has time to clean up his evidence. He leaves his gun on the counter. David manages to crawl across the floor. He gets the gun and knocks the Reverend unconscious."

"If he has a gun, why not shoot him?" Shane asked.

"He's right," Beth said. "I wouldn't take that risk. I'd want to make sure he couldn't do any more damage to me or my lover."

"This is a frickin' mess," Nick said, then pointed at Lola.

"You and your people are to blame." He turned to Jerry. "Let's call this in and deal with it as it goes."

Lola took a step forward. "If my people hadn't been here, David and Gabriela would be dead and the Reverend would be free to kill again."

"You aided and abetted a criminal. If you'd come to us the moment David confessed, none of this would've happened."

"I didn't know until this evening. Trust me, if I could do it all over again, I would have gone with my first instinct and turned him over to you. Since the damage is already done, let's clean it up and get them to a hospital."

"Listen to Lola," Dr. Adams said. "My prints need to be on the gun. Let me hit the bastard and knock him out." He winced and pressed the bloody clothing against his stomach. "Everyone will need to leave, I'll call 911 and act like it was just the three of us in the room."

"Fuck you people." The Reverend used his forearms and knees to push himself upright. Ryan pressed his booted foot against the man's back and forced him to remain on the floor. "I'll lawyer up," the Reverend continued. "I'll tell everyone about what y'all did here."

"Who's going to believe you?" Jerry asked. "Elizabeth Neal's family? Or how about the Samuels and Oakley's?" He looked to Nick. "What do you think?"

"What about David's crime?"

Jerry glanced to Dr. Adams. "We'll need to destroy Gabriela's phone. There are several homicide cases David worked that I don't want to see re-opened. If his credibility is questioned, you know damned well it's a strong possibility."

"Jesus, Jerry," Nick said. "We're tampering with evidence and a crime scene."

"From where I'm standing the only innocent person in this room is Gabriela." Jerry sighed. "I think we can all agree that other than David, Gabriela and the Reverend, none of us were here tonight."

"I'll take care of the phone," Lola said. "I don't want you caught with that evidence and having to explain it." She held up another phone. "This one is the Reverend's. We'll need to keep this, too."

"How can we trust this woman?" Nick asked.

"Beth," Jerry said. "Have you been working with Lola?"

"Just on the necrophilia case, and I trust that she and her people will not leak what's happened here," she said, choosing her words carefully. Did she honestly trust Lola? To a degree. The woman had her own agenda, and Beth believed Lola would do whatever it took to achieve it.

"Since I trust Beth," Nick began, looking to Gabriela, "I say we get this done and get them medical assistance."

Jerry nodded, then pulled a pair of latex gloves from his pocket. After he snapped on one, he had Ryan and Shane haul the Reverend near Dr. Adams, while he retrieved the Reverend's gun off the counter.

"This is against the law," the Reverend shouted, and fought against Ryan and Shane's hold.

"Call the cops on us," Jerry said, and careful of the blood on the tile, crouched next to Dr. Adams. "I considered you a friend. What you did was despicable, especially when we depended on you for answers. If it wasn't for your position as ME, I'd ruin you." He handed Dr. Adams the gun. "Make it quick."

As Dr. Adams turned the weapon in his hand so the barrel faced him, not the Reverend, the Reverend swore and tried to roll. Ryan placed his foot on the Reverend's back again to keep him still, but Dr. Adams shook his head. "In case there's cast off from the blow to the head, you're going to need to step far away."

"Do it," Jerry ordered, and they all moved behind the kitchen island.

"This ain't right," the Reverend shouted, and scooted away from Dr. Adams. "He done those dead women wrong."

"You should have killed me instead of those women," Dr. Adams said, quickly swiveled the gun in his hand and aimed it at the Reverend.

"David, don't," Jerry yelled.

Beth flinched as the gunshot echoed through the kitchen. Her skin crawled with dread and her heart raced as the acrid smell of gunpowder filled the room.

Nick rushed around the island and stared at the Reverend. "He's dead."

Beth glanced to Shane, but his focus was on the ME. Lola, tapped Shane's shoulder, drawing his attention. "Get out of here," she said, and, pulling a key from her pocket, moved toward Nick.

Shane nodded, then, without looking at Beth or saying anything, he walked down the hall and out of the house. Shoving aside the hurt and how easily he could dismiss her, Beth followed behind Lola, then stopped and stared at the gunshot wound to the Reverend's temple.

"What are you doing?" Nick asked, as Lola bent next to the Reverend.

"Taking my handcuffs with me," she said. Then, after removing them from the Reverend's lifeless body, she pulled a knife from her boot and cut the duct tape from the man's ankles. "David, where's your cell phone?"

"My bedroom, on the nightstand."

"I'll get it," Ryan said, and stepped through the obstacle course of blood, then rushed up the steps.

"Now we don't have to worry about the Reverend disputing our story," Dr. Adams said, and still holding the gun, rested his hand in his lap.

"You didn't have to murder him," Jerry said.

His chin trembled and his eyes filled with tears. "Actually, I did," he said, and looked at Gabriela. "Look what he made me do."

Ryan returned, and used the front of his shirt to hold the phone. Jerry, who still wore one glove, took it, then handed it to the ME. "Do you think Gabriela will make it?" Jerry asked.

Dr. Adams let go of the bloody cloth he'd been pressing against his stomach, and took the cell phone from Jerry. "I hope so."

"Will she tell anyone what you've done?"

Tears slid down the ME's face as he shook his head. "If you were engaged to a necrophiliac, would you tell anyone?" He tapped at the phone screen. "Better go."

"Everyone out," Jerry said, and they quickly rushed from the house.

Once outside, Jerry stopped Lola. "We need to talk. Follow us out of here." He turned to Beth. "Plan on meeting with us in the morning."

She glanced to Nick, who looked as if he wanted to say something else, then she opened her car door, and climbed inside. As she drove off, the other two cars trailing behind her, she heard sirens in the distance. Gabriela had to have sustained her injuries more than ninety minutes ago, and she prayed the woman survived. Even if she did, she would have to recover from more than her physical injuries.

Gabriela had discovered that the man she loved not only had a disgusting fetish, but had been the catalyst that had caused the Reverend to resurface and kill again. Beth couldn't begin to imagine what must have gone through the woman's mind when Dr. Adams had been forced to cut her, or how she would cope with all that had happened tonight. Like Dr. Adams had said, Beth doubted Gabriela would tell anyone that he'd been the necrophiliac they'd been looking for. Talk about a dirty secret.

Suddenly chilled, she put on the heater and tried to ignore the nausea weaving through her stomach. She knew the signs of an adrenaline crash, and was glad she was halfway home. The hour had grown late and exhaustion had started to make her lethargic. Considering she'd worked today, then had sat through a four-hour class, she should sleep well tonight. Since she'd possibly ruined her relationship with Shane, and had witnessed, then covered up a man's murder, she knew she'd do nothing but toss and turn. While she was worried about what Jerry and Nick might say to her tomorrow, she was more worried about how Shane would react when she went to see him. And she would go to him tomorrow. She owed him an apology. Whether he'd accept it or not was the question that would likely make sleep elusive tonight.

Or, she could take advantage of their argument and walk away permanently. Cutting ties with Shane meant she'd cut ties with Lola and ATL, which, for her current and future careers, would be in her best interest. Severing their relationship also meant she would no longer have to worry about how to deal with Shane's past.

The nausea increased, and an ache developed in her chest. Breaking up with Shane would mean she'd never see him again. She would miss their late night talks. Holding him, loving him, listening to his dreams, while she shared her own. There wouldn't be a future filled with hope and love. Instead, she'd have to deal with the heartache of knowing that she was too much of a coward to accept the man she loved for who he was, too afraid to tell anyone who thought she was insane to risk her career for him to kiss her butt.

As she pulled into her development, tears blurred her vision. She blinked them away, but as she pulled into her driveway they came faster and harder. A small part of her had hoped Shane might have decided to come back to her house to talk, but the sensible side of her had known he wouldn't. She'd acted as if sex had been her sole reason for being with him, then had given him the impression that he embarrassed her. Never in her life had she treated someone—especially a man she loved—so cold and callously.

After she walked into her empty house, she went straight to the fridge and pulled out a bottle of wine. If the Reverend hadn't tortured Dr. Adams and his fiancée tonight, Shane would be here now. Probably in her bed, or snuggling on the couch as they finished a movie. She pulled a glass from the cupboard and filled it. Instead, her only company was the wine and self-loathing.

She'd only known Shane for two weeks, but she wasn't ready to let him go.

He might not give you the choice.

She took a long drink from her glass, then set it on the counter. Staring at her couch picturing him there, determination swelled in her belly, knocking aside the queasiness. All of her life she'd set goals for herself, then had worked and fought damned hard to achieve them. She'd fight for Shane, not out of guilt for what she'd said, but out of love. If he still wanted nothing to do with her, the one thing she'd take away from knowing him was that there were no rules when it came to loving and caring for someone. No timeline or schedule that needed to be followed.

Shane had also taught her that life was too short, and she didn't want to spend the rest of hers wondering what could have happened if she hadn't risked her heart and told him the truth.

She wanted him. She needed him. She loved him.

Lola's Rental House, Everglades City, Florida
Friday, 8:22 a.m., Eastern Standard Time

Lola tightened her grip on Ryan's hand as they walked up the steps to the porch of the rental house. She hadn't slept well last night, the bags under her eyes the proof. After she and Ryan had met with the detectives, she'd gone home, poured herself a shot, chased it down with a beer, then had sat on the couch and cried. Ryan had held her, had told her none of what had happened at David's had been her fault, but his reassurance hadn't helped. She'd made several rookie mistakes during this case. While a killer was now dead and no longer a threat, so many lives had been ruined. And she had to live with that.

When they reached the door, Ryan placed his hands on her shoulders and forced her to face him. "Remember, no self-doubt, only confidence."

Last night, as she and Ryan had discussed what had happened, he'd reminded her that she needed to be confident in herself in order for the rest of ATL to be confident in what they were doing. Although she agreed with Ryan, she knew in her heart she had to admit her mistakes to her crew. These people weren't just employees, they were family. She cared for each one of them, even Mel. Every family needed that one crazy relative to spice up Thanksgiving.

Since Lola had grown up with only her mom and dad, and had lost her dad at a young age, being with Ryan, Shane, Barney, Vlad, Harrison and Mel had been an invigorating and spiritual experience for her. She looked on Barney as the uncle who loved to tell stories around the dinner table. Vlad and Harrison had become brothers to her. Shane...she hadn't handled his relationship with Beth well. At all. But she cared for him. He was Ryan's brother, and had paid a terrible price for his mistakes. She hoped one day soon he would look at her without questioning her motives, and accept her into his and Ryan's family.

As for Mel... Growing up, Lola had invented several imaginary sisters. Mel wasn't one of them. The woman might have a bit of crazy running through her genes, but she was sweet and loyal to Ryan, Shane and Barney. Mel gave Harrison and Vlad a hard time now and then, which, at first, had made Lola want to go all sister-bear on the woman and let her know she needed to back off her boys. But during the time Lola, Harrison and Vlad had been working at Ryan's boat shop, Mel had, time and again, gone out of her way to make them all feel welcomed.

"I know," Lola finally said, then kissed Ryan on the cheek. "No self-doubt, only confidence is my mantra."

Ryan took her hand in his again, then opened the door to the rental house. As they walked inside, she realized the rental house needed a name. Many of the vacation homes in the area had names, and while their headquarters was by no means a vacation spot, it deserved to be called something. When Harrison had given their group the Above the Law title, he'd suggested that if the Super Friends had the Hall of Justice, why couldn't ATL have a kick butt headquarters, too. At first, she thought Harrison was being a little ridiculous, but now she agreed with him. They were a family, a tightknit group who stood behind one another and who needed a safe place to always call home. The rental house was that safe place. It kept more than their equipment, and was more than a roof over Vlad and Harrison's head. It held their secrets and was the place where they could assemble in good times and in bad.

Instead of looking at this current meeting as one of those bad times, she needed to make her crew understand that there were going to be plenty of ups and downs ahead of them. That no organization hit the ground running without a few mistakes along the way, and she'd made quite a few during this case.

She stepped into the living room and saw that everyone was seated at the dining room table, Styrofoam coffee cups and paper plates in front of them, and two boxes of donuts at the center of the table. Not only did they need to name the house, but she needed to purchase kitchen supplies.

"Good morning," she said, drawing their attention.

"Morning," Harrison greeted her. "Vlad made coffee and Mel brought donuts."

"Sorry, honey," Mel began, "they were all out of the glazed jelly donuts, but I did snag a couple of apple fritters."

Her second favorite over jelly. That Mel would know and remember this, that all of them, with the exception of Shane, had greeted her and Ryan with a smile boosted her confidence. "Thanks for thinking of me, Mel."

"Why wouldn't I?"

"Because I didn't handle this case very well," she admitted, and looked to Shane, who stared at her with both appreciation and understanding. "I've done things that I can't take back, but can only learn from."

Ryan pulled a chair out for her, and she took a seat at the head of the table. Once he'd settled in the chair next to hers, she asked, "Has everyone been brought up to speed on what happened last night?"

"Harrison and Vlad told us what they saw when they got there," Barney began, "and Shane filled us in on what happened after the boys left."

"It's almost as bad as what happened here," Mel said, referring to the jackass they'd been forced to hunt last

November.

"Unfortunately," Lola said. "Since everyone knows what happened, let me start by apologizing to Harrison and Vlad. I'm sorry I placed you two in a bad situation."

"We didn't see it that way." Harrison picked up his cup. "How could you know the snake guy would be at David's?"

"True. But if I'd let Shane give Beth what we had on David, last night wouldn't have happened." She held up a hand, stopping Harrison from speaking. "I get that if we'd betrayed David, the killer would still be free. But I also can't help thinking that if we'd worked with the Collier County Sheriff's Office on this, we could have had deputies or detectives staking out David's house. They could have stopped the killer before he'd had the chance to go inside and torture David and Gabriela. Instead, I'd allowed my ego to get in the way. This was our first case, and I needed to prove to Ian that he didn't make a mistake when he asked me to spearhead our group."

She leaned back in the chair. "You all know that I was a CORE agent, but remember, I'd only been with the agency for six months. There've been times where I've wondered if Ian gave me the position to keep me off his regular team."

"Why would he do that?" Barney asked.

"Because he's marrying my mother. Before he gave me this position, he admitted to assigning me easy cases. He'd worried that if something happened to me, my mom could blame him and walk away."

"So you think Ian planted your butt in the Everglades to keep you out of trouble?" Mel asked, with a grin. "'Cause if that's the case, he didn't do a very good job."

"Vlad remember talk with Ian and Cami about Asian Lola. Ian and Cami treat Asian Lola like helpless baby."

"You're right, they did."

"Vlad not done. Vlad think Asian Lola not baby, but spoiled child."

"Geez, dude," Harrison said. "Not cool."

"Vlad not try to be cool. Vlad honest. Asian Lola cannot win all times. Vlad do not like this pouty Lola."

"I agree with Vlad," Shane said. "Get over yourself. You've been given a job, do it. Like you said, you can't take back the mistakes you've made, but you can learn from them. Now it's my turn to be honest. I was surprised Ian gave a rookie this position. But from what I've heard about him and CORE, and the agency's success, I doubt the man would've risked his reputation if he didn't have confidence that you could handle the job. So, like I said, get over yourself."

"That's right." Barney leaned forward and pulled one of the boxes of donuts toward him. "Back when I was in 'Nam—"

Vlad groaned, while Harrison let out a sigh.

"What? You two boys got a problem with my stories?"

"I love your stories," Mel said, and flashed Barney a smile. "I could listen to you talk all day."

Barney stared at her. "I hate it when I can't tell if you're yankin' my chain."

Ryan chuckled. "Don't we all. Barney, make your point without a story. Lola and I met with the detectives last night after we left David's, and we have things to discuss."

"All I was gonna say was that never once did I think things would go smooth. All you gotta do is look around the table. We've got a room full of different and strong personalities, but we work well together, and I'd do anything for each one of you no matter if you screwed up or not. I love what we've got here, and don't regret tellin' Ian I wanted to be part of it—with Lola at the helm."

Lola's throat tightened. "Thank you, Barney." She looked to Shane. "You're right. I need to get over myself. Moving forward, I might be the one in contact with Ian, but since we're in this together, I would like for everyone to be in agreement on decisions that pertain to our group as a whole. Starting with working with the two detectives we met last night."

"What about Beth?" Mel asked. "I thought she was our liaison."

"That's up to her. Shane, how did Beth feel about what went down last night?"

He looked away and reached for his coffee. "Don't know."

The room went silent, and Lola realized she probably screwed up Shane and Beth's relationship. She'd talk to him about it once they were alone, and would even go to Beth if necessary. Shane and Beth were good together, and she hated to see them split.

"Well," she began, "regardless of what Beth wants to do about ATL, the two detectives, Jerry Tennyson and Nick Wagner, were not happy with us. After we talked, and Ryan and I explained what we're about, Jerry liked the idea of having us at his disposal."

"At *his* disposal?" Harrison shook his head. "I don't like the sound of that."

Ryan grinned. "Lola didn't, either. She told Jerry we wouldn't work for him, but we would help them if they needed it."

"I also asked that they do the same for us. Jerry agreed. His partner wasn't as enthused with the idea, but by the time we'd left, he seemed good with working with us from time to time."

"Can we trust them?" Shane asked.

"I'm certainly not going to give them any of your names, the location of our headquarters, or that we're associated with CORE."

"You didn't answer the question."

She sighed. "I should be in county lock-up right now, and David should be under arrest. Since that's not the case, for now, I trust that it's possible we can have a good working relationship with them."

"I'm gonna take that as a maybe," Barney said.

"A definite maybe. Since Jerry and Nick are now aware Beth knows about us, working with the two detectives will take pressure off of her." She looked to Shane. "Despite how I'd initially reacted to you dating Beth, I don't want problems for her."

"So how's this going to work?" Harrison asked. "I'm assuming you didn't tell them that I hacked into their computer system."

"God, no. I said nothing about that, or how we'd coerced

Dustin Williams into going to them with his body-snatching story. I made it clear that we won't have a problem giving them information, but it's none of their business how we acquire it. As for how this will work, it'll be the same deal we had with Beth. If Jerry and Nick have something they'd like us to look into for them, we'll choose whether or not we want to be involved, and vice versa."

"So we can break a few laws and still be legit," Harrison said.

"I doubt the detectives would like for us to break any laws, but I think if it's low risk to them, and if they get what they want out of it, they'll overlook some of our activities." She leaned forward and rested her hands on the table. "We'll take our partnership with the detectives case by case, that is if you guys are good with working with them."

"As long I don't have to deal with the detectives, I'm good," Harrison said. "I don't want them knowing who I am."

"Vlad agree with Harry. Detectives cannot know Vlad."

"I ain't got nothing to hide," Barney said. "Mel does, though."

"Either Ryan or I will be the only ones who will talk to the detectives."

"I'm fine with it," Mel said. "How about you?" She elbowed Shane.

"I have no problem helping with transportation, or if you guys are in a pinch, but I don't want ATL taking away time from my business. I'll be reopening soon, and need that to be my main focus."

Good. Shane could remain in the know without heavy involvement. From the start, this had been exactly how Lola had envisioned Shane's contribution to ATL. "That works for me," she said. "Okay, now that we've agreed on that...Jerry called me this morning to update us on what happened after we left the crime scene. Both David and Gabriela had surgery during the night. Gabriela's still in ICU, but David is already in a regular room and scheduled for release in a few days."

"It bugs the crap out of me that David isn't going to be

busted for what he did to the dead women," Harrison said.

"I think his punishment is better than prison, plus by keeping his crimes secret, Gabriela's name won't be dragged down with David's." Lola let out a breath as she remembered the recording they'd watched on Gabriela's cell phone while in the parking lot of the diner. "Ryan and I saw David's confession. Apparently David had performance anxiety. He wanted to please Gabriela and keep her happy, so he turned to necrophilia, hoping the time he spent with the dead women would help his sex life."

"What a thoughtful man." Mel rolled her eyes. "I'm sure Gabriela took his confession well."

"In the recording, she went off on him," Ryan said, and shook his head. "So in trying to save their relationship he destroyed it, and plenty of other lives."

"Jerry also told me that he forced David to either resign from his position as ME and promise to never work as one again, or he'd leak his confession."

"I thought you took Gabriela's phone," Shane said.

"I did, but gave it to them. They need the leverage against David, not us. I don't care what happens to the man from here."

"It's too bad about David," Harrison said. "It would've been cool to have an ME in our pocket."

Lola smiled. "Instead we now have two detectives, and that works for me."

"Vlad wonder about snake man."

"The snake man referred to himself as the Reverend, but his real name was Deacon Rhodes, and his last known address was Columbia, Alabama, where he lived with his father. According to Nick, Beth took the file we'd given her and dug deeper. She discovered that Katie Reed's father, Harlan, was originally from Easterville, Tennessee, and had belonged to the Church of the Living God, which was rumored to use venomous snakes as part of their religious activities. Beth found the name of the former pastor."

"Deacon Rhodes?" Harrison asked.

"No, his father, Malachi Rhodes."

"Wow," Mel said. "If only she could have talked to the dad. Last night could've been avoided."

"Jerry and Nick don't agree. Once they ID'd Deacon Rhodes, and Nick connected his name back to the pastor's from Beth's report, they contacted Columbia, Alabama police. Since Columbia is a small town, police were able to confirm that Deacon and his father both live there. The officer offered to go to Malachi's house and be there when Jerry called to inform him about his son's death. The pastor took the news hard and said this couldn't be true. His boy was a gentle soul and wouldn't hurt anyone. Since Deacon had never been fingerprinted and had a clean record, and Malachi was confined to a bed, Jerry suggested they get a DNA sample from the father, and compare it to the son's, just to be one hundred percent certain they had the right man."

"If Deacon lived with him, wouldn't the dad question where his son had disappeared to for the past couple of days?" Harrison asked.

"Jerry asked him that, and the pastor claimed that his son, who was also a preacher, had traveled to Georgia, not Florida, to visit members of their congregation. Meanwhile, the dad's a mess over this, so Jerry tells him they'll talk more the next day. About an hour later, Columbia police called Jerry to let him know Malachi's live-in nurse found him dead."

Shane frowned. "How'd he die?"

"Rattlesnake bites."

"Suicide by venomous snake." Barney snagged another donut. "Fitting."

"Especially because that's exactly how his wife had died twenty-eight years ago."

"Vlad at loss for word." The Russian stood. "Polina need feeding," he said, then looked to Lola. "Unless Asian Lola have more?"

"Two things. The drug dealer, Smitty. Vlad and Harrison are planning to leave for Siesta Key next week. Mel, were you able to get in touch with your contacts there?"

"All set," she replied.

"Yeah, Mel's already given us names and numbers," Harrison said. "I need to finish my research on the dealer, but other than that and packing, we'll be set to go."

"Good. Okay, the second thing I want to discuss is this house. Barney and Vlad, the kitchen is looking fabulous. Great job. How long before you're finished?"

Harrison waved a hand. "Hello? I painted the kitchen."

She smiled. "And you did a great job, too."

"He whined the entire time," Barney said. "Kitchen will be done by the end of next week."

"Excellent. Then you all have a week to vote on a name for the house."

Harrison tapped the table. "I knew you liked my idea."

"I do. We need to name it and have a plaque made, then display it on the porch. But I will veto anything that's a spinoff of The Hall of Justice or Bat Cave or—"

"Vlad have name."

Oh, boy. "What's that?"

The Russian grinned, then stepped into the kitchen. After a minute he returned with his alligator, thankfully with the rubber band around its snout. "Polina's Paradise."

"Damn, boy." Barney stood and gave the gator's head a quick rub. "We're gonna start calling you Alligator Vlad." When Vlad furrowed his brows, Barney said, "You know, like the movie, *Crocodile Dundee*."

"Vlad know not this *Crocodile Dundee*."

"You don't know any movies."

Vlad stroked Polina's back. "Vlad have better thing to do than watch TV."

"And that is?"

"He reads," Harrison answered for the Russian.

"*Penthouse* don't count for reading," Barney said with a chuckle.

"Vlad know not this *Penthouse*, but Vlad intrigued."

"On that note." Mel rose, and turned to Vlad. "You're weird, but I like Polina's Paradise."

"Would Ice Cream Mel like to touch Polina?"

"You can keep your gator relationship to yourself." Mel slung her leopard print purse over her shoulder. "Ice Cream Mel has something to do before work. I'll see y'all at the boat shop."

"Mel's right. You are weird," Harrison said. "But I like the name, too. What about you, Shane?"

"The name is fine." Shane stood. "What's weird is that we went from discussing a necrophiliac and murder investigation to naming a house."

"That how ATL roll over," Vlad said.

Harrison also rose, and made his way to Vlad. "Dude, you're cool without trying to be. So please don't try."

The Russian grinned, and as the two of them made their way back into the kitchen, Lola heard Vlad ask about *Penthouse*. She covered her mouth to keep her laughter contained.

God, had she needed this moment. After what they'd witnessed last night, after the stress of dealing with the detectives and the worry over the mistakes she'd made, she had needed a bit of silliness. She needed to know they could work together as a team, yet treat each other as a family. And what family wasn't weird?

Shane started for the door. "I'm heading to the airpark."

"You're on the schedule today. Need me to get your boat ready this afternoon?" Barney asked.

"I should be on time. I'll call if I'm running late."

As Shane left, Barney adjusted his eye patch. "That boy isn't in a good place."

"I'll go talk to him," Ryan said

Lola stopped him. "Let me."

Ryan kissed her cheek. "If he's a dick to you, I'll kick his ass."

"If he is, I think I probably deserve it," she said, then hurried out of the house. She caught up with Shane as he was sliding into his truck. "Have a sec?"

"Just a few," he said, and turned the ignition. "What happened with Beth?"

"None of your business."

"Let me guess. She's mad at you for not telling her about David, right?" When he didn't answer, she said, "Tell her it was my call. Put the blame on me."

He shifted the gear. "Would you have kept that information from Ryan?"

"That's different."

"And that's a shitty answer." He tilted his head against the headrest and let out a sigh. "I want Beth to trust me and love me as much as I trust and love her."

Oh. My. God. She'd totally, unintentionally made a mess of Shane and Beth's relationship. "I'm so sorry," she said, reached through the opened window and touched his arm. "My intent was to keep her out of trouble."

"I know it was." He rolled his head and looked at her. "It was mine, too. She didn't see it that way."

"Let me talk to her and explain."

"No." He sat upright and gripped the steering wheel. "Don't get involved. Too many things were said. It's done."

Her heart broke for him and for Beth. "Are you sure?"

"Positive. Like I said, don't get involved."

She stepped away from his truck. As he backed out of the driveway, she thought back to when Beth had showed up unexpectedly at her door, Shane at her side. The cop and the ex-con. A mismatched pair. Yet, she'd seen the way the two of them had looked at each other. Considering she'd only known Ryan for less than forty-eight hours before deciding she wanted to be with him, she had no room to judge their relationship, but maybe she could fix it. Would Ian? Would he interfere with his agents' love lives?

"Don't think about it."

She swiveled and faced Ryan. "What are you talking about?"

"Don't," he said, and pulled her into his arms. "My brother will figure this out on his own. He doesn't need you in his business."

"*I'm* the reason they're having issues."

"You're not." He kissed her forehead. "Honey, Beth's a cop. Shane's a felon. No matter what you've done, it doesn't change that. This isn't about you. It's about them. I think it's mostly about Beth.'"

"Do you think she's using what happened last night as an excuse to end things with Shane?"

He kissed her again. "Only Beth can answer that."

CHAPTER 20

Shane's House, Everglades City, Florida
Saturday, 6:12 p.m., Eastern Standard Time

BETH PULLED INTO Shane's driveway and let out a shaky breath when she saw his truck. She'd called and had sent him a text yesterday. When he hadn't responded, she'd tried him again today before and during her shift. Still nothing. She hated to pop by his house unannounced, but he'd left her no choice. She needed to see him and apologize. If he refused to accept her apology, then at least she'd tried.

As she approached the door, a swarm of hornets, not butterflies, filled her nervous stomach. He might slam the door in her face and not even give her the chance to say anything at all. She hoped that wouldn't be the case. She'd take an argument over the silent treatment he was giving her. While she didn't want to fight with him, at least if they argued there'd be some line of communication open between them.

Drawing in a deep breath, she pressed a hand to her chest where her heart raced and knocked on his door. After a minute or two, she knocked again and rang the doorbell. Still nothing.

Maybe he wasn't here. Maybe Ryan or someone else had

picked him up and they'd gone to dinner. She started down the porch steps. Since the boat shop closed at five, he wouldn't be there. He could be at the airpark, which was a short drive from his house. She could go there, but also didn't want to look like a stalker. She could—

The door opened. She stopped and turned. Shane stood in the doorway wearing athletic shorts, and nothing else but a scowl on his face. She wanted to smooth the crease along his forehead, kiss the rigid line of his mouth and make him smile again. Although it had only been less than two days since she'd seen him, she'd missed his smile. She'd missed him.

"Hi," she said. "Can I come in?"

He slicked back his wet hair and blocked the doorway. "No. What do you want?"

She'd expected him to be upset with her, but not so damned cold. She glanced away and willed herself not to cry in front of him. Shane was a strong man who deserved a strong woman. "I want to talk."

"I don't.

She met his gaze, saw the hurt and anger in his eyes, and let the tears fall anyway. "Too bad." She rushed up the steps, and pushed by him.

He caught her arm, stopping her from moving past the threshold. "I didn't invite you inside. The calls, texts and now barging into my house—it stops, or I'll file a restraining order against you."

She let out a nervous laugh. Despite the range of emotions, the sadness, the guilt running through her, she couldn't help it. "That's ridiculous."

"You bothering to come here is what's ridiculous. I don't want to talk. I don't want your apologies. You said what you meant. It's over, so let it go."

She gripped his bicep. "But I didn't mean any of it."

"Rolled off your tongue easily enough."

"I was angry, and admit that my reaction was immature and mean."

"I see. So whenever your mad at me, I can expect you to

throw my felony in my face."

"I didn't throw it in your face, I pointed out a fact. I didn't want you near Dr. Adams' house. Not with two detectives there, and not without knowing exactly what Lola planned to do to the killer." She tightened her hold on him. "Shane, I don't want you to go back to prison."

He let go of her arm, and shook her hand off his bicep. "No one wants that more than me."

"Yet you went to Dr. Adams' anyway."

"To make sure nothing happened to my brother," he said, and stepped away from the door. "I didn't know if I could trust Lola to do the right thing."

"I meant what I said about staying with ATL. Lola isn't fit to run your group, and by staying part of her team you're running the risk of going back to prison."

"Lola's all right. She admitted she made mistakes, and although it doesn't change what happened, I respect her for that."

"So you'll continue to work for her?"

He shook his head. "If ATL needs a ride, that's about all I can give them. I work for myself. My business is all I care about."

She looked away to hide her trembling chin. "Is that all you care about?"

"Yes."

Tears swam in her eyes, clouding her vision. With her heart breaking, her future with Shane evaporating, she faced him. "When I found out about your record, my first instinct was to walk away. "

"Thanks for the reminder. If I recall correctly, you let sex warp your judgment." He shrugged. "I get it. You're a good girl, and you wanted to be bad. What better way than screwing a felon?"

God, she'd said horrible things to him. Determined to at least finish the apology she'd started before she left, she took a step forward. "I did want to be bad. I wanted, for once in my life, to do something wild. When we went to dinner, then up in your plane, I realized I wanted more than just a good time, that you were more than a sexy guy, that I could fall hard for you." She brushed the tears from her face. "That I already had."

He looked to the floor. "After only two dates? Now *that's* ridiculous."

"Is it? You wanted me to commit to you after a week."

"When a guy is getting laid regularly, he'll—"

"Stop it," she shouted. "Just stop. If you're trying to hurt me, it's working. I came here to apologize and hoped we could work things out, but can see I was wrong."

"Work things out?" He shook his head and half-laughed. "How? You don't even want your parents to meet me. Or were you just being immature and mean when you said that, too?"

She hugged herself. "I do want them to meet you. I want them to…" *Love you as much as I do.* She couldn't bring herself to say it and needed to leave. His feelings for her obviously didn't run as deep as hers. Staying here and arguing with him would only lead to more hurt.

"You want them to what?" he asked.

She dropped her arms and moved toward the door. "It's not important. I'm sorry for what I said the other night. Right now, I'm sorry I didn't walk away sooner."

"I wish you would have," he said, his voice strained. "You knew the risks, you knew my past, so you had to know we couldn't work. I warned you. I told you this would happen."

"You also told me you wanted more than tomorrow or the next day. But apparently not that much."

"What does that mean?"

"Look how easy you're ready to forget about us."

"I never said I could forget you," he said, his eyes intense with raw emotion. "I just can't be with a woman who's ashamed of me."

She choked back a sob and turned away from him. "I'm not ashamed of you, I'm ashamed of myself for the way I treated you." She gripped the doorknob. "I wanted my parents to meet you so they could know and love you as much as I do. I'm sorry I hurt you," she said, then opened the door.

He came behind her and slammed it shut. "You did hurt me. I know why you did it, but it stung all the same."

She rested her forehead against the door. "You chose your loyalty to Lola and ATL over me. It hurt that you didn't trust me enough to tell me about Dr. Adams until it was too late. What you did or didn't do doesn't justify how I treated you." She dragged in a deep breath as more tears streaked down her cheeks. "I wish I could take back what I said."

"The part where you love me?" he asked, and settled his hand on her shoulder. "Beth, look at me."

She shook her head. "Please, let me go home."

He turned her, and pressed her back against the door. "Answer me," he said, his eyes hopeful, yet wary.

"Of course not." She shoved him and let out a small sob, the anger suddenly rising inside her. "I love you." She pushed him again, forcing him to step back. "But I wish I didn't because I had no idea how bad losing you would hurt."

His hands fell to his sides. The tension etched on his face and the pain in his eyes only compounded the ache in her chest.

"I think you decided we didn't have a future before I blew up at you the other night," she said.

"That's not true."

"Are you sure? Because you tried to talk me out of being with you before."

"Yes, I'm sure. I love you, damn it," he shouted. "That first kiss and I knew I was screwed. You were too good for me, but I didn't care. Selfish or not, I knew what I needed and that was you."

He loved her. Hope swelled in her chest, and renewed her need to fight for them. "I told you to stop putting yourself down. I'm not too good for you. *We* were good together. And how were you selfish when you tried to push me away because you worried about my future?"

He swore and shoved a hand through his hair. "Because maybe I worried about mine, too. Maybe I was scared one day you'd wake up and realize you'd made a mistake, that being with a guy with a prison record was going to mess up your career. Maybe I thought it'd be easier to stop what we were doing before I got in too deep."

"Did you get in too deep?" she asked, and stepped toward him. "Or are your feelings for me only on the surface?"

He ate up the distance between them and cupped her cheeks. "I wish I didn't love you so much, because I had no idea how bad losing you would hurt," he said, echoing her words with love and worry in his eyes.

She placed her palms over his hands. "You haven't lost me."

"Eventually I might."

"After the years you've lost, do you want to spend your life worrying about what might happen? Or do you want to take a chance and spend it with me? The man I fell in love with went for what he wanted."

"And I want you. But I don't want you to ever regret being with me, or resent me if something happens with your job because of my past. I don't want to come between you and your parents."

God, she loved this man. Time and again, he put her before himself and his needs. "It's just a job, and no one needs to know our business." She took his hands in hers, and drew them to her chest. "I would never treat your past as a dirty secret, but I see no reason to advertise it, do you?"

"Not at all. I prefer if people didn't know. Does this mean you wouldn't tell your parents?"

"I think I should, but I won't if you don't want me too."

"One day I'm going to ask your dad for permission to marry you. I think your parents have the right to know who their daughter is spending the rest of her life with, don't you?"

Her heart raced as she let go of his hands and twined her arms around his neck. "We met two weeks ago and you're already talking marriage?"

"The man you fell in love with goes after what he wants, and I need you in my life." He inched his face closer to hers. "I'm sorry I said your feelings for me—after only two dates—

were ridiculous. I didn't mean it."

She brushed her lips against his. "I know you didn't."

"I'm sorry I didn't call you as soon as I found out about David."

"I know you are." She kissed the corner of his mouth, and ran a hand along his chest. "I'm sorry that you're too busy apologizing to kiss me."

He grinned. "Yeah, I think we've both apologized enough."

Regret nudged her. "Did I? Again, I can't take back what I said, but I—"

He kissed her. "Do you love me?"

"Yes."

"Will you stay here tonight? I missed sleeping next to you."

"I was hoping I could. I missed you, too."

He kissed her again, then started walking her backward toward the bedroom. "Will you make me a promise?"

With the way he was already pulling her shirt over her head and unhooking her bra, she'd promise him just about anything. "What is it?" she asked, and slid her hand in the waistband of his shorts, then shoved them down.

"Let go of what you said in your garage. I have. No regrets, Beth." He pushed her shorts over her hips, then tilted her chin. "I spent seven years regretting and counting. Counting down the days until I was free and the cracks in the cinderblock walls to keep from going crazy. Now all I want is to count on having you beside me."

She stared into his eyes, eyes that held the love and trust she hadn't realized she'd been looking for all her life, but was so thankful she'd found. "I'm yours, and you're mine. Together, we've got this," she said, and kissed him. As she hugged him close, skin to skin, chest to breast and stripped of the labels that should have kept them apart, she didn't worry about the ups and downs they might face.

Shane was her future, and that was all that mattered to her.

****

Naples Community Hospital, Naples, Florida
Saturday, 8:02 p.m., Eastern Standard Time

As the nurse knocked on Gabriela's door, David's injured stomach grew queasy with dread. He hated himself. Hated the man he'd become and how he'd allowed himself to veer onto a selfish and self-destructive path, a path that had destroyed his and so many other lives. But he needed to face Gabriela one last time. Redemption wasn't something he deserved or expected. Neither were understanding or forgiveness. He deserved nothing but punishment.

The nurse opened the door and pushed his wheel chair into Gabriela's room. "Good evening, Miss Fuentes, are you up for a visitor?" the nurse asked.

Gabriela glared at him, the hatred in her eyes killing him. "Come get him in ten minutes."

"Will do," the nurse said, and gave him a worried look before leaving the room.

Once they were alone, he stared at her. Considering what he'd put her through, she still looked beautiful to him. He ached to touch her. To see her pretty smile. To hear her tell him she loved him one last time.

"Why are you here?" she asked, her tone emotionless and cold.

"I know it's over between us."

"Permanently. If I could erase the years I spent with you from my mind, I would. For now, I plan to pretend you never existed. Once you leave this room, you're dead to me."

He swallowed. Hard. "Your doctor said you should recover just fine. No damage to any of your internal organs, only minor scarring."

She shoved her blanket aside, along with her hospital gown and revealed her stomach. "Would you call this minor?"

As he stared at the stitches her doctor had given her, at the puckered skin around them, he hated himself even more—if that was even possible. The scar would not be minor. It would remind her of what he'd put her through until the day she died.

421

She pulled the blanket over her. "I suppose things could be worse. The Reverend could have cut me and, instead of looking at you, I'd be dead. Thank you for making sure that didn't happen. I'm sure taking a kitchen knife to me was difficult."

She'd thanked him as if she were thanking a butcher for the right cut of meat. He had no right, but his temper flared. "It was utter hell. I've kissed and tasted every inch of your body. From the moment I met you, I knew I'd never love another. What he put us through, what he'd forced me to do…" He leaned into the wheel chair and fought the sob lodged in his throat. "I'm so sorry, Gabriela."

"The detectives told me he made you cut yourself," she said, and there was no sympathy in her eyes. "I imagine that was also difficult."

"It was nothing compared to hurting you."

She kept her narrowed, hate-filled gaze on him. "The detectives also told me you killed him."

"I shot him in the head."

"Good. He deserved to die."

"He deserved to be gutted." The Reverend had forfeited the right to live the day he'd murdered Katie Reed.

She gave him a slight nod and rested her head against her pillow. "You had to know I didn't want to see you. The doctors obviously told you how I was recovering, so there's no reason for you to be here. Say what's on you mind, then I want you out of my life."

"I wanted to thank you for not telling the detectives about my crimes." Although Jerry and Nick were the lead detectives on the investigation, and had planned to keep what he'd done to the dead women from their reports, Gabriela could have changed that.

"I didn't keep my mouth shut for you. I preferred to keep my humiliation to myself, not have it splashed on national news." She fisted her blanket. "The trip to Africa. You knew then that the Reverend was after you, correct?"

"I wanted to protect you."

"And I just wanted us to be together," she said on a sob. "Damn it, David. I loved you. I truly, deeply loved *you*. Not for sex, but for the good man I thought you were."

"I *am* that man. But I wanted to make you happy on every level of our relationship."

"By fucking a dead woman? Do you realize how *sick* that is?" With her head against the pillow she looked to the ceiling. "Were there others?"

"No," he answered honestly.

"Did you really go to a funeral home and view a random dead woman, then masturbate in the bathroom?"

Oh, God. He *was* sick.

"Answer me," she demanded, and winced as she raised her head.

"Yes, damn it. I did it. But I did it for you. For us. I've tried drugs, therapy, toys to help fix my anxiety issues, but nothing worked. What I did was wrong, but I was desperate and needed to do something to give you the pleasure you deserve."

"For us," she echoed. "You're such an asshole. My *pleasure* came from being with you. If you had bothered to ask, I would have told you that I was satisfied with our sex life. Now I'm disgusted. Knowing that you put your penis in a dead body, then in mine, repulses me." She rested her head against the pillow. "I'm done with you."

"I love you."

"I don't care. You and your love means nothing to me now." Tears streamed down the side of her face. "You'd made me so happy." Her face crumpled as more tears fell. "I loved you so much."

He didn't bother to wipe his tears or hide his emotions. "I still love you."

"I still don't care. People died because of you."

He hung his head in his hands and cried. "I know. I never meant for that to happen. Please tell me you believe that." Needing to hear her say it, he looked to her. "Please."

A hint of the love she once felt for him shined in her eyes. "I know you never meant for those women to die, but after the first murder you could have done something to prevent the next." Her eyes hardened. The minute amount of love in them disappeared and was replaced with disgust. "Instead you led a killer to an innocent pregnant woman. That shows me just how selfish you are. You might be sorry for those women, but I think you're more sorry that you were caught."

He wheeled the chair closer to her bed. "I know I can never make up for what I did, but I want to try. Sell the engagement ring. It was appraised for twenty-five grand. I also want to give you money to help pay down your mortgage, or for whatever you need."

She glared at him. "I'll definitely hock the ring, but you can keep your money. All I want from you is your promise to stay out of my life."

"You have my word. I'm going to sell everything I have and still move to Africa to work with my family's foundation. If and when I return to the States, I'll move to Tampa, where the foundation's headquarters is located."

"All I wanted was your promise to leave me alone. I don't care what you do with the rest of your life. Like I said, once you leave this room, you're dead to me."

He sucked in a breath, and wiped his tear-soaked face. "I'll never forget the first time I saw you. You were so—"

"Stop," she cried, and pressed on the nurses' call button. "I don't want to hear any of this."

Knowing this would be the last time he'd ever see and speak to Gabriela, his chest tightened with panic. "I love you. I'll always love you." The door to the room opened. "Please tell me you believe that. Please tell me you'll remember me for more than this. Please try to forgive me."

The nurse stepped inside and glanced at the two of them. "Everything okay?"

Gabriela sniffed and brushed a tear from her cheek. "He's ready to go back to his room." As the nurse began to move his wheelchair, Gabriela said his name. The nurse stopped, and David stared at the woman he'd once planned to spend his life with and would forever love. Not with hope, he knew there was no hope for him, no happiness in his future, only pain and sorrow.

"I believe you," Gabriela said. "The only reason I would ever forgive you is so that I could move on and forget that you ever existed." She turned her head and looked away from him. "*Adiós*, David. *Espero que los pecados que manchan el alma serán limpiados antes de que Dios te lleva en sus brazos.*"

I hope the sins staining your soul will be cleansed before God takes you in his arms.

"I do, too," he said. "Good-bye, Gabriela."

EPILOGUE

Five months later...

Cap'n Ryan's Airboat Tours, Everglades City, Florida
Sunday, 3:34 p.m. Eastern Daylight Time

SHANE HELPED BETH, along with a handful of her nieces and nephews, off the airboat, then onto the dock. Beth's oldest nephew, Robbie, turned to him as they made their way down the pier to where Beth's graduation party was in full swing. "Thanks, Uncle Shane. That was awesome. You have the coolest jobs," the boy said, while the other kids agreed, and also thanked him.

He did have the coolest jobs. He was able to either take people flying or boating, and made a lot of money doing what he loved. If they knew he flew a secret organization around from time to time, they'd probably think *he* was cool. "You're welcome," he said, and spotted Vlad passing Polina over to another one of Beth's young nephews. "Looks like Vlad finally got here with his gator. Head on over for a turn to hold her."

As the kids rushed off, Beth wrapped an arm around his waist. "Well, Uncle Shane, you and my parents were right. This is the perfect place for my graduation party. Thank you." She rose to her tiptoes and kissed him.

Uncle Shane. From the moment Shane had met Beth's brothers and sisters-in-law, they'd welcomed him into the family, just as her parents had. Their kids had immediately begun calling him Uncle Shane and had acted as if he'd always been part of their lives. It probably helped that he was engaged to their aunt, could take them in a plane or on a boat, and that he knew a Russian guy who owned an alligator. Still, he'd take their smiles and the way they, along with their parents and grandparents, had accepted him.

"I'm going to see if Mel needs any help," Beth said, then after another quick kiss, she headed inside the ice cream shop.

He owed Ryan for shutting down the boat shop early and letting him erect a tent and tables in the parking lot. He owed Lola and Mel even more. Between the two of them and Beth, they'd come up with the menu, but Lola and Mel had been the ones to make enough food to feed Beth's large family, along with his own.

Beth had insisted that Ryan, Barney, Harrison and Vlad come to the party. At first, he hadn't been comfortable with that, especially since she'd also invited her friend Erin, her former partner, Ricky, and his family, as well as the two detectives, Nick and Jerry. Although Ricky had no idea about ATL, the detectives were well aware of them, and they'd already made use of their team several times. Lola had also taken advantage of their arrangement with the detectives. The first time had been when Vlad and Harrison had traveled to Siesta Key to go after the drug dealer, Smitty. Jerry had a few friends within the Sarasota County Sheriff's Office who had been more than happy to arrest Smitty, once Vlad and Harrison were able to locate the man and gather enough evidence to put the dealer away for life.

Yeah, things were working well. The renovations for Polina's Paradise had been completed months ago, which had given Barney time to help Shane work on and finish making cosmetic updates to the rental house he had bought from

Ryan. Since Beth's last day as a Collier County deputy had been two weeks ago, and she now no longer had to live within a certain radius of the sheriff's office, she'd finally moved in with him. Thank God. They were both tired of driving forty minutes to see each other. Plus, with the sale of her townhome, she'd been able to pay off her student loans. Between the money she had left over, and the way his aircraft business had taken off, he'd purchased another Cessna and hired a pilot. Lola was thrilled, because this meant he could transport ATL whenever they needed him without interfering with his business.

Laughter and kids' voices floated from the dock. He turned just as Barney was assisting Beth's parents and grandchildren from his airboat. As kids raced past Shane, Irene and Ed Price approached him, smiles on their faces.

"Now I know why Bethie loves going on that thing," Irene said, then squeezed his arm with both hands and kissed his cheek. "We had so much fun."

"Grandma, come hold Polina," Robbie's six-year-old sister, Meagan shouted. "Hurry, she's so cute."

Irene wrinkled her nose. "Cute, huh? Coming, sweetie," she said, then walked toward where Vlad showed off his gator.

"You did good today," Ed said, then dabbed at the perspiration along his forehead. "I'm still a little ticked off that you won't take my money."

Irene and Ed had insisted they pay for Beth's graduation party, since it had been their idea to have it. Now that he had plenty of his own, he didn't need their money. "Just a little?" he asked with a grin.

"Because we'll need to throw you and Bethie a wedding, I'm not too broken up about saving my money."

"Ed, I already told you that Beth and I will take care of all the wedding expenses. We're not getting married until Beth passes the Bar and finds a job anyway. We have time."

"I don't know about that. When you asked for permission to marry our daughter, you promised us grandbabies. We're not getting any younger and we want those babies."

Shane chuckled. "I'll make good on my promise. In the meantime, maybe you should quit talking to me and go enjoy the ones you have."

"I might have to go back to the airboat and borrow the ear protection. I love my grandkids, but they're damned loud." He looked away from where the kids played and his children sat at the tables talking, then turned to Shane. "Irene and I decided not to tell Beth's brothers about your past."

Shane stared at his future father-in-law. "I thought you felt they should know."

"At first we did, but not anymore. We're happy you and Beth are together. Because of you, she was able to quit a job neither me or Irene liked. We have and always will support Beth's decisions, but we hated that she was a cop. You have no idea how much we worried about her safety."

"Is that the only reason you're not telling your sons about me?" Shane asked. The day he'd first met her parents they'd drilled him about his murder conviction, his time in the Army, and about his past and current aircraft business. After several exhausting and stressful hours of questioning, he and Beth had left, both of them unsure of where he stood with her parents. He still wasn't one hundred percent sure, but since he and Beth had spent almost every Sunday evening at her parents' for dinner, and they'd given him permission to marry their daughter, he'd figured they were okay with their daughter's choice.

"Son, if I could've handpicked a husband for my daughter, you would have been my first choice. You're a hell of a man, and you're part of our family. My sons don't need to know anything more than that. No one does." He wiped the sweat from his forehead again. "I need to get out of the sun. Let's grab a beer."

Ed reminded Shane of his own father. Accepting, blunt and to the point. "I'm going to see if they're ready to bring out the food first." Before Ed walked off, Shane stopped him. "Thanks for what you said. It means a lot to me."

Ed grinned. "So does our daughter's happiness. I'll keep a

beer on ice for you," he said, then headed toward one of the large buckets Harrison and Vlad had filled earlier with ice, beer, sodas and water bottles.

As Shane made his way up the porch steps and toward the kitchen, Ryan's dog, Sadie, came out of the souvenir store. He looked to the door, and saw Ryan at the threshold studying him. "Something wrong?" Shane asked, and approached his brother.

"From where I'm standing I'd say everything's great. Beth has a nice family. I heard the kids calling you uncle, it's got a nice ring to it," he said with a smile.

"Lola's pregnant."

Ryan's eyes widened and he suddenly paled. "She is? Oh, my God. How do you know, and not me?" He gripped the doorjamb and turned. "I've got to talk to her."

"Wait." Shane grabbed Ryan's arm. "I thought that's what you were going to tell me. You did say uncle has a nice ring to it."

Ryan let out a breath. "You scared the hell out of me. No, I just meant it's good to see you a part of Beth's family."

Shane rested a hand on his brother's shoulder. "It's not like I don't already have family. Thanks for everything you've done for me—before and since I came home."

"Is this the point where you tell me you love me and then give me a hug?" Ryan asked, and grinned.

"Hell, no." Shane let go of his brother. "You smell like BO."

Ryan laughed, and gave him a bear hug anyway. "I love you, bro."

"You, too, man," Shane said, and took a step back. "We did all right."

"More than all right. All those people who thought the Monahan brothers would amount to nothing can kiss our asses."

"Who can kiss your ass?" Lola asked as she came around the corner, followed by Beth.

"It's nothing," Ryan said, and kissed his fiancée. "Is

everything ready?"

"Yep, but we can use help setting the food out on the table." Lola tugged Ryan's hand. "Come. I've already recruited Harrison."

"I'll help, too," Shane said.

"No, you stay with Beth and entertain your guests," she said, and dragged Ryan into the kitchen.

Once they were alone, Shane turned to Beth. "I'm not sure if your dad told you, but he and your mom aren't going to tell your brothers about my record."

"He told me. And like I'd hoped, they love you just as much as I do."

"Say that again."

She smiled. "The whole thing or just part of it?"

"The last part."

"I love you."

He'd never grow tired of her saying she loved him. He'd never grow tired of her. When he'd been in prison, he'd spent seven years dreaming and imagining what his life would be like once he was on the outside. Beth hadn't been part of those dreams, because he'd never thought he would find a woman like her. Now that he had, he'd never let her go.

"I love you, too," he said.

"Uncle Shane," Meagan called, and stepped onto the porch. "Vlad's not sharing Polina."

"Little yellow hair girl need stop tattle on Vlad. Vlad have share enough. Polina need to feed." The Russian eyed Meagan, and held Polina close. "If little yellow hair girl not good, maybe Vlad will feed—"

Harrison came out of the ice cream shop with a tray of rigatoni. "Vlad, put the gator in her cage and help us with the food."

Vlad gave the girl a dirty look and stalked off with his gator. Meagan stared at the Russians back, then ran off to the tent.

"Was Vlad going to threaten to feed my niece to his gator?"

Shane glanced to Harrison, who shook his head. "The no smoking thing has him a little edgy. He wouldn't really feed her to Polina. Vlad loves kids," he said, then walked off with the food.

Beth took Shane's hand. "When we have kids, Vlad is not allowed to babysit."

Shane laughed and let Beth lead him toward the tent. As the afternoon turned into evening, and their guests left, Shane sat next to Beth at the table and looked around at the mess they'd have to clean up. Barney, Vlad, Harrison, Ryan, Lola and Mel joined them, each with a beer in their hand.

"Hell of a party," Barney said.

"Except for little yellow hair tattletale girl, Vlad agree."

"Vlad, she's six," Beth said. "Don't be so sensitive."

"Vlad sorry Kiss Beth."

"That's okay." She smiled, then looked at the others. "Thanks again for everything you did for Shane today."

Lola shook her head. "We did this for *you*." She raised her beer bottle. "Congratulations on your success, Beth, and welcome to *our* family."

THE END

LOOK FOR MEL'S STORY…

PERFECTLY TOXIC

BOOK TWO
C.O.R.E. ABOVE THE LAW

OTHER C.O.R.E. TITLES
BY KRISTINE MASON

ULTIMATE KILL
BOOK ONE OF THE
ULTIMATE C.O.R.E. TRILOGY

When the past collides with the present, the only way to ensure the future lies in the ultimate kill...

Naomi McCall is a woman of many secrets. Her family has been murdered and she's been forced into hiding. No one knows her past or her real name, not even the man she loves.

Jake Tyler, former Marine and the newest recruit to the private investigation agency, CORE, has been in love with a woman who never existed. When he learns about the lies Naomi has weaved, he's ready to leave her—until an obsessed madman begins sending her explosive messages every hour on the hour.

Innocent people are dying. With their deaths, Naomi's secrets are revealed and the truth is thrust into the open. All but one. Naomi's not sure if Jake can handle a truth that will change their lives. But she is certain of one thing—the only way to stop the killer before he takes more lives is to make herself his next victim.

ULTIMATE FEAR

BOOK TWO OF THE ULTIMATE C.O.R.E. TRILOGY

When a deranged mother's grief drives her to replace her dead son over and over, obsession leads to murder...

Chicago detective Jessica Donavan will never stop looking for her missing daughter. Her obsession has destroyed her marriage, but the search is the only thing that helps keep her sane and her mind off of everything she's lost—her husband and her baby girl. When she uncovers a string of unsolved disappearances and reappearances of a number of baby boys, Jessica turns to her soon to be ex, Dante Russo, a former Navy SEAL turned investigator for the private agency, CORE, to help her fit together the pieces in this perplexing puzzle. But as Dante helps her, she realizes just how much she still craves his support—and his touch.

Dante is still in love with his wife and would do anything to have her back in his life again. He's been miserable since she left him to deal with the grief over their daughter's abduction, never understanding how much he grieves as well. When Jessica tells him about the case she's working, he jumps at the chance to take part in her investigation. He's hoping not only to save their marriage and ease his personal pain over the loss of their daughter, but to stop a serial kidnapper from taking another victim.

As Jessica and Dante work side by side, pregnant women begin to turn up missing or dead, and they start to uncover the consequences of another woman's unfathomable grief. The childless mother doesn't just want a baby. She wants a newborn straight from the womb.

And when forced to confront the dark and twisted perversion of a mother's obsession, can Jessica and Dante find their lives again...or merely more death.

KRISTINE MASON

SHADOW OF DANGER

BOOK ONE OF THE
C.O.R.E. "SHADOW" TRILOGY

Beware of what lurks in the shadows...

Four women have been found dead in the outskirts of a small Wisconsin town. The only witness, clairvoyant Celeste Risinski, observes these brutal murders through violent nightmares and hellish visions. The local sheriff, who believes in Celeste's abilities and wants to rid their peaceful community of a killer, enlists the help of an old friend, Ian Scott, owner of a private criminal investigation agency, CORE. Because of Ian's dark history with Celeste's family, a history she knows nothing about, he sends his top criminalist, former FBI agent John Kain to investigate.

John doesn't believe in Celeste's mystic hocus-pocus, or in her visions of the murders. But just when he's certain they've solved the crimes, with the use of science and evidence, more dead bodies are discovered. Could this somehow be the work of the same killer or were they dealing with a copycat? To catch a vicious murderer, the skeptical criminalist reluctantly turns to the sensual psychic for help. Yet with each step closer to finding the killer, John finds himself one step closer to losing his heart.

SHADOW OF PERCEPTION

BOOK TWO OF THE
C.O.R.E. "SHADOW" TRILOGY

What happens when negligent plastic surgeons receive a taste of their own medicine...?

Chicago investigative reporter, Eden Risk, receives an unmarked envelope containing a postcard ordering her to watch the enclosed DVD...or someone else dies. No Police. After Eden watches the DVD, a gruesome, horrifying surgery, she turns to the private criminal investigation agency, CORE, for help. Only she hadn't expected that help to come with a catch. Her former lover, Hudson Patterson, has been assigned to the case.

Hudson would rather have another CORE agent handle the investigation. Two years ago, he'd screwed things up with Eden...bad. And as more DVDs arrive, Eden and Hudson find themselves not only knee-deep in a twisted investigation, but forced to deal with their past, and the love they'd tried to deny.

SHADOW OF VENGEANCE

BOOK THREE OF THE
C.O.R.E. "SHADOW" TRILOGY

Welcome to Hell Week. You have seven days to find him...

At Wexman University, male students will do anything to get into a top fraternity. They'll prove their worth during Hell Week by participating in various physical, psychological and even juvenile pranks. But those shenanigans aren't so funny when pledges start disappearing. What kind of evil has stalked this small Michigan university for the past two decades? Theories range from obscene scientific experiments to grotesque satanic killings...but they're all wrong. The murdered boys serve a single purpose...the ultimate revenge.

Rachel Davis, forensic computer analyst for the private investigation agency CORE, has been itching to leave her desk behind and work in the field. When her brother Sean, a student at Wexman, is found beaten and his roommate kidnapped during Hell Week, she gets her chance. Only her boss insists former U.S. Secret Service Agent, Owen Malcolm, helps her with the investigation. Owen is the last person she wants on this assignment. She'd been secretly half in love with him for over four years, until the night he'd crushed her ego and destroyed her hopes for any kind of future with him.

For his own reasons, Owen refuses to risk becoming involved with a coworker. Now that he and Rachel are stuck working side-by-side to solve this perverse investigation, he's having a hard time fighting his attraction to her...an attraction he's tried to deny from the moment they met. But time is ticking. They have seven days to find the missing pledge and catch a killer. Seven days before the body count rises and the pledge ends up another victim of Hell Week.

CELESTE FILES: UNLOCKED

BOOK ONE PSYCHIC C.O.R.E.

Some secrets should remain locked in the past...

Celeste Kain hasn't had a psychic vision in two years. After being brutally attacked while helping criminal investigation agency CORE stop a serial killer, her mind repressed her clairvoyant abilities. Married to CORE agent, John Kain, mother to their toddler, Olivia, and owner of an up-and-coming bakery, Celeste has been doing fine psychic-free. Only now the dead are using her body to tell their stories again...putting her new life and family at risk.

Haunted by a murdered woman, Celeste turns to a psychic mentor to learn how to control her gift, protect her family and bring justice to the dead. But the more she digs into the dead woman's past, the further she slips into the unknown, unlocking secrets literally worth killing for. As the body count rises, it becomes clear: someone in the dead woman's family is deeply, violently wrong. And Celeste needs to be careful, before she loses something more precious to her than her life.

Celeste Risinski, the heroine of Shadow of Danger (Book 1 C.O.R.E. Shadow Trilogy), is back with her own series. Join her as she learns how to deal with being a wife, mom, baker and...psychic investigator.

CONTEMPORARY ROMANCES
BY KRISTINE MASON

KISS ME

PICK ME
BOOK ONE OF THE REALITY
TV ROMANCE SERIES

LOVE ME
BOOK TWO OF THE REALITY
TV ROMANCE SERIES

ABOUT KRISTINE MASON

Kristine Mason is the bestselling author of the popular romantic suspense trilogies C.O.R.E. Shadow and Ultimate C.O.R.E. She is currently working on her next trilogy, C.O.R.E. Above the Law, along with a series of Psychic C.O.R.E. novellas.

Although Kristine has published a few contemporary romance novels, she focuses most of her energy on her romantic suspense stories, which she loves for their blend of dark mystery/suspense and sexy romance. She is fascinated with what makes people afraid, and is famous for her depraved villains whose crimes present massive obstacles for her heroes and heroines to overcome.

Kristine has a degree in journalism from Ohio State University and lives in Northeast Ohio with her husband, four kids, and two dogs. If she's not writing, she's chauffeuring kids, gardening, or collecting gnomes. Oh, and she makes a mean chocolate chip cookie!

Connect with Kristine on Facebook, Twitter or by email at authorkristinemason@gmail.com. You can also find out more about Kristine's books by visiting her website: www.kristinemason.net.

Kristine will raffle off one $50 gift card among all subscribers of her newsletter each month. To sign up for Kristine's email newsletter please visit her website: www.kristinemason.net.